PRAISE FOR **BLOOD**

"This intriguing tale of magic and mayhem delves deep into the human psyche and shows what great writing and characters are all about. It grabs you by the throat and heartstrings and won't let go. If *Blood of the Four* isn't on your must-be-read pile, it should be!"

—Sherrilyn Kenyon, #1 *New York Times* bestselling author of
the Dark-Hunters & Nevermore

"*Blood of the Four* is magnificent! Epic in scope, grand in execution, and majestic and bloodthirsty in equal measure."

—Sarah Beth Durst, author of The Queens of Renthia series

"There's something for everyone here, including some subtly feminist themes and several spectacular displays of magical conflict. This novel is an expert crowd-pleaser."

—*Publishers Weekly*

"Golden and Lebbon pull off pure magic with *Blood of the Four*. Easily one of the best fantasies I've read in the last ten years. *Blood of the Four* kicks all kinds of ass!"

—James A. Moore, author of the Seven Forges and Tides of War series

"*Blood of the Four* is definitely fantasy on an epic level, contained in an over-whelming single volume for the reader's convenience."

—New York Journal of Books

"Your excitement over a new literary fantasy world may wane a bit when you realize the world is part of a long series with no end in sight. It's one reason why standalone high fantasy can be a treat, and that's exactly why we're so pumped for *Blood of the Four*."

—Nerdist

"Epic. Horror titans Golden (*Ararat*, 2017) and Lebbon (*Relics*, 2017), who previously teamed up on the YA series The Secret Journeys of Jack London (*The Wild*, 2011), meld their talents again in this fantasy of madness and war."

—*Booklist*

"In a genre overcrowded by ever-expanding series, this book demonstrates that there is plenty of room for action and intrigue in a stand-alone. . . . A nicely self-contained and kinetic excursion into political fantasy."

—*Kirkus Reviews*

"Thoughtful and thoroughly entertaining."

—*B&N Sci-Fi & Fantasy Blog*

"If you love epic fantasy, especially if you are looking for one where you can read it all without endless waiting for a next volume or spending a year of your life wading through a dozen or more doorstops, grab a copy of *Blood of the Four*."

—*Reading Reality*

"This book blew my expectations away, making me extra glad I actually read it! I would wholeheartedly recommend this, especially since it's not like a ten-book commitment—it's a standalone after all! 5/5 would book-push this book. 5/5 would read again."

—*Power & Page*

"What do you get when you bring two skilled authors together and they write a book? The answer is simple: something rather wonderful."

—*The Eloquent Page*

"Christopher Golden and Tim Lebbon are a formidable pair of writers of fantasy stories. They have total control over their characters and the character arcs are finished perfectly. It is a real treat for all those who enjoy reading fantasy fiction."

—*Washington Book Review*

"*Blood of the Four* is a fun read. The partnership of Golden and Lebbon has resulted in a stylistically seamless narrative. . . . The attention paid to gender makes the book refreshingly contemporary and adds important intellectual and cultural heft to an entertaining tale."

—*Bookreporter*

BLOOD OF THE FOUR

Also by Christopher Golden

Ararat
Snowblind
Dead Ringers
Tin Men
Don't Go Alone
. . . and many more

Also by Tim Lebbon

Relics
The Silence
Coldbrook
The Family Man
The Hunt
. . . and many more

BLOOD
OF THE
FOUR

CHRISTOPHER GOLDEN

AND

TIM LEBBON

HARPER Voyager

An Imprint of HarperCollins*Publishers*

This is a work of fiction. Names, characters, places, and incidents are prod-
ucts of the author's imagination or are used fictitiously and are not to be
construed as real. Any resemblance to actual events, locales, organizations,
or persons, living or dead, is entirely coincidental.

BLOOD OF THE FOUR. Copyright © 2018 by Daring Greatly Corporation and
Tim Lebbon. All rights reserved. Printed in the United States of America.
No part of this book may be used or reproduced in any manner whatsoever
without written permission except in the case of brief quotations embod-
ied in critical articles and reviews. For information, address HarperCollins
Publishers, 195 Broadway, New York, NY 10007.

HarperCollins books may be purchased for educational, business, or sales
promotional use. For information, please e-mail the Special Markets De-
partment at SPsales@harpercollins.com.

Harper Voyager and design are trademarks of HarperCollins Publishers
LLC.

A hardcover edition of this book was published in 2018 by Harper Voyager,
an imprint of HarperCollins Publishers.

FIRST HARPER VOYAGER PAPERBACK EDITION PUBLISHED 2019.

Designed by Paula Russell Szafranski
Maps by Eric Gunther and copyright © 2017 Springer Cartographics

Library of Congress Cataloging-in-Publication Data has been applied for.

ISBN 978-0-06-264140-3

19 20 21 22 23 BRR 10 9 8 7 6 5 4 3 2 1

For my daughter Ellie, in her first year of university life. Be brilliant!
—TL

For my daughter, Lily, in her first year of high school.
Find your joys and follow them.
—CG

Pirates

Tan Kushir

Igler's End

VOLCANIC ISLANDS

SUSKMOUTH

Lartha

RIVER SUSK

Skarroth

THE SPINE

Quandis

INNER RING

OUTER RING

REEF

The Hotlands

Map by Eric Gunther
Copyright © MMXVII Springer Cartographics LLC.

Lartha

Map by Lori Gunther.
Copyright © MMXVII Springer Cartographica LLC.

SUSKMOUTH 30 MILES

RIVER DEFENSES

SALT BATHS

Clan Daklan Hill

RIVER SUSK

Clan Kallistrate Hill

Temple

Yaris Teeg

Clan Ellstir Hill

Clan Hartshorn Hill

BLOOD SPIRE

SCHOLAR'S BRIDGE

BONE SPIRE

Clan Burnwell Hill

Palace Hill

HERO'S SQUARE

To the Spine Mountains

BLOOD OF THE FOUR

BOOK ONE

1

In the darkness Phela heard a laugh, a sigh, and then a groan of passion, and shadows came alive with the hint of possibilities.

She might have been a princess bound by tradition, and no longer a child, but Phela still had a desire for fun and a love of games that belied her age. Some of those games were played all across the island kingdom of Quandis. They were passed down from parent to child, rules malleable and changing from one generation to the next. They were a rite of passage, a learning process, and the means by which a youngster was introduced to the politics of interaction and the art of conflict.

But young Phela had also contrived her own games, whose rules also shifted over time. And each time, her activities found new aims and new purpose. They all led to the same outcomes, though: manipulation of circumstance, the power of words, the molding of wills to her own desires. She often broke rules, but for a princess, such transgressions were generally overlooked.

As time passed, she had abandoned most of her games, but one lingered, her interest never waning. Phela called it Whispering. It was the gathering of secrets, the harvesting of hidden truths and forbidden knowledge. Whispering required stealth, agility, and determination, and the ability to hold on to the knowledge she collected until its true value became clear to her. It had begun as a child's game, but as an adult she had come to recognize what Whispering could gain her.

She believed that one day her game would make her the most powerful royal ever.

Phela's Whispering took her through forgotten passages and into dark spaces no one else in the palace knew about or remembered. She found her way mostly by touch. Though she carried candles and flints, she rarely risked giving herself away. These places were hers, and she meant to keep them.

Another sigh was followed by the steady creak of a wooden bed shifting beneath a couple making love. Phela felt nothing—no surprise, no sense of arousal. No shame that she was listening to her mother having sex. The queen's chambers were well guarded and isolated deep in the heart of the vast royal palace, but Phela's Whispering passages twisted around this heart like great veins.

The blood they ran with was the knowledge of what she might discover.

She edged forward. Her hands pressed through webs, and they tore with soft ripping sounds. Creatures scampered in the darkness, mostly away from her. A few came close, but they did not bother her. She was used to such things by now, and they seemed to know she too was a hunter—and respected that. Phela sensed their calm observation, watching her with eyes that could see in the dark. She wondered what they saw. Not a girl any longer. Not for some time.

A woman who knows her own heart. Someone determined to find her own way.

Her life and future were regulated and dictated by the fact that she had been born into royalty. She did not begrudge that entirely—

she quite enjoyed the wealth and privilege that came with her position. Yet from an early age, Phela chafed at the *idea* of strictures and had been committed to finding and forging her own path. Exploring these forgotten byways through and beneath the palace had made her feel that she was commencing this journey. There were tunnels and sewers; crawl spaces and voids left between one period of construction and the next; basement areas and hollows beneath great, ancient foundations. She had found whole series of long-abandoned rooms known only to rats, wraiths, and other creatures of the dark . . . and now to her. This was her world, full of shadows and echoes, and it had become the only place where she truly felt free. She could exist here without question, shedding the protocols or traditions that might affect where she went next, and when. She could lay her plans and construct her schemes.

Someone cried out. A woman's voice, high and unguarded.

The princess moved quickly, climbing a series of ancient wooden struts that took her up above the wide, arched ceiling of her mother's private chambers. Phela's feet were clad in thick stockings, and on her hands she wore soft leather gloves. The rest of her clothing was tight and smooth, with no buckles or belts to knock against wood or stone to give her away. Even her hair was twisted into a tight bun and knotted atop her head. She was built for surreptitious movement, and as her mother's cries of pleasure came faster and higher, Phela flowed across the ceiling structure of her chambers.

She was heading for a place she had been many times before.

The cries were now joined by deeper grunts, the serenade of a man lost to pleasure. Linos Kallistrate was her mother's lover. Once their involvement had been secret, but now many people knew of their trysts. It didn't seem to matter. Linos was a nobleman—Baron of Clan Kallistrate—and his wife, Carina, seemed to accept the fact that her husband was fucking the queen. In truth, there was little else she could do. Who would dare speak against the lovers? Queen Lysandra was strong but harsh, and many noble families had witnessed the power she was willing to exert to gain what she desired.

Desire, Phela thought as she heard her mother and her lover reaching their crescendo below her. She lay across the network of timber ceiling struts and peered through a crack in the old plaster beside one of the heavy arching beams. This desire was animal, and the sight of the sweating, naked bodies in the huge round bed below illustrated that better than any sounds or cries ever could. They writhed and thrashed, limbs entangled, slick skins slipping against each other. There were no words, only indeterminate sounds like those of creatures in the wild. Eventually these cries faded away into heavy breathing, and their bodies seemed to slump as if deflating. They spread across the bed, and Linos rolled from the queen and fell onto his back, arms and legs wide, staring up at the ceiling.

For a moment Phela felt that he was staring right at her, and she held her breath. Then he turned his head to stare at his queen.

"You're a beast," Queen Lysandra said, her chest rising and falling with rapid breathing.

"And that's why you love me," he replied.

To Princess Phela he *did* resemble a beast. She wasn't inexperienced with men—there were young noblemen living and working in the palace who could vouch for that—but Linos was something else. Hair covered his body, sprouting from his toes and legs, swathed across his stomach and chest, and his beard was full and dark. His hair was also long and usually braided, though when he was in her mother's bed, he often seemed to delight in letting it free. Between his legs he also possessed something beastly. Even now, wet and waning, his cock was larger than any Phela had ever seen.

"Do I love you, Linos?" Lysandra asked.

"Madly, my queen," he said. He reached across and clasped her thigh in one huge hand, squeezing as if to prove ownership.

Phela willed her mother to slap his hand away. It was an unspeakable liberty, and despite what she had just witnessed them doing, the simple act of him holding her leg like a chunk of meat offended Phela deeply.

It seemed her mother did not think the same way.

Phela perused their bodies for a moment more, then shifted position slightly so that she could survey the rest of her mother's private chambers. She visited often enough, but viewing from this angle felt like seeing the place in all its brash, ostentatious honesty. When she was there in the queen's presence, all her attention was on her mother. She was a strong woman, assured and confident, harsh when the situation required it, loving in her way. Yet even from her daughter she demanded total attention.

Now, secreted away, Phela could look around.

Linos's clothing was deposited in an untidy pile near the heavy, closed door. His sheathed ceremonial sword stood propped against the wall. He must have entered the chambers and stripped off immediately, perhaps at his lover's request. The queen's clothing was neatly folded on a chair close to the large bed. Beside the bed, on a low table, was a carafe of wine with two fine crystal glasses, both still reflecting a deep ruby red from wine not yet drunk. Phela knew that her mother only touched wine in her most unguarded, private moments, and even then she only drank small quantities. She preferred to remain clearheaded.

Also on the table was the paraphernalia of spiza—several small glass vials, a mixing globe, and the familiar crumbled remains of the drybread usually eaten with purified spiza. That was also a vice belonging solely to Linos. If her mother was cautious of wine, she hated spiza. It took you away and opened you up. It made you vulnerable.

Phela knew all too well. She had tried it. Whispering in passages deep beneath the palace, she'd found a small room left over from construction works a thousand years ago. It was here that she'd hidden away to take spiza for the first time. One of the weaker blends used by many, it had still opened her mind and eased her down into a comfortable fugue. She had felt safe taking it there, alone and concealed from prying eyes. Yet, even so, she'd felt a rush of paranoia as the spiza faded from her system and senses, and the once-friendly darkness had seemed laden with threat. It was the one and only time she had fled her secret network of passageways and crawl spaces in fear.

She still wasn't sure whether the spiza had caused her to imagine the presences watching her or had allowed her to sense them.

Linos rolled onto his side and stretched for a pinch of the drybread. He ensured some of the refined spiza was sprinkled on top, then relaxed back onto the bed.

He didn't eat it, though. Instead, he dropped the drybread and spiza onto his hairy, muscled stomach.

Phela frowned. *What is he waiting for? Wait . . . no, the queen would never—*

But the queen did. She leaned over Linos and ate the mixture, and even from high above, with the heavy plastered ceiling between them and only a narrow crack to view through, Phela heard the crunching as her mother swallowed it down, not only demeaning herself before him, but also ingesting enough spiza to open her mind and let it drift.

Oh, Mother! she thought, but then she smiled through the shock. It was moments like this that made her Whispering so much more than a mere pastime. Such knowledge was the fuel to her future.

She settled down to watch for a little while longer.

⁓

An hour later, with the queen and her lover sleeping wrapped in each other's arms, Phela decided it was time to work her way back to her rooms.

Just as she moved she heard her mother's voice from below.

"The Four will be mine."

Phela frowned in the darkness. Surely she'd misheard? Either that or her mother was dreaming. She edged to the ceiling crack again and stared down.

The queen was seated, blanket drawn around her shoulders.

"The Four are always yours," Linos said. "You're queen."

Lysandra laughed, voice tinged with bitter humor. "That's a title. I have plenty. Do you want to hear some more?"

Linos waved a lazy hand.

"Figure of Nine," Lysandra said. "That means I'm patron of the greatest dance school in Quandis. Lady of Fields, which apparently means I oversee the farming needs around the Northern Lakes. Queen of Strikes, Honorary Beneficent Leader of Larks, Commander of the Army, Navy, and City Guard." She trailed off, hugging the blanket tighter. "Chief of the Silent."

"Of course," Linos muttered. His voice carried through the queen's chamber and up to its high ceiling. In the stillness, nothing existed but their words.

"The Four draw me," Lysandra said. "I've been there, you know. Down. Farther down than any royal before me, drowning in the shadows that have haunted the depths since before the Four created the world and cast the Pent Angel out. I've been . . . *deep*."

Linos was fully alert now, eyes wide at this dangerous talk. Phela considered warning her mother. A shout, a thump against wood, something to startle her out of her hazy, unguarded speech.

Something to stop this heresy.

Because the queen was not allowed to touch the magic of the Four. Though the royal bloodline was the bloodline of the Four, their magic was not meant for any mortal soul other than select priests of the High Order who had spent many years preparing. Even then, they only inhaled the dregs of that ancient magic.

And *none* of them went down to where the Four were alleged to lie.

"Mother, what have you done?" Phela said in a whisper too quiet even to disturb the dust inches from her lips.

"Tell me," Linos Kallistrate breathed, and in those words he revealed his true self. If he had loved Lysandra, he would have been begging her to stop.

"It's been too long," Lysandra said, her voice low and even, almost hypnotic. "Too many years Quandis has suffered its wars and conflicts, revolutions and strife, and all the while magic lies dormant in forgotten caverns, in the lost chambers of the fallen First City. If they truly loved us, wouldn't the Four share the magic they wielded when they forged this land? It's a question I've asked myself many times. I'm sure my father asked it as well, and the kings and queens before us. But asking the question goes no way toward answering it, whatever the priests of the High Order tell us. Honoring magic's existence and yet not seeking its touch is like . . . knowing the air is here, but not inhaling. Suffocating. Letting yourself die when all you need to do is open your mouth and *breathe*."

Lysandra was rocking now, moving side to side as the spiza surged through her veins and her mind opened up, gushing forth its thoughts into this otherwise silent room. Phela desperately wanted her mother to cease, because Linos could not be trusted.

But she also wanted her to reveal everything.

"And I'm going to breathe," Lysandra continued. "The High Order knows that magic is rich and full down there, they've known for generations. That old bastard Per Ristolo, he's over two centuries old, and magic has done that to him. I've been down there, Linos. Not as deep as I *will* go, given time, because as yet my body and mind can't take the rawness of the magic. But slowly I'll go deeper until . . . until I can . . . And then I'll truly be a royal of the bloodline of the Four. I'll bear the magic they once used to mold this land. The heat of the fire, the solidity of the earth, the strength of the wind, the power in the water. Imagine all that in your veins, Linos."

Phela glanced at Linos again and the change in him shocked

her. He was scared. Not just disturbed by what his lover was revealing to him, but properly afraid. As if he'd only now realized how
dangerous this talk really was.

"My queen . . ." he said, reaching and touching her shoulder.

She shrugged him off. "I feel . . . tired . . ."

"You should sleep," he said. "It was a mistake to give you so
much spiza."

"I don't make mistakes!" she said, but she let him pull her down
so that she was curled against his side, the blanket tucked around her
so that Phela could only see her mother's long golden hair splayed
across the pillows.

Linos lay back, still naked, staring up at the ceiling and frowning deeply.

Now he'll see me, Phela thought, and that twining of past and
future excited her. But he did not see her. He was focused on something much further away than these royal chambers.

She grinned in the darkness. The pompous prick had believed
he knew the queen so well—her intimacies, her body, her sexual
preferences, all laid out for his use. Now, he'd discovered far more
than he could have ever wished.

He knew her *true* secrets, of activities so forbidden that even a
queen might face trial and punishment.

And he was now *part* of them.

There were islands on the Ring where it was rumored scores of
High Order priests lived out their lives, banished because their initial contact with magic had driven them insane. There were many
unbelievers who thought magic to be a myth, tales left over from
older, less enlightened times. Yet anyone other than those of the
High Order who dared pursue magic was executed. On the main
island of Quandis, throughout the islands of the Ring, and even in
the Outer Territories, the pursuit of magic and the worship of the
Pent Angel were the only two crimes still punishable by death.

In all the history her tutors had ever taught her, all the journals and edicts she'd read in the Archives of the Crown, Phela could not think of a single instance when a royal had attempted to gather magic for themselves.

As she lay in her secret place, she sensed a new history unfolding around her.

⁓

A Bajuman dreams . . .

Blane's mother dresses him from head to foot in rough, itchy material. She sings as she does so, an old lullaby in a language he doesn't understand, and he smiles as the words flow from her mouth. His mother has a beautiful voice, and sometimes she sits by the side of the road leading from the port of Suskmouth to the capital city of Lartha and sings for their supper. More often than not she comes home with a few coins. Enough for some bread, fruit, and nuts, at least. Sometimes she returns with nothing. On those occasions she and her two children go hungry, and the past few days have been like that.

His mother's smile is a tight mask, and her singing now is ragged, her voice wandering away from the melody and struggling to return.

On the other side of their one-room hovel, his sister, Daria, is dressing herself. She's three years older than him, and she understands just how the material needs to fold and hang so that very little of her body and face is visible. People don't like seeing Bajumen, don't like to see the brands seared into their forearms to mark them from birth. They're slaves, lower than the lowest. Not everyone hates them, but many do, following a tradition of hatred that extends back generations. At best, they are ignored.

So the Bajumen make themselves invisible. The quieter they are, the smaller, the more likely it will be that they'll go a day without being abused, spat upon, or even beaten.

Blane sees his older sister like this on the day she dies. Her carefully arranged clothing, revealing only a sliver of cheek and her pale, piercing eyes—the eyes of all Bajumen, the deep blue shade that many have grown to hate. Winter eyes, people call them. She makes sure to cover the serpentine brand on the inside of her left forearm too. The serpent slithers upon its belly in the dirt, the lowest of all animals just as the Bajumen are the lowest of all peoples.

Blane waves good-bye as Daria leaves their hovel and goes to work for her master. She does not wave back. She is already out the door by then, and once in the open street a Bajuman rarely does anything that will draw attention. He remembers watching her for a moment longer, and then turning around to allow his mother to complete dressing him, covering his brand just as his sister had done her own.

She does not return that night, and it takes three frantic, worry-filled days to learn her fate. News filters through, whispers carried from person to person, that Daria's master has beaten her to death and disposed of her body in the sea. Blane never knows what imagined slight was the cause of such a beating. No one investigates. The seas around Quandis are often home to Bajuman dead.

"There is one way to escape," his mother says. She reaches for him, still mostly hidden in the shadows. When he takes her hand, it feels heavy and cold, so unlike her.

Squeezing his eyes closed, he wonders whose hand he is really holding.

A Bajuman dreams . . .

Blane and his sister are walking along a street somewhere on the outskirts of Lartha. In obscure dream-knowledge he understands that Daria has been dead for ten years, but still she walks with him, grown into a woman he will never know. Swathed in Bajuman clothing, they walk in silence, trying to be less than shadows. Yet something about her is far less Bajuman than he.

The street bustles. Traders have set their colorful stalls along either side of the road, leaving just enough room for rattling wagons to pass by in both directions. They attempt to sell trinkets made here in Lartha or hundreds of miles away on some of the more remote islands of the Ring. Or wine brewed on the mountainous slopes of the Spine to the south, and rarer drink imported from across wide oceans. Or food cooked and wrapped on the street—fried meats and spiza, pickled fruit, vegetables and grains he recognizes, and many more he does not. Blane doesn't approach any stalls. To be seen trading with a Bajuman will ruin their business for the day, something very few traders will risk.

If he and Daria wish to eat, it'll be by barter, later on when they're returning home and most of the traders are packing up for the evening.

He blinks, and every other person on the street is Bajuman.

The shouting and laughter fades to nothing, and the only sound is the shuffle of feet, the soft whisper of rough clothing against skin. The brightly colored stalls are now faded, displaying rotten food, broken jewelry and trinkets, wine gone to vinegar. Wagons no longer move along the road. He can see one in the distance resting on a broken axle, the skeletal remains of two dead horses still harnessed to the front.

"What is this?" he asks. He turns to Daria, but she doesn't seem to hear him. He reaches for her, but she brushes him off, his hand barely touching her rough garments.

Blane tries to keep up with her as she moves away, but even though she still only walks, she is much faster than him.

Others around the street are staring at him. He knows their eyes and their looks, because they are his own—the deep blue eyes that mark them as Bajuman; their branded flesh; the worried, cowed expressions that beg not to be challenged.

And then they all change.

The frowns turn into wicked grins. The eyes blaze fire that stills his heart, freezing it between beats. The people lower their hoods and fling open their garments, revealing naked bodies glorious in their health and ruddiness, no longer the sickly slaves they have always been. There's nothing sexual about the gesture. It's an expression of freedom.

His sister no longer flees. Instead she has turned around and is also fully revealed, and hatred blazes within her.

Blane looks down at himself and realizes that he is no longer Bajuman.

He is a priest, and preaching the word of the Four means he has betrayed every last Bajuman who has ever suffered in their age-old persecution.

They despise him for that. Even his long-dead sister, standing before him now with hatred burning at the very heart of her.

She hates him.

⁓

Blane woke into the welcome chill of dawn, troubled by his dreams. He knew they were little more than a manifestation of subconscious guilt. He'd had similar vivid nightmares many times before, and on the path he'd set himself he knew that they would recur. He also had no doubt that they would fade, given time.

He breathed in deeply and prepared himself for a day like the hundred before and hundreds that would follow. The days would gather and drift, but he knew that one day all Bajumen would recognize him for what he had achieved. This was the sole tenet of his singular, unique faith, the belief for which he suffered.

Until then, he could live with the guilt.

Blane sighed and swung his feet from the bed. The chill of the stone floor drove away the final vestiges of sleep, and then he heard the familiar sounds that had greeted him every morning since coming to Yaris Teeg, the home of those novices aspiring to join the priesthood of the Faith.

"Wake up, you nobodies! Rise with the sun. Bathe and do every disgusting thing you have to do, but be at breakfast by second dawn, or I'll have you scrubbing down the floor of the Chapel of the First till your fingers bleed and your knees powder to dust!"

"Per Santoger's in a good mood this morning," Gemmy said from Blane's left.

"Isn't he always?" Blane replied. Gemmy smiled and stood to dress, and Blane did the same. Throughout the dormitory fourteen other novice priests rose from their single cots, groggy, rubbing sleep from their eyes, dressing, shuffling slowly toward the bathrooms at the room's far end. The nudity had quickly become routine. *Everything* was routine. That was how Yaris Teeg worked. The Faith crafted novices into priests through simple repetition, so that each meal, prayer, and lesson became a groove in the soul, worn down the way a constant trickle of water might carve the path of a river over time. Repetition became faith in such a way. Routine became all a priest might know. It cut wounds that became scars, and scars were certainties.

But not for Blane. He promised himself he would never succumb to routine, and that he would only ever wear this faith like a mask.

"It's a good day to find the gods," Gemmy said, splashing cold water over her face. She and Blane shared a bowl, as was often the case. Having arrived at Yaris Teeg together they had quickly become friends. At least, as friendly as the instructors would allow.

She was right. It was a good day. Sun streamed through the high, unglazed windows in all four walls of the bathroom area, and Blane could see clear blue skies beyond. A few birds circled, soon lost behind the stone walls. The windows were quite narrow. Their view was restricted.

Blane splashed more water over his face to hide his tired sigh. The serpent on the inside of his left forearm stared back at him in accusatory fashion, as if disdaining his pursuit of the priesthood. He pushed such doubts away, as he did every day.

The novices filed through their routines with drilled efficiency. Then, after an hour of prayer in Yaris Teeg's main chapel, Per Santoger faced the novices and recited passages from the Covenant of the Four. His leather-bound book was old, and some said it had been used at Yaris Teeg for over six hundred years. Its pages were sometimes replaced with fresh rubbings from the Covenant castings in the Temple of Four, facsimiles of ancient instructions supposedly hacked into the rock of the land by the gods eons ago. But the book as a whole was original, and its leathery cover was stained dark with the hand sweat of countless teachers.

Per Santoger made the words his own, booming them out so that they echoed from the chapel like the voice of the gods themselves.

A basic breakfast of bread and goat's milk followed. After that came a period of silent, personal prayer, and many chose to perform these prayers in private. The instructors allowed the isolation, because they maintained it was good for the soul and permitted each novice to find his or her own path to the gods.

For Blane, the path was somewhere secret. Parting from his small group, he slipped off and made his way through Yaris Teeg to one of the smaller libraries. He waited until the librarian's back was turned and breezed through, passing between ranks of packed shelving and isolated lecterns bearing ancient tomes, and heading toward the back of the large room. Down a circular set of stairs, through a narrow, low corridor formed of shelves that had slumped and fallen into one another, he entered part of the library that was rarely visited. Most books and scrolls here were written in languages he did not understand, and if they were studied, it was not by any novices he knew. Perhaps the High Order came here to delve into the deep past, or the writings of civilizations from far away or long ago.

That was why he came. While the others undertook private prayer, Blane entered into solitary study. He might spend hours here and find nothing overtly useful, but he still believed that his knowledge was expanding with every visit to this place. There were other libraries uphill at the Temple of Four, places forbidden to novices, but he had explored there as well. He had to. He was seeking hidden truths and had long been convinced that the secret ways to the magic he sought were buried in ancient wisdom.

If that magic even existed.

It had always seemed to him a thing that occurred only in folktales, like stories about ghosts and the Phage, and the Pent Angel, and monsters that populated legends about the islands of the Ring. Most of what he'd gleaned suggested that very few truly believed in magic anymore, but some priests of the High Order were said to have the power to influence the elements, communicate with spirits of the dead, and cast illusions. Blane didn't know what to believe, but if magic existed—if the High Order had access to that kind of power—then he wanted it for himself.

No. Not for himself. For his people.

The Bajumen had their own legends, the prophecy of the Kij'tal chief among them. The Kij'tal was a savior imbued with godlike power who would rise from within their own ranks to free them from slavery and build a new Bajuman nation. Nonsense, of course. Even his mother had not believed such foolishness, though many of their people did. And yet if the Kij'tal was never to come, then *someone* among them must rise. Blane believed that if he could advance within the Faith and become High Order and access their arcane magic, then he could use it to free the Bajumen. The Kij'tal might be a myth, but if magic existed, Blane might wield it to force the bigots to truly see his people for the first time.

He looked at an old book from close to the bottom of a pile, forced out by the weight above it. Pages were swollen with damp, the cover soft and pulpy. Much of the print had faded to nothing, but he found some pages that were still willing to reveal their secrets. There were images drawn in a style he'd never seen before, symbols that might have been a form of writing. He studied the pages until he found similar patterns, trying to find a rhythm and sense to the language. There was none to be seen, but still he spent time with the book open in his lap. Sometimes an image or meaning would bloom in his mind hours or days after viewing, as if his mind continued working on the question subconsciously.

If the magic was real, he *would* find it in time.

Later, he slipped from the library and rejoined his companions. Gemmy had spent the time alone in their quarters, and she smiled a contented smile when she saw him, face awash with joy at her communion with the Four. Her smile made her beautiful, but he pitied her blind, foolish faith.

They trooped down a series of open staircases to their gardens beside the river at the base of Temple Hill. Though this was only one of the Seven Hills that comprised the core of the capital city, and though bridges connected Temple Hill to its nearest neighbors, most thought of it as separate. Indeed, it did not look at all like the other six hills. Over centuries the sprawl of civilization had covered the others, and Temple Hill seemed simple and bare by comparison. There were storehouses and stables, two breweries, a book bindery, and a handful of smaller temples dedicated to one discipline or another, all of them in the shadow of the Temple of Four, which stood high atop the hill with its four grand towers casting their shadows down upon the city. And on the far side of that hill, as if hidden away from the rest of the capital, there was Yaris Teeg.

At the foot of Temple Hill the river Susk flowed into the city, and there were fertile fields where the novices nurtured crops, tended to orchards, and grew flowers whose beauty had earned renown even on distant shores.

Blane, Gemmy, and the others worked for several hours in the blazing sun, maintaining a respectful silence so that the work would itself become a form of relaxation and prayer. It was nearing the end of the Planting Season, and there were still seeds to sow, weeds to dig out, new beds to plow over, water to fetch from the river, and a dozen other tasks to ensure the gardens provided the entire priesthood with enough fruit and vegetables to last through the winter. The Growing Season would officially begin in three days' time, and then their work went from planting to tending these new crops.

Blane liked it down by the river; it soothed his turbulent heart. The shush of the churning water cut out sounds from the city, iridescent birds swooped and fished, dragonflies buzzed the banks and plucked insects from the air. Here, at work in the Faith's gardens, Blane felt almost at peace.

In truth, he'd been more at peace since he'd been at Yaris Teeg than ever before, because none of the instructors from the priesthood looked upon him as Bajuman. That had been a shock upon arriving, almost disconcerting, and it had taken some time to get used to being treated the same as all other novices. Slowly, Blane was becoming used to being a person, not a thing.

Still, he didn't let himself forget.

Because even his first day here he'd seen the familiar look of disgust and contempt that he'd grown up with. From Gemmy. It was in her eyes as she had gushed the usual bile. Words of hate had lost meaning for him long before, but their tone was always poison.

He'd blinked and looked aside and down, a familiar tactic to turn his Bajuman gaze from anyone looking directly at him.

A sigh had followed. When he looked back, Gemmy had been crying.

"It's going to take me some time," she'd said.

"Time for what?"

"To unlearn."

⌒

Pausing close to the river, empty buckets ready to be filled with water once again, Blane stretched his back and looked up the hill. The towers of the Temple of Four rose high above them, crowning the hilltop, taller even than the Blood Spire and Bone Spire that soared above Palace Hill. Each of the temple's towers had been built in dedication to one of the Four, which in turn proved how the Four had been an integral part of Quandis history for millennia.

"Don't slack, Blane," Per Santoger said. The old priest walked the gardens, taking time to work now and then, but spending more time overseeing the novices' digging and hoeing, planting and watering. Blane often saw him standing or crouching by a worker, talking with the person about the Four, quoting words from the Covenant that he always carried. He sometimes sounded gruff, but he was a man dedicated to his cause. Some said he'd been a priest since he was seven years old.

"Just stretching my back, Per Santoger."

"Physical work is good for the soul."

"And bad for the back."

Per Santoger smiled, then crouched down and beckoned Blane to do the same. He was a big man, taller than most, girth expanded by many years of priests' ale, yet he was as devout as any, and renowned for his affinity for novice priests.

"You seem troubled," the old priest said. "Sometimes distant. As if your whole heart isn't here."

"I'm very much here," Blane said, trying to sound sincere. "Every part of me."

The priest nodded slowly. He was rocking back and forth, his robes trailing in mud, the various chains of his office clanging gently. He did not take his eyes from Blane's. Staring into the deep blue eyes of a Bajuman, the old man betrayed no distaste. Blane truly was an equal here, and that still troubled him.

"You're more special than most," Per Santoger said. "Someone who has further to climb achieves a greater purpose. In most people's eyes you started lower than low. They see a slave, not a person. In some ways that makes things more difficult for you."

"Not more difficult," Blane said. "There's simply more to strive for."

"Finding the Four is never easy," the priest said. "I shout at you all and berate you, and tell you that your days are not yet simple enough, your piety is uninformed, your quest for the Four is a journey you've only just begun. But you must also know that I want the best for you all. The journey to the Four is long, and even my own path is only just begun."

Blane was not sure how to reply to that. So he simply nodded and looked at the ground between his feet.

"You'll learn not to look aside," Per Santoger said, and it was as if the priest understood Blane's true desire. "Now help me up. My old man's knees are about to seize."

Blane helped the priest to his feet, then went back to work. His back continued to ache, but he no longer paused. He enjoyed sweating, relished the heat of the blazing sun on his back.

After lunch they were allowed a brief period of rest. The male and female priests overseeing their training expected that this period be filled with personal prayer, but on occasion social contact was also allowed.

Blane did neither. He sat on one of the many sets of steps in the shadow of the Temple of Four and closed his eyes, face tilted slightly toward the sky. An observer might have believed him at prayer, and though his thoughts concerned the gods, he was not seeking them out.

I shun Lameria, god of the Bajumen, he thought. *I shun the Four, gods of Quandis. I shun the Pent Angel, the fallen god. Unencumbered, free and clear, I set to my work.*

Other Bajumen might believe he had betrayed them, but it was for them that he did this. If the price of his quest for freedom was their rejection and hatred, he could live with that.

I suffer for us all so that, one day, none of us will suffer again.

Later, Per Santoger rang his bell, and Blane made his way back to the others. Tired from the morning's work, they climbed the stairs cut into the face of the hill and passed through the walls of the temple. They gathered in a small courtyard, waiting for the priest to lead them to one of the great libraries for an afternoon of quiet reading and contemplation of the Covenant.

Instead, he spoke.

"News has reached me of troubling events," Per Santoger said. "Linos Kallistrate has been arrested. He is charged with blasphemy and treason, and being a worshipper of the Pent Angel." A hush of whispers went through the trainees. "His execution has been scheduled for dusk in Hero's Square."

"There hasn't been an execution for years!" Gemmy said.

"Nine, to be precise," Per Santoger said. "You understand what this means. Novices from Yaris Teeg traditionally provide a choir at executions. So now I'm troubled with teaching you all to sing."

Blane and Gemmy swapped glances.

"Will Apex Euphraxia be there?" Gemmy asked. Euphraxia was almost a mythical figure, Voice of the Four and yet rarely seen by anyone other than the nobility and members of her own household. Some said she was two hundred years old. Some said she was a ghost.

"The apex's movements and intentions are not mine to know, nor to speculate upon," the old priest snapped.

"What song do we sing?" Blane asked, but Per Santoger had already turned and was making his way inside the temple.

"It's called the 'Mournful Quell,'" Gemmy said. She surprised him by taking his hand. Her excitement surprised him more. "Come, Blane. We're going to make history!"

2

Demos Kallistrate stood hunched in his cell, staring at the heavy wooden door that barred him from freedom, his breath coming in angry huffs. His fists were clenched, his knuckles bleeding, so swollen that he could barely open his hands. He'd shouted at first, screaming at his jailers to release him, demanding to see his surviving family and know what had become of them. But the iron-grated window set into the stone wall let more than the breeze into his cell—it brought him the mocking cries and excited chatter from the road below. Dirty children, belligerent daytime drunks, and ill-tempered rabble had gathered to collect every scrap of gossip and sorrow they could find. If he had learned one thing in his time sailing as part of Quandis's navy, it was that horror always brought carrion, and those black-hearted creatures rejoiced in picking at its bones.

So he kept his voice silent, even as he stepped forward and began to beat on the heavy door again. His fists crashed against the wood, his boots kicked at its bracings, his shoulder shook the door in its frame, but he knew he would never break it down. The Guards understood their duty and would not be summoned by his pounding. Still, what could he do but try? He didn't belong here. He was Demos Kallistrate, son of Baron Linos of Clan Kallistrate, Supreme Admiral of the Navy. Though no official announcement of betrothal had been made, surely the entire capital knew he was the intended of the Princess Myrinne, youngest child of Queen Lysandra.

How could they do this to him?

He couldn't feel his hands anymore and wondered if his knuckles were broken. Exhausted, he staggered backward and rested against the stone wall, closed his eyes, and felt the breeze. The afternoon shadows were long, dusk not far off. It had been a beautiful morning, and then the day had become a nightmare. A detachment of the City Guard had marched up Kallistrate Hill and burst into his family home without warning. Demos's father had flown into a rage, ordering them to stand down. Instead they had beaten him with cudgels and bound his hands, and when Demos and his younger brother, Cyrus, had attempted to defend their father, they had been beaten as well. Demos had heard the snap of breaking bone before his brother cried out and cradled his arm to his chest. One soldier had taken their mother, Carina, by a fistful of hair and dragged her from the house.

Once his whole family had been removed, the City Guard had set fire to the house, the noble seat of Clan Kallistrate. Cyrus had been unconscious by then, dumped into the back of a jail wagon, and their father had a black sack over his head, cinched tightly around his throat. So neither he nor Cyrus had witnessed the family home engulfed in flames as the horses drew the jail wagon downhill and across the bridge to Palace Hill.

Demos had seen. And they had all heard his mother screaming at the sight.

Now, in this small cell, Demos's ears echoed with the memory of his mother's cries.

Breathing deeply to steady himself, he stared at the locked door. The split in his upper lip had reopened and fresh blood trickled. His skull and back throbbed from the beating he'd taken. He'd been in the navy five years, doing the hard labor of sailing, fighting island savages and lunatic Penters, and repelling pirates determined to string his intestines from the rigging of his own ship. Demos had been hurt worse than this.

His pride, though—that was where it stung. That, and not knowing what was happening with the rest of his family.

Outside, the sweet, angelic voice of a little girl rose in a lovely melody, a tune about the Seven Deaths, the variety of execution methods that were once employed by the Crown and the Faith. She must have learned that in school. The fact that there had not been an execution since before she was born made the song and its possibilities even more chilling.

He started for the door again, fists raised.

The lock rattled.

Demos stopped and took a step backward as the door creaked inward. A tall Guard with a thin beak of a face ducked his nose into the cell. Demos readied himself to attack, but the man put up a finger to hush him and withdrew into the corridor.

The door swung farther inward, and a woman wearing the rough, wine-red cloak common to the Crown's healers stepped in. He was ready to tell her to get out when she drew back the hood.

"Thank the Four, you're all right," Demos breathed.

Princess Myrinne shot a look at the Guard. "You watch this door, Konnell." She gave the man a shove, closed the door behind him, and put her back to the bloodstained wood. Finally she looked back at Demos.

"*You* were worried about *me?*" she asked.

"They came for my family, Myr. They burned our home. If they could do that—"

She crossed the cell in two long strides, grabbed his head between her hands, and kissed him deeply. Demos moaned from the pain of his bloody mouth and from the emotion that threatened to spill from him, but he drove them both away, grabbed her shoulders, and held her at arm's length.

"Myr—"

"They're all alive," Myrinne said. She knew his first question, of course. "I'll tell you quick, because I can't stay."

Demos released her. "You can't get us out?"

All his worst fears seemed to be true. *No, not your worst fears— they're all alive, she said.* But if not the worst, then near enough. Myrinne was a princess of Quandis. If she could do nothing . . .

"It must be some error," he went on. "Your mother has given our betrothal her blessing. She has had my father in her bed and my own mother hasn't raised even a whisper of objection, if only to save the future you and I have together. At first I thought I might've done something to turn her against me, but I've only been home from sea a single night. I meant to visit my family and then surprise you, and if they didn't know I'd be here, surely the queen—"

Myrinne grabbed his arm to still him. "Quiet, boy," she said. They were same words she'd been using to hush or calm him since they had both learned how to speak. They had played together even as toddlers and had known each other forever. "It's not you who's enraged her."

Demos knew, then. "Father."

"He's accused of treason and blasphemy—"

"Blasphemy?"

Myrinne glanced away, unable to meet his eyes. "Worshipping the Pent Angel."

Demos grabbed hold of his skull as if his head might topple from his shoulders. "Gods, no." He ought to have known. They didn't burn the houses of common criminals. But this? It wouldn't just be his father who suffered if the accusation could be supported.

What are you thinking? Of course it can't! "My father's no Penter. And he's no traitor, either."

Myrinne rose to her full height, an inch taller than Demos. Her black hair framed her pale face, and in the failing light of day, in the golden gloaming, she seemed a ghost of the beautiful life he'd imagined.

"He's been accused by the queen herself, my love," she said stiffly, almost formally. "It doesn't matter if the charges are true. His execution will be—"

"*Execution?*" Demos said. He shook his head, trying to loosen the idea and let it fall away. The idea of his father's death. Such a big man, strong, proud. "There hasn't been an execution in years."

"My mother is making an exception in this case," Myrinne said.

Demos turned from her. He leaned a shoulder against the wall, fists throbbing where the feeling had begun to return to his swollen knuckles. How would he fight this? He'd been in battles in distant lands, brought pirates to justice as an officer of the navy, grown up as companion to Myrinne and friend to her siblings, Phela and Aris. He'd trained in swordsmanship under the same masters as the children of the Five Great Clans, side by side with the three young royals. But this was a different kind of fight.

"You know he's not a Penter," Demos said. "And so does she. She's punishing him for something else. What could he possibly have done to warrant this?"

"I've no idea. But we'll think of—"

The lock rattled. The door creaked open. The bird-beaked City Guard, Konnell, ducked his head in.

"Dusk approaches, Princess," Konnell whispered. "I hear boots on the stairs."

She cursed. When she spun toward Demos again, he saw the

pain in her eyes for the first time. Up to this point she'd been full of grim purpose, but now she shuddered and wiped dampness from her eyes.

Myrinne put a hand behind his neck, pressed her forehead to his. "You're to be taken to Hero's Square for judgment and the pronouncement of your father's execution date. The whole family."

"All of this in public," he said numbly. "The nobles . . . the Five Clans . . . they won't stand for it. My father is a baron."

"Highborn or lowborn, we're all just flesh and bone," she said, her tone heavy with warning. "These are dreadful hours, and you'll need to be smart instead of proud. I'll do whatever I can, but in the meantime, promise me you won't fight them."

He imagined his mother stripped and flogged, imagined Cyrus branded. "How can you ask me that?"

"Because I know you," Myrinne said. "In your whole life, you've never encountered an obstacle you couldn't remove by pulling rank, starting a fight, or turning on the charm."

He managed half a smile. "You want me to try charming the hangman?"

"If it were possible, yes! But you know it won't work, and fighting or trying to pull rank won't work any better. I'm trying to save your life, Demos. Don't make the job any harder."

She pushed him away, tugged up the hood on her wine-dark cloak, and then swept past Konnell into the hallway and was gone. When Konnell closed the door and Demos heard the lock fall into place, all he could think was that he wished he had kissed her one last time. Just in case.

From outside his window came the voice of the little girl again singing about the Seven Deaths. Jeers and laughter rose up from the road, too, and he heard the clatter of hooves and wagon wheels. And for the first time it actually dawned on him:

Perhaps the judgment on the whole of his family would be

more than flogging, more than branding. More than the mere breaking of bones.

Perhaps Queen Lysandra meant to execute them *all*.

Demos hurried over to the window, grabbed the high sill, and pulled himself up so he could see outside. He saw torchlamps igniting along the road, throwing strange shadows upon the faces of the milling crowd and against the shops and homes and other structures as evening crept over Lartha. The people did not disperse. They could sense the spectacle coming.

They smelled blood.

The lock on his cell ratcheted again and he turned, hopeful. But this time it wasn't Myrinne that Konnell brought with him. Two of the new arrivals were City Guard, but they were mere shadows at the corners of his vision compared to the third person Konnell led into the cell. Demos's blood ran cold.

Shome of the Silent stood six and a half feet tall. The tattoos of her order marked her face and the left side of her scalp, which she kept shaved. Shome led the cadre of mute women assassins who served Queen Lysandra. Their existence was rumor to most, but not to Princess Myrinne's intended husband.

"Demos Kallistrate," one of the soldiers said, "you will accompany us now. Your arms will be bound, but not your legs, unless you fight us or attempt to escape."

He ignored them and focused solely on Shome. In the golden light her eyes appeared orange.

"What is she doing here?" he asked slowly, chin raised in the defiant pride that noble birth had bred into him. Myrinne had said pulling rank would be useless, but surely his nobility had *some* meaning to these people.

The Guard who had spoken sniffed a bit and shifted his feet nervously. "I see no one," he said. "We see no one."

"*No one*," Konnell echoed. His eyes narrowed, his gaze heavy with caution.

"Cowards," Demos whispered, a thin smile of defiance on his lips. "I mean, I have known some cowards in my life," he said, louder. "I've killed dozens of them. But even *those* cowards weren't as pathetic as you lot."

Despite his disdain, he meant to cooperate. He would allow them to bind his arms but leave his legs free. Bruised and bloody, he would have that dignity, at least. But then he heard the sound of his mother screaming from farther down the corridor. She was screaming not in anguish or fear this time, but in fury, and he knew she had chosen to fight the soldiers who had come for her. His muscles tensed, his bloody hands fisted once again.

When they finally dragged Demos from his cell, they had bound him at the wrists and ankles and his clothes were stained with fresh blood, not all of it his own.

Fuck dignity.

⁓

The dusty shelves of the Archives of the Crown had vanished into shadow as the last light of day faded. Phela sat hunched over an ornately carved wooden table laden with yellowed scrolls and heavy tomes full of crumbling pages. Something her mother had said the night before had set her off on this latest excursion into the archives. As evening arrived, she bent farther to bring the words closer to her eyes. She was so intent upon her task that it was only when the writing on the pages became illegible that she realized how dark it had become.

Tutting at the inconvenience, she slid back the chair and stood, glancing about the room for a lamp. She searched past shelves and tall storage units, in nooks and cupboards, and around where the true crown lay beneath a stone altar, hidden from all eyes. She found one eventually on a small table near the massive archive door. From its weight alone, she knew it needed refilling, but a bit of oil still splashed in the well, so it would do for now.

Just as she opened the wooden matchbox beside the lamp, she heard the low rumble of voices beyond the door and froze. One voice was deeper and louder than the others, more irritated, more in command.

Her nose wrinkled in disdain. It was her brother, Aris. The prince who followed his prick.

Her footsteps soft, Phela crossed back to her chair and stepped up onto it, then onto the table, and from there into the towering bookshelf beyond. The archives were full of such impressive shelves, but this bookcase had come to serve another purpose for the princess on more than one occasion.

Aris hammered on the door. "Sister! Open this door!" A pause, then another round of banging followed. "I know you're in there. We've looked every other gods-damned place."

Like a spider, she clambered up the tall bookcase and reached for the balustrade of the narrow balcony above. She hoisted herself up and over, then perched there, her breathing as quiet and unlabored as her thoughts.

"Open it," she heard Aris say, beyond the door.

There came the rattle of a key and a thump as the ancient lock turned. The door drew open and the archivist, Samnee, entered. She was an old woman with skin the same rough yellow as the parchment paper that filled these rooms, her vast domain.

"Out of the way," Aris said, brushing the crone aside as he barged through the door with a lantern held high. In its glare his face appeared waxy and sick, not the handsome features of the stalwart and forthright Prince Aris, beloved of all Quandis.

Almost *all,* Phela thought.

"I told you she wasn't here," Samnee said in the snide tone she'd used on Queen Lysandra's offspring ever since Phela could remember. Though mostly on Phela herself, since neither Aris nor Myrinne had ever spent more than an hour in the Archives of the Crown by choice. Phela was the sponge who soaked up knowledge.

Aris sniffed the air like a hunting dog and strode toward the table. Phela stiffened then. She didn't like the idea that he might take a close look at the scrolls and books that had seized her attention.

"Prince Aris—"

"She's here," Aris said. "Or she was."

Samnee sighed irritably. "As I've told you, nobody enters the archives without my key, and it is still safely with me. Princess Phela is *not* here."

Phela couldn't help smiling at the archivist's utter dismissal of her brother. Very few of the Crown's subjects would dare speak to a royal that way, even Aris, so beloved for his kindness and fairness and his insistence on all things being neat and orderly. But Samnee had never been fond of the prince, partly because he had no interest in enriching his mind, and partly because he could be an utter bastard when his adoring public was nowhere to be found.

Aris raised the lantern high, its light throwing ghostly shadows all around the sprawling archive chamber. Phela hunched lower, though she knew he couldn't see her where she hid up high.

"Have it your way," he said aloud to the room. "But if you are here, hiding among the stories of the dead the way you did as a girl, you should know that both Mother and Myrinne have asked me to find you, each for her own purpose. The queen has asked because there's to be a public spectacle in Hero's Square a short while from now. Perhaps even an execution, if the presence of the hangman is any indication. Myrinne, on the other hand, has asked for you because the family facing justice tonight is dear to her. I believe Mother intends to have Baron Kallistrate killed. Maybe the wife and sons as well."

Phela went numb. She stared into the darkness of the narrow balcony that ran around the dome of the archives. It was a place where no one came anymore, not even old Samnee, whose knees could no longer endure the climb. She'd probably forgotten that this place even existed. Phela should have felt safe, but even up here the world intruded.

Linos? she thought. *The baron's entire family? Surely not.*

The grunts and slapping of flesh from the previous night's adventure returned to her, but it wasn't the rutting she'd witnessed that mattered here. The queen had taken spiza, urged on by her lover, and she'd confessed to a crime that might threaten to destroy her. But that would never happen if the only witness had already been hanged in Hero's Square. Clearly she hadn't been so addled as not to remember what she had said.

Gods-damn it, Phela thought, and she stood up to reveal herself.

Aris had already left the room, taking Samnee with him. As Phela opened her mouth to speak, the door slammed shut and the key turned in the heavy lock, leaving the princess to stare into the darkness. Which was for the best, really. After all, what would she have said? She needed a few moments to gather her thoughts, to consider how this evening's horrors might unfold.

She slipped along the bookcase-lined balcony and found the little door leading to the tight spiral stairs back down into the archive. Beside the door, behind a curtain, she entered a narrow recess that seemed nothing more than a storage space or a vent for air, perhaps a flaw in the design of the room, some unfinished bit of architecture. To anyone else it would seem odd but uninviting, but Phela knew better. These passages were vital to her Whispering. Such secret labyrinths that existed behind, above, and beneath the places most eyes could see cradled her and gave her time to think.

There was no time now, though.

Princess Phela hurried back to her quarters to change her clothes. She had horrors to witness. She had not believed it would come to this, but if her mother's indiscretions led to public executions, she might use even that to her own advantage. There would be no more Whispering tonight, but she had a feeling there might be screams.

_cᴖ_

Torches poured smoke into the night sky and set shadows dancing around Hero's Square. Demos blinked blood out of his eyes as the City Guard dragged him out of the jail wagon. His brother, Cyrus, had sobbed in fear and confusion throughout the short ride from the jail, nursing his broken arm and worrying over their mother. Carina Kallistrate had been beaten unconscious by Guards after she had clawed their faces. One of them had been rushed away to healers, likely to lose an eye. *Served the bastard right,* he thought.

Bumping along the street in the back of the wagon, Demos had eased Cyrus aside and checked his mother's pulse, searched her skull for softness or indentations, and pulled back her eyelids to examine her pupils. In the Crown's navy he had seen many injuries, and he was certain she would live.

Which meant that she was still fit enough for them to kill.

Cyrus struggled against his captors as the City Guard pulled Carina from the back of the wagon and dropped her to the ground. One of them dumped a bucket of water over her head. Shocked to consciousness, she sputtered and swore and tried to attack them again.

"Mother, enough!" Demos snapped.

Carina grew still and looked around the square. Demos watched her take in their surroundings. Rage bled from her face, replaced by shock and a flicker of something that might have been hopelessness. Whatever fate awaited, she knew it could not be avoided. Demos felt proud of his mother, but he could not say the same about Cyrus.

His brother wept.

Demos understood those tears, but he would not give Queen Lysandra the satisfaction.

Hero's Square—halfway up Palace Hill—had been used for centuries as the site of celebrations honoring military heroes returning home to Lartha. Demos had twice been decorated here by the queen for courage in naval combat. His father had even received the Silver Spear, the highest military honor the Crown could bestow, forged in the catacombs beneath the palace from the ruins of the Silver Citadel, bloodied in battle generations ago and blessed by the apex.

No one was being honored tonight. Demos's proud father stood battered, bloody yet defiant, as tall as his abused body would allow. He looked straight ahead into some indefinable distance. Perhaps to meet his family's gaze would break the last shred of control he had.

The torches flickered, the fire jumping and sparking like living things. The smoke created a veil in the breeze that shrouded Queen Lysandra's personal guard. The queen herself stood on a platform her servants had carried with them, three steps and a dais decorated with inlaid gold feathers and the symbol of the Crown. It elevated her above the masses that had gathered, several hundred eager faces who were joined every moment by many more. Soon there would be thousands, coming across the bridges from the other hills and up from the valley and the river's edge. The crowd had seen public punishments before, but never in Hero's Square, and never of a noble clan. And definitely not of a clan whose baron had been so close to the queen, and whose eldest son had been rumored as the future husband of a princess. This felt like an evening when history would be forged.

Prince Aris joined his mother on the dais, one step behind her. A moment later, Demos saw Princess Phela climbing the platform to join them. Two members of the Silent flanked the dais, standing on the ground—they could not be elevated with royals. Regardless of where they stood, Demos felt shocked to see them there, so publicly associating with the queen. The assassins were rarely seen, and only spoken about in whispers to frighten those who might raise their voices against the Crown. It was more evidence of how much had changed in a single day.

Of Myrinne, there was no sign.

The hangman, known to most as Death's Hand, stepped into the clearing the crowd had left in front of the dais. His last execution had been almost a decade ago, and Demos found himself wondering what the man had been doing all this time. It was a strange thought. He didn't really want to know.

As Death's Hand raised his right fist, the crowd fell silent.

"Linos Kallistrate!" he said, his booming voice carrying across the square. "You are accused of treason against the Crown, and blasphemy against the Faith, and named as a worshipper of the Pent Angel. If you wish to speak against these accusations, do so now."

The crowd all turned to stare at the pale, shaking form of Baron Linos Kallistrate. His clothing was torn. He'd been beaten, his face bloody and so swollen that his left eye seemed to have vanished. Now he stood up, his spine rigid, and his guards held him tightly as he opened his mouth to mount a defense.

But nothing came.

Or, rather, what came was a series of ragged, unintelligible noises. Demos saw his mother sag against her guard, and his brother issued a plaintive cry for their father's anguish. Blood spilled from Linos's mouth as a black, mangled stump of muscle tried to form some recognizable language.

Death's Hand had cut out his tongue.

Demos saw the glint of cruel amusement in the executioner's eyes, and he turned to stare at Queen Lysandra. *No, not just the queen. Myrinne's mother,* Demos thought. Seeing her delight in this cruelty, he didn't know how that could be possible.

Queen Lysandra stood on the dais with a look of calm satisfaction. Demos saw the way Princess Phela shifted behind her, watching her struggle with this proclamation as if she might speak against it, and he allowed himself a flicker of hope.

"As the queen herself is your accuser," the hangman continued, "there will be no trial. Tomorrow at dawn, you will be executed for your crimes, and your family—"

Linos cried out in that ragged voice and struggled against his captors.

That was quickly drowned out by a chorus of soft dissent rippling through the crowd. Many of those in attendance were of noble birth themselves, members of the Five Great Clans, and they were used to feeling safe. Untouchable. Now the unimaginable had begun to unfold and they all felt it.

To execute the baron of one of the Five Great Clans without trial was an affront they could not countenance. The anger and shock rapidly cascaded around him, a contagious epiphany spreading by whisper—especially among the nobles from the other clans. Because while the Crown had the right to summary judgment, under the law, the crowd knew—as did Demos himself—of no instance in which any king or queen had exercised that right, at least not since the Josqueni uprising nearly a century before. If Lysandra would order the murder of Baron Kallistrate, what was to stop her from having any one of them executed if they spoke against her?

Not a gods-damned thing.

Carina began to shout words of denial, and Cyrus cursed Lysandra's soul. But Demos felt none of their heat. Rather there was a cold distance between himself and his own bones, as if his ghost had separated from his flesh and time had slowed to a snail's crawl. He allowed himself to breathe, staring at the queen and her children standing with her. Phela had a slender, vulpine beauty, her copper-red hair cut short but somehow still a mess of unruly tufts. Aris had a darker aspect, neat and handsome and orderly, the sort of future monarch one would never imagine might support murder and conspiracy. Yet that was precisely what they were all witnessing. Whatever the real reason, it was clear Queen Lysandra had finished with Demos's father and now she wanted him out of the way. Perhaps he truly had offended her, or maybe he knew things that might endanger her, but Demos was confident that his father was no traitor and certainly no Penter. His execution would be murder, pure and simple, in public and in service to the Crown.

Aris touched his mother's arm and Queen Lysandra turned to leave the dais. Her personal guard closed in around the bottom of the steps with the two Silent watching the crowd for potential threats. Death's Hand barked an order and two soldiers wrestled with Linos, trying to drag him from the square. He roared, spitting blood through the air and refusing to be taken away, and Demos found himself stepping forward. His mother shouted her husband's name, trying to shake loose her Guards so that she could lunge for him, but she was held back.

"Where is she?" Demos shouted, staring at the queen, furious and defiant. "Where is your daughter, Princess Myrinne? She would be here if she could, and she would speak against this, unless you have locked her up as well. Is that it? Are you too ashamed to allow Myrinne to witness this *atrocity*?"

The queen tried to ignore him, but Demos saw a subtle waver as she stood on the top step, as if she'd become light-headed. Phela took her arm and steadied her.

As Demos's words echoed in the silence of the square, it was clear they had an effect. The City Guards holding Linos had stopped to listen. Even Linos himself had gone quiet. The gathered masses awaited some reply from the Crown. Queen Lysandra took the second step.

"What are you hiding?" Demos screamed at her when they got none. "What does my father know that you would cut out his tongue to keep him from speaking?"

Prince Aris had also been steadying his mother. Now he turned and stalked to the edge of the dais, looming above Demos Kallistrate, who only hours before had been like a brother to him.

"My sister is not here because she could not bear to look at you, who she once loved so deeply," Aris said, sneering in disgust. "She is not here because she's ashamed to be seen and to have the good people of Quandis—highborn and lowborn alike—remember that she nearly made the mistake of marrying herself into a family so full of disgrace, a family of traitors and heretics—"

"Lies!" Cyrus screamed, tears streaming down his face. "You lie!"

A Guardsman threw him down, smashing him face-first against the stones of the square. Cyrus didn't cower, though, and instead twisted, reaching for the dagger at the Guard's hip. He managed to draw out the blade and was squaring himself up for a lunging attack when he was struck again. The Guard twisted the blade out of his hand, forcing Cyrus back to his knees, and savagely kicked him in the head once, twice, a third time, each blow punctuated by cries and gasps from the crowd. Screaming Cyrus's name, Carina shook off the soldier holding her and ran to her younger son, but the Guardsmen quickly converged and dragged the two apart. They stood Carina on her feet and tried to do the same to Cyrus, but even though his eyes were open, there was no light coming from them. His face had already begun to swell, blood ran from his nose, and he clearly couldn't stand on his own. The Guards had to prop him there as if he were some farmer's scarecrow.

Demos felt sick. He knew he ought to be silent now. If the queen would countenance such treatment of his brother, she would certainly not hesitate to have her City Guard kill Demos himself. And yet he took two steps toward the dais and glared at Aris.

"My brother is right," Demos said. "I don't believe you, and neither do these people. The whole city knows that the queen took my father into her bed! There's something more here, something she—"

"Enough!" Aris thundered. Taking that as an order, one of the soldiers guarding Demos thumped him in the gut, winding him. As he bent over and gasped for breath, Aris leaped from the dais and dropped into the square only a few feet away.

The prince drew a dagger from the sheath at his hip as the soldiers pulled Demos upright. He did not struggle against them. Whatever fate had in store for him, it had already been written. Aris gripped Demos's hair in one hand and yanked his head back, pressing the dagger against his throat.

"By your words alone you prove your family's disgrace," Aris said. "To speak against the Crown is treason. If you attempt to do so again, Death's Hand will cut your tongue out as he did your father's."

"We were to be brothers, Aris," Demos said. "You stinking piece of shit."

"Brother implies equal, Demos. And we were never going to be equal."

With that, Aris released him and sheathed his dagger. Jumping back onto the stage, he turned to face the crowd as he passed down a fuller judgment.

"Tomorrow you will all bear witness to the traitor's execution. Following that, the traitor's wife and sons will be sold at auction." He smiled at Demos as he said, "I think people will pay a handsome sum for such trophy slaves. All of your personal wealth and property is forfeit. You're lucky your clan name isn't erased from the annals of our history, but Kallistrate Hill remains, and I'm sure there are enough cousins to squabble over the smoking ruins of your family home and control of the clan's interests."

As Aris's words spread through the crowd, Demos heard spectators' voices raised in horror. To highborn and lowborn, the idea of execution would be terrifying enough, but to sell nobles into slavery was almost unthinkable. He looked at his family, still not quite sure how to connect Aris's words with what it would mean for them. His brother . . .

Cyrus remained upright, but only because of the firm grips of the Guards who held him. He sagged in their arms, and his eyes were closed and his face had gone pale; Demos feared he was unconscious. Other soldiers held their mother, and though she wasn't badly hurt, she slumped nevertheless at the prince's so-called justice. The Guards themselves remained vigilant, and Demos knew he could not fight. Not with his family in peril. A time would come, but this was not it.

With nothing to lose, however, his father had no such compunction.

Baron Kallistrate's wordless scream punctured the night sky above Hero's Square, the ululating cry of some savage beast. Demos twisted in time to see Linos drive his elbow into a female soldier's throat, and then overpower a towering male. Blood sprayed from his mouth as Linos ripped the soldier's sword from his scabbard.

"Father, no!" Demos lunged, but his arms were held in place. Someone kicked the back of his left leg and he dropped to his knees.

The hangman faced Linos Kallistrate in the torchlight. The queen had reached the bottom step, but she paused, startled, as Death's Hand drew his own sword. At first it looked as if they were evenly matched, but an executioner's victims are rarely allowed to fight back, and he was facing one of Quandis's greatest warriors. He didn't stand a chance. In two swift strokes Linos cut the hangman's throat and opened his belly from chest to balls, and Death's Hand's innards spilled out wet and stinking onto the stone. Dead on his feet, the hangman toppled forward into the pile of his own viscera.

Shock held sway, keeping the crowd silent. Linos breathed wet, ragged, bloody breaths. No one screamed. No one spoke.

Until Carina whispered. "Linos, my love." The words traveled throughout the square on shadows and smoke.

Linos looked at her as if seeing her for the first time, and Demos could see both betrayal and forgiveness in his mother's gaze. His father had tears in his eyes and seemed torn between listening to his wife and killing the woman he thought he had loved. Linos glanced back and forth between Carina and the queen, and when Demos followed his father's eyes and looked over to the dais, he saw that

Princess Phela was going to say something, only to have Queen Lysandra forestall her with a raised hand.

"It's done," the queen said. "Kill him."

The City Guard soldiers moved in, surrounding Baron Linos Kallistrate. The queen didn't even stay to see her order carried out, as her personal detail escorted her away, the prince and princess in tow, the swords and daggers fell. The people of Lartha watched as dozens of blades glinted in the torchlight. Men and women in the uniform of Quandis, many of whom had once been under his command, took their turns with Baron Kallistrate.

They murdered him one hundred times.

While the queen was saved this gruesome sight, Demos and his family were forced to watch. When they were dragged away at last, the City Guards were still hacking at his father's remains. Demos went willingly, turning his back on his father's corpse because Linos's spirit had already gone. Only then did he see that the Guardsmen who'd been holding Cyrus up had let him fall and were dragging him by his feet back toward the prison wagon. He couldn't be certain his brother was dead, but he feared it. He felt it to be true, and that feeling left him numb inside.

As Demos made his way up into the wagon, his mind seemed detached from his body, and the only thing he could think was that now it would be up to him to find a way to avenge both Linos and Cyrus.

Demos didn't know how such a thing might be done.

But he knew it began with Princess Myrinne.

3

Sometimes, days went by without her remembering that she was Bajuman. She would never have believed it possible back when she was a child, beaten by her owners, abused, vilified, then ignored. Back then, her heritage had always defined who and what she was. There had been no escaping the deep blue truth in her eyes, the brand on her arm, or the familiar sense of unbelonging that dogged every day and haunted her dreams at night.

Surviving that life had made her a different woman. Stronger in many ways. Fairer in others. Yet it all shaped who she was. So today, when she had a punishment to deliver, her memory of being a Bajuman was rich and close.

"Admiral Hallarte, the hearing is ready." Shawr stood at her cabin door and held it open. Her steward was small for his seventeen years, his feminine features attracting a certain amount of abuse from some of the sailors, and a different kind of attention from others, both male and female. But appearances could deceive. The admiral had once seen Shawr cornered by two pirates, and he'd gutted them both with his curved blade without giving them a chance to blink. He had a fast hand and a good heart, and in the three years that he'd been serving aboard the battleship *Nayadine*—as well as being her steward, spy, bodyguard, and valet—he had become her friend.

He was also yet another person she continued to deceive. Once simply the slave Daria, now Admiral Daria Hallarte of the Royal Quandian Navy, her whole life was built upon a carefully constructed sham. Over the years Daria had learned to dismiss any guilt. Fate had brought her here, not intention. She had simply grabbed the hands of chance and let them haul her from death and into a brand-new life.

She sighed and stood, and Shawr shifted from foot to foot by the door.

"What will you do with him?" he asked.

"Sugg? He's to be judged and punished, of course. He betrayed us to the Skull Raiders for a handful of silver pieces." Daria saw Shawr's eyes flicker to one side, the sadness in his face. She knew that Shawr and Sugg had been friends. The seaman was known as a friendly, garrulous type, and that made his crime even more difficult to fathom. It also made what she had to do all the more painful.

"What punishment?" Shawr asked. He was overstepping his mark. Daria was an admiral with six ships under her command. The steward might have been her friend, but even attempting to question her decisions, however subtly, constituted gross misconduct.

Perhaps he knew her too well.

"Sugg conspired with a pirate clan, Shawr. What punishment do you think appropriate?" She shrugged on her cloak. She'd never grown used to the fine material and delicate weave. "He sold our location and intentions to a Skull Raider spy. If that spy hadn't been caught and interrogated, we might have sailed into an ambush that would have seen many Quandian sailors killed." She examined herself in the mirror. Even after all these years, sometimes she did not recognize the eyes that stared back at her. They had given her freedom, yet they were not hers. "He sold us out for a handful of riches, giving no thought to the lives he put at risk. We may never know his reasons. Was he drunk? Blackmailed? Mind altered by bad spiza? It doesn't matter. For that crime, what would you consider a good and just punishment?"

Daria knew that she could be a powerful speaker, a formidable presence. Add in her scars and her silvery-gray eyes and few would stand in her way. She saw the effect her words had on the young man.

"I . . ." he began. "Of course, whatever punishment you sentence him to is the right one."

"A wise answer," she said. Then, softly, "You know what must be done."

Daria left her wardroom, walked along the hallway and up the narrow flight of stairs leading to the ship's topmost deck, and Shawr followed. He carried her weapon belt, heavy with sword, blades, and throwing stars. On occasions like this, she preferred to don her weapons where everyone could see. She could rest the belt on her hips and clasp it closed without it making a sound. It showed her skill as a warrior, and her breadth of experience.

"A keelhauling," she said as sunlight touched her face. "Haven't had one of those for a while. Or a flogging. I'll have Seaman Guye do it; he's strong and has a good whip hand." She paused before stepping up on deck and glanced back down at Shawr. "Or maybe I'll make him eat every coin his betrayal earned him, until his stomach is heavy, and then throw him overboard."

Shawr blinked up at her. The smile that formed on his face was hesitant, but firm.

"You're a good person, Admiral," he said. "You'll do the right thing."

"Thank you for your vote of confidence," she said. And she knew that Shawr was right.

∽

Daria sensed a shimmer of anger in some of the ship's crew. News of her judgment had already been sent to the fleet via message hawks, and she could see crews gathered on the other vessels' decks as they prepared to witness Sugg's fate. Many sailors watching now might have been dead if Sugg's betrayal had not been thwarted. Most of them would have been happy to dish out summary punishment with their own hands. But they kept their anger to themselves because the respect they held for their admiral was absolute. Their surprise at her choice of punishment would soon fade away.

Daria knew that this moment was another tale that would build upon the legend of her command.

"Under the gaze of the Four, have you any last words?" she asked.

Sugg stood naked before the ship's crew, shivering in the cool breeze that blew down from the north. Wind whistled in the rigging. Waves slammed against the ship and threw a haze of spray across the decks. Bad weather was on the way, and the fleet's ships would soon be turning their noses south to try and outrun it. Perhaps her judgment was not so merciful, after all.

"You should have killed me," Sugg said.

"That would make me as heartless as you." Daria raised her voice. "Before the Four, and bearing witness to their mercy, let your punishment be met." She nodded at the six sailors gathered around Sugg. "Put him in."

A small rowboat had already been lowered over the side, and now the swell banged it against the hull, as if eager to welcome its occupant. She'd instructed it to be provisioned with a bladder of water and a pouch of dried pulses. It was enough to keep him alive for seven days, maybe more if he could gather rainwater when the storms came.

That is if the waves didn't overturn him, or lightning didn't strike and sizzle him to a crisp, or some sea creature didn't reach out and pluck him from the boat with tentacles or spiked limbs . . .

But that was up to the gods now. He had almost left the fleet dead in the water. It was fitting that his punishment fit that crime.

Sugg did not resist. He walked to the railing, climbed until he was balanced on top like only an experienced sailor could, and held out his arms. He glanced back at Daria and Captain Gree, the *Nayadine*'s commanding officer, then performed a perfect dive into the sea. He disappeared from view and Daria heard the splash. The rowboat's fixed line was cut, and the six sailors remained at the railing to ensure the guilty man did not cling to the *Nayadine*'s hull as the rowboat fell quickly behind.

"Captain Gree, you have your orders," Daria said.

"Yes, Admiral. I've communicated them to the fleet. We're heading south from the storm, and then west again, toward our target."

"Journey time?"

"If the storm doesn't surprise us by also turning west, nine days."

Daria nodded at him and saw the respect he held for her. For the briefest instant she experienced a flash of her Bajuman past and glanced aside and down, averting her eyes. When she looked up again, the captain had gone about his duties, and she cursed herself for that moment of weakness.

She walked to the railing and looked out across the sea. Sugg and his boat were already far behind them, riding the swell close to the churned trail left by the *Nayadine*'s passage, and the horizon in that direction was a boiling mass of heavy, high clouds. Lightning sparked deep within the cloud bank like a living thing, raging and furious at their escape. Sugg in his small craft had no sail—had no oars, for that matter—and no such means of escape.

"I knew you'd do the right thing, Admiral," Shawr said. He

joined her at the railing and leaned out and over, looking down into the sea.

"I'm the admiral," Daria said. "I always do the right thing."

"Even if it's wrong?"

"Shut up or I'll push you overboard as well."

Smiling, Shawr touched his chest in a casual salute.

"Prepare my wardroom for a conference," Daria said. "Tomorrow morning at dawn, once we're away from this storm, I want all six ships' captains aboard."

"It's another nine days until landfall," Shawr said.

"I'm aware, Shawr. We're sailing to war," Daria said. "And the Skull Raiders now know we're coming. Could be they'll sail out to meet us. Either way, I want to be prepared."

"I'll make sure it's ready." Shawr gave another salute, crisper this time, and left her alone at the railing.

She looked past the bow and ahead, in the direction of Quandis six hundred miles to the south. She had the respect of the crews, the captains, and even her sometimes troublesome valet. Most importantly, she maintained respect for herself.

Daria had killed many people in her time at sea. Her reputation as a warrior was well earned; her strength, fearlessness, and skills as a tactician were spoken of in ships' quarters and wardrooms across the Quandian fleet, not to mention the dank places pirates hid to lick their wounds. These aspects were part of the reason for her rapid rise through the ranks, until she became an admiral while still in her twenties. But this forward momentum through her career was also driven by a factor that no one knew and which she could never reveal—a desire to flee her past. The faster she moved forward, the less chance the past had of catching up with her.

She thought about submitting Sugg into the hands of the ocean, and she couldn't help but dwell upon what had become of her from that same situation.

From the cold clasp of the sea, to the leader of armies.

Fate and Lameria sometimes acted in curious ways.

⌒

A Bajuman dreams . . .

Daria's master beats her one more time. He's a fat man, rich but bitter, dressed in finery yet stinking of sweat and filth. He's been her master for half a year. Hatred is a constant fire in her gut, burning brightly, searing her from within. More than once, she's been beaten for a glare he didn't like, or because she'd tried to run, or simply tried to shield herself from him. The blows still hurt, the bruises still sting, her blood still flows, but the beatings have become almost routine now. They're no easier—if anything, they've become more savage—but she retreats within herself every time he raises a hand to her. In that interior space, she kindles the fires of her hatred and waits for her master to grow tired. She prays to Lameria to send the bastard a killing stroke or fatal heart attack from the exertion required to keep hurting her, but that justice never comes.

Her master's anger and fury is never richer than it seems today. She cannot even recall what she did wrong, which makes her think she did nothing. There is not always a reason for such abuse. He seems to enjoy it more when there *is* no reason.

She starts to sense that today is different when he grabs her by the hair and drags her across his land. He is a trader, an importer of animal pelts from islands of the Ring, and as such his home is close to the northern coastal port of Suskmouth. Too pompous to live in the town itself, his house sits upon the clifftop, a drafty and creaking place that looks far more comfortable than it is. He's all about appearances.

Daria closes her hands around her master's and pulls back, trying to lessen the unbearable tension on her scalp. This makes him even angrier and he jerks, hard. She screams. This is a pain she can't shut out. Other slaves working at drying racks see her and look away. They feel sorry for her, but at the same time they're glad it's not them. Daria understands. She often feels that way herself.

Leaving his land, being hauled over a low stone wall and scraped across rougher ground, she realizes at last that he is dragging her toward the cliff.

Her heart flutters. Fear bites in cold. Every roar of rage from her master's fat mouth is matched with the impact of waves against the rocks far below . . .

He stands on the cliff edge and watches her fall, these final few seconds of her life long and rich. Her senses are alight—the salt tang of spray on the air, the warm breeze in her mouth, the sound of gulls mimicking her master's final, scornful laughter. The feel of her body impacting violent waves, somehow missing the rocks. The sight of the world being washed away as she goes under, dragged against cruel rocks by the churning tide, flesh scoured and torn, traceries of her blood spreading in the water, pinking the surf.

She floats. Adrift. The sun scorches her, salt water bleaching the colors from her shredded clothes, the life from her soul. She prays to Lameria that she might die, and then wonders if she is already dead. She tries to look around to find land, but there is none to see. The forceful tides around Quandis have clutched her to themselves, carrying her away from the vast island and giving her the freedom she has always sought . . .

She floats. Thirst swells her tongue, sun and salt burn her eyes, and she wishes she could die. Yet she clings to life with every fiber of her body . . .

In these moments before death I am more alive than ever before, she thinks, and a shadow falls over her and blots out the sun, even though there is not a cloud in the sky.

A Bajuman dreams . . .

The sea nurses Daria, lifting and swaying, yet the surface beneath her back is solid. She can hear the creak of straining timbers and the sound of voices in a language she does not understand. Rough hands touch her body, tending wounds that burn like fires ignited beneath her skin. Shadows move across her vision. She cannot see.

She smells the rich odor of sea spiza being burned, and she knows now where she is. Such spiza is forbidden on Quandis because of its supposed connection with Pent, the fallen god who fled across the ocean in its flight from the Four. The spiza was seeded by Pent's shed, damaged skin as the god was driven from the main island, past the Ring, and out into the wilds of the ocean.

She can hear the laughter and sense the peace, and the smell of sea spiza being smoked gives her some peace too. She is on a pirate ship. She's being nursed and tended. If they were going to kill her, they would have done so by now.

A Bajuman dreams . . .

. . . of smoke and fire, screams and death, and the eventual embrace of the sea once more. It burns her eyes and sets her wounds aflame again, and when she is next dragged from the sea, she prays that it is into the hands of death. She never believed that such pain could be endured, even by a Bajuman. *Brother,* she thinks, and Blane is there in her memory bidding her farewell that final time. She wishes she had turned around to wave.

"Her eyes," someone says, "look at her eyes!"

And now they see me for what I am, she thinks. *They rescued a drowning wretch from the hands of pirates, only to discover that I am Bajuman.* She almost smiles. Perhaps the final cut—a blade plunged into her heart or drawn across her throat—will free her of this pain.

But Fate and Lameria act in mysterious ways.

"I've never seen gray eyes that shine so."

"Not gray," another voice replies. "That's the silver hue of ancient ice, and I've seen it before. She's a highborn of Tan Kushir."

Her body is badly scarred, left side so scoured by coral and bleached by the sea that there is no trace of her birth brand, no evidence of the slave she was. And so Daria the Bajuman dies, and Daria Hallarte, last survivor of the noble family Hallarte kidnapped from the island of Tan Kushir by pirates two hundred and seventy days before, is born.

It takes a long time, days or even weeks, but when her sight begins to return, it welcomes in a whole new world.

∽

Bajuman-fucking prick, Phela thought. Her brother, Prince Aris, a weak man given to cowardice and pettiness, was acting like a dog awaiting the whip. Four days after the execution of Baron Kallistrate and they'd seen little of their mother in that time.

"But I've heard the whispers!" he said.

"Don't talk to me of whispers, Aris," Phela said. He looked at her wide-eyed, knowing who she was and what she could do. She'd made sure he knew. They had been close as children—she had adored him the way the rest of Quandis seemed to—but now he disgusted her. Aris sensed it, but he never asked her what had changed between them, and Phela never explained it to him. She liked the fact that her older sibling was afraid of her and liked it even more that the mystery of her disdain made him so uneasy.

If only he knew the extent of what she could *really* do. One day she might ask him what had happened to those Bajuman bitches he fucked and made with child. She suspected he didn't even know himself. Bajumen came and went, appeared and disappeared, without anyone really caring. Some bleeding hearts might cry out about the injustices heaped upon the Bajumen, but to most, one more dead slave floating downriver to the sea was simply fresh food for the fish. If she was clinging to a dead baby, that was more food. Nothing more.

Phela saw it as cleaning up her brother's mess. He went out and fed his addiction, she followed on behind and made sure no embarrassments were left behind. Their mother knew of her actions and agreed with them, though Lysandra kept herself one step removed. She was the queen, after all. She was also one of the most devout people Phela knew, and her fear that Aris's coupling was offending the royal bloodline—and thus the holy bloodline of the Four—meant that the actions of the killers Phela engaged were necessary. The assassins of the Silent were only too happy to slink through the shadows and slice a Bajuman throat.

And now she wished they'd slit her brother's throat, if only to stop him from prattling on like this.

"Nevertheless, the nobles are muttering among themselves," Aris was saying. "It's to be expected from Clan Kallistrate—if they can stop squabbling about who will inherit the barony long enough to be enraged—but I fear the other great clans may also mount a protest about the fate of Linos and his family. And who can say how such a protest might end?"

She knew how it would end. Gods, they were surrounded by the proof of it all around them. They were walking through the corridors of the palace, passing paintings, sculptures, and other works of art that told stories of Quandis's past, one not always made of sunshine and peace. Surely Aris understood that. Or maybe not. Her brother was never really one to take heed of his lessons, let alone his surroundings.

But Phela loved the history embedded in such artifacts, and from a young age she had enjoyed hearing those stories told. As she grew older, she discovered places where other items that told darker tales were often hidden away. She might only have been in her twenties, but she knew better than most that Quandis had a rotten heart. When she was Whispering, she often spent long periods in hidden places. She had run her fingers over old royal armor holed by pikes and still rusted with blood. She had stared at paintings of a king no one now remembered, and whose name had been scrubbed from the land's history. One deep room held a series of unfinished sculptures, their subjects twisted and deformed by eldritch magic. That a land like Quandis might take measures to conceal its dark heart, rather than destroy all evidence, fascinated her even more.

"Let them protest," Phela said finally. "They can object, have their say, wave their arms in the air. Nothing will come of it."

"Really? You seem to forget the strength in numbers our nobles have, Phela."

"I forget nothing, but I have every confidence in our queen's rule."

"She'd better be here," Aris said. "If she isn't . . ."

"If she isn't, the situation can await her return," Phela said.

"Return? From where?"

She did not answer him, biting her tongue instead. She'd said too much. She knew very well that her mother was not in her chambers, and she had a good idea of where the ailing woman had gone. To give that knowledge away was a weakness.

But it was only Aris. He'd never been the sharpest arrow in the quiver, and his mind was usually so addled by wine, spiza, and sex that tomorrow he'd forget today.

I still have to guard my mouth, Phela thought. *Perhaps not around Aris, but why risk it?*

Knocking on her mother's chamber doors, hearing the echoes reverberate around what she knew was an empty room, she allowed herself a momentary release of excitement.

So much was happening so quickly that her life's ambitions were sprinting ahead. She had to keep up with them, grasp hold and rein them in. Control them. All her life she had wanted only to be queen and make Quandis great again, greater than it had ever been, and recent events had started to show her how. Part of her wanted to forge on, but she knew that a slow, considered approach was best. That way, no mistakes could be made.

"Mother?" Aris called through the door. He rapped on the wood.

"She's not here," Phela said.

"She might be; perhaps she's—"

"There are no Guards at the door," she said. "The room's quiet. She's not here, Aris, and you know why."

"Why?" he asked.

Because she's gone down seeking more magic, Phela thought. "Because she's feeling conflicted and disgusted at what she did," she said. "Imagine discovering your lover was a Penter? She's drinking and spizing, making herself ill. Abandoning Lartha when the city and Quandis need her most."

"Mother is queen. She wouldn't abandon her people. Not for anything."

"Then where is she?" Phela asked innocently, to which Aris had no answer.

And he was wrong anyway. *Not for anything? What about for magic?* Phela thought. *Oh yes. I think for magic, our mother would do anything.* The bloody actions in Hero's Square four days earlier had already revealed that fact to the world, though no one but Phela knew exactly why those events had taken place.

"We need to do something," Aris finally said. He shook himself down and stood taller, perhaps remembering that one day soon he was destined to be king. There were many who believed that he would make a good ruler, though no one knew him quite as well as Phela. She knew the deep, sordid truth of his life and lies and lack of anything remotely resembling competence to rule. She knew that in truth, the very *last* thing he wanted was to be king.

Once she would have stood by and watched him ascend to the Crown, even with his inability to control his prick. Bided her time. But her mother's spiza-induced mutterings to Linos Kallistrate had changed everything. Now, whole new possibilities she had only ever dreamed of were opening up for Phela.

"We *will* do something," she assured him. "I'll wait for Mother here. You go and arrange an audience with the heads of the Five Great Clans. They'll listen to you, Aris, because they respect you." He soaked up her praise like the weak man he was.

"Will Mother be all right?" he asked.

"Of course she will," Phela said, and she kissed her brother on the cheek. "She'll be fine. Now go." She watched him walk away along the wide hallway, trying to find an ounce of feeling for the man, a sliver of sibling affection. There was nothing.

It's him, not me, she thought. *I'm not unloving. It's that he's unlovable.* She loved her sister, Myrinne. She loved her mother, the queen. And she loved Quandis more than anyone or anything. More than life itself. She had more than enough love to go around, but she bestowed it only where and when it was deserved.

She told herself this and took comfort.

When Aris was gone, Phela rested her forehead against the door to her mother's chambers, ruminating again upon the admissions she'd heard from the queen's mouth a mere five days earlier. Events were moving apace. Her mother had sparked the fire of change, and Phela's machinations would spread the flame. Soon, she would speak to Shome, head assassin of the Silent, and make her most decisive move. But for now she would wait, knowing that the perfect moment would come when everything was in place.

Yet it wasn't easy. Part of Phela was desperate to go in pursuit of her mother. Down deep into forbidden places.

Into the deep places where Phela so wanted to go.

Phela the Whisperer knew of three secret routes leading from beneath the palace, the heart of Lartha's greatest hill, and ending deep under the Temple of Four. Over the past year she had followed two of them, and both times her journey had been halted when she'd found herself plunged into dire danger. Pure luck had seen her through. The first time, a passageway carved through the subterranean stone had twisted and turned its way down, following seemingly random changes in direction until the ancient route was blocked by a rockfall. Living within the tumbled rocks was a herd of ghost spiders, blind arachnids as big as her fist that each carried enough venom to kill an army. One touch of their poison on human skin, one spray, and the victim would die an agonizing death over several hours as their organs liquefied.

On her second expedition, Phela had found herself in a great carved chamber at the base of which lay an underground lake. She thought perhaps the chamber was a remnant of the First City, and several stone bridges spanned the space. There was evidence that one of them had been used before—hooks were affixed into the rock, with rotten ropes slung between them.

Halfway across, the sound of rock cracking and crumbling had caused her to pause. She'd backtracked carefully. A few chunks of stone had splashed into the lake far below.

Something else splashed down there, as well. In the weak light from her blazing oil torch, she saw long, slick limbs exploring upward toward the bridge. Their tips touched the stone, moving along with a delicate caress, before pausing where she had been crouched moments before. Sensing her heat. Sniffing, perhaps tasting her. In the archives she had encountered mentions of the Gods Unnumbered, the deities of prehistory, countless horrors worshipped by the First People before the fall of their society and the rise of the Four. Whatever had been in that lake, she wondered if it existed alone or if it might be one of the Gods Unnumbered. For once, Phela had no desire for an answer.

Her journey back up into the light had felt like being born again, yet such fear was a constant part of her Whispering. Any knowledge that did not kill her made her greater.

She was aware of the beginnings of the third route but had not yet explored it. She'd discovered its existence in ancient books in the darker corners of the Archives of the Crown, the place where many of her Whispering journeys were initiated in her imagination. The library itself was an adventure, a labyrinthine place with more books than anyone could read in a lifetime, many of them long forgotten and piled away in dark, rotting corners. Phela found such secrets in that place. Never more so than in these recent days.

She fought the urge, though. The time for her to make this journey was not now. But it *was* close. Soon, she would give in to her desire, and it would be her greatest Whisper yet.

The time when the secret places she knew would lead her to become queen.

Until then, there were events to set in motion.

⁓

Into her own chambers, past the bathing area, removing a wooden screen hiding the complex plumbing and pumping systems that fed her large bath, squeezing past the pipes, climbing down a narrow vertical shaft with feet on one wall and back braced against the other, Phela Whispered her way into hiding once more. She loved moments like this, when only the gods knew where she was. It was when she felt most free, and she vowed that she would continue to Whisper even when she was no longer simply a princess.

In a way, it was what her mother was doing. Going down deep, probably with help from members of the High Order, she was finding her own secret places.

Phela lit a torch and twisted her way through a wrinkle in the foundations of the palace. The next thirty feet were tight and narrow, and she had to crawl on her stomach, pushing the torch ahead and letting herself slide down the gentle slope. The first time she came this way she had no idea what lay at the end, or whether the crack in the land would grow tighter, narrower, eventually constricting around her until she was trapped, destined to starve to death as darkness enveloped her. Not knowing had brought a delicious fear. Its memory tingled, sending a cold chill through her veins.

She emerged from the space and stood upright again, in her cave of trophies. Of everything she knew, and all the things she had done, this was the one place that, if found, might offend enough to cast doubt on her royal morality.

Because for every one of Aris's Bajuman whores she had ordered killed, she had kept something to remember them by.

The preserved objects hung from a mesh of wires wound around rocky protrusions on one high wall. A hand, withered and dried. A sagging breast, leathery and shapeless. A string of knuckle bones. A set of pouting lips sewn together to mimic a smile. Four toes, all of them big toes from left feet. A flap of skin, a shriveled liver, a scalp of still-lustrous hair. A fetus, wrapped in burlap and black with rot. A fleshless head, the soft child's skull molded into a long, thin shape.

There were no eyes here, and no branded parchments of human skin. Nothing to betray the victims' Bajuman heritage. That was for Phela to know.

Every one of these women, every would-be child, offended her. Each time Aris pumped his seed into a Bajuman womb, the royal bloodline and bloodline of the gods was corrupted.

Her hatred of the Bajumen was never deeper than when she saw these remnants of her brother's mistakes.

She knew that there were likely more trophies to be harvested, but not many more. Aris's secret habit of fucking Bajuman women was almost at an end. Soon she would be able to pay this cave one final visit and then she would leave it alone, just one more secret place fading away into Quandis's history, never to be seen again. A dark history hidden, not expunged.

Casting one backward glance, Phela left her trophy chamber and embarked on another short journey.

৵৩

Shome never seemed surprised when Princess Phela appeared in the Silent's quarters in the basements beneath the royal palace. Though she had not passed through their doors or crossed the bridge that spanned the underground chasm separating their rooms from the rest of the palace's subterranean domains, her arrivals always seemed expected. This often troubled Phela, and she had begun to suspect that Shome was aware of some of her Whispering routes. Yet that should hardly be a surprise. The Silent were shadows themselves, so of course they would know the best ways to remain hidden.

The head of the Silent stood and pressed her arm across her chest in a salute, bowing her head.

"Shome," Phela said. "I know I've asked a lot of you in the past few days, but I need to speak with you one more time." The big woman towered over Phela, and her appearance always made the princess's heart thunder with dread. The tattoos, the shade of her eyes, her demeanor exuding danger and violence. She was scarred and battered from decades of combat, most of it destined never to be recorded in any official Quandian history texts or songs. Yet Phela knew that those who went against Shome were more scarred, if not dead. There was a good reason why she'd been captain of the Silent for over two decades.

Shome inclined her head slightly at Phela's statement before turning and leading the way through a large hall toward a wall of doors at its rear. Several more Silent sat around the hall, some drinking and eating, a few reading, and a couple of them performing exercises together. They all averted their eyes when Phela looked at them. What they did not see could not trouble them.

She was always disturbed by how quiet their rooms and great

hall were. It was one thing to observe their vow of silence in singular moments, but collected here, the hush was almost oppressive. The exercising pair moved with a fluid grace, leaping and lifting, rolling and bracing themselves in stress positions without making a single sound. Even the fires in braziers affixed to the carved cavern walls blazed without spitting and popping. Perhaps they chose the wood and oils they burned with care, so that there were no knots to spit under heat, no corrupted oils to sizzle. But even that attention to detail was alien, and despite being someone who normally embraced the quiet, she did so to hear the whispers.

Here the only sound was the beating of her heart and the thunder of her furtive glances.

Phela took off her shoes and walked with care toward the line of doors. She followed Shome through the door farthest to the left, as always, and they entered the captain's private chamber.

The cave was small but surprisingly well appointed. A pipe wound down from the ceiling to provide running water, a wide shelf on one wall was covered with a thick mattress and comfortable cushions, and the floor was carpeted with rugs and throws. A single low table had a chair on either side, and Shome indicated that she should sit.

While Princess Phela made herself comfortable, the assassin prepared a drink of fruit-flavored water.

"Things are going well," Phela said. Shome nodded and sat, tattooed head tilted to one side in invitation for her to continue. "Whoever you chose to do my bidding performed admirably, and in just a handful of days. Whispers of revolution are spreading among the Five Great Clans. When my mother returns, I'll greet her with the news, and those who rise will be cut down. We'll remove the weak, unfaithful heart of our noble society, and those who harbor grudges against my family. I know who they are. I know what they're saying. Thanks to you, they'll reveal themselves."

Shome bowed her head in acknowledgment.

"I know this goes without saying, but I must emphasize it none-theless: no one can *ever* know what I asked of you. And this final favor I have to ask must remain our greatest secret, Shome. Do you . . ." Phela paused, feeling the weight of the deed like a rock in her heart. Could she really ask this? *Should* she? Once asked it could not be unsaid, and her life would move on the inexorable course she had laid out.

Yes. She could. She *must*. Her mother's dabbling in magic and sex-crazed admission to Linos Kallistrate had merely brought for-ward what Phela had planned for so long. And her whispered knowledge about the incredible age of Per Ristolo . . . well, that had ignited ambitions even Phela had never before imagined.

Ambitions of magic.

"Do you love your queen?"

A nod, slow and deliberate.

"Do you love the Crown more?"

A nod, more assertive.

"My mother is well on the way to killing herself," Phela said. "She's growing mad and poisoning herself, rotting from the inside with spiza and guilt over what she did to her lover." *And the magic,* she thought, *that's the worst of it, the greatest cause of her growing instability. But I can't spread that, even to the Silent.* "If she dies . . . *when* she dies . . . Aris takes the throne."

Shome glanced aside, a brief gesture, but so telling.

"Exactly," Phela said. "I can't allow that to happen. For the good of the Crown, and for the sake of Quandis, Aris cannot be king. He's too weak. His habits would be revealed, and the Blood of the Four would stink with the taint of Bajumen."

Shome was expressionless, waiting to hear what Phela was head-ing toward.

"Aris has to go," Phela said. "But in a very particular way. Find a Bajuman woman of particular beauty. Lure Aris to her. And while they are fucking, kill them both."

Shome drew in a sharp breath. It might have been the loudest sound the princess had ever heard from the Silent assassin.

"You *will* do this," Phela said. "You serve the queen, Shome, and you've served her well for many years. But you recognize strength, and you know what's best for Quandis. In your silence, you take everything in and give away nothing. That's *your* strength. Not only physical might and the ability to fight, but knowledge. In that way you're much like me."

Shome blinked slowly, then sat back in her chair.

"So you know this is the only way. The only way to save our country and our traditions. You will do this for me, the queen to be, but even more, you will do this for Quandis."

Without hesitation Shome stood, pressed her hand across her chest, and bowed her head.

Phela closed her eyes and felt the faint shift in the air that indicated Shome leaving the room. For a while the princess remained there, eyes closed, breathing softly through her mouth, relishing that brief, silent peace before the storm that was to come.

The storm she was creating.

4

To most of the people of the city, the grand towers of the Temple of Four were a comforting sight, visible from nearly every square and alley. They were a beacon to those nobly born and to the filthy beggars in the streets alike, as they worshipped the Four.

Anselom, god of Earth and Love.

Bettika, god of Wind and War.

Charin, god of Fire and Secrets.

Dephine, god of Water and Beasts.

To the Bajumen, however, the towers were symbols of oppression, and the root from which prejudice grew.

Yet faithful and heretical alike believed that the work of the priesthood went on within those towers, that priests gathered there to commune with the gods of Quandis and to pray for the health of the people and the wisdom of the Crown. Once, Blane too had believed this. But now he knew better. Yes, there were prayer chambers, vast libraries, and chapels of silence and abasement within the towers, as well as the sleeping quarters of priests who had been anointed to serve the tower of one of the Four over the others.

But like all secrets, the true secrets of the temple dwelled below.

Blane had been searching for those secrets carefully and quietly since arriving at Yaris Teeg. In its basements were passages into deeper levels, as well as tunnels and stairwells that ventured into the hill itself and wound their way upward, underground steps that led to the Temple of Four. Blane had explored those tunnels he could enter without a key and had gone back and forth to the Temple of Four during the night, while all others were sleeping, just to know that he could.

That morning, a temptation had presented itself. Blane and the other novices had been brought up the hill to the Temple of Four and paraded through the corridors from one tower to the next, receiving lectures from four separate priests about the history of the Faith and the particular miracles of the god of their choosing. Those of the High Order were required to worship all the gods, but also to dedicate themselves to the glory of one, favoring a single deity over the others, thus determining the tower in which they would reside. Per Ristolo waxed lyrical about Charin, which surprised Blane. The wizened old priest did not seem the type to have chosen the Tower of Fire and Secrets for his home.

But as interesting as that information was, it was what happened after that passionate speech that woke something in Blane. They were moving through the corridors when Per Ristolo's old knees gave way beneath him. Blane knelt beside him, steadying the priest as the rest of the novices continued on toward the Tower of Wind and War.

Per Gherinne—a silver-haired owl of a woman—had hesitated. Blane saw the question in her eyes as she considered admonishing him, and then the softening there as she decided that his kindness to Per Ristolo mattered more in this moment than the rigidity of their instruction. She had nodded and followed the novices.

Per Ristolo had injured his wrist when he'd fallen. Blane eased the man to his feet and helped him along by the elbow, escorting him through the twisting hallways to the healer's room. The ancient priest had mottled skin, brown age spots giving him an almost reptilian aspect. A few strands of hair lay gossamer thin upon his pate. Weak and trembling, nevertheless he had the strength to be furious with himself for the failings of his body. Such anger would be frowned upon by his fellow priests and by the Four, but in front of a mere novice he did not bother to hide his pique, nor to hesitate in chiding himself for not traveling the safer Elders' Corridor. He'd even gestured in the general direction of the door.

The Elders' Corridor. Blane's eyes had betrayed nothing, but the excitement in him blossomed as he considered its possibilities. A more direct route for the most ancient among them to travel from one tower to the next, a path through the heart of the Temple of Four. A secret place, even the knowledge of which was forbidden to novices. Per Ristolo's expression had rippled with instant regret, but the look had vanished just as quickly. The priest's tongue had slipped, but he passed it off as nothing. After all, it wasn't as if a novice offering up the rest of his lifetime in service to the Four would risk their wrath by trespassing in a space forbidden to him.

Unless, of course, that novice did not believe the gods existed to rain their wrath down upon him in the first place.

Now, in the darkest part of the night, what Bajuman mothers had always told their children was called the Creeping Hour, Blane padded quietly along the Elders' Corridor. His heart hammered in fear. It was one thing to be caught out of place during his Solace, and if questioned, he could always say that he sought a space most conducive to his prayers. But this was entirely different. If he were discovered by a sleepless priest, any claim that he had come there searching for Solace would be dismissed immediately. Blane ought to be at the bottom of the hill, asleep on his mat in Yaris Teeg, not up here in the temple, and certainly not in a place forbidden to all but the eldest among the High Order.

He was here, though. And the thought frightened him as much as it excited him.

He held his breath, not daring to make a sound as he reached the door at the far end of the corridor. Ornate and lovely, inlaid with sea glass and hammered metal, the door had a simple latch for the ease of old men and women whose hands had been turned to claws by age. Slowly, Blane exhaled. He thought of his mother, long dead now, and of the tales she had told of the Creeping Hour, that time when doubts of the soul manifested in flesh and bone and walked the world, when the moonless breeze carried the sins of the past, when the ghosts of shamed ancestors tempted the living with acts of dishonor. He remembered her words to him and his sister, Daria:

No child should be awake during the Creeping Hour.

In terror, Daria had mumbled a question. She'd been having trouble sleeping and feared she might be awake through no fault of her own. Night haunts had often plagued her, and they'd only grown worse that winter. Their mother had leaned in, eyes full of pity and love. *Then keep your eyes closed and lie as still as the dead, your face like a mask. Any trace of emotion will give you away. Play at sleep if you can't achieve it. Play at death if you mean to avoid it. Lameria save you, otherwise. Nothing good walks the world in the Creeping Hour.*

Blane believed in neither sin nor soul, nor the ghosts of his ancestors. But like the sister he'd loved, he too was plagued by night haunts, and sleep often evaded him. Somehow, belief or not, he still felt the frisson of guilt along his spine and the flush of it in his cheeks. Not because he was breaking every rule being here in the Elders' Corridor, but because he walked the world during the Creeping Hour.

A smile touched his lips. *I love you, Mother,* he thought. *I miss you, Daria.* Those thoughts gave him strength. He was doing this for their memories, as much as for the thousands of Bajumen still alive. He steeled his resolve and reached his hand out.

He touched the latch on the beautiful, narrow door and opened it to discover himself in the heart of the ocean. The chamber seemed vast at first, but as he took several steps inside he realized it was instead a miracle of architecture. The walls and curving ceilings were blue-and-green glass in delicate hues—windows into mystical, nonexistent skies. Gentle sunlight seemed to gleam behind that stained glass, and yet he knew the Creeping Hour lingered and outside it was dark. It didn't bother him, however, for within this chamber Blane felt as if he stood at the bottom of a shallow sea, gazing up from below at the surface, with the sun glinting off the waves overhead. In his entire life, he had never been in a place of such elegance and peace. For a moment he loved the priesthood for what they had made here, but then he remembered he wasn't even supposed to be able to see this. Moreover, he recalled the humiliation of his mother's every waking moment until her death, and his sister's murder.

The hate rushed back in.

Quietly focused, Blane examined the room, so much smaller than the mirrors and glass made it appear. The floor had been inlaid with true sea glass, but within it he saw a pattern, a shell-like spiral turning inward. Blane followed that spiral on silent feet. He felt absurd but pushed that awkwardness away. He knew the priests by now, knew their devotion to ritual and to movement. This spiral was no accident.

In the center of the room, he reached the last narrow sea glass tile. The moment his foot came down upon it, he heard a soft exhalation of air behind him. The sound grew to a longer breath, perhaps a sigh, but it came from no human throat. The spiral had begun to slide downward without any rumble or grinding of stone, lowering to form a circular stairwell that descended deeper beneath the temple. Blane knew he had found what he had been searching for.

This was the secret entrance to a realm of further secrets, where the priesthood conducted its most ardent business and where, perhaps, they even indulged in the magic that whispered rumor said remained their sole province.

Blane took one step down and froze. How foolish it would be to go now. He calculated how long till the priests might stir to begin performing their rituals. Were they down there even now, seeking echoes of a magic he still did not truly believe in? He couldn't be sure, but he also couldn't chance it. Whenever he finally descended, he would have to take that risk. But not tonight. It was enough to know that he could find this place again and gain entrance into the subterranean chambers. For now, he needed to think and prepare, and when he returned, it would be with hours to spare.

And with a blade, just in case.

He retreated up that single step and immediately the quiet hiss began again, the swirling stairwell rising back into place, until in moments it was only the sea glass floor once more. Bathed in the light of the blue dream of an ocean, Blane slipped softly back through the door and into the Elders' Corridor, making his way through the Temple of Four, then down the hill through those subterranean stairwells to Yaris Teeg and his own bed. As he laid his head on his pillow, he knew that sleep would not come.

Play at sleep if you cannot achieve it, his mother had said. *Nothing good walks the world in the Creeping Hour.*

This night, he had to believe that she was wrong.

⌒

The Blood Spire pierced the dawn sky above the capital, rising from the heart of the palace to a needle tip. As a little girl, Phela had marveled at the architecture, trying to imagine how its builders had constructed scaffolding so high above Lartha and its people, nobles and rabble alike. In those years she had asked her favorite teachers where the Blood Spire had received its name, and each of them had given a different answer. The most obvious was the scarlet hue of the spire itself, but others had suggested darker origins, inspired by dungeons below the palace where prisoners had been tortured and executed. The spire rose so high that its foundations went deep into the ground, so the explanation had some logic. Others were more poetic in their musing, calling the Blood Spire the heart that grew from the core of the empire.

Whatever its origins, Phela hated the place. She found its color unnerving and sometimes thought she heard the echoes of ancient, pained cries in the curving stairs that twisted round and round within it. She'd rather visit the Temple of Four with its haunting, horrific gargoyles than this place. The Blood Spire had only one way up and down, and it was this she hated most of all. There could be no Whispering here, no sneaking. Not even the Silent could come and go without being seen by someone.

But when summoned by the queen, one simply had no choice but to answer. And Queen Lysandra loved the damned Blood Spire for all the reasons Phela despised it.

The sun had barely risen when she made her way up through the spiral, forcing herself not to fall into her childhood habit of counting the stairs as they wound upward. She already knew that there were two hundred and ninety-eight, and she had more important things on her mind. A light sheen of exertion coated her skin, and her heart beat loudly in her chest. When she was Whispering, she crawled through hidden spaces that provided her at least three or four possible escape routes at all times, but not here on these narrow stairs, where she was forced to duck her head, and where the hidden corners of each landing might hold assassins lying in wait.

Don't be stupid. She has no reason to want you dead. Not yet. Not unless Shome had betrayed Phela and her schemes to her mother.

In that event, these steps she climbed were the ascension to her own death, but there was nothing to be done about it anyway.

The shuffle of her feet upon the stone stairs echoed in a quiet slither, as if serpents nested in the shadowy eaves of the spiral both above and below. Her eyes were tired and her skull hurt and she thought she must be too young to feel so old. As unusual as it was for her to be up with the sun, it was even more so for Queen Lysandra.

Stooping to get beneath the last curve of the stairs, Phela started at the sight of the City Guard waiting on the sliver-thin landing.

"Princess," the Guard said, inclining his head.

She felt her face flush as fury blossomed in her chest. Phela studied the Guard's face, his long nose and sharp jaw, and committed them to memory. She did not like the idea that a man had seen her so vulnerable and would be able to share that tale with others in the palace, or out in the taverns of the city. She believed this one was named Konnell, a Guard favored by Princess Myrinne. She would remember him.

"The door," she said.

The wind whistled through the cracks around the door, but when Konnell opened it, the cold barged into the stairwell like a starving, howling wolf. Phela hated having to pass so close to the man, but there was so little room on the landing that she had no choice. To his credit, he stood aside and tried to make himself as small as possible, and yet she was still forced to brush against him.

His credit meant nothing to her.

The morning sun gleamed off the scarlet tiles of the Blood Spire, turning its surface darker, bloodier. Here at the pinnacle was a platform that ran around the whole circumference, a balcony that looked out over the entire capital.

The view was spectacular, and no more so than when she looked east. Crowning the seventh hill of Lartha, the four towers of the

Temple of Four cast their shadows down across the city. The priesthood's spires were the only structures higher than the Blood Spire, and that had never sat well with Phela. She disagreed with her mother on a great many things, but on this they were in accord.

Another Guardsman waited on the balcony. The wind pushed against Phela, but she waded through it, ignoring the uniformed man as she followed the railing around the spire's high balcony and came upon the small gathering that had arrived before her. The queen stood against the railing, gazing out across the city, as she had done a thousand times before. *Mother always* did *love it up here,* Phela thought. It took much of her will to keep a sneer from crossing her face as she thought about why.

The truth was, the queen reveled in her subjects' obedience and felt she could drink it in from up here. As if her power came from physical prominence, and not the exaltation of her blood. She loved their *love,* whether it was real or presented to her as such by courtiers, and the very idea disgusted Phela, even as she more than a little craved it.

But that wasn't the only reason the queen chose to meet here. She also loved the balcony of the Blood Spire because it was inconvenient, and because it was truly secure. One way in, and one way out. The only people who would ever know what words were spoken and what commands were given out here on the balcony were those she had summoned to join her. The power over their bodies. The power over their minds.

The power that Phela was so close to taking as her own.

All that flashed through her mind as Phela studied the faces of those present, trying to decipher what their presence meant.

Commander Kurtness of the City Guard stood with Dafna Greiss, Voice of the Queen, who communicated edicts to the functionaries responsible for the governing of the kingdom. Phela had been summoned by a pounding upon her door that morning, with the dawn light just edging the horizon. The urgency meant a crisis in the city or the empire, and so it did not surprise her to see Dafna the Voice and Commander Kurtness present. She had also expected to see her brother, Aris, but he was not among them.

The faces she had not anticipated were those of Shome, and her own sister, Myrinne. Tall and red-eyed, Myrinne had tied her hair back in a simple knot and wore a thick coat and loose trousers ill-befitting a princess. Physically and intellectually, Myrinne had become a formidable young woman, but her kindness had always been her undoing, and it stood in the way of greatness. Phela knew it would always be so, and as much as she loved her sister—as far as she considered herself capable of love for another individual at all—she was happy to take advantage of that.

"You've dried your tears," Phela observed. "I'm pleased to see you out in the sunshine."

Myrinne cast a dark look her way, but Phela neither blamed her for that glower nor felt the sting of it. The pain carved into Myrinne's features and glistening in her eyes caused Phela a pang of regret, but she had not been the cause of her sister's sorrow. Why should she feel the weight of it? It complicated things, love. But not overmuch.

"Where is Aris?" the queen asked, without turning.

It was an excellent question. But Phela didn't focus on that. Her mother's words had a strange shape to them. The wind had gusted in that moment and Phela shivered with its chill, so she could not be sure if that odd slur had been a trick of the breeze.

"As I said, Majesty," Commander Kurtness replied, "my captains have gone to his door, but he does not respond." He sounded nervous.

Queen Lysandra had been bent forward over the railing, but now she stiffened. "I wasn't speaking to you, Kurtness. The question was for my daughters."

"And I've told you, Mother—" Myrinne began.

"Where *is* he?" the queen shrieked, and she twisted herself around to glare at the princesses.

All of Phela's cleverness failed her in that moment as she stared in shock at the change in her mother. Lysandra's cheeks were hollowed and the skin beneath her eyes sagged. Her whole body seemed to have grown frail and the left side of her mouth was frozen in a half scowl. But worst of all her left eye had gone an opalescent white, and a trickle leaked from its corner.

"Mother . . ." Phela began.

This crone who had been the queen crossed the space between them like some horrid spider and took a fistful of Phela's hair. Myrinne gave an audible gasp as Phela froze, neither of them knowing how to respond. None of them did, for no one had ever seen the queen lay a hand on one of her children except to admire Aris's handsome face.

"Where . . . is . . . my son?" Queen Lysandra rasped.

Phela looked the queen in the eye. "I have not seen him since yesterday."

The half of Lysandra's face still capable of expression turned crestfallen. She seemed more like a child or a woman in the midst of a dream than a queen. Her fingers opened, releasing Phela's hair, and she turned to stare at nothing with her good eye, the ruined one still weeping.

"They've got him. I'm sure they've got him. My baby boy."

Queasy with horror, Phela tried to figure what had happened. No spiza could do this, not so quickly. In the space of three days, her mother had gone from indulgent, perhaps addicted, to ruination. Such an erratic, feverish state might be temporary, but there was no way the physical transformation was anything but permanent. Her beauty had been taken from her. Queen Lysandra's power had been in her vibrancy and the iron strength she exuded. Now she seemed nothing short of mad.

This isn't only spiza, Phela thought. *This is magic!* The faces of those around her reflected her horror, but that was probably as much from the queen's appearance as it was her actions against Phela. Surely not all of them could know of the queen's dabblings in magic, if any? Dafna loved Queen Lysandra without reservation, and of all of them perhaps she might be aware of her mistress's habits. But Commander Kurtness had come to the City Guard as an army veteran, loyal to the Crown but not necessarily to the woman who wore it. *And Myrinne,* Phela thought. *Myrinne, whose dreams have been torn asunder, her lover in chains?*

She's too caught up in her own problems to know what's truly wrong with our mother.

"This is hardly the first time Aris has vanished on us," Phela said, with far more calm than she felt. "His prick leads him to wander, but he always wanders back."

She glanced at Shome. Surely, the captain of the Silent had not yet murdered Prince Aris, but Shome could have already found him a Bajuman whore to get lost with. It wasn't the first time Aris had disappeared into the arms or between the legs of some blue-eyed bitch.

Shome noticed her attention and Phela arched an eyebrow ever so slightly, asking the question without words.

The assassin gave just the slightest nod of her head. So she *had* already put the plan for Aris's fate in motion. Phela's heart quickened.

The queen didn't accept Phela's explanation, though. "No. *They've* got him," she whispered, placing her hands on the smooth scarlet of the Blood Spire as if she were speaking to it, confiding her secrets again, even more irresponsibly than before. And perhaps she was. She pressed her ruined cheek against the bright red structure and the wind gusted, blowing her hair across her face, pasting her skirts to her body. "The traitorous fuckers have got him."

"And which 'traitorous fuckers' are these?" Myrinne shouted, no longer able to contain her rage at their mother. "More imaginary enemies like Linos Kallistrate?"

Phela shot her a withering glance. "Nobles have been coming to the palace doors every day since Baron Kallistrate's execution, sister. You know this. It might be possible to mollify them if we didn't simply turn them away every afternoon. Unrest is growing. There's no telling where it might lead."

In the fog of her madness and paranoia, sick with magic and spiza, the queen barely heard them.

Queen Lysandra turned first to Dafna the Voice, but then her single good eye cleared and the old cunning crept back into that gaze, and she looked at Commander Kurtness. "The clans talk among themselves and they believe I can't hear them. But I hear plenty, Commander. I hear plenty."

"Yes, Majesty, of course," Kurtness replied. "But if you believe harm has come to Prince Aris in the capital, it's more likely to have been back alley brigands or some Bajuman cutthroat than one of the clans. The noble families are already uneasy after the execution of the traitor . . ." He glanced apologetically at Myrinne. "That said, I've already dispatched the City Guard to search for him, but—"

The wind died. Even the sunlight seemed to fade for a moment. The wall of the Blood Spire glistened, as if truly painted with blood. Queen Lysandra rose to her full height, and more, somehow taller than she had ever been, and the ruined side of her face drew up in a grotesque half smile.

"Traitors," the queen snarled. "Are you one of them, Commander?"

"No. No, Majesty, I have served you faithfully for—"

The queen sagged. A tendril of black smoke curled from the corner of her mouth and was whipped away on the breeze. Startled and shocked, Phela drew in a sharp breath and felt something enter her mouth—a taste on her tongue like incredible age; a caress of something on the inside of her cheeks, stroking deep memories from somewhere she could not have been. *What have I tasted?* she thought, and then a surge of potential swept through her and she felt, just for a second, that she might be able to lift the weight of the whole world.

As the feeling passed she closed her eyes and breathed deeply, craving another taste. But whatever had leaked from her mother was now gone. Phela caught her breath and wondered whether anyone else had seen, and if they had, what they had believed it to be. She looked around, but she was closest to her mother, and in the others she couldn't see any suspicion—if they'd marked the presence of the smoke, it would have almost certainly caused a reaction. She alone had seen.

She had *tasted*.

Magic! she thought, only to have her excitement dampened. *But black, dead.*

Rotten.

What would true, living magic feel like?

With that exhalation, the queen was herself again, although her opalescent eye had a tinge of pink now, and the trickle of tears left a bloody trail. The magic Phela's mother had tasted had not only ruined her.

It was clearly *killing* her.

"Send the Guard to every noble household," Lysandra said. "Begin with those of the barons, but send them to the homes of every cousin, niece, and uncle—every member of the Five Great Clans. Search every room. Drag them into the street and flog them in front of their own slaves if they attempt to interfere. If you need assistance, send word to Apex Euphraxia that the Phage are commanded to aid the City Guard—"

"The *Phage?*" Kurtness asked, evidently shocked.

Phela shared the sentiment, even though she managed to keep herself far more composed. Still—*the Phage* . . . Did that mean they were real? Most believed the legendary soldiers to be a myth. Yet even if the Phage were not merely a convenient fiction, the Crown wouldn't actually be able to command them.

Still reeling from her brief taste of magic, Phela held her tongue as they all waited for her mother to speak.

The queen seemed about to say more, but held back, looking out across the city. Perhaps it was confusion, or a moment of lucidity and doubt in the events she had already set in motion. Eventually, though, she turned to Shome, now so drained that she could not even lift her gaze to look upon the assassin. "Listen to me, Shome. The Silent are to follow along, linger in shadows, seek the traitors. The City Guard are sent to find my son. You are tasked with making certain that anyone of noble birth found plotting against me is dead or imprisoned come nightfall."

With eyes downcast, the queen did not see Shome's quick glance at Phela. It could have ended then. Shome might have drawn a dagger and cut Phela's throat, spilling her treacherous blood before her mother. But the captain of the Silent kept still, and Phela knew then and there that Shome truly was her ally . . . at least for the time being.

Diminished, Queen Lysandra gestured toward the door. She did not turn to the railing again, did not look back out over her city and empire. When the Voice—who had remained strangely silent all this time—opened the door for her, the queen stepped into the darkness and began the long spiral down the gullet of the Blood Spire. Kurtness and Shome followed, and in moments only Myrinne remained on the balcony with Phela.

"What has happened to Mother?" Myrinne asked. Her shock was rich and deep.

"Too much spiza," Phela said. She watched her sister's reaction, eager to see whether she also knew of the forbidden magic their mother had been seeking. It seemed not.

"Do you think there could be anything to it?" Princess Myrinne asked.

"To her taking spiza?"

"Well, yes. But more to what she was saying. Do you think the noble houses could be so afraid now that they would revolt?"

Phela reached out to move an errant lock of hair from in front of her sister's eyes, and she smiled. "Is that worry I hear in your voice, Myr, or hope?"

She expected Myrinne to be scandalized by the suggestion, to babble some demurral. Instead, the tired beauty grew as still as the Silent, there on the tip of the Blood Spire, with the cold wind stealing their words and their secrets.

"I would never betray the queen," Myrinne said firmly. "But I will fight for Demos's freedom, and the freedom of his family."

"I'd expect no less," Phela replied. "You have always been the best of us."

Myrinne's face crumpled, but only for a moment. She fought the fresh tears that welled at the corners of her eyes, tightened her jaw, and turned on her heel. In a moment she had vanished through the door, following their mother and the others down the spiral.

Alone, Phela went to the railing. She looked out over the city, the villages beyond, and at the hint of ocean on the horizon, and she smiled. The wind whipped at her hair and her clothes, but it wasn't the breeze that quickened her heart, nor the tantalizing drop that loomed beyond the railing. The horrors she had both feared and anticipated were unfolding so much faster than she would have imagined.

And that taste . . .

She thought again of Myrinne and her smile wavered.

Phela realized she *did* love her sister. She only hoped that when all this was over, the Princess Myrinne could be allowed to live.

∽

The brand still burned. Demos lay on the cold floor and forced himself to stare at the scabbed, swollen symbol burned into the back of his right hand. Four small interlinked rings represented both the gods and the divine right of the noble families of Quandis to own slaves. The Bajumen had their own brand, one that marked them as the lowest of the low, but all the noble houses could brand their slaves if they so wished—that same symbol, the four rings, in the same place on the back of their right hands.

How can this be? he thought. The pain of the brand had been searing and intense. The pain afterward had lingered and ached. But there was a deeper pain, an anguish and a shame, that he knew would echo forever. He was Demos Kallistrate, not only the son of a baron and betrothed of a princess, but a respected sailor and warrior. *Not just respected,* he thought. *I'm a fucking hero.*

A little voice in the back of his mind cackled at the arrogance of the thought, but that didn't make it less true. He'd saved Admiral Hallarte's life. He'd killed a hundred pirates by his own hand and helped quell the uprising on Yitka Isle on the Outer Ring.

Yet the shame kept burning. He stared at the brand. *I'm . . .* his thoughts began again, but then he shook his head. Whatever he'd been once, right now he was nothing more than someone's possession. He'd never felt comfortable around his family's slaves, had tried to be kind to them, but staring at his brand, he felt himself hideously diminished, and he began to wonder how they'd perceived themselves.

I can't stay like this. I'll get out. There must be a way to eradicate the brand.

And yet he knew that to do so was a crime. Even former slaves still wore the brand, along with a brand of freedom that went on the back of the opposite hand. Still, there must be exceptions for people of noble birth, people who . . .

People whose fathers were executed for treason and blasphemy?

Demos stared at his brand and knew that he was going to have to get used to it. Even as he knew that he never would.

He heard footsteps and sat up quickly, hands curling instinctively into fists, pain flaring in his brand. Five days had passed since his father's execution and he still saw the man's dead eyes whenever he closed his own, still heard the hopeless scream that had issued from his mother's lips. Now he stared at the rough-hewn door of his cell, ready for whatever might come through it. His tongue passed over swollen lips, finding the copper taste of his own dried blood.

Until his arrest, he had never been inside a room as rough as this, as bare and cold. Even the chamber in which he'd first been imprisoned had been a luxury in comparison. His present cell measured five feet square. He had no clothing and no bedding, only a bucket for his waste and a small pile of old hay that caused him to itch and sneeze and barely kept him from the cold hardness of the stone floor.

He'd fought the slave traders. When the auctioneer had brought his gavel down and announced the sale of Demos's flesh and bone, he had roared and lunged while they'd dragged him away. They had sold him dearly, his heritage and name making him perhaps the most desirable trophy slave sold in that square for many years. He still did not know what had become of his mother and brother. Three quiet men had thundered their fists down upon him, rained kicks at his back and skull, and chained him in to the back of a closed wagon. When they had reached their destination and they had pressed the white-hot brand to his flesh, he'd struggled so much that they had beaten him unconscious, and when he woke inside this cell, he had no idea where in the city he might be. If he was even *in* the city. Questions had raced through his head:

Where was he?

What noble had purchased him?

Who would stoop so low as to prey on the misery of a once proud family?

The lock tumbled with a clank, and he wondered if some answers might finally be coming. Demos sniffed, tightening his fists, and glared at the door. One of his eyes had swollen mostly shut, and he still ached from the beating he'd taken. He was weak, too, from the meager food and water he was occasionally granted. Yet if an opportunity presented itself, he would fight.

To do otherwise would be to betray his mother and brother, whom he was desperate to find.

The door scraped across the floor as it opened.

Demos's one good eye went wide, and for a brief moment, he could only stare at the ice-blue gaze of the woman who stood in the doorway. There was no sign of the three gray-garbed brutes who'd been there every other time the door had opened. Only this woman, with her hair like dirty wheat and those winter eyes. Demos had encountered pirates and wandered the shores of distant islands, he'd beaten Penters for information, and he'd breathed the same air as men dying of disease. But as quickly as the shock hit him, now his nose wrinkled, the muscles in his neck tightened, and he averted his gaze from this woman he had been raised not to see.

Bajuman.

His fists opened. He would not fight her.

"Good morning, slave," the Bajuman said. "I am Mouse."

Demos stared into a corner of the tiny cell. Black mold grew on the wall. The mortar between stones sweated with moisture, and the blocks themselves were rimed with the yellow accumulation of decades of spiza smoke. A slave he might now be, branded forever, but he had been taught to never acknowledge a Bajuman.

She apparently had no compunction about acknowledging him. Moving so swiftly he did not have time even to blink, she caught him

with a single blow to his face before grabbing him by the hair and
the wrist as she drove him against the wall.

All hesitation gone, Demos bucked against her, striking out
with his free hand, but she just bounced his head off the wall again.
With a snicker she reached down and took his balls in her grasp,
squeezing enough to make him freeze in place, as if time itself had
halted.

"I don't want to waste time playing with you, Demos," she said.
"Look at me."

He averted his eyes once more.

Her grip tightened.

He allowed a groan to escape his lips, but it wasn't the pain that
made him finally turn to see her. It was the familiarity in her voice,
as if she knew him.

"My face, slave. Look at my face."

Demos shivered in pain, inhaled sharply, and finally met her
wintry gaze.

Mouse released her grip and stepped back, wiping her hand on
her trousers. "There. Was that so difficult?"

Confused, he began to look away, but she clucked her tongue
and he focused on her again, hating his obedience. Something about
the curve of her jaw, the shape of her shoulders, and the ridge of her
nose . . .

"There it is," she whispered. "Recognition."

How could it be? he wondered. All his life he'd been taught that
Bajumen were untouchable, invisible, beneath the lowest born. He
was a reasonable man, and had never found reason to hate them, but
his gaze shifted away from them like rain running off a roof. This
woman . . .

"Hello, boy," she said, and the two words echoed down through
his lifetime to childhood. They unlocked memories of laughter and
hiding places in his family home, and blood in his mouth from the

punishment his father would mete out every time he learned of his son playing with the thing in their darkest cellar, the child of the Bajuman who butchered the animals for their table.

Hello, boy.

Demos frowned. Somehow the pain of the past few days sank its claws deeper into him.

"Hello, girl," he whispered, as he had when they were children. He frowned, not understanding so many things. Every instinct told him to turn away, but he kept his focus on those deep blue eyes. "I . . . I don't even know your name."

He remembered the way they had once run from the cook when they'd been discovered hiding among meat hung to cure in the room behind the cellar chimney. Despite his pains and his loss, the memory softened Demos enough that the left side of his mouth edged up into the beginning of a smile.

She struck him with such force that his head snapped backward and he crumpled to the floor. For unknown seconds the world went black, and then vision and sound returned. He groaned and rolled onto his side, curling up. He had never been ashamed of his nakedness, but his balls remembered how willing she was to make use of their vulnerability, and he made to protect them.

"Mouse," she said, crouched beside him. "I told you. I am called 'Mouse.' It's the only name you need, and more than you deserve. It's important for you to understand your position in the household, so let's begin there." Her voice hushed. "You are nothing. Less than nothing. Beneath Bajuman."

"How can you be here?" he asked.

Mouse cuffed his ear. Hard enough to start it ringing, hard enough to draw a trickle of blood, but Demos thought perhaps not quite as hard as she *could* have hit him. He wanted to think some lingering childhood fondness held her back, but his skull throbbed and warm blood slid along the curve of his chin.

"For the same reason you're here," she said, and she hit him again. Harder. No trace of sentiment there. "I am here because I'm a slave. Soldiers came and took the slaves from the Kallistrate household, claimed us for the Crown, and I promise you they did not treat us with the tenderness that I've shown you."

"If you've tenderness to offer, perhaps you left it elsewhere?" he suggested. "What I've seen thus far—"

She smacked him across the face. "Is more kindness than you deserve." Mouse stood and he flinched, thinking she meant to kick him. "You'll stoke the fires and powder spiza for the chimneys. You may be allowed to butcher an animal the way my father did, if you prove adept at it. But you live in this cellar now. This room is your home."

Demos exhaled, taking that in. He had assumed it a holding cell, but this box had just become his world.

Mouse moved to the door. She opened it, and the stink of piss wafted in again, with the aromas of spiza smoke drifting in behind it. The combination made him want to retch, but his eyes were on that door. The three who had taken him, who had beaten him, were nowhere to be seen. She was strong and fast, and he at least temporarily weak and slow, but if he could make it past her . . .

"You'll wash yourself every third day," she said, ghostly eyes shining in the shadows. "Twice a day you'll be fed whatever scraps the household has left behind. If our master has guests, you will often be hungry, but when her house is quiet, you may have enough to sate you. Do not meet the gaze of anyone other than another slave, and even then, I'd watch yourself. Do not speak to anyone other than another slave—again, I'd suggest you keep most of your thoughts to yourself. Are these instructions understood?"

Demos swiped at the blood trickling from his ear. "They are."

He did not stand.

"Good," said Mouse. "Remember them well. They are about to

be tested. I'll take you to the slaves' bath. You will wash quickly and dress in the tunic I provide and then I will lead you through the kitchen and to the quarters of Vosto, the praejis."

"As you say," Demos replied, mustering as much dignity as he could manage while still keeping his gaze mostly averted. Each noble house had a praejis, a slave who had risen over time to become the virtual head of the household, the only slave who had regular contact with his or her owners.

Already he imagined himself supplanting the one called Vosto as praejis. Existence as a sailor had scoured from his spirit most of the whimsy that life in the nobility had inspired, but Demos had always been a pragmatist. He hoped that Myrinne would be able to prevail upon the queen to hold himself and his family innocent of whatever offense his father might have given, real or imagined. But until such time, he had to walk the path before him, and find a way to thrive.

Mouse eyed him up and down, then stepped into the corridor and gestured for him to follow. Though the stink of spiza hung oppressively in the air, and though his new keeper had just outlined the constraints upon this new life, still he felt his spirits lift as he left the square box of his room behind. This meager dram of freedom would not quench his thirst for it, but it was refreshing.

"Go on." Mouse pointed to the left. "Your bath awaits." The corner of her mouth lifted in rueful humor. How many times had she used those same words to one member of his family or another, but under vastly different circumstances?

Demos lowered his gaze to the floor. "May I ask one question?"

He steeled himself, prepared for punishment. Prepared to bleed again.

"Carefully," she warned. "You may."

Demos glimpsed those winter eyes, but only for a moment. "If

I'm to meet with the praejis, is there anything else I must do to avoid angering him?"

"I'm taking you to the quarters of the praejis, but it isn't Vosto you will meet there." Mouse shoved him, and he caught himself on the wall as he staggered toward a set of stone stairs. "This one time, you'll meet your mistress."

5

It wasn't the first Bajuman mouth he'd had wrapped around his prick. It wasn't the twentieth, nor the fiftieth. One hundredth? Perhaps. Prince Aris had lost count long ago.

But that initial touch of moist mouth and warm tongue always felt like the first.

He groaned and lay back on the heavily cushioned bed. The delicious flick of a tongue across his balls sent a shiver through his body. Then another, licking at the same time, and when he looked down he saw all three of them bent over him, one from the left, two from the right. They were naked, oiled, beautiful Bajuman women, proud of their brands and relishing this moment of power he allowed them. Sucking and fucking a prince. Being naked and unashamed before Quandian royalty. What they knew, and what he didn't mind them knowing at all, was that it also afforded *him* a deep sense of power.

Free from the bindings of princehood, there was power in doing whatever he wished, whenever he desired. He would never love a Bajuman, but neither could he bring himself to hate them.

How could he? They were gorgeous, and they set him free.

While the women to his left and right worked on his balls, the one suckling on his manhood lifted her leg across his body and presented herself to him. For the thousandth time Prince Aris wondered whether a royal tongue lapping at them felt any different from a slave's or a fellow Bajuman's. And for the thousandth time that thought lost itself in the delicious moment.

Aris groaned and writhed, abandoning himself to wonderful sensation. Good Xhenna Pan wine warmed his stomach and freed his mind to concentrate on nothing but here and now. The spiza these three Bajuman women had ground, combined with oil, and spread on their bodies for him and each other to lick off, coursed through his veins, setting his senses alight and sparkling across his skin, heightening every sensation to almost unbearable extremes. Yet Aris bore it well. He always did.

He closed his eyes and flowed with what made him feel most alive. The room was warm with body heat and the flickering fire from the torches in sconces on the walls. The air hung heavy with the aromas of lovemaking, spiza, and spilled wine. The walls were splayed with Bajuman artwork, harshly carved figures performing arcane rituals. He knew that such expressions of their history and beliefs were banned, but few people ventured into Bajuman homes, and the practice was widespread. He sometimes wondered what these figures were doing, and why their representations were so basic and formless, almost as if the Bajumen chose to draw like children. But he did not wonder for long. In truth, he didn't care.

He didn't come to places like this to admire their artwork.

The woman squirming on top of him tensed and squealed, releasing him from her mouth as she found her own shuddering release. She moved aside, her sweat-slicked body slipping from the bed to lie on the rug-covered floor. Pushing himself up onto his elbows, he looked down at the two women still working on him. One was tall and thin, her piercing eyes closed, but in pleasure, not shame. He found no shame in these wonderful women. He treated them as equals—perhaps the most terrible, damning secret for a man who concealed so much—and before and after their lovemaking he would talk to them, honor them, and put their concerns at rest. He always did. He found a satisfaction in their gratitude and humility that was almost as great as . . .

. . . almost . . .

"Carry on," he gasped. "I fear it's just the two of you now."

The woman on the right grinned up at him. She was shorter and far more voluptuous, and it was she who opened her mouth and swallowed him down, never once losing eye contact.

And such eyes. Like winter aflame, their deep-blue coolness caught the candles set around the room and scorched into his soul, setting fires deeper than any he had ever known from any woman other than a Bajuman. Aris did not fool himself—these women were no more skilled at sex than any other he could have chosen to sate his needs across the kingdom. But their unbridled joy at his acceptance of them gave them an almost animal passion, a primeval need to enjoy him as much as he enjoyed them.

He'd had two many times before, but three . . . never. This was a first. When opportunity presented, he was not one to turn it aside.

The fires were building, within him as well as deep in the Bajuman women's eyes. Wine soothed him, spiza tingled his senses, and he felt himself surging toward a release, the first of many, and if that meant he remained here a day and a night, then—

The heavy curtain covering the door was swept aside. A draft of air flushed into the room, flickering the candles, a frigid jolt on sweat-soaked skin that sent sharp shadows jerking across the walls. The woman to his left sat up and turned toward the doorway, and—

Aris could not understand quite what happened next. At the exact moment of his explosive release, the woman's head snapped back and her throat was open, blood splashing across his groin and stomach to merge with his seed, and his mind shrank back from the harsh truth of what was happening. The voluptuous woman to his right rolled onto her back, her legs and arms straightening upward as the figure thrust a heavy sword into her gut.

She screamed.

The woman on the floor stood, darting for the edge of the room, but was swiftly caught by a fist wrapped in her hair.

Shome, Aris thought, and against all possibilities he knew that he was right. Shome, captain of the Silent, taller than most men and tattooed with promises of horror, pulled the woman back by her hair until she landed across Aris's blood-splashed legs. The first woman thrashed on the floor, bleeding out from her gashed throat. The woman to his right was spluttering, the sword now hacked upward into her rib cage.

The woman pushed down across his legs lashed out with her hands and caught Shome across the face. Skin parted. Blood dripped.

"No," Aris said, still not quite understanding. "No, what is this, what's . . ."

Shome looked down upon him with disgust. She let go of the sword and reached for the third woman with both hands, pushing her against Aris's thighs, pressing down and twisting until she snapped the Bajuman's neck.

Aris felt the break transmitted through his legs. She was looking back and up at him when the fire went from her eyes and they turned paler than ever before. Not pale. Dead.

"No," Aris said again. He made no effort to cover himself. He could not comprehend what was happening. Wine and spiza merged and confused. He was not a fighting man, and he carried no weapons, but he knew they would not have been any use.

Not against Shome.

She stood upright and stared down at him, blood dripping from her face. She took a long, frank look at him, from head to toe, and Aris felt a sudden rush of rage. How dare she look at him like that? How dare she intrude upon a prince's private moment and . . . and . . .

His cock was waning. Blood was already cooling across his body, even as the other two Bajuman women quivered their last.

And then he knew how she would dare.

She would dare because she had been sent with this task in mind.

"My mother?" Aris asked. Shome blinked. "My . . . my sister?"

Shome grabbed the sword and tugged it from the dead woman's body. It dripped. She raised it back over her left shoulder, tensed, determined, silent as ever. Her muscled arms shone in the candlelight. Her tattooed face and scalp told stories of agony and death. The killing blow would take only a second.

The seconds passed.

"I am your prince," Aris whispered. His voice was shaking, and he hated that, but it could not be helped. He was not brave.

There'd never been a reason for him to be.

Shome tensed again, pulling the sword back a little more as she prepared to swing it down and onto his body. He could not bear to imagine the pain of metal cleaving flesh, the thought of his insides turned out, but he was so petrified that neither could he move. But, for a few more seconds, nothing happened, and that emboldened him just a bit.

"I am your *prince*!" He injected as much righteous anger into his voice as he could, pleased that the shaking was gone, his tone lower and more commanding.

And Shome gave pause once more. She frowned, glanced aside, and lowered her heavy sword. How many it had killed, Aris could not guess. Three more than yesterday, with the Bajuman women who lay dead about this room.

But no more today, thank the gods.

Shome placed the tip of her sword on the floor and rested her hands on its hilt. She was still frowning, turning over some inner conflict. Aris recognized the doubt in her eyes, and he released a held breath he hadn't been aware of holding.

He closed his eyes and prayed to the Four for their kindness and mercy . . .

. . . only to feel a large, calloused hand close around his cock and balls. And even as Aris's eyes snapped open again, and his mouth dropped wide to yell, the shout froze in his throat when Shome sliced her sword through his manhood's root.

Aris had never known such pain. Such shock. The scream might remain locked in forever. *Kill me!* he wanted to shout. *Finish what you started!*

But Shome did not kill him, and that was somehow worse.

She threw his severed genitals to the floor between the dead women and sheathed her sword, and Aris wondered if it was over. But then she drew her knife and as he tried to scramble away, she slashed across his forehead and cheeks, his nose and lips, long, deep cuts that he knew were enough to scar him hideously. The pain was white-hot and ice-cold and warred with the agony between his legs. Then she grabbed him around one foot and dragged him from the bed. His head struck the floor, dazing him.

For minutes or hours Aris floated on planes of blinding agony. Light and dark played before his eyes. They merged and pulsed, each throb matching that of his hammering heart. As Shome dragged him he felt carpets and rugs beneath him, then wood, then naked stone, and then the thump-thump of a long staircase leading down, down, *down*. Splinters dug into his back and thighs, and then stone abraded his skin. He heard only her steady footsteps and his own nails clawing at the ground, trying to hold himself back until they ripped from his fingers, causing a new wave of horrific sensations to burn through his body.

Shome was breathing heavily. Though still daytime, they were surrounded by a deepening twilight.

When she stopped dragging him at last, Aris lay still. Disbelief and agony provided a temporary buffer of shock between reality and his senses. He opened his eyes and looked up at a stone ceiling. It was festooned with moss and filth, and many-legged creatures crawled there. He heard rats and gutter vipers. He smelled shit through his ruined nose.

Shome picked him up by the throat and stared into his eyes. The pain stole away much of his perception, concentrating everything on the raging agony at his core. She reached her free hand to the small of her back and produced a small dagger, its blade so sharp that it felt like nothing more than a whisper on his skin as she slit his throat.

Aris gasped for air, eyes wide, the stink of his own blood filling his nostrils. Before she let him go, he saw something in Shome's face that broke through the incredulity and pain.

He saw pity.

Then she released him and he dropped. Light receded above and away from him, a pale circle marred only by Shome's face watching him fall.

He struck water as cold as ice, so cold that it numbed his pain, but not his terror. The water swept him away into a darkness so profound it had weight and texture, but another darkness crept in at the edges of his eyes and his thoughts began to float away from him.

Aris, Prince of Quandis, unmanned and cast down, pumped his blood out into the waters beneath the city, and was gone.

‮ᴄᴐ‬

Mouse watched him bathe. Before, Demos had often bathed in front of Bajumen, unabashed and unashamed at his nakedness because he'd hardly even acknowledged their presence, and if he had, then their gaze had meant nothing. Many times he and Myrinne had made love while Bajuman slaves were still in their rooms, tidying away clothes or feeding the fire. It meant nothing. *They* meant nothing. It was no different from washing or fucking in front of a dog.

Now, Mouse stood in the room and ensured that he cleaned himself properly, and he was aware of little else. Still, he took in the bathing room, wondering if there was anything he could use. But there wasn't much. It was a dank, echoing chamber, windowless and lit only with several oil lamps in recesses in the walls. The water was cold and slimy, cloudy from previous use. The soap pot was slick with oil and lined with hairs. It was a grim scene that seemed to echo in his mind, and perhaps Mouse was also there to ensure he didn't slip under the water and stay there.

"Wash your balls," she said.

Demos scooped soap and raised himself from the bath, smearing the cool, oily mix across his genitals. He washed and submerged again, and he wasn't sure whether the whisper he heard was water splashing against stone, or the Bajuman's soft laughter.

He paused and looked down into the water, letting it settle so that he could see reflections in the scummy surface. The lamps cast rainbow splashes across the oily water, and he saw Mouse's inverted shadow motionless in the corner, watching. In another world—the world reflected in the bath, perhaps—she would be waiting to do his bidding. In this world, everything had changed.

He closed his eyes and remembered his father's cruel death, before blood-hungry crowds and with false allegations ringing in his ears—

"Out!" Mouse snapped. Demos flinched, expecting another punch, but for now she seemed to have ended her physical abuse.

I should have fought back, he thought. *I should never allow a slave to treat me like this!* But he had fought back, from the moment the Guards had first seized his family to the moment Mouse had entered his cell, and every time he'd been beaten down. The brand still ached on the back of his right hand, marking his defeat. Declaring his shame. Announcing that he was worthless, like any other slave. He knew he ought to keep fighting, his spirit raged inside, but weakened by days of incarceration, hunger, thirst, and constant beatings, he knew how it would end. If Myrinne could not free him, he would have to escape, and if he hoped to escape, he would need to bide his time. He had to be careful. In his time Demos had seen slaves come and go from his own family's grand home, and he'd rarely considered why the new faces were there, nor where the old ones had gone. The Kallistrates were not a cruel family, but he knew that life among slaves was cheap. People treated like nothing often resorted to treating each other like nothing too.

Mouse could just as soon kill him as look at him. He feared that their shared history made this likely.

He climbed from the sunken bath and wiped his hands across his body, flicking away the slick remnants of oily soap. Mouse threw a tunic at him and he caught it, slipping it over his shoulders. It was itchy and rough, but it protected him from the cool breeze breathing through these subterranean chambers.

He still wasn't sure where he was, nor which family had dared purchase a former noble to add to their retinue of slaves, which family could sink so low as to burn the slave brand in the flesh of one of their own. He could have queried Mouse about the identity of his new mistress, but he feared that such a question would not be welcome. And he was intrigued enough not to wish to endanger this meeting.

"Follow me," Mouse said. She turned and left the slaves' bathing rooms. In the hallway outside there waited a man and a woman. They were dressed in tunics identical to his own, and they barely met his gaze. They carried burlap sacks on their shoulders, and Demos recognized them as the pale gray bags used to store recently harvested, unground spiza. The man was Bajuman, and the woman was of one of the races brought to Quandis as slaves from some far-away land. Demos didn't even know the name of her people. He felt a spark of shame at that, and when they glanced at each other, it was he who averted his eyes.

Mouse ignored the two and led him up a curved stone staircase into a wide, better-lit room. There were still no windows, but oil lamps in steel baskets hung around the walls and sat in low braziers spaced regularly around the large space. There was no ornamentation here, no nods to aesthetics. It was a purely functional room. The sudden expanse came as a shock to Demos's senses after days incarcerated in cells, though, and he let out a surprised grunt that echoed around the hall.

Several slaves glanced up at the noise, then down again at what they were doing. Mouse glared at him.

Four fire pits were being tended, each by two slaves. The pits were sunken into the stone floor and filled with burning hardwood and chunks of coal. That in itself was an indication as to the standing of his new master. Coal was an expensive import into Quandis usually used by one of the Five Great Clans, and even then most often in the homes of the barons.

Only four barons now, he thought. *At least until a new Kallistrate baron is named.*

The clan members were probably already squabbling among themselves to choose a new leader. Perhaps they'd already chosen one. It disgusted Demos to think about which cousin had presumed to take on the mantle of Kallistrate leadership. He wondered if they would try to revitalize the remains of his father's estate on the hill at the northern edge of Lartha. It was painful to think of, almost as painful as memories of his father's death, and his mother's and brother's beatings. He tried to cast it from his mind, but he could not help remembering their great, ancient manse ablaze, and the rest of their hilltop estate being fought over by lesser relatives eager to climb Lartha's social hierarchy. The idea was unbearable.

"Move on!" Mouse said, slapping him across the cheek. "Pay attention!" Demos glanced up, and her chilling eyes reflected the oil lamps like white fire.

They crossed the room, passing close to one of the pits. Demos had already smelled spiza in the air. Now he saw why. While one slave tended the fire, the other used a hand grinder to turn dried spiza into a fine powder. They then scattered it into the flames, and the carefully managed fires sparkled and emitted a blur of heat haze filled with spiza fumes. Almost completely smokeless, the haze was captured by circular metal hoods suspended above the fire pits, and from these hoods rose narrow pipes that disappeared into the stone ceiling. Demos could imagine heat from the fires driving the fumes up through the floors and along a network of pipes and ducts. He suspected that there were grilles throughout this building, perhaps subtly hidden behind furniture or in dark corners, and that the whole place had a constant level of spiza in its atmosphere.

It was intriguing, because he also recognized the spiza being burned. It was a calmer, used to settle nerves, relax the body, ease worries from the brain, not the kind of mind muddler that had become almost taboo in Larthan society. Whichever noble had bought him liked to spend time in his own home relaxed, but still keep his wits about him.

The slaves worked with smooth efficiency, their pupils deep, dark holes, their mouths slack. Some of them drooled. He held his breath as they walked by.

Mouse led him across the room and through an archway. They moved along a hallway, passing several closed doors on either side, until they reached the door set in the hallway's end wall. Beyond the door was another circular staircase, and this time he counted nineteen worn steps until they emerged into a small, plain room.

Mouse headed left, but just before following her Demos glanced right.

A heavy wooden door had been left ajar, and through it he saw the interior of a dwelling the likes of which he'd never seen before. The room appeared vast, with high arched ceilings and elaborate carved columns at regular intervals. Between these columns, where the ceiling curved up to its highest point, colorfully glazed rooflights let in splashes of brilliant sunlight, casting patterns down across the stone floor. It was the first daylight he'd seen in several days, and he had the strangest feeling that he was viewing the light of a different world. Things had changed, events had moved on, and Demos and his family now had no influence over the land that this sun continued to bathe. It was a depressing thought, and he vowed to cast it aside.

If only it was that easy.

They moved on.

At a lower level in the huge room, curtains hung between columns on invisible lines. They were beautiful, elaborate pieces of material, each of them from a different place of origin, each displaying artwork, decorative techniques, and histories from lands near and far. He recognized scenes of snow and ice from Tan Kushir's troubled history, the angular blue shading of Herio artwork, character studies of shaman and mythical demons from Xhenna Pan, and the mystical, ever-changing colors of a Penperl-leni tapestry. Each curtain represented a piece of high art, and he was stunned by the opulence and riches so casually on display. Not the Hartshorn clan, then, this house. The Hartshorns were never this ostentatious. He tried to narrow it down in his mind.

"This way," Mouse said, but she kept her voice low, and by that he knew that they were almost there.

She stood before a door in the small room's far wall. She waited until he joined her, then glanced sidelong at him. He saw a flicker of something in her eyes—memory, perhaps even sorrow—then she grew hard and distant once more. Mouse pushed the door open and signaled for him to enter.

The praejis's room was windowless but well appointed, but as Mouse had told him, the praejis was not present. And the woman who sat waiting inside was the last person Demos expected to see.

Euphraxia, Apex of Quandis, Voice of the Four, offered him a humorless smile.

"Kallistrate," she said, the word dripping from her mouth like poison. He'd never heard one word, one name, imbued with such venom. And such hatred. "Kallistrate . . ." The apex *hated* him.

The apex *hates me?*

Demos had seen her many times when she conducted worship in the Four Square, that vast expanse of rooftop contained within the boundary of the massive spires rising from the Temple of Four. Only nobility attended services in that place, and the apex regularly preached to several hundred people while the shadows of the spires held them in their cool embrace. To him she had always seemed an intimidating woman, both grand and severe, and her age only exaggerated those attributes. With her sitting before him now, he felt humbled in her presence.

Yet the hatred emanating from her . . . he couldn't parse it.

"Your Holiness—" Demos began, and Mouse slammed him across the side of the head with a tight fist. He stumbled sideways into the open door and almost slid to the ground. His vision blurred, eyes watered. When he could see again, Euphraxia had not moved. She stared at him expressionless.

"Do not speak unless spoken to," Mouse hissed into his ear. She tugged at his arm and he stood, leaning against the door to maintain his balance.

I am Demos Kallistrate! He breathed deeply. He could barely believe that the apex of the Faith could allow slaves in her household to be treated like this. But then he would not have believed that such wealth would be evident here, nor that she would exist in private in a constant state of subtle intoxication from the calming spiza.

It seemed that behind closed doors, even the greatest in the land harbored secrets.

Euphraxia said nothing else to him. She merely stared, seated, while Demos and Mouse stood just inside the open doorway.

Demos risked looking around. Euphraxia sat on a wooden bench beside a square table, upon which were piled many cooking and eating utensils and vessels. There was no food evident. The rest of the room was neat and well-kept, and he imagined the praejis lounging on his bed while a slave swept and polished around him.

He could hear the apex's heavy breathing. She was very old, yet she sat stiff and upright, proud. Maybe it was her age that necessitated the constant miasma of calming spiza throughout her home.

"I summoned you here so that I could see your face," Euphraxia said at last. "So I could study the eyes of a Kallistrate brought low and see that brand on your flesh."

Demos flinched at the disgust in her voice, and shame flooded through him. The brand. The gods-damned brand. Was that all it took to turn the highest of the high into the lowest of the low? It seemed so.

"That's why I'm here? You have some vendetta against my clan?"

Mouse struck him again, so hard that his vision blurred and fresh blood ran from his split lips.

"Do not speak, you fool! And lower your damned eyes!"

Demos spat blood onto the floor and glared at Mouse. He would not let them erase who he'd been, brand or no brand. "The apex wanted to *study* my eyes. Perhaps you should listen more closely to your mistress's—"

Mouse hit him again—and again—driving him to his knees with punishing blows until Euphraxia herself barked, "Enough!"

Demos kept his head down. Not that he had much choice—he could barely lift it. His blood dripped to the floor, but he felt a smirk form on his broken lips. To hell with both of them. Perhaps in his life he had earned Mouse's ire—perhaps he had this coming from her—but he owed the apex nothing.

Euphraxia approached him. Demos only stared at her feet, at the elegance of her boots, the dyed leather, the symbols of the Four etched there.

"You're wondering why I hate you," Euphraxia rasped. "You're wondering why I bought you, why I brought you here, what will become of you. Well, you should know that I will enjoy having you here, in the bowels of my house, toiling and bleeding and seething in fury every moment. You cannot fall from such heights and live in such misery without praying for answers, and what better place to pray than the house of the apex? Your prayers will be wasted, of course. I brought you here to tell you *nothing*! I know that the mystery of it will only add to your suffering as you wonder why for the rest of your wretched, painful life."

The apex spat upon him. He watched her feet as she turned away in dismissal.

"Take him out of here," she sneered. "But harm him no further. He is the lowest of my slaves, but still a slave in the household of the apex. I want his life to be insufferably long, full of days of drudgery and nights of indignity. The slaves are to treat him as if he were their own slave."

Her boots clicked on the floor as she walked away, and a distant door opened and closed.

What of my mother? he wondered. *What of my brother, Cyrus? How did this happen?*

Demos dreaded the answers. He looked up at Mouse, expecting triumphant disdain, but instead he saw sympathy there and had no idea what to feel.

"Time to start work, slave," she said.

Averting his eyes, Demos stood and walked from the room.

Once Mouse started leading him into the cellars, though, he glared at the back of her head. *I am no one's slave,* he thought, vowing to keep hold of such defiance.

It would probably be the only fire he had to keep him warm.

6

Phela's skin felt flushed, though she could not see her own hands in the darkness inside the walls. A ghost of herself, invisible to all—even her own eyes—she nevertheless felt more alive than ever before. What was this feeling, this tremor in her heart, this prickling at the back of her neck? She had been in danger before, but she thought this must be what true peril felt like. Yet at the same time, she'd never felt more in control. The whole world seemed soft and yielding, and it was her touch that might keep it propped up, or bring it tumbling down.

Aris had never had the patience even to play cards, never mind to build little houses out of them, but Phela had played that game with her sister when they were small girls, and Myrinne had been the master of it. She had the patience and dexterity not to even breathe, for fear an errant exhalation might bring the entire house of cards down. Phela had not realized then how much she had learned from watching Myrinne work with those cards and helping her set them in place. But learn she had.

The Crown was as fragile as the structures she and Myrinne had built. According to legend and faith, the royal family had the Blood of the Four in their veins, and the people needed to believe that for the Crown to remain strong. Phela needed to believe it herself—not only to believe it, but to confirm it. Her family had become a house of cards. The entire kingdom rested atop it. Phela had spent years Whispering behind the walls, studying what history she could find, learning all she could about her family. She knew that the trick now would be to dismantle the house while leaving the kingdom itself unharmed. If she could do that, then she could rebuild the *Crown* into the shape she desired using far sturdier materials.

Namely, myself.

Behind the walls, she listened as the slow collapse of her mother's house began to gain speed.

"Speak the truth to me now, Commander," Queen Lysandra said, her raspy voice edged with warning. "I know the Five Clans are rife with treachery and treason, and I must know who among them are my enemies."

"Majesty, I always speak the truth to you," Commander Kurtness replied. The wariness in his voice would be plain to anyone who had not lost the ability to gauge the behavior of those around them. "Members of the City Guard have spent the past two days out among the Five Clans. In uniform they have searched every room of every noble household, and out of uniform they have gone quietly onto the hills and into the streets and listened to the mutterings of nobles and rabble alike. We've found no evidence of a significant uprising. What we've found more than anything is fear. The execution of Linos Kallistrate and the enslavement of—"

"Liar!" screamed the queen.

Phela flinched. Even with long years of practice remaining still while Whispering, the pain and panic in her mother's ragged voice startled her. She could only imagine what it had done to those in the room with her. In addition to Kurtness, Shome was there, of course. But who else? Phela had only started listening a moment before, and now this.

"Majesty . . ." Kurtness murmured.

"Don't try to mollify me!" Queen Lysandra screamed again, and then her voice dropped low, as if she spoke only to herself. "I have been ill, Commander, but don't confuse illness with weakness. My beauty may be ruined, but I have all the cunning I've ever had."

"My queen," said another, and Phela recognized the Voice, Dafna. "You have always relied on Commander Kurtness's guidance and loyalty. If he says—"

The queen actually *hissed*. "Don't speak to me as if we were *friends*, Dafna. I put words in your mouth and you speak them. Those are the only words I want to hear from you, the ones that echo my own. You *have* no opinion. Now shut up!"

A moment passed in awkward silence. Phela could imagine them all wondering what to do next, wondering just how mad the queen had become. Then she heard a loud sniff, and she could smell the sharp odor of burning spiza, and she knew that her mother must be indulging. Throughout her life Phela had learned many things about her mother while Whispering, and until she had seen the queen taking spiza with Linos Kallistrate, she'd thought there had been nothing left that might shock or disappoint her. But this . . . in front of *others* . . . Her nostrils flared in revulsion. Phela felt sick as she waited for one of the queen's advisers to speak up in objection, or at least to question the wisdom of partaking at this time.

No objection came, though. Instead, the next voice surprised her. It belonged to a man of whose presence she had been entirely unaware, and that unsettled her.

"The City Guard are not the only ones who move among the people," the man said. It took a moment for Phela to place him. She recalled a long, black, braided beard and a scarred face. A shaved head. The air of a soldier never quite comfortable with his role of priest, though he had changed the path of his life from the worship of war to the worship of the Four decades earlier.

Per Ostvik was one of the High Order. Phela frowned. If Ostvik was here, where was Euphraxia? The High Order were a clan unto themselves, fiercely secretive and protective of their own ranks, but surely Euphraxia, the apex, would not approve of her subordinates meeting with the queen without her present.

"All right, priest," the queen said, her voice dripping with uncommon disdain. "Tell me what you holy ones have learned."

Where had that disrespect come from? Phela had believed her mother intimate with the apex and the High Order. In seeking magic, surely Queen Lysandra had conspired with them to break the laws of both Faith and Crown? Nothing about this meeting made sense to Phela and, more than anything, that bothered her.

The cards teetered . . .

"Majesty," Per Ostvik said warily, "you must trust someone. If you cannot trust those who speak for the gods, who else remains?"

Phela heard her mother whimper, then, and she knew the house of cards must truly be at its end. The last few walls were falling, or else Lysandra would never have shown such weakness to anyone.

"You have been my friend, Ostvik," the queen said. "But I've put too much faith in you already. If you tell me there is no conspiracy—"

"Quite the contrary, Majesty," the priest said, his voice ringing loudly. Even from the other side of the wall, Phela could feel his voice inside her chest. There was a deep power there. "There are conspirators all around. But most of those voices are easily silenced. Clan Daklan fears for their foreign trade and the safety of their merchant ships abroad, but they will be loyal if they believe the Crown can keep the economy stable. The same is true of Clan Ellstur, who care only about the product of their farms and mills, and Clan Burnwell, who give their loyalty always to strength, to command. I worry more about Clan Hartshorn—"

"Poets and teachers?" Commander Kurtness sniffed dismissively. "We're to fear *them*?"

Phela could almost see the way Per Ostvik would be narrowing his eyes now, angry at the interruption.

"Artists," Per Ostvik said. "Historians. You dismiss them so easily. The women and men of Clan Hartshorn are, and always have been, the most suspicious of the Crown. But there's a reason they're a Great Clan. Because knowledge is power. *Words* and *influence* are power, as much if not more than the swords your soldiers hold. Trust me when I tell you rebellion is there, simmering quietly in the cellars and alleys of that hill, behind the stained-glass windows and beneath the lyrics of each new song being sung there today."

"My queen," Dafna said, "I believe it would be an error to make rash generalizations about—"

"But of course you know the real problem," Per Ostvik cut in.

No one said a word. Stuck between the walls, Phela exhaled and a small cloud of dust danced away from her lips. Her ear remained pressed to the wood and her feet ached with the cold of the stone beneath them. She felt the solidity of wood and stone as if they were her own limbs, and the entire palace was her flesh and blood. But to those within the queen's chambers she remained a phantom. Even in their silence, they would never hear.

Except perhaps Shome. But the captain of the Silent would not speak against her.

"Clan Kallistrate," the queen said at last, revealing that despite her paranoia and failing health, she had not completely lost her senses. "Killing their baron has left a void."

"Kallistrate Hill is in disarray—" Commander Kurtness began.

"Chaos, you mean," Per Ostvik said. "It isn't merely the execution of their baron. It's the enslavement of the rest of the baron's immediate family. Half of Clan Kallistrate is talking open revolt against the Crown, or some kind of secession of their hill from the kingdom."

"And the other half?" Dafna asked, perhaps because the queen had again fallen silent.

"Fighting over the barony, of course," Kurtness said. "If Demos Kallistrate were free, he would inherit the title. If his brother were alive, he'd do the same. But they're not, so what remains is yipping and nipping at one another like hungry dogs over a scrap of meat. They're furious, but much more focused on who will be baron than on any kind of uprising."

A hiss halted any further conversation. Phela shivered behind the wall, knowing that hiss had come from the miserable thing her mother had become.

"Majesty?" Kurtness ventured.

"The Kallistrates are furious, you said. And Ostvik says they speak openly of rebellion."

"It's only talk, my queen," Kurtness replied. "As I said—"

"Only *talk*? The City Guard ventured onto the Seven Hills out of uniform in order to learn what is whispered among the other clans. You've just said as much. But we know there is unrest. Disloyalty. And your Guardsmen, Kurtness, have done *nothing* to suppress this and have not arrested those who foment talk of rebellion. You've listened as Quandians openly disparage their queen."

"No, Majesty," Kurtness said. "It isn't like that—"

The slap echoed even inside the walls where Phela hid. She flinched again, so startled that she did shift a bit, a tiny brush of her knee against the wall, evidence of just how deep her shock was that her mother would strike the commander of the City Guard.

"I wear the crown. I am queen," Lysandra said. "In my veins runs the Blood of the Four. To speak against me is to speak against the gods themselves, to blaspheme against the Four. Would you not agree, Per Ostvik?"

Phela held her breath. Surely, this priest of the High Order must see that magic and spiza had not merely addled the queen's mind, they had broken it. That her judgment could no longer be trusted. Gods, the sweet and acrid stink of spiza even permeated the walls. Phela could hear her mother inhaling noisily, like a pig at the trough. This was what the great Queen Lysandra had come to. Ostvik couldn't agree to—

"Of course, Majesty," Ostvik said. "The Four live through your bloodline. Those who speak against you are not only rebels, they are sinners."

"There," Queen Lysandra said, almost too quietly for Phela to hear. "Rebels and sinners. And if the City Guard is too hesitant or too incompetent to do what must be done, then there are other ways."

In the Whispering space between walls, Phela felt that prickle at the back of her neck again. She flushed with excitement, sure that something remarkable was about to happen, after which nothing would ever be the same. Linos Kallistrate's execution had set these events in motion, but her mother's addiction and dissolution were her own doing.

And they would be her undoing.

"Shome," the queen said, breaking protocol merely by acknowledging the presence of the captain of her assassins. "Tonight you will take the Silent to Kallistrate Hill and extinguish the spark of revolution. You will display the dead, and make an example that will silence any disloyal tongues among the other clans. Now go, all of you. All but you, Per Ostvik. There is much to discuss."

Phela heard footfalls and the creak of an opening door. She needed to go and speak with Shome before she left to do the queen's bidding, but she delayed a moment to listen and was rewarded with a final exchange that gave her pause.

"I'm going to have to tell Euphraxia what transpires here and among the clans," Per Ostvik said.

"You'll say nothing!" the queen snapped. "We have kept many things from your apex, Per Ostvik. We both have secrets we'd rather she not know. So for now you will say *nothing*. There'll be time for truth later, after we have decided just what that truth ought to be."

Phela heard another huff, another sniff of spiza, and then she Whispered away in disgust.

She met Shome in the alcove behind the door to the Servants' Stairs. The captain of the Silent stood studying a dusty carving of one of the early kings, so old now that nobody recalled which monarch it represented, so that in some ways it had come to represent them all—all of those who'd worn the crown and ruled in a time when there were still men and women alive who remembered the Four as living gods. Legend said that Quandis had once belonged to the Bajumen, that their ancestors had been the indigenous tribe here until the clans had come with their worship of the Five, who became Four when the Pent Angel turned on the rest. That was nothing but legend, though. Folklore. Myths now known only to a few, and mostly ignored by them. Except that this dusty, forgotten king would have known better.

"King Nothing had his time," Phela said quietly.

Shome turned to her, blinking in irritation. The Silent were known for their stealth, and it was good to know that Phela could still surprise her.

"That's what I've always called him, in my head," Phela went on. "King Nothing."

She had prowled these corridors and stairwells all her life. King Nothing's timeworn stone features were intimately familiar to her. Sometimes she had spoken to him as if he were a friend, there in the alcove at the top of the Servants' Stairs. But Phela had no friends today. Not even Shome. Not even her sister, Myrinne.

She searched Shome's eyes. "Is it done?"

A slight knitting of the assassin's brow made Phela wonder, but then Shome gave a single, slow nod, and she knew that her brother was dead. Prince Aris, no longer destined to be King Aris. Shome glanced down the Servants' Stairs before reaching inside her tunic and drawing out a rough cloth bag, which she handed to Phela. Its strings were not knotted, so it was the work of only a moment to open the bag and peer inside. Phela's stomach gave a sickened twist when she identified the shriveled, bloody flesh inside that bag. Her nostrils flared and her eyes welled with tears, mourning for the brother Aris had been in their childhood days. She had done this for Quandis, she told herself. For the health of the land and the glory of the Four. She promised herself that, and when she glanced into Shome's eyes again, she thought perhaps the captain of the Silent was making similar vows to herself.

"We do only what must be done," Phela said quietly, though to persuade Shome or herself, she was not sure. "When you carry out my mother's orders on Kallistrate Hill, make it very public. The word will travel fast. I want the Seven Hills and beyond to know that the *queen* sent the Silent to exact her vengeance."

Shome nodded again, then turned and descended those darkened stairs, leaving King Nothing and the future queen behind.

Phela cinched the drawstring bag and left the alcove, moving through a doorway and back into the corridor that led to her mother's chambers. As she went, she let her grief come to the fore, let it show on her face, so that when she approached the two Guards on sentry at her mother's door, they could see the pain and urgency in her.

She let them see her tears.

"I'm sorry, Princess Phela," one of the men said. "The queen is not to be—"

"Trust me," Phela said, wiping at her tears as she shot him a withering glance. "You do not want to trifle with either one of us today."

The Guards glanced at each other. The queen's instructions regarding her privacy and her children had been inconsistent over the years, so it was no surprise that they relented. They bowed their heads to her and opened the twin doors as quietly as they could. Phela entered, padding quietly through the entrance hall and standing outside the door to the audience chamber. Inside, she could hear her mother and the priest arguing.

"—cannot take you below again," Per Ostvik was saying, his voice both firm and pleading. He did not want to defy the queen, of course, but he sounded as if he had made up his mind.

"But you will!" Lysandra commanded. "You will take me tonight, priest, or you won't live to see morning!"

"Don't you understand that I am trying to save you, Majesty?" Per Ostvik beseeched her, clearly seeking a way out of this task. "I can feel the magic lingering in you, suffusing you in a way it could not have if you'd gone through the proper preparatory steps. It's eating your mind and destroying your body. You went too far this last time, and I'm afraid—"

Phela felt a momentary recollection of that taste of magic on the Blood Spire, leaking from her ailing mother's eyes and drawn into Phela's mouth with her gasp of surprise. Its intimacy. Its power. She knew what and where Per Ostvik spoke of when he mentioned going below, and Phela felt an intense excitement prickling at her, as if he spoke those words directly to her.

But not yet, she thought. *Mother rushed. I have to be careful and methodical if I'm to succeed where she has already failed.*

Phela entered the room. She'd thought herself prepared for the sight of her mother, but Lysandra looked worse than ever. Her ruined eye continued to weep. The smell of spiza in the room barely covered another stench, a darkly sweet body odor that made her think of rotting things. Bent and too thin, skin hanging loosely on her frame, Queen Lysandra turned and pointed at her, jabbing the air with her finger as if it were a dart.

"This conversation is *not* for you."

Per Ostvik said nothing, and Phela ignored her mother's anger and admonition. Instead she allowed her grief to flow forth again as she crossed the room to hand the drawstring bag to the Queen. The coarse cloth rasped on the older woman's skin as Lysandra took it in confusion.

"What are you doing? What is this?"

"Prepare yourself, Mother," Phela said. "It . . . it is from Aris. That much has been confirmed."

Queen Lysandra faltered. She whimpered like a wounded beast and sorrow twisted her already ruined features into something even uglier, a contorted sculpture of human pain. Phela watched as she opened the drawstring bag and peered inside at the bloody, shrunken lumps of flesh that had been Prince Aris's manhood. The bag slipped from the queen's hands and slapped to the stone floor. Per Ostvik reached for it, but the queen turned on him, yelling, "Don't you dare!"

Then she froze, as if time itself trapped her between moments. As if neither past nor future held refuge, and so she refused to move. Phela moved up beside her, put a hand on her narrow shoulder, and tried not to breathe in too deeply the sickness nesting within her.

"He was in bed with three Bajuman whores," Phela said. "All three are dead, murdered by whoever killed him. The assassin took his body, but left his manhood behind."

Queen Lysandra inhaled sharply, as if waking from a trance. She shot a dark look at Per Ostvik, who seemed to wish himself anywhere but in that room. Phela didn't blame him.

"Witnesses?" Lysandra asked.

"Only Bajumen, but they confirm the tale. Aris is dead, Mother. The prince is gone. Rumors already rise that the Bajumen are taking advantage of the confusion caused by the turmoil among the Five Clans to stage their own revolt. They're going to try to kill their masters. They're going to defy the Crown and the Four."

"No!" Lysandra screamed. She kicked the coarse cloth bag and it tumbled across the floor, Prince Aris's shriveled cock and balls spilling out, leaving a trail of crusted blood clots on the stones. "No they will not!"

She began screaming for the Guards. Magic sparked in her eyes, misting from them, and smoking tendrils leaked from her open mouth.

There! Phela thought, breath freezing in her chest, but she resisted the temptation to inhale, dragging the shreds of dark stuff from the air.

Her mother's lips turned an ugly golden hue as she screeched. Per Ostvik approached her, perhaps trying to calm her down, but the Guards rushed in and Lysandra kept screaming, and then the queen's face went slack and she began to tremble. A stain spread on the front of her dress, painting a damp wishbone on the fabric. The stink of urine overwhelmed the other odors in the room as she turned and staggered toward the small table where she'd left the small chunks of green-and-yellow spiza.

"Majesty," Per Ostvik whispered, but he made no move to help her, or touch her. His disgust had paralyzed him.

Queen Lysandra collapsed, one hand still outstretched for her addiction, ignoring the trophy her son's killer had sent. Black tears ran from her ruined eye.

"The Bajumen," she said to the City Guards as they approached her. "Tell Commander Kurtness to kill them. Send him to me if he wants the order from my mouth but . . . kill them.

"Kill them all."

And Phela's hands deftly shifted the cards a little more.

⁓

Admiral Daria Hallarte breathed deeply and the smell of wood smoke, sulfur, and burning flesh filled her nose.

The battle had been over for an hour, but her blood was still up, and her breathing was short and harsh. With one pirate ship sunk and the second set aflame, the outcome was not a surprise to her at all. She had killed two pirates with her own hands, and that did not trouble her. What *did* disturb her was the message that had arrived by seagull from the queen, commanding all ships not engaged in vital defense of the kingdom to return to the capital to put down what the message called "a simmering insurgence." Even though Daria had already made her decision about how to respond, uncertainties bit at her, and she was not used to that. Daria had come as far as she had because she was decisive and firm. She did not like harboring doubts. It made her feel like a Bajuman.

She looked from the windows at the rear of her wardroom. The burning pirate ship was half a mile astern, its rigging and masts now little more than stark lines against the flames reaching ever higher. It was listing to starboard, and soon the sea would rush in, extinguish the flames, and claim the ship for its own.

Out of two pirate crews there were only five survivors, and now it was time to interrogate them. They waited tied up on the deck of the *Nayadine,* the finest vessel in the Crown's fleet. They knew that their time was short. She would promise them a quick, painless death if they answered her questions, but the task did not fill Daria with glee, because she had questioned pirates before. It was very unlikely that they would talk. It was highly probable that they would die in terrible agony rather than betray any secrets about the pirate guilds.

Still, she had to try.

The way the *Nayadine* rolled and creaked felt familiar and reliable to her, but the boards breathed with the ghosts of sailors past, and she felt them with her, from captain down to deckhand. The men and women who had rigged the sails and plied the waters on this ship would not judge her. They had fulfilled their duty and expected nothing but the same from her.

Which begged the question, what was her duty today? She had never been very good at trusting people. Most of the officers in her command had earned the faith she put in them, but it was one thing to trust your subordinates to follow orders and to be competent, and another thing entirely to rely upon the wisdom and counsel of another. She trusted Shawr to be loyal and brave, but in the end he was merely her steward and hadn't the breadth of life's experience to offer real perspective. For the past two years, whenever she had a difficult decision to make, Daria had relied on the counsel of one man—Demos Kallistrate. She could never share the core truth of her life with him, or with anyone. But her doubts and fears, her hesitations when it came to decisions regarding her command, were things that she could trust Demos with. And something like this order from the queen . . .

Four curse you, Demos, she thought. *You had to be on leave now, of all times?*

When he returned from leave, Demos would be given the captaincy of the *Breath of Tikra,* the oldest ship in her fleet of six. If Daria didn't think it would cause a mutiny, she'd have given him Captain Gree's job. Her sailors loved and admired Demos, but he had been with them too short a time to be raised above so many far more experienced women and men.

Unless I arrived back in the capital while he was still on leave, she thought. *Wouldn't that surprise him?*

A knock on the door did not make her turn. She knew that knock, its scuffle, and knew Shawr would come in whether or not she bade him enter.

"Captain Gree has gathered everyone on deck," Shawr said. "The prisoners are still aggressive and defiant. One of them has already killed herself."

"How?" Daria asked. "I ordered that they were to be bound and kept alive for questioning."

"And bound they are," Shawr said. "Best guess, she had a capsule of redfish venom somewhere in her mouth."

Daria raised her eyebrows. She'd seen someone die of a redfish bite. "She'd choose that over a quick death?"

"She's still smoking," Shawr said.

"Such dangerous enemies we have to fight."

"Which makes the decision about the queen's order a real dilemma, Admiral?" Shawr asked.

"More than you know," Daria said quietly.

"But we'll go, surely," Shawr replied, coming to stand at her elbow, where he placed himself so often in hopes of being useful. "The message carried by that gull made it plain there is strife at home. The queen—"

"—has instructed her army to send whatever forces we can spare without interfering with our existing missions," Daria interjected. She did not need to remind Shawr that he ought not to question her. Her tone said enough. "I'd much rather be out across the sea, attempting to find the Far Shore or to reestablish relations with the Chilkot people, but our orders to confront the pirate threat brought us closer to home. And this mission is vital."

"It's pirate raiding parties, Admiral. Nothing more. The islands around the Ring have fought off pirates before and they will again, with or without our help."

"You're young, Shawr. You see the current threat, but you're not good at looking forward. If these pirate guilds ever banded together, they could pose a threat not just to the Ring but to all of Quandis. Now this dog who claims to be Kharod the Red—"

"Who has been dead for five centuries," Shawr interrupted.

"I'm not suggesting he is *actually* Kharod the Red. But whoever this new pirate chief is, he knows how to inspire the guilds. Which is why we can't return to Lartha. We've still work to do here, and questioning the captives—getting every ounce of information we can from them—is only the beginning. The queen will have to get along without us."

Shawr nodded grimly, as if all the wisdom of the ages weighed upon his head. "So you've decided."

"I have."

Daria would tell the captains what she had told Shawr. Like him, they would accept her reasoning. The logic was sound, after all. If this new pirate chief who fancied himself a figure out of legend managed to persuade the various guilds to band together, they might turn themselves into an effective army of thieves and cutthroats, and the Quandian navy could not allow that. In the name of the Crown, they had to track down and destroy this new Kharod the Red.

"Some of the captains will balk," Shawr said. "There are some among them who will want to rush to the queen, out of loyalty or seeking glory."

"You mean Captain Gree." A flicker of a smile crossed Daria's face. Shawr disapproved of anyone he thought might not be completely dedicated to her. Given the life she'd been born into, she didn't like comparing a person to an animal, but he did have a singular loyalty she'd only ever seen in dogs. She was grateful for the fierceness of his friendship.

"Perhaps."

"I know how to handle Gree," she said. "That's why I'm an admiral." She smoothed the front of her jacket, ensuring that her sword and throwing stars were secure in their sheaths. She might be using them again soon. Daria led by example, even more so if that meant interrogation and torture. It was yet another reason that she was held in such high esteem; though an admiral, she was not afraid to get her hands bloody.

Up on deck, the stench of battle was even stronger. The bodies of seven Quandians killed in the skirmish were being washed and prepared for a sea burial on the foredeck, their wounds sewn and bound, fine clothing laid out ready for dressing. Soon they would be lowered into the hands of Dephine, god of Water and Beasts. It was a sad accompaniment to the scene immediately before her.

The five pirate captives were lashed to the railings amidships. One of them, a woman, was scorched lobster-red by the redfish venom she'd managed to swallow, and a pool of blood still bubbled on the deck around her. Hair hung low over her face, obscuring much of the dreadful damage from view. Her arms were stretched out to either side. The ropes securing her to the railings smoked.

Daria was glad her corpse had been left among her companions. They could smell the sweet cooked-meat stench of her death, and two of them were even now trying to move themselves aside from her spilled blood. If it touched their skin, it would burn.

She walked slowly along the line, pausing before the dead woman, drawing her sword, and using its tip to lift the corpse's head so that all could see her disfigured face. Some of her own people looked away. None of the pirates did.

"This could be you," she said.

"We'd welcome it," one of the pirates said. He was a big man, heavily tattooed, serpents and suckered sea creatures squirming along his limbs from beneath his sleeves and short trouser legs, a sea dragon twisting around his neck and across his face. Its open mouth sat around his own. When he spoke, the dragon roared.

"Your name," Daria said.

"Phyllips. I knew a Quandian like you once, only not as ugly. I took out her eyes and ate them while I skull-fucked her. She was still alive. She lived for a few days after that, and the rest of my crew—"

Daria flicked her sword and sliced it across his cheeks and through his nose. His cheeks fell open, blood bubbling around the split in his nose as he tried to calm his breathing. At least it had stopped his foul words.

"I'll kill you all quickly if you answer my questions," she said.

"Where's the honor in a quick death?" Phyllips asked, spitting blood. "Give me hours. Give me days." He stared right at her as he shuffled sideways, laying his leg flat in his dead companion's toxic blood. His skin began to sizzle. Phyllips grinned.

"I'll have your leader on my sword before the summer's out," Daria said.

"Kharod the Red has been on many swords!" Phyllips shouted. The pain seemed to be feeding him, fueling his anger and fury. "King Kharod will eat you all, he'll chew you up and—"

Daria turned her back on the pirates and faced her crew and captain. Gree was smiling, and his smile widened as they locked eyes. She knew that her decision to remain at sea, rather than sailing for Quandis, was not his favored one. But she could also see that he understood her reasoning.

Having Captain Gree maintain his trust in her gave Daria strength. She knew that she was going to need it.

Incensed by her turning her back on him, Phyllips the pirate ranted and shouted some more. All to no avail. She waited until his ravings quieted, then turned around to continue her questioning. She had prepared herself for this. It would be a long, bloody afternoon.

The heavy beating of wings interrupted her. A huge albatross appeared from around the ship's bow, circling the *Nayadine* once before drifting down to land on the railing, tucking in its enormous wings. The symbol of Clan Daklan was painted in blue upon its proud chest, and the bird cocked its head and stared at Daria and her crew.

The gull that had arrived earlier still was exhausted and waiting for a return message. Gulls were typically used to deliver messages within the confines of Quandis, or sometimes as far out as the Ring, so when one arrived this far from home, Daria knew that there were only two explanations. Either whoever had sent that message had been an amateur, or all the Crown's albatrosses had already been employed.

This new arrival was not from the Crown at all. Clan Daklan were foreign traders, merchants and explorers, and so they had many albatrosses of their own. Using one to send a message to one of Quandis's military vessels was unheard of.

Shawr started toward the bird, but Daria held up a hand. "No. I'll get it."

The moment she approached, the albatross froze. It stood patiently as she reached out, unwrapped the leather covering on its left leg, and peeled away the heavy parchment rolled within. It was addressed directly to her. Daria unfurled the parchment and stood staring at the words scrawled there, her pulse quickening.

> *Baron Kallistrate executed. Family enslaved.*
> *If you come home, do not speak of your friend and my son*
> *Demos or you risk yourself.*
>> *With respect and in mourning, Carina Kallistrate*

Daria stood still for a few beats of her heart, blinking away the shock.

Then she held the parchment up and let it go, watching it catch a breeze and drift up, then down into the waves. She turned toward her crew, who waited expectantly. Captain Gree was frowning.

"Shawr, kill that bird and take it to the cook. The captains and I will have it for dinner."

"Yes, Admiral. Of course." Shawr eyed the big bird—its vicious beak and heavy wings—and rested his hand on his knife.

Daria hefted her sword. She started with the pirate closest to her, slicing his throat and stepping back so that the blood did not spurt onto her boots. She moved down the line, and when she reached Phyllips he was grinning at her, head back to expose his neck.

"Hail King Kharod the Red," he said.

"Yes. I'm sure." She stabbed him through the heart, then turned to face her shocked crew once again.

"Captain Gree, send signals to summon the other captains to the stateroom. Prepare the fleet. We're done here. We're sailing for Quandis."

As she went belowdecks, Daria's loyalties fought within her. Sailing for Quandis, yes, and into a time of turmoil and mystery. But who she might serve when she arrived was a question yet to contemplate.

∽

Phela had mastered the art of being still, yet she despised the act when it was forced upon her. She sat now in a ferrowood chair, its seat and backing so rigid that such chairs were most often used by the priesthood. They found something like grace in their own discomfort. Phela had always disparaged this foolishness, and yet wasn't she doing something quite like that tonight? This very moment? *Who is the fool now?* she thought.

The thing that lay in her mother's bed did not resemble Queen Lysandra. Withered, arms folded defensively around her chest, her mother was curled on her side, dragging in quick, shallow breaths as if each one were precious to her. And perhaps they were. Only her ruined eye remained visible, the other buried in the pillow beneath her head. Her hair had gone thin and waxy and fallen out in hanks. Tears still wept from the ruined eye, but the wondrous magic that had snaked from within her to be whipped away on the breeze had given way to a thick, yellow pus.

"Majesty," said Dafna the Voice, shifting on the end of the bed, perhaps under the illusion that the queen still needed her. "Can I get you anything?"

"Hush, fool," Phela said. "Don't you see she's beyond needing things this world can provide?"

Dafna glanced at her, stung. Phela ignored Dafna's hurt feelings and grief, wondering what might become of her now. She supposed she would have to endure the woman for a little while, so that the transition of power seemed respectful. Peaceful. Dafna might even prove useful in the long term—the people had faith in her, and she did have an uncanny ability to project calm even when delivering dreadful news. It might be worth keeping her around.

She would think on it.

Standing sentry at the head of the bed, Shome watched over Queen Lysandra and barely lifted her eyes toward Princess Phela or Dafna. Her loyalty remained invested in the Crown itself, not the woman wearing it, and her obligation tonight was to her current monarch. She watched over Lysandra with a looming, monolithic devotion.

A breeze eddied along the floor and Phela relished it. Before she had stopped speaking entirely, the queen had asked for the room to be warmer, and so Dafna had instructed the servants to bank the unseen fires higher and to vent the heat into the queen's chambers. It was insufferable. The breeze was a relief, then, and moreover meant that another mourner had arrived.

Myrinne entered the room. She moved with a grace and power that Phela admired, quiet out of respect rather than a desire for stealth. The princess Myrinne hated their mother now—she must, Phela reasoned, given the fate of the Kallistrates—but still she behaved as if grief had her in its grip.

Phela did not rise from her chair. Dafna slipped off the end of the queen's bed and retreated to the archway around a recessed window, as if she wished to vanish there. Myrinne knelt at the queen's bedside, staring at the wreckage of the woman who had raised them with a stern hand, profound expectations, and cold wisdom, when she had bothered to raise her daughters at all. Aris had been her golden child.

"Is that . . ." Myrinne began, then turned to look at her sister. "Do I smell spiza, Phela?"

"She begged the healers. They relented. If that's what brings her peace." Phela shrugged.

Myrinne nodded. "No harm in it now, I suppose."

"We all know her body's more than familiar with it," Phela said bitterly, surprising herself. Quite undisciplined of her to allow her true feelings to show. That wouldn't do at all.

Myrinne bent and whispered something to their mother. For several minutes they remained like that, all of them as silent as Shome, only the breathing of the heat vents and the queen's ragged exhalations breaking the quiet. And then Myrinne glanced at her older sister again.

"Where is Aris? It's unthinkable that he should be anywhere but here."

Phela let her gaze drift to Shome before focusing on Myrinne once more. "Myrinne, our brother is dead."

Myrinne had been kneeling, but now she sagged to one side, gripping her mother's bedclothes. Sitting on the floor, back to the bed, she stared at Phela.

"Take that back. Say it's not true."

From the window archway, not as hidden as she'd like, Dafna spoke up. "I'm afraid it is. Prince Aris has been murdered by Bajumen. An edict has been issued by the queen to execute them all to be sure that his killers will die."

Myrinne hung her head. "It makes no sense. Why would they—"

"Perhaps they were tired of him fucking their women," Phela said. "Three Bajuman whores were murdered with him, all in the same bed."

"No," Myrinne said, squeezing her eyes shut. "How can this be happening?"

Phela frowned. "You act as if you loved our brother. Aris was horrible to you."

Lysandra moaned softly. Dafna emerged from her redoubt, eyes hopeful. "Majesty?"

"Leave us," Phela said without turning toward the Voice.

The room held its breath. Phela kept her gaze on her sister, but she could practically hear the Voice stiffening.

"You do not command me," Dafna said.

Such temerity, Phela thought. She glanced at Shome, who moved instantly out from behind the queen's bed and stood staring at the Voice of the Queen. Phela had to give her that: Dafna had spine, for she stood facing Shome as if fear had not begun to chill her bones. Myrinne watched it all happen, and a light of epiphany flickered across her face. She rose shakily to her feet.

"It would seem that she does, Dafna," Princess Myrinne said, smoothing her coat. "Based on my mother's condition, it seems unlikely she will linger more than a few days, at best. The healers tell me they have no experience with whatever ails her and cannot forecast her fate with any certainty. But . . . look at her, Dafna."

Myrinne herself did as she instructed the other woman, turning to face the queen. "My mother is dying. My brother has been murdered. Perhaps Princess Phela does not command you today, but she will be Queen Phela soon enough. Yet if nothing else, respect a daughter's wish to be alone with her dying mother."

The Voice did not speak again but quietly retreated from the queen's chambers. A cool breeze danced along the floor, and then there came the soft thunk of the doors closing in the anteroom.

At last Phela rose from the chair. Heart quickening, she stood beside Myrinne and the two princesses looked down upon the ruined shell of their mother. Phela remembered callousness in her childhood, but there were kindnesses as well. There had been laughter. Even honor, once upon a time. She had learned vital lessons from Lysandra when she'd been just a girl. If that woman had lived on, strong and wise and ruthless, Phela would never have desired the Crown. At least, that was what she told herself. But the Blood of the Four ran in their veins, and the Crown deserved more than the selfishness and corruption that had replaced Lysandra's better traits. Quandis deserved a queen willing to do anything to maintain its grandeur and honor, to restore both the fear and the faith of the people. She would be that queen, and that brief taste of magic on the Blood Spire had shown her how.

Their island state shone brightly, an example to the world. Other nations wished to trade with her, or go to war with her, or desired her protection. The Four had smiled upon this place, had carved it from the land with their own hands, planting their seed in its people so that the crown would always rest on the head of one of their own descendants. Phela knew she was doing what must be done.

Yet it hurt her, just the same.

For the first time in years, she took her sister's hand.

Myrinne glanced down at her. "This will be better for Quandis," she said, as if reading Phela's mind. "We both know that. Her mind has been unraveling."

Phela studied her, wondering just how perceptive her sister might be. "It was never my dream to be queen."

Myrinne's gaze flickered toward Shome, but only for a moment. "Until it was."

Swallowing down a smile, Phela gave the tiniest nod. "Until it was."

"When you're queen, you'll undo the horrors of these past weeks. You'll order the Kallistrates released."

"Order Demos released, you mean. Does that mean you've learned who purchased him?"

"Euphraxia has him—"

"The apex?" Phela said, interest flaring. "Why would she—"

"His mother is enslaved to Clan Daklan and his brother is dead," Myrinne finished.

Phela nodded, understanding immediately. Daklan and Kallistrate had been allies for many generations. It seemed likely Carina

Kallistrate had been purchased by their old friends in order to save her from suffering at other hands. Which could only mean that Euphraxia had outbid them for Demos, a strange turn indeed. Unless one considered history.

"You must order them both freed immediately," Myrinne said. "We can't bring Demos's father or brother back, but you can at least give him and his mother freedom."

On the bed, Lysandra sighed and shuddered, almost as if she could hear their conversation and it revolted and infuriated her. Phela thought perhaps she could, and didn't mind.

She smiled and turned to her sister. "I know you're good with a sword, but I always wondered if you'd have the stomach for actual combat. Now I think perhaps you would. It seems you have a stiffer spine than I've given you credit for. I'm proud of you."

Myrinne squeezed Phela's hand. "You'll do it, then?"

"You have my word I will try."

"Try?"

"Euphraxia is the apex, and I suspect she has . . ." Phela shrugged. "A peculiar hunger to make Demos her slave."

"But why?"

"I've heard rumors of an old grudge," Phela said. As usual, she did not let on any more than was required. In her Whispering she had heard fragments of conversations, and putting them together she'd constructed an incomplete picture of Euphraxia's hatred of the Kallistrate name. But this news seemed to confirm it all. Sometime long ago—long before most alive now were even born, save perhaps Per Ristolo and some others of the High Order, whose advanced ages even she did not know for certain—Euphraxia's family had been a part of Clan Kallistrate. The tale involved a Kallistrate ancestor who had ruined Euphraxia's former family name. The exact nature of this offense Phela still did not know, but it was enough to cause the family to be banished from the clan. Euphraxia's ancestors, and consequently Euphraxia herself, had been encouraged to join the priesthood to make ends meet. The whole event had inspired a deep-seated hatred that persisted down through the generations and must still burn bright and hot in Euphraxia's heart today.

Phela wondered how well this intense hatred sat beside the apex's worship and love of the Four, gods of fairness, forgiveness, and mercy.

"Grudge or no grudge, you have to try," Myrinne said.

"I'll do my best to release them," Phela said thoughtfully, pieces falling together in her mind. "But not immediately. First, there is something Demos must do for me."

Suspicion clouded Myrinne's eyes. "What is it you want, sister?"

So Phela told her, in detail. Myrinne protested at first, but eventually she relented as Phela knew she would. What choice did she have?

Extracting a promise to be kept apprised of their mother's condition, Myrinne glared at her sister one last time and then hurried from the queen's chambers. *Running to Demos, no doubt.*

"Now, Shome," Phela said when she was certain Myrinne had gone, "it's time we eased Queen Lysandra's burden. There is much to be done, and Quandis won't benefit from a long, uncertain wait. There's no need for my mother to suffer anymore."

The captain of the Silent might have been carved of stone for all that her expression gave away in that moment. But when Phela went to the hutch where the healers had secreted the queen's spiza inside tiny drawers, when she brought it back and began to administer the spiza to her mother's lips, Shome gave her assent simply by remaining still.

Soon, Queen Lysandra was also still. Also silent.

And so she would remain forever.

7

The novices of Yaris Teeg were walking in pairs through the bustling Larthan streets and squares north of Temple Hill. Ahead of them, across a wide, shallow valley, loomed the hill of Clan Daklan, its sheer eastern cliff evidence of some ancient cataclysm that must have split the hill in half, all the other slopes heavily built up with colorfully rendered structures—homes, shops, restaurants, storage buildings, schools, and its renowned hospital. At its top was the sprawling castle housing the greater families of the clan and its wider network of friends and advisers. Down at the base of the hill, lining the bank of the river Susk where it cut through the city, were the offices, warehouses, jetties, and docks used by Clan Daklan to marshal and organize their extensive trade operations. Several large ships were moored, and countless smaller vessels came and went up and down the river, many of them docking beside the trading clan's hill. Business was done, money changed hands, promises were made, and deals forged.

It was so different from the quiet of the temple.

Away from their quiet studies, the novices were told they could look, but never speak. These times outside Yaris Teeg were part of their initiation into the priesthood, because it involved levels of self-control and adherence to their teacher's strict instructions.

Gemmy was failing her test.

"See the way they're looking at you?" she whispered.

Blane frowned and glanced sidelong at his friend.

"All around," she continued, "mothers with children, traders at their stalls, teenagers, and soldiers—they're looking at you as I've learned to."

"Quiet!" he urged. "Per Santoger will hear, and we'll be—"

"They're looking at you not as a Bajuman, but as a priest."

Blane drew in a sharp breath. His anger at Gemmy simmered away to nothing, and he wanted instead to reach across and grasp her hand. He didn't, of course, but he still marveled at the idea that she was a friend. It was taking him some time to grow accustomed to the fact that he had a friend with brown eyes. Most Bajumen never had the chance to entertain such friendships, other than during the innocence of childhood, and his own reaction to it was unexpected. For a man so focused on his own separate purpose, he felt deeply touched and moved by something as simple as Gemmy's smiles.

"That's because we are priests first and foremost," Per Santoger said.

Blane flinched, waiting to be berated. Beside him, Gemmy pursed her lips into a tight smile. But Per Santoger, walking close behind them, did not tell them off.

"If you know deep inside that you serve the Four, then however damaged your soul—however set upon, abused, mistreated, or twisted by guilt—the love of the Four will repair it. They will reforge it with a passion and drive to serve them. That's why they look at you as a priest, Blane, even if they glimpse your brand or your eyes. Because you're starting to believe it yourself."

The old priest's words startled Blane, but he nodded his thanks.

"Now, as I recall, my instruction was that we should walk in silence," Per Santoger said, and he hurried past them, huge girth swaying, to the head of the line of twenty novices.

Blane glanced at Gemmy, and when she smiled, he could not hold back his smile in return. It was honest and heartfelt, and he let himself enjoy the moment.

With that newfound confidence, he let himself look for the first time at the many Larthans in the streets and squares they passed through. It was a stance he was not used to—usually as a Bajuman he walked with his head bowed, averting his eyes from others in case their gazes accidentally locked. If that happened, some would choose to beat him for his audacity, while others might simply shout and rage. Not everyone hated the Bajumen from birth, but tradition was a powerful force.

So powerful, apparently, that the simple tradition of the priesthood was enough to overcome generations of bigotry and intolerance.

They passed into a warren of narrow streets—high buildings shutting out the view of the Temple of Four and associated smaller temples behind them—and onto the gently sloping route down to the river in front. Per Santoger hadn't revealed their destination, but that was not his way. For him, every walk was a journey, every day a new adventure, and he lectured that moving closer to the Four meant identifying and embracing opportunities to learn more about those ancient gods.

Their time at Yaris Teeg was all about discovering these opportunities, and Per Santoger's way was often to let realization dawn, rather than try to force it upon them.

The streets were relatively quiet. These were residential districts, and many people were either away from their homes at work or school, or sleeping off a night's activities. Those they did pass were women, young children, and old people, and almost all of them performed the sign of Four as the trainee priests and their tutor walked by.

Blane looked at an attractive woman and glanced away, but not before he caught her smile. He looked up again. She was still looking at him, holding her hand to her throat in the sign of Four. She held the hand of a small child, a young boy picking his nose and watching this strange procession with wide eyes.

Blane smiled back and continued on his way. Fifty days ago, he might have been arrested and flogged for such a smile.

They passed through several more narrow streets until he could start to taste the unmistakable hint of the river Susk, the mix of salt water and silt the great river carried up from the sea and back down from the uplands twice each day.

He liked the river. It reminded him of his mother, and the times she had taken him and his sister there to bathe when their day's work was done. *The land has a long history and a deep memory, and the ebb and flow of these waters is like its heartbeat,* she would say. *Strip, bathe, wash, and feel its pulse.*

"It's the salt baths," Gemmy whispered.

"What?"

"That's where he's taking us."

"What're the salt baths?"

"Didn't you ever . . . ?" She trailed off. She no longer got embarrassed when she forgot his ancestry. "No, of course you didn't. You'll see. Fed by the river, heated from deep vents in the caves below, lit by burning sky moss permanently aflame on the ceilings . . . it's quite a place."

"Why would we be going there?"

Gemmy's sidelong smile turned into a grin. "To sing!"

During Blane's time training for the priesthood, Gemmy's love of singing had quickly become apparent. She was good at it, and the first time they sang together with other priests he realized that she reveled in it too. She loved it so much that she'd expressed disappointment that Linos Kallistrate's execution had been so abrupt that they'd never gotten to sing the "Mournful Quell." Blane's look of shock had drawn a contrite apology from her, but he still wondered whether it was heartfelt.

Blane was tone-deaf and didn't know most of the songs they sang, yet he was grudgingly starting to enjoy it. There was something about opening your lungs and singing to the sun, moon, and stars that felt like freedom.

At the edge of a larger square, Per Santoger paused at the head of their column and turned to address them. Past the priests in front of him, Blane could see across the square to a tall, elaborate façade that he had never given a second glance before. He'd known it was used for something he would never be able to experience, so he had closed it off from his mind. It was simply a weighty shadow casting down on him just as his eyes were cast to the ground.

Now he saw it properly, and he realized what a beautiful structure it was. Cornered with pillars, faced with colored timber paneling carved and painted into scenes from histories that Blane could only guess at, the river shushed by behind the building, and a shimmering haze rose from six tall chimneys extending thirty feet above the high domed roof.

"Today, I have brought you to the—" Per Santoger began, but then a commotion across the square caught everyone's attention. Blane shifted sideways to see past those in front of him.

A squad of City Guards emerged from behind the salt baths building. There were at least a dozen of them, heavily armed and armored, and between them they were dragging six frightened, scrawny slaves, all Bajuman. None of them struggled. They knew better than that.

The squad's captain strode to the center of the square, a group of small children scattering before him, their mothers or nannies scooping them up in their arms and backing away to the square's edges. The sun beat down and larks still sang as they danced above the city capturing insects from the air, but the atmosphere had changed.

Something dark and cool settled around the square, like invisible shadows anticipating night.

"What's happening?" Blane asked. Per Santoger did not turn around to reprimand him. Other trainee priests were also chattering.

"They use slaves to shovel the salt up from mesh collection grids on the riverbanks," Gemmy said. "I wonder why—"

The captain drew his sword and planted it point down in the pavers at his feet. As the six Bajumen were thrown to their knees in a line ten paces behind him, the captain addressed the crowd.

"For crimes against the state," he said. His voice sounded relaxed, not agitated. It was the voice of a man who had already said these words before, perhaps many times that day. And for the first time Blane noticed something else about this contingent of the City Guard—blood smeared their armor, dulling the usual shine; their hair hung in sweaty bunches, as if they had been exerting themselves, or running; and the captain carried a looped wire ring hanging from his belt.

Blane couldn't be sure what the things threaded onto this wire were, not from this far away. But he thought they looked fleshy. Pale.

"And for crimes against our queen. And against the Four. And against . . ." He waved a hand, as if at a fly buzzing around his face. He sounded almost bored. "Their sentence is death."

At that final word, six City Guards drew their own swords and slashed them through the air.

Blane would never forget that moment. It happened in the blink of an eye, but something slowed it in his perception, as if the hot summer air was too heavy to allow such movement, too oppressive to entertain such rapid, sudden violence.

The swords sang the same notes as they connected with the Ba-jumen's necks.

Four heads spun and rolled, hitting the ground and spilling blood.

Gasps went up from some of those spectators who had retreated to the edges of the square.

Gemmy grasped Blane's hand, but it was him who squeezed.

"Anyone owning a Bajuman slave is to submit them to the Guard for judgment," the captain said as the bodies fell. Soldiers stood over the two twitching, still-whole Bajumen and finished the parting of heads from bodies.

"Failure to comply will result in arrest and imprisonment."

Other soldiers gathered up the heads that had rolled and sliced off their left ears.

The captain looked directly at Per Santoger, only thirty feet separating them. Gemmy shoved Blane sideways, only half a step, but enough to nudge him behind a taller novice in front.

"The Crown will compensate for lost slaves, and where new slaves cannot be supplied, a mutual recompense will be agreed."

The captain took the wire hoop from his belt and held it up while six ears were threaded onto it. They joined many more.

"You," the captain said, pointing at a small group of men and women huddled beneath an overhang in front of a café. "Throw the bodies into the river."

Their task here finished, the soldiers re-formed into a tight line behind the captain. He took a small scroll from his pocket, consulted it, grunted, and then started walking briskly from the square.

"What just happened?" Blane breathed. "What did he mean?"

Gemmy remained pressed tight against him, as if shielding him from the sun. The two men in front of him glanced back, and Blane could even see Per Santoger turned around and looking down the line toward him.

All pretense had gone. They still knew that he was Bajuman. Of course they did, and of course they would give him away, old prejudices driving them, instinct pulsing through their blood and souls more powerfully than the worship of the Four ever could. That was what made his real aims and intentions as a novice priest so meaningful, and so important.

No one would ever forget.

Blane prepared to run, squirming to free his hand from Gemmy's. Blinking, he saw the swords whisking through the air and parting skin, flesh, bone. Breathing, he heard the dull thuds of heads hitting the ground. He could almost smell the hatred, and he wondered why he'd ever believed that scent could be purged from his nose.

A hand closed around his upper arm, holding him tight.

"We have to go," Per Santoger said. "You have to hide. Gather around, everyone. Huddle in. We have a friend to return to Yaris Teeg."

Blane opened his mouth to speak but found that the words would not come.

Moving back through the city, up from the river and toward the mighty hill that was home to Yaris Teeg and the Temple of Four, Blane saw signs that every nightmare he had ever feared was coming to life.

Close to Quanar's Corner, a popular place for orators, seven Bajumen were hanging from ropes strung over the lower branches of a singkoot tree. Six were dead, and one still kicked her legs feebly. All of them were missing ears. People hurried by, a few throwing nervous glances at the hanging dead, but most just kept their heads down.

A little farther on, they crossed a footbridge over one of the artificial canals snaking out from the river and into the city. Surrounded by his fellow novices, Gemmy closer than all of them, Blane could not see much, but he could hear the collective gasp from his companions as they crested the bridge. Even Per Santoger grunted, his deep, old voice sounding a brief pause in their journey. Needing to know, Blane edged closer so he could see down into the canal below.

It was clogged with bodies.

Its gentle flow was halted, and piled against a silty bank at the tight corner downstream from them were dozens of corpses. All of them were naked, all Bajuman. They showed signs of terrible violence. Some were missing heads, others were cut and hacked. None of them moved, but river-things moved over them. Perhaps not yet even cold, these dead Bajumen bodies were already being consumed or made into homes by the baser creatures of Quandis.

"What's happening?" Blane said. "Why?"

"Crimes against everyone," Gemmy said.

"What crimes?" His voice was rising, but a glance from a couple of those around him silenced him. He had no choice but to place a deep trust in his new friends, and he could not betray that trust by giving himself, or them, away.

In one narrow street, blood smeared the stone pavement, lapped at by several straggly dogs.

Beside a building undergoing restoration, three Bajumen sat against the scaffold, heads in their laps, signs tied around their necks. KILLER OF PRINCES, the signs said. Blane did not understand.

Shouts echoed through the streets. Some screams. Later, a few cheers. When they were finally close to Yaris Teeg, Per Santoger ushered them on ahead, past the gates and up the steps carved into the hill.

"We're going to the Temple of Four," the priest said, already panting with exertion. "Safer there than Yaris Teeg. More secure. And the Guard will never enter that sacred place."

He hurried them all the way up the high hill until they reached the gates of the Temple of Four. They were already open as they so often were, a sign of welcome for any of the faithful who might care to visit.

Once through, though, the old priest called out for the gates to be closed. They hurried inside, milling in the wide courtyard known as Four Square, and Blane looked up at the four towers. The rising sun framed them so that it looked like the whole temple was aflame. Their shadows stretched out like the gods reaching long fingers across this city in turmoil.

⌒

Per Ristolo emerged from a tall arched doorway in the shaded half of the courtyard, walking slowly with the aid of a stick. Yet he looked determined. Per Santoger gestured to the young priests to remain where they were, then went to meet him, and the two old priests stood conversing quietly while the trainees lingered in a small group. Even inside the walls of the Temple of Four, they kept Blane in the center of their huddle.

Blane might have cried tears of joy if his heart had not been burning with rage.

"I have to know why," he said. He shoved his way out of the group. Gemmy grabbed his arm to hold him back.

"Per Santoger told us to stay here!" she said.

"And do nothing? Can't you see how scared he is?" Blane said. In truth he wasn't sure if the old priest was showing fear, or surprise, or a shocked resignation at the things they had seen. It didn't matter. He shrugged Gemmy's hand from his arm and walked slowly across the courtyard, not quite approaching the two old priests, but getting close enough so that he could hear their exchange.

". . . seen the fires myself from the towers, all across the city," Per Ristolo said.

"How many?" Per Santoger asked.

"Too many to count."

"Rebellion?"

"Perhaps, but I think not," the older priest said. He saw Blane's approach and caught his eye, but did not react. Whatever news they shared was too harsh for secrecy. "I think genocide," he said. His eyes glimmered with tears.

"What's happening?" Blane asked. Per Santoger threw a stern look his way, but his old companion placed a hand on his arm.

"More than anyone, he should know," he said. "There's no distinction within these walls, and that makes it a good place. But not everyone accepts that. We've known that forever, and now perhaps our openness will be put to the test."

"You have to hide," Per Santoger said to Blane.

"What's *happening*?"

"Exactly what you saw on your way back. A slaughter of Bajumen," Per Ristolo said. "All across the city, on the queen's orders. Bajuman whores killed Prince Aris and unmanned him, and word has spread that it was the start of an uprising by those lowborn."

"Word spread by who?" Blane asked.

"Ah, that's a real question," Per Ristolo said. "But there are fires all across the city, and—"

Something banged against the gates. At the same time, Blane saw a strange expression pass across Per Ristolo's face. It was a fleeting, shocking twist of his features into an almost animal snarl . . . and then Blane realized that the priest was wincing in pain.

Something dark flowed across the whites of the old priest's eyes, darker than blood, deep as night. Then they were the pale yellow of age once more. Yet he was no longer the mumbling, befuddled old man Blane had taken him to be. He was something else. He was *strong*.

In the archway behind Per Ristolo, the shadows seemed to flow in response.

Blane's eyes opened wide. *Phage!* He'd heard whispers about these soldiers of the Faith, but had never seen them, and therefore had never believed in them. Some said they were ageless creatures given long life, spending most of their time hibernating beneath the Temple of Four until called upon to protect against threats to the priesthood or attack its enemies. Other rumors suggested they were wraiths of dead priests. There were some tales of them being used in Blane's lifetime, but eyewitness accounts were varied and confused, and the priesthood remained silent on the matter, even among themselves. Older myths told of greater conflicts, either expanded in the telling or relating stories whispered down through the generations.

However the rumors changed, the idea of magic behind them remained consistent. And whatever they had been, the Phage were *here*.

Per Ristolo had summoned them as if from nowhere, and they were wraiths indeed. Shadows given substance, they hung back inside the archway, unnoticed by most of the novices in the Four Square.

Blane was close enough to see.

"Per Santoger is right," the ancient priest said to Blane, "you should hide."

But it was too late.

"I ordered the gates locked!" Per Santoger bellowed. His only answer was the heavy creaking of stiff hinges as the two wide, heavy gates swung inward, revealing the view of the city and river below. Far away, smoke rose from several unseen fires, caught and smeared across the sky by windstreams higher up. Closer, so close that Blane could still see blood on their swords and sweat knotting their hair, stood six members of the City Guard.

Their captain was a short, squat woman, her braided hair wound into a bun and pinned with a pale blue blade to match the uniform colors of the Guard. Her five soldiers were spaced behind her with weapons ready. They exuded authority, a casual confidence that was matched in the slow manner in which they walked into the temple grounds.

The captain surveyed the courtyard, eyes lingering for a moment on the two elder priests. Then her gaze settled on Blane.

He saw nothing in her eyes. No triumph, no hate, no excitement or trepidation. Only a sense of duty. In a way, that scared him more.

She gestured toward Blane and asked, "Is he the only one?"

"Of course not," Per Ristolo said. "You can see there are other novice priests all around you."

"You know that's not what I meant."

"He is one of us," Per Ristolo said, "and the City Guard are not welcome within the temple walls."

"I'm not asking for your welcome," the captain said. "Is he the only one?"

Blane started backing away, even though he knew that if he turned and ran, they'd shoot him down with the small crossbows they kept primed on their belts. The captain motioned three of her men forward.

"He's no longer Bajuman!" Gemmy shouted, and he wanted to deny that claim, scream in the faces of these Guards and priests that with his brothers and sisters dying in the streets, he was more Bajuman than ever before. Yet he also didn't want to die.

"There'll be no murder on these grounds," Per Santoger said, voice low but carrying across the courtyard. He stepped toward the captain, and she held up her hand, palm facing him.

"It's not murder," she said. "It's orders."

"Then why not do it yourself?" Blane asked. "Or are you afraid I'll take your sword and stick it up your arse?"

The three soldiers closing on him stopped, an almost comical look of shock on their faces. Even the captain appeared startled by his defiance. Perhaps he was the first Bajuman to talk back at her today, let alone fight.

But fight he would. He knew it then, and he was prepared for it, although his stand would be brief. He'd spit and bite and punch, and when he felt the metal in his flesh, he'd fight until he couldn't fight anymore. That was why he was here, after all. He'd just never expected it to happen so soon.

Blane glanced at Per Ristolo again, and the dark seepage around the high priest's eyes seemed to be shading his face, as if denying the sun access. Blane's heart beat faster. *I'm seeing it,* he thought. *I'm here, bearing witness, and I'm about to see—*

Magic. He was seeing magic. That thing he had never believed, but always hoped was true. And it meant that he didn't fight alone.

The specters in the arched doorway manifested, flowing across the courtyard, parting around the two elderly priests, and coming to a halt before the three soldiers advancing toward Blane. They were heat haze, shadows, dust devils. They were dreams. They were real, and their reality meant that his sacrifices had not been for nothing, that his ambitions could be achieved. But first he must survive.

Blane couldn't discern their sexes. They moved like fluid creatures, graceful and silent, their weapons the most solid things about them, gleaming in sunlight and seeming to glow with something brighter and hotter. Long, thin, curved blades in their left hands, shimmering whips in their right, the tendrils made of fine chains that flexed with a life of their own. Their armor was pale and supple, like thick leather, and, where exposed, their skin was inlaid with tattooed designs that made it difficult to focus on them. Camouflage, perhaps. Or maybe something more.

"We desire no conflict," Per Ristolo said. It was clear that he commanded these Phage warriors in some way, and he made no attempt to hide the fact. Blane had thought Per Ristolo just an old, decrepit priest, a teacher, but if he controlled magic he had to be one of the High Order.

The Guard soldiers and their captain had plainly never seen

anything like the Phage, and they stared wide-eyed at these warriors arrayed against them. Yet their training was strong, and their sense of duty remained.

"This isn't conflict," the captain said, a touch of strain in her voice. "If your . . . *soldiers* don't stand down, this is defiance of the Crown."

"The Crown's military doesn't have any place, jurisdiction, or rights on temple grounds. The queen knows that. You know that."

"I know what's happened," the captain said. She took a step forward, sword drawn, and her troops followed.

"I had nothing to do with it," Blane said.

"Your people did."

"How many times do I have to tell you: he's of *our* people," Per Ristolo said. "Captain, you know as well as I that provenance should have no bearing on how one is perceived. Don't you?"

The captain froze and glared at the priest.

"I see outlander features in your face," Per Ristolo continued. "You're shorter than most Quandians, more heavily built, your skin a shade or two darker, though you use pigments. Somewhere in your past—perhaps not your parents, but your grandparents' generation, for sure—one of your ancestors lay with someone from beyond the Ring."

The captain glared.

"From the far south, I'd guess," Per Ristolo said. "The Hotlands."

"I'm going to count to three," the captain said, and now her simmering anger was plain. It was not against Quandian law to have children with someone from the Ring or the lands far beyond, so long as they had not been brought to Quandis as a slave. But questioning someone's background, even suggesting this was an issue, was a certain way to cause offense.

"Consider your actions carefully . . . *outlander,*" Per Ristolo said. "One."

Blane felt the eyes of the novices upon him. They had withdrawn to the edge of the courtyard, leaving him exposed close to its center, the Phage and Guardsmen before him.

He wanted to look over and spare Gemmy a brief smile, but he dared not look away.

"Two."

Whatever happened next would be fast. If fighting began, he would run for the archway from where Per Ristolo and the Phage had appeared. He knew where it led. The Temple of Four. There were a hundred places to hide.

"Three," the captain said. "Take him."

It was even faster than Blane had expected.

As the soldiers of the City Guard stepped forward, the Phage seemed to flow, moving like breath on the breeze. As they attacked, they and their weapons grew more solid and defined. Metal clashed, and someone cried out. Blane didn't even have a chance to run, frozen in place until Per Santoger pulled him down. From that position, all he heard was a grunt, a thud, and the impact of someone falling. He tried to watch three points of combat at once, but at each, two Guards took on one Phage, the fighting fast and furious, and he could make very little sense of anything.

Per Santoger crouched beside Blane, wincing as his old joints creaked. He grasped his student's face between old, gnarled hands.

"Run and hide," he said. "You, and the other priests who were once Bajuman. Find them all, run with them, and *hide*. Go now!"

Jolted from his shock, Blane rushed for the doorway, expecting a crossbow bolt in his back at any second. None came. At the opening he paused and looked back, past the bodies on the ground, past the violence cutting the air, to Gemmy and the others. Every one of them had stood with him, and for that he owed them everything.

Gemmy raised a hand, and Blane waved back.

Then he ducked inside and was welcomed by the temple's cool interior. He lost sight of the chaos outside, and soon he could no longer hear it. The heavy walls of the temple swallowed the sound, and they would swallow him, too.

Blane already knew where he needed to go.

ᴄ◌

News of the slaughter of the Bajumen must have been spreading rapidly through the priesthood. Minutes after entering the shadowy temple proper, Blane rounded a corner and ran into a small group of novices. Most of them were Bajuman. Frightened, like him. Wide-eyed and lost, they had heard what was happening, but they hadn't seen what he had seen. Most of the teaching took place down in Yaris Teeg, but this group must have been summoned to the Temple of Four for some lesson or another. Blane's was the only group of novices who had left Temple Hill today, and he was lucky to still be alive.

There were five Bajumen in the group, and a few more Quandians. No instructor. In these desperate hours, they had been sent on their own to find somewhere to hide.

"Into the libraries!" Blane said. "Through the general sections and—"

"Who are you to tell us?" a woman asked. She looked older than Blane, and he could tell from her robes and the chains she wore that she was more advanced in her training.

"Someone who's seen," was all he said. His haunted eyes must have convinced her because she and the others nodded.

"I know a place," the woman said. "A scroll chamber, sealed from the outside to maintain a dry atmosphere. The entrance is well hidden down behind the History of the Ring section." She frowned at Blane. "You'll be coming?"

"Of course," he said, at the same time thinking, *Of course not.* He knew of a far better hiding place, but he would share it with no one.

They set off, passing through some living quarters, kitchens, and a dining area, wending their way through the interior of the temple and toward its northern edge. They left the courtyard and violence far behind, but Blane could still hear the sound of metal on metal, and see the Phage dancing on sunlight as they attacked.

To protect me.

Whatever else he might think of the priesthood and their out-dated beliefs, at least they were true to their word. He felt a pang of affection for grumpy, old Per Santoger, and then a cool flush of concern as he wondered whether the priest was even still alive.

News like that would have to wait until much, much later.

As the group passed through a courtyard overgrown with lush grape plants and orchid poles, Blane slipped away. No one saw him go. Even if they had, it would not have mattered—Bajumen had learned to mind their own business, even among their own kind. He often thought that was one of the greatest tragedies of their race's de-cline and subjugation—the loss of curiosity, and the lack of knowl-edge required to simply survive in this cruel world. They held up their foolish hope that the Kij'tal, the Bajuman savior, would one day appear and free them all, but Blane had always viewed this as nothing more than an excuse for not rising against their oppressors. They were waiting for the moment, waiting for the leader foretold by the ancient prophets. But where was the Kij'tal now? If a savior were ever to appear, wouldn't this be the day?

Right now, he had other things on his mind, as did the group of Bajuman novices. *They have their own safety to consider. I have my future to face . . .*

A couple of times he was forced to slip into open doorways when he heard voices farther along the corridors, hallways, and staircases. Not hiding, as such. Not really. Just . . . keeping his pres-ence silent. He waited until the priests or helpers walked by, then continued on his way.

He wondered how many of Quandis's Bajumen would be

dead by the end of the day, but he tried to shove that thought from his mind. In this hour of their greatest need, Blane's hand had been forced at last. He had seen the Phage fighting with unnatural strength and grace. He had seen that strange smudge of darkness around Per Ristolo's eyes as he gave them silent orders to confront the City Guard.

He *knew* what he had seen, and he knew what he could do to show his people that he was no traitor to them or Lameria.

He eventually found his way to the secret passage and was soon walking the spiral and standing on the central piece of sea glass, hearing the breath of air and the almost imperceptible sound of the spiral staircase dropping open beneath his feet. Blane took in a deep breath and inhaled the forbidden scents of this temple's deepest places.

Blane had never believed in the gods. But now, after so much investigation and secretive research, the sight of the Phage had solidified a suspicion he had hoped was real.

Now, he believed in magic.

8

A strange calm had settled over Demos after his encounter with
Apex Euphraxia. He knew it might have been the spiza smoke
that lingered in the air and coated the walls of the stone box where
he'd been quartered, and if the spiza had been helpful, he welcomed
it. Myrinne would not leave him here. She would do something to
effect his release. Even branded and shamed, he trusted their love
enough to know she would not abandon him. But that would take
time, if she managed it at all. Myrinne's influence only stretched so
far. Which left it to him to contemplate another plan, to watch and
wait.

Slaves in the household of the apex had a hierarchy all their
own, with the praejis at the top, the maids and kitchen slaves below him, the spiza burners and coal shovelers next, and then the
ones the nobles called muckers, who cleaned filthy bowls and pans
and who scrubbed shit and piss out of broken pipes and emptied
chamber pots. In that hierarchy, Demos fell somewhere beneath the
lowliest mucker. He wasn't even welcome in the kitchen. Most of the
household slaves treated him as invisible, speaking to him only to

give orders. He had bleached vomit from carpets and thrust his own hands into a backed-up sewage pipe, and that had been on his first day working in the house of the apex.

Whatever reason the apex had for hating him and his family name, she'd made sure the rest of her slaves felt it as well. They all bore brands, either that of the slave or the Bajuman, but somehow he bore another, invisible to the naked eye, and they despised him for it.

Which made him wary of today's work. On the surface, it seemed less revolting than other tasks he'd been assigned, so why choose him, the most despised among Euphraxia's slaves?

Now he understood. The task had been passed down from one tier to the next because the others were afraid of it. And no wonder.

Demos knelt on the filthy cellar floor with a rag tied over his nose and mouth. The air in this dark grotto at the back of the house hung thick and damp around him, a warm miasma of smoke and stink. There were four large coal hearths in different corners of the cellar, though the weather had not yet turned cold enough for them to be lit. In Euphraxia's home, however, the spiza chimneys burned all year long, all day and night. There were six of them, much narrower than the hearths used for coal, and this filthy grotto contained the open mouths at the base of two of those spiza chimneys, as well as a coal hearth and a massive store of coal at the bottom of the chute used for its delivery. The spiza stores were vast and diverse and kept behind a thick, locked wooden door with iron strapping.

Demos had his upper body inside the open trap of a spiza chimney, his neck and shoulders aching from the two hours he'd already spent scraping years of accumulated rime off the stone. The whispers that made their way down through the hierarchy said the apex had complained that the spiza smoke wafting through her curtained corridors had a sour tang. That was all it had taken—a sour tang. The praejis, Vosto, had decided this ancient rime detritus must be tainting the scent of each day's burn and thus it had to be removed. The perfect job for the one face nobody in the house wanted to see.

In better days, Demos had risen quickly in the ranks of the navy and in the estimation of his commanding officers because he never shied away from work. Now, he would have gladly given this task to another. With every scrape of the flat iron blade against the inside of the chimney, thick dust clouded around his head. His work disturbed generations of spiza rime, old and thick and caked with mold, and there was no telling what hours of inhaling that dust might do to him. The stink of it choked him and muddled his thoughts. He paused now and then to withdraw from the chimney and clear his head, but he put his strength into the work. The only alternative would have been to refuse, and he knew Vosto would have relished any new opportunity to beat him.

The spiza made the edges of his world blur and momentary introspections seemed to last for hours. Yet he somehow maintained his focus, or at least kept his hands working. Beads of sweat trickled down his forehead. Voices whispered in his brain—words of love from Myrinne, childhood assurances from his mother, barked commands from the officers of Admiral Hallarte's fleet, his own quiet prayers from years long past. He felt his heart beating in time with his efforts, and the whispers fell into the same cadence, until his life had diminished into nothing but this echo-dance between muscle and memory.

When something nudged his hip, it felt like nothing, barely there.

The next nudge came harder, made his ribs hit the inner wall of the chimney, broke his rhythm. The blade slid sideways and he raked his knuckles. Demos thrust himself backward, out of the chimney, and turned to face his attacker. The flat blade had gone dull, but he held it like a weapon.

Mouse stood over him. "Go on. Try it. Take a swipe at me with that blade and I'll open your throat with it."

Demos wavered. He'd moved too fast with all the spiza he'd inhaled and now his gut roiled and he felt himself blanch. He shook his head, trying to clear it, as his lips went dry.

"What do you want?"

Mouse's eyes narrowed. "Are you ill?"

He felt the sweat on his forehead and the back of his neck, but he would not give her the satisfaction of revealing precisely how much the spiza had undone him. Demos tossed the blade into the open mouth of the chimney. The corners of his vision blurred and the colors of the dingy cellar seemed brighter and more vivid, but he took a deep breath and stared defiantly at Mouse. He'd averted his gaze enough in the aftermath of his father's execution. The murder of Linos Kallistrate had turned his son into a boy again, but now Demos the man had begun to remember himself.

"I'm fine," he replied.

"Your words are slurred. Too much spiza." Mouse sighed. "You should've said something. I'd have gotten you to a window. The spiza they used in those chimneys a hundred years ago was much more potent and not nearly as refined as what is used now. There are tales of madness, of minds unraveling—"

"And tales of those who saw the faces of the gods," he said, the words like moths fluttering from his lips. "I know the stories."

Her hand lashed out and he felt the crack of her knuckles across his face, but the pain was remote.

"Do not speak to me as if we're equals!" she snapped. "We will *never* be that!"

The words hung in the air as if they had substance, the layers of their meaning ready to be peeled away and examined.

"We were equals once," he said quietly.

His voice brushed at the stone walls around them, and Mouse

glanced over her shoulder as if to make sure no one would overhear before glaring at him.

"Never equal," she said. "Only too young and foolish to recognize what we were."

"We were friends."

"We were slave and master. If you think laughing together as children erases all the years of indifference that came afterward—"

"I don't." Demos drew a deep breath and let it out. A veil of glittering light seemed to fall upon the whole scene, and Mouse's eyes were brighter than before, as if the blue winter within them blew across the cellar. "Society bent us to its roles. Tradition forged us. But I was never cruel to you, Mouse. Cold, but never cruel."

Mouse struck him so hard across the face that he thought his cheekbone might have cracked. He rocked backward, staggered against the chimney, kicked over the bucket of spiza rime, and nearly hit the ground. The vivid colors were bleached from his vision and the dreary gloom of the cellar returned. Mouse's knuckles had split and blood dripped from them as she loomed over him.

"I'm sorry," Mouse said.

She hit him again. Demos saw it coming. Confusion cost him a sliver of a moment, and he paid the price. Mouse struck him three times in quick succession, then hurled him against the stone wall. He fell in the spilled spiza dregs, the chalky dust of centuries coating his clothes and hands as he scrambled away. Mouse kicked him, but he turned with the blow, and shot out his own foot and hooked her leg out from beneath her. She fell, and he was on her. Demos struck her twice before he saw the resignation in her deep blue eyes, and he hesitated.

A mistake.

Mouse snapped out a kick, shot her heel into his balls, and Demos went down again. Wheezing, he tried to curl up and protect himself, but she dragged him to his feet. Examining him as if searching for places he didn't appear bruised, she struck him again, just at the edge of his left eye, and he felt it begin to swell.

Panting, Mouse said, "Your princess is on her way here."

Myrinne! A flush of elation rushed through him.

"Euphraxia wants Princess Myrinne to see what her intrusion has cost you. Vosto ordered that I be the one to beat you."

Spiza had blunted the pain before, and now hope helped Demos separate himself from his bleeding, bruised flesh.

"Do what you must," he said. He'd been in his share of brawls, proving himself a more than capable warrior and sailor. If he'd chosen to fight now, the moment of surprise no longer in Mouse's favor, he could have killed her. Instead, he would take whatever physical punishment he must endure in order to see Myrinne.

Mouse licked the blood from her knuckles, ready to come at him again, but a sudden clatter made them both turn in time to see a body tumbling down the old coal chute. Demos rubbed a hand over his eyes and wondered just how much the spiza had affected him, but as he rose shakily to his feet, Mouse rushed toward the coal bin and he knew he had not imagined this.

"What are you doing, you little fool?" she barked. "What idiot thief would break into the home of the apex?"

The idiot thief struggled to right himself in the shifting coal, a thin arm flailing before he got hold of the edge of the bin and poked his head up. Smudged with black coal, his pale features were even more striking, his blue eyes more vivid. No more than twelve years of age, the skinny Bajuman looked stricken with fear. Tears rolled down his face, streaking clean lines through the coal smudge.

"Mouse," the slave boy said. No idiot thief after all.

"Tollivar?" Mouse said, gaping in shock. "What are you *doing* here? You can't . . . if you're caught, Euphraxia will claim you."

"Tollivar," Demos whispered, recognizing the boy. His mother had been a slave in the Kallistrate home. When she'd died, the other slaves had taken to looking after the boy so that he could remain among them. To his shame, Demos did not recall the dead woman's name.

Tollivar dropped his gaze, wiping at his tears, inclining his head in subservience to his former master.

"No!" Mouse growled. "He is a slave now, just like me. You do not bow to him!"

Tollivar glanced up doubtfully. Demos walked toward them until he had come abreast of Mouse.

"It's the truth," he said, showing the boy his brand. "In this house, I'm meant to bow to Mouse. But tell us, boy, what's got you so terrified?"

"You were supposed to stay with my uncle. You were supposed to stay hidden," Mouse said sadly.

Tollivar swiped at his tears, smearing coal dust. Then his face crumpled as he tried to speak, but sobbed instead. Mouse lifted him from the coal bin and held him as if he were her own son, shushing and comforting until he had his tears under control.

"Your uncle . . . your uncle is dead," Tollivar said.

Mouse raised a hand to her mouth to hide her horror.

Tollivar glanced at Demos, then back to Mouse. "They're all dead. The Guard is moving through the city executing every Bajuman they find. The queen's ordered them to kill us. All of us."

Demos wanted to argue, to say the queen would never give such an order. But that was the queen as she'd once been, not the woman who had executed his father. Yet it still seemed absurd.

"That makes no sense," he said. "The damage to the city's economy, to all of Quandis . . . it will take years for the noble families to recover—"

"The noble families?" Mouse spat. "There are many thousands of Bajumen on the main island. How long do you think it will take *them* to recover once they've had their heads removed?"

Head ringing from the beating she'd delivered, and still muddled by spiza, Demos knelt beside them. "As long as it will take for my father."

"Your father was a prick," she rasped.

"And yet he was my father, and Lysandra murdered him. Whatever madness has claimed her, we're all in danger because of it." Demos put a hand on Tollivar's shoulder. The boy flinched back, staring at him, stunned by this tiny expression of compassion. "They can't come for you here, Tollivar. Not in the apex's home."

"He's not even meant to be here," Mouse hissed. "He can't stay or she'll—"

"Then we'll hide him," Demos said. "He's safer here than on the streets. And you're safer here than you would have been with Clan Kallistrate. The Crown has no official authority in this house. For the City Guard to take you, Euphraxia would have to surrender you."

Mouse held the boy tighter for a moment, then nodded.

"First we hide him," she said. "Then I'm going to clean myself up. If Euphraxia realizes you struck me, she'll have you killed. She hates you, Demos, for whatever reason. So let's move, and quickly. Any one of us might still be dead before the day is out."

⁓

Demos waited in the piss-stinking corridor outside Mouse's room as she washed her hands and face in a basin. His mind had begun to clear a bit, enough that the throbbing pain of the beating she'd given him broke through. In her doorless room, she stripped off her tunic and replaced it with one devoid of any blood. Her muscled torso had been made hard by years of hard work and he saw scars that were not fresh, wounds that could only have been given to her in the Kallistrate household. It hardened Demos in a way he'd never imagined—hardened him to his own life, to his own family, to the traditions whose destruction he'd been mourning.

They'd hidden Tollivar in the one place nobody would look—

Demos's cell. Only Mouse and Demos ever went there now. In time they would find another place for him. There were other Bajuman slaves in the house and they would have to be warned. Surely they would help. But that was for later.

Mouse emerged from her room and led him to the praejis's room. Vosto stood outside his own door and looked Demos up and down with a sneer.

"Only cuts and bruises," the praejis said, disappointed. "I was hoping for some broken bones, at least, Mouse."

"I don't want to do his work for him while he heals."

Vosto considered this, then waved her away. "Go. The princess has already arrived and the apex is impatient to have her gone."

"Yes, praejis."

Then she was gone, and Demos found himself standing in the corridor with the praejis, eyes downcast, paying obeisance to a slave who despised him for his noble birth. Vosto knocked once and entered. Demos followed with his head down, still able to taste his own blood from the beating Mouse had given him. He held his left hand over his right, covering his brand, yearning for a moment with Myrinne but hating for her to see him brought low.

"Well," he heard Euphraxia say, "at least the time I've been waiting here was time well spent for my slave."

Myrinne said his name, anguish in her voice, and he heard the rustle of her clothes as she rushed toward him.

"No!" Euphraxia barked. "You will be seated!"

Demos snapped his head up to stare at her. When he began to speak—forbidden, unless he had his owner's permission—Myrinne was the one who hushed him.

"Did you just command the Crown to sit?" she inquired, taking a step toward Euphraxia. Myrinne's skin had a dusty, almost ghostly quality, and her hair was in disarray. Everything about her spoke of frayed nerves, and yet as she glared at the apex, towering over the much older woman, she might have been forged of iron.

"This is my home," Euphraxia said. "The Crown has no authority here."

"Leave this room," the princess said.

Euphraxia flinched. "I've just reminded you—"

"You are apex of the Faith, yes. Your home is meant to be treated with the same sovereignty as the Temple of Four. But rules once thought to be forged in fire and carved in stone are crumbling all around us, as I'm sure you know."

"The Bajuman slaughter?" The apex shrugged, unconcerned. "And I'm aware that the queen has been testing the loyalties of the noble families. She suspects treachery among them and I share her fears. Your mother has put her trust in me and I in her, and the value I place in that trust is the only reason I allowed you into my home again."

With the apex only feet away, Myrinne reached out and touched Demos's face, kissed his bruised cheek. For a moment he could see just how much the sight of his blood unsettled her.

"How dare you?" Euphraxia whispered. "He is my slave."

"I've always wondered how it is you're allowed household slaves," Myrinne said. "From novice to High Order, the rest of your priesthood abase themselves. The very idea of a slave undermines what it means to serve the Four, and yet here you are—the apex from whom the greatest devotion of all ought to be expected—with slaves, and spiza, and luxury."

"What are you playing at, girl?" Euphraxia said. "You need no lesson from me in the relationship of the apex to the Crown. I'm the bridge between the royal line and the Faith, between the people and the Four. I'm part of both worlds. And you have already outstayed your welcome."

Myrinne reached out and took Demos's hand. Whatever knowledge gave her strength, he drew from it and lifted his gaze in defiance again, staring at the apex. His owner.

"Your good relationship with the Crown no longer depends on earning my mother's trust," Myrinne said.

Understanding dawned on Euphraxia's face. "The queen has passed, then. Tragic, but not unforeseen."

"Only a short time ago," Myrinne said. "As I left the palace to come to you."

"I will pray that the Four welcome her into their realms, and I offer my condolences to your brother, Prince Aris. Now King Aris."

"That will be very difficult, as my brother is also dead. Gone before my mother, in fact."

Demos stared at her. "Myrinne . . ."

She squeezed his hand but kept her focus on Euphraxia.

"Your sister—" the apex began.

"My queen, and *yours*," Myrinne corrected. "Many things will change, now. Everything might change. And even if Queen Phela continues respecting the house of the apex as part of the sovereign property of the priesthood, unless you choose this place as your prison, you will leave it one day, and whatever protections you enjoy do not exist outside these walls."

Euphraxia stood rigid. Hate radiated from her. She pointed at Demos.

"*That* is mine. My slave, by all the laws of Quandis and by the decree of the queen. Unless Queen Phela wishes to undermine her mother's decree—"

"It is *my* wish."

This confirmation put a smug smile on Euphraxia's face. "Well, Princess. Until then—"

"Until then, you will see that he is not harmed again, by your order or any other."

Euphraxia said nothing. Only smiled.

Myrinne stepped close to the apex. "Now get the fuck out of the room."

౧

At first, Demos only held her. In spite of his bruises and the blood on his face and clothing, even in spite of his brand and his humiliation, Myrinne had suffered far worse, learning of her brother's death and then losing her mother on the same day. All the spite and hatred he had been nursing toward Queen Lysandra vanished upon hearing of her death. The pain of his father's execution remained and he had nowhere to expend his grief, no one left to blame.

Myrinne kissed his cheek, kissed his lips, but he tried to pull away when she turned over his hand and went to kiss the symbol burned there.

"No," he whispered. "It's not right."

"It's a scar," she said. "We all have them."

"Not this one."

"Please let's not compare our suffering," Myrinne said quietly. "What little time we have together now must be our medicine, not further injury."

She was right, of course. As she always seemed to be.

"I'm sorry," he said, and he kissed the top of Myrinne's head and held her quietly for a long minute, until she steadied herself and gently pushed him away, holding him at arm's length.

"We must speak," she said. "Euphraxia won't forgive the insults of today, and there's no way to predict what she'll do now. Her faith runs deep, but in her way she's as mad as . . ."

Myrinne left the words unspoken, closing her eyes tightly a moment, but Demos heard them in his own mind. *As mad as your mother,* he thought.

"Surely everything will change now," he said quietly. "Phela keeps her own counsel, and she despises me—"

"She doesn't like your arrogance, but she doesn't despise you."

"She despises me because once upon a time she was the object of your adoration, and then you fell in love."

Myrinne gave a nod. "All right. That's probably true."

"Regardless," Demos went on, "I've never doubted her love for you. She's cold, but not heartless."

"I wish I had your confidence. Once I would have, but now . . . there are days I fear I don't know my sister at all. And she's Queen Phela now. She is the Crown, and the Crown needs no approval."

His heart sank. "You're saying she won't free me. That my mother and brother and I are to remain slaves, even though Phela knows you and I were to be married? Yes, she's not fond of me, but does your happiness mean nothing to her?"

Myrinne had flinched at his words. Now her eyes filled with sorrow. "My love, I thought you knew. I'd have said it first, before anything—"

"What?" Demos said. "What is it you thought I knew?"

She put a hand on his chest, fingers splayed as if to feel the beat of his heart. "I'm not the only one who's lost a brother."

Demos felt himself shrink. "Cyrus."

"His injuries on the night of your father's execution were too dire. He lingered for a day and then . . ."

"He died a prisoner. Before he could be sold into slavery," Demos said, his own voice hollow in his eyes.

"Your mother has taken it poorly," Myrinne went on. "My friends in Clan Daklan tell me she's ailing, though she's safe enough for the moment."

"Clan Daklan . . . bought her?" Demos asked, though he knew the answer and understood. His mother had friends among the Daklans. If they'd bought her, it had been more for her protection than the status conferred by trophy slaves of such notoriety.

"At auction," Myrinne confirmed. "They outbid Euphraxia."

Demos nodded, taking it all in. So much death and so much fear, in both of their lives, but he and Myrinne would endure. He promised himself that.

"What will Phela do now?" he asked.

"The new queen is nothing if not cunning," Myrinne replied. "She won't simply wave away our mother's decrees, because to do so would undermine the strength of the Crown. But she *will* be methodical and, if needed, ruthless. She *has* promised to free you and your mother, but not yet. Phela doesn't trust Euphraxia. She wants to know the secrets of this house."

Demos licked his dry lips and tasted spiza and blood. "I'm to be her spy."

"For a time," Myrinne said. "She needs to understand Euphraxia's loyalties. She wants news on the apex's reaction to her becoming queen. And as insurance against any negative reactions, anything you might learn of Euphraxia that can be used against her . . ."

"Will all be currency for Phela," Demos finished. "Leverage, if the queen has cause to go against the apex."

"I suppose so," Myrinne said. "Our fates are in Phela's hands. We have no choice but to obey and be patient. When the time comes, Demos, and she fulfills her promise to free you, that's when we run."

"Run?"

"Together. You and I. And your mother, if I can free her, too."

The idea of fleeing Lartha, and Quandis, was a shock to him. All his life, he'd wanted to be a warrior like his father. His time under Admiral Hallarte's command had helped him to forge his own identity. He'd had a future mapped out in his head. But with everything that had happened, and these new events that had fractured the Crown and must surely be sending shock waves through the land, he saw that Myrinne was right. It might be the only way for them to have the life together that they longed for.

"The beatings will continue," Demos said. "Euphraxia hates me, for reasons I don't yet understand. I can endure them, but she'll do everything she can to keep you from me, now."

"No doubt. But can you find a way to get messages out, and for me to get messages in?"

Demos thought of the tear-streaked coal smudges on Tollivar's face, and Mouse's wintry eyes. She'd beaten him more than once, but he'd seen her regret and anger, and he'd had a tiny taste of what it meant to be a slave.

To be beneath notice.

"Perhaps," he said, his thoughts racing ahead. He kissed Myrinne's hands. "But tell Phela I have a condition."

"Demos—"

"You're aware of the Bajuman purge your mother ordered?"

"Of course."

"*Queen* Phela must stop it. Rescind the execution decree. And she must keep the City Guard away from this house—"

"She'll never agree," Myrinne said. "I've just told you, she won't want to undermine the primacy of the Crown. The Blood of the Four runs through us, Demos. The Crown is meant to be infallible. If Phela suggests that our mother's decree was wrong, the public will be encouraged to question—"

"Myrinne," Demos said softly, "Phela's fears are not my concern. Our future, and that of my family, is. Tell her my price."

"She'll have you killed herself if I put it to her that way."

"Then tell her the truth, which is that the only way for me to guarantee that I'll be able to get messages in and out of this house is if she spares the lives of the Bajumen. If they're all dead, my presence here is useless to her."

A heavy fist pounded on the door, and then it opened without further warning. Vosto stood there. He bowed his head in obeisance to the princess, but his manner belied that gesture of respect.

"My mistress tells me the slave Demos must return to work."

Myrinne kissed Demos tenderly and he winced from the bruising on his face. She told him that she loved him. And then she left.

When Myrinne had gone, Vosto stepped inside and closed the door, and the day's beatings recommenced.

～

Alone, hidden away, and somewhere that felt apart from the rest of Lartha and Quandis, rage and grief coursed through Blane.

The deep shadows of this subterranean place were his only company, and he felt no shame in letting them see and hear his tears. It felt good to let such emotions flow. As he descended the spiral staircase into levels where only the High Order priests were allowed, his vision and hearing were blurred by his own quiet sobbing.

Each time he tried to blink away the tears he saw the Phage, and the signs around Per Ristolo's eyes that could only have been magic. The priest-wraiths had moved with unnatural grace, speed, and strength, and it had been Ristolo guiding their actions. Blane was sure of that, just as he was certain that today, Quandis had changed forever. He was living through turbulent times, and he hoped that such upset might provide enough confusion and distraction for him to do what he intended.

Blinking away his tears, he went down and down. The staircase was long, and when he thought it ended, there was merely a wide landing area and another spiral shape inlaid in the floor. He followed this circular path and a second staircase fell away beneath him.

He thought of his sister, Daria, and wondered whether her violent death had been something of a blessing. She had not suffered many more years of abuse. She would not be alive through whatever was to come. Because the one thing Blane was certain of as he descended toward mystery was that this was only the beginning. And while he was no godlike Kij'tal, no savior, he might yet be the person the Bajumen had been waiting for. And if that was what they needed to believe in order to fight, perhaps he could give them that. Perhaps he could be the only Kij'tal they required.

He felt nowhere near ready, yet his time for standing still, learning, and absorbing information had ended. It was time to act.

The staircase ended in a small room with several tunnels leading away into darkness. He placed the blazing torch he'd lit up above in an alcove and picked up one of the more effective oil lamps stored there. He shook it and heard oil swishing around, glad that it was full. He had no wish to be trapped down there in total darkness.

There was no telling what else might be there with him.

He lit the lamp from the torch and took a few steps from the staircase. His surroundings were altogether more functional than the sea-glass-decorated room high above. Walls were smooth rock with a few carved sigils, faded and obscure. The floor was stone, polished over time by countless feet, inlaid here and there with curious, arrow-shaped stones of different colors. He suspected they might be directional indicators pointing to each of the several doors leading from the circular room, but he had no idea what each color or arrow meant. The air was heavy and still with the taint of undisturbed ages, as if the same air had persisted down here for eons. Somehow, it was warm. That surprised Blane, and troubled him also. It was as if something alive was heating the air with body heat, or perhaps these rooms and tunnels were themselves alive, and he had entered the belly of the beast.

A whisper sounded behind him. He spun around, crouched low, and wished he'd brought a weapon. There was nothing there. He breathed a sigh of relief, then realized what he'd heard: the whole spiraling staircase enclosure had risen into the ceiling, forming a flush surface that he could just touch on tiptoes.

Trapped! he thought, and from higher up he heard a few soft thuds as the structure collected itself into its static form. He looked around in a panic, moving back and forth across where the staircase had come to rest, shoving shadows back with the lamp. Then he glanced at the floor and saw the same spiraling shape left behind. It was fainter that the one he'd first seen above, and carved into the stone rather than formed of colored sea glass. But he was sure it was a similar mechanism, and when the time came to walk it, the same effect would occur.

He was deep beneath the Temple of Four, and the temple had sections that were almost three thousand years old. Some of these subterranean spaces might be older still. And deeper—perhaps there were even remnants of the First City. As he descended he had felt the weight of the hill and the deep history it carried above him, crushing down and at the same time drawing on him with its unknowable gravity. What secrets might this place hide? What stories might be lost down here, forever drifting with no ears left to hear, and no voices able to speak? He wondered if he was alone in this maze of rooms and tunnels. He hoped so, then immediately upon that hope came fear that it *was* so. If no one knew where he was, no one could help him if something went wrong.

But what can go wrong? he thought. *I'm used to being alone. It's where I need to be if I'm going to do this.*

Blane chose an opening from the circular room at random and started walking.

He entered a wide hallway that continued so far that the lamplight did not reach its end, and he was immediately comforted by signs of regular activity. Several hooks on the wall to his left held robes and belts, and a scattering of small alcoves contained the melted remains of candles. Farther along the hallway, an open doorway on his right revealed a dark room that grabbed his attention. At first glance he thought it contained balls of thick snakes, a great mass rolling and churning in the faint light from his lamp. Then he gathered himself and moved closer to see a dozen coiled ropes hung from hooks on the wall, nets filled with wooden pegs and mallets, and bags leaking powder slung from a rope line across the room.

Blane frowned. Climbing equipment, down here? Confused and troubled, he moved on.

The hallway curved to the left and down, and as it grew steeper the flat floor turned into a series of wide steps. Channels on either side carried away moisture condensing and running down the walls. An occasional shadow skittered out of the light, and Blane kept alert, wary of the ghost spiders he had heard lived in such places. He passed several more open doorways and peeked inside the rooms. A couple were sleeping quarters, cots neat and unused. One was a dining area, with a small table of neatly stacked crockery. One room was used for prayers, with several ornate rugs spread across the floor and a symbol of the Four cast into one wall, an elaborate design of sea glass, carved wood, and heavily layered paint.

Blane stood there for a while staring at the decorated wall. He wondered how many High Order priests came down here and knelt before this image, baring their souls to imaginary gods. He had once secretly mocked them, all the time, as he also chided his own people for their continuing belief in Lameria.

How can our god be watching over us when we've been tortured, abused, and murdered as slaves for the past thirty decades? he had once asked his mother.

Lameria tests us in life so that we might triumph and sit by her side in death, she had replied.

Well, fuck that. Since his teenaged years, Blane had no wish to believe in a god who sought to put her followers through a life of constant pain. And if she did exist, he'd hate her.

And yet . . .

And yet, he had seen the dregs of magic evident in Per Ristolo's eyes when he had commanded the Phage. Only recently, he had heard whispers among the novices of magic being harvested and absorbed by only those priests most ready to receive it—old High Order priests, the most devout, and those wholly dedicated to the Four.

Blane had no choice but to believe in magic now, but still he refused to believe it came from any god. He understood the contradiction, but he was a pragmatist. Like the seasons and the tides, perhaps magic *needed* no gods but was simply some force as yet unexplained. Whatever it was, *wherever* it was, he had committed himself to finding it. Gods be damned.

Soon he reached a large double doorway at the end of the winding corridor. Two heavy wooden doors filled the opening, braced with elaborately worked iron banding, the hinges the length of his forearm. A large split panel at the door junction held a keyhole on one side, and he didn't think for a minute that he would be able to get through. Yet if the High Order had something to hide, he wanted to see it.

Blane grabbed one of the door handles, turned it, and stood back as a series of metallic clunks and clangs echoed from within. Whatever process he had begun took several seconds to end, and it finished with a heavy thud that he felt through the stone floor.

Surprised, holding his breath, he held the handle again and pushed. One door swung open. From beyond came a waft of must, and a splash of shadow that seemed almost solid, washing the lamp light back as if extinguishing the flame with its coolness. Blane took a couple of steps back and gathered himself before stepping into the open doorway.

At first the room beyond looked empty. Square, fifteen steps to each side, it was merely four walls and nothing else. No furniture, no adornments, nothing to suggest why it was hidden behind such heavy doors.

Such heavy unlocked *doors,* he thought. The High Order must have been so confident of the secrecy of this place that they did not deem it necessary to use locks.

As he stepped into the room he noticed something strange. The far wall had a deep shadow at either side and across the top. It was only as he moved closer that he saw the shadows were openings. It was a false wall, hiding something beyond.

Blane had lost track of time. He might have been away from the others for two hours or six, there was no way of telling. There was also no way of knowing what was happening far above. Per Santoger and the others might be looking for him even now. Or they might be dead.

I'm here, he thought. *No turning back. Not until I've found something . . . anything . . . that might make this forbidden journey worthwhile.*

He skirted around the end of the wall, holding the lamp out before him so that the space beyond was illuminated. It looked just like the other half of the room, except there was no door. Nothing particular set it apart. He aimed the light around, turning slowly, and then lifted it toward the freestanding wall that split the room in two.

He gasped. At first he only recognized one small panel, a page from the Covenant of the Four known as the Promise in Red, a recitation that everyone was required to read aloud on their birthday each year. It was accompanied with images of the Four as pillars set at the corners of the world, holding up the full weight of existence. The Promise in Red was meant to provide strength to those pillars.

As he moved the lamp back and forth, its light seemed to spread, and he realized that this was much, much more than just a simple wall.

This was the fabled Wall of the Four, upon which those ancient gods had supposedly carved their own Covenant with the future inhabitants of Quandis. He frowned and stepped back so that the light would reveal more.

There were parts missing. He had seen many bound copies of the Covenant, and each tile here equated to one page from the book. Every copy of the book contained eleven blank pages, each one representing one of the eleven lost passages supposedly hidden or stolen away from the Covenant over the millennia.

On the wall were eleven blank spaces where tiles had been removed.

Disbelief vied with something else in Blane's mind. He wanted to scoff at the folly of this place—buried so deep, and in worship of false gods, the effort of people to excavate and build this room, construct the wall, and carve the tiles was immense. Yet there was something about the wall that unsettled him, an otherness in the way the carvings cast shadows, repelled light, as if they were existing only halfway in this world. It was like looking at something made by no man.

Perhaps his senses were so heightened that he was imagining things. *Foolish fantasies,* he thought, and he berated himself for being so twitchy.

He wondered where the lost pages were. If anywhere, surely they would be down here. If they even existed at all. Much had been written about what those eleven lost pages might contain. Blane believed none of it, because he had always assumed that the Covenant was something written down by humans, not gods.

The words and images seemed to shift and flow before him, like a viper hypnotizing a rodent, taunting his disbelief.

The oil lamp sputtered, faded, flared again.

Blane held his breath. The wall had receded from view, and just for a moment he felt its weight before him. Solid, dark. When the lamp brightened, it was almost the same as it had been before.

He squeezed past the wall standing in the middle of the room, exited the door, and swung it shut behind him. The lamp spat again. He swilled it and heard plenty of oil still in its reservoir. Perhaps the air was growing thinner. That might have been why his mind was playing tricks on him. He felt a heavy presence behind him, and when he turned quickly and aimed the light back into the shadows, it remained behind him, just out of sight over his shoulder which-ever way he turned. Footsteps followed his own. He paused, and the echoes went on just a little too long.

Walking quickly, then running, Blane took a series of turns. He only realized he was lost when he came to a junction he hadn't seen before, with three tunnels heading away from a central core. Col-ored arrows were set in the floor here, too, although he could not even recall which color arrow he'd followed the first time.

Something thudded in the tunnel behind him. Perhaps it was his heart pumping blood through his ears, but whatever the mes-sage, he listened, turning left and fleeing the junction before his fear could catch up.

This is foolish! he thought, skidding around a corner. *I'm running from myself!* However much he knew that to be true, calmness eluded him. He had no idea how extensive this underground warren was, and the more he ran, the more likely it was he would become truly lost. The High Order believers might encounter him down here in days, curled in a dark corner with his lamp long since extinguished, drooling and shivering and unable to shed the shadows no matter how much light the priests shone upon him. Or they would find him in many weeks' time, dead and cold, withered, life fled forever into the deepest night.

Slowing, grasping hold of sanity and striving to give himself the peace and sense he required to find his way out, he fell.

As he rolled, he somehow kept hold of the lamp and prevented it from breaking. Light and shadow danced as sharp edges bit into his shins, back, shoulders. He hit the ground hard, and looking back and up he saw the old staircase he'd just tumbled down. Very old. The steps were dipped and worn from countless feet and endless years, and behind him . . .

Deeper, darker shadows drew him with terrible gravity. There was a stillness all around him now, as if whatever imaginary danger he had been running from had brought him here on purpose. This felt like a much older place than those above, and less frequented. Dust layered the floor, unmarked by feet. Spiderwebs blurred sharp corners. Long, thin stalactites hung from the ceiling.

Stretching away from him was a tunnel formed in the solid rock of the land. This was no finished structure, but rather a cavern, a crack through the world that might have been here even before humans first appeared on Quandis, before the First City. And something was down there, no longer behind him, but beyond, pulling at him. A great power lured him in, like a moth to a flame, except this flame was night, this moth a man. It was a promise of something unknown, but he also sensed a startling intelligence, a dreaming presence that exuded the whole world as its dream dregs. It was humbling and belittling, and the sheer weight of that unseen thing threatened to crush the breath from his lungs.

Finally, he thought. *All the mystery of Quandis, all the magic that's talked about and dreamed about in the land, it's down there and it's calling me.*

Blane stood, wincing, holding bruises and cuts but ignoring the pain, because beyond the reach of the light in that deep tunnel, something was moving.

He held his breath. The fear was different this time, more solid and tactile, because he knew this was not his imagination.

This was real.

The skittering, crawling things were coming toward him from deep darkness, lamp light glittering in countless blind eyes. Ghast spiders. He counted ten, but there might have been twice that many. Each one was as big as his fist, and any one of them could have killed him with its venom a hundred times over.

They were not rushing. Perhaps they knew that their victim had no hope.

Blane turned and ran back up the staircase, slipping, almost smashing the lamp, rising and running again. He dashed through corridors and hallways, crossed junctions without pause, constantly terrified that the spiders would catch him or his light would go out, or perhaps both.

When he collapsed at last into a gasping, sweating heap, struggling against the sobs that threatened to rack his body, he pressed his face to the floor and felt a ridge cutting into his cheek. Lifting himself up, he saw a familiar spiral design.

Blane laughed until he could no longer hold back his tears.

9

Queen Phela stood atop the Blood Spire, the wind rushing around her, robe whipping at her legs. The crown felt strangely light, but she had no fear of it flying off. The girl she'd chosen as her chambermaid had woven it into her hair. It was so strange to gaze out across Quandis, at the stripe of blue ocean in the distance, and to know all this was now her domain. So strange to think that Phela the Whisperer would find it much more difficult to come and go unnoticed, to vanish into the walls, or anywhere at all. And yet she was queen now, which meant that no doors would ever be closed to her again. Her mother had loved the Blood Spire and Phela had always hated it, but now she understood the power of standing here and gazing out at a land that was hers to command.

"Phela?"

The newly crowned queen laughed softly and shook her head. "You're going to have to get used to calling me—"

"Majesty, yes. I'm sorry."

Queen Phela turned to study her younger sister. "We're alone, Myrinne. I don't mean now, although getting into the habit would be wise. You're still my sister, and I don't expect you to use the honorifics when it's just the two of us. But in front of others . . ."

"Yes, yes," Myrinne said, unable to hide her urgency.

"What of Demos?" Queen Phela asked. "Demos and his 'demand'?"

"It isn't a demand. He has a plan, a way to help, but he can't manage it if all the Bajuman slaves are——"

Queen Phela held up a hand, eyes narrowed. Something had shifted in the shadows against the spire. A moment later the door swung open, and Dafna the Voice showed herself.

"Your Majesty," Dafna said, tucking a lock of hair behind her ear as she bowed.

"What is it? I gave instructions that my sister and I not be interrupted."

The bony, hawkish little woman nodded. "Yes, Majesty. And I'll retreat if you prefer, but I thought you would like to know that representatives from each of the Five Great Clans have arrived together, presenting a single envoy. They wish to offer their condolences, and they are requesting an immediate audience."

Phela arched an eyebrow. "Are they really? Only hours as queen, and already so many are making demands." She glanced at Myrinne. "Perhaps they need to be reminded what it means to be queen."

Dafna the Voice stood rigid, awaiting instruction. Phela wondered how much she had overheard.

"Go on, then," she said. "Take them into the audience chamber and tell them I will hear their entreaties shortly. And Dafna?"

"Majesty?"

"If I ever suspect you are listening to conversations not meant for your ears, I will have the Silent carve those ears from your head."

Dafna flushed, nodding and mumbling as she retreated and closed the door behind her.

"Come," Queen Phela said, taking Princess Myrinne by the

hand and following the Voice. "We'll discuss Demos more soon. For now, let's see what surprises the day has in store."

c⌒⌐

Each of the Five Great Clans had indeed sent a representative. Per Ristolo was also there to represent the Faith, and Phela marveled that the shuffling old man had the energy to make the trip across the city from the Temple of Four. She sat on the High Seat in the audience chamber, struggling not to feel that the throne still belonged to her dead mother. Down inside her soul a thin stream of grief trickled. Not guilt, but certainly a sadness. Phela had loved her mother once, had believed her to be strong and courageous and just, and now she told herself that Queen Lysandra *had* once been all those things. But time, spiza, and a taste of forbidden magic had destroyed her and endangered Quandis.

Phela had acted to preserve the kingdom and save the memory of the woman her mother had been. In her heart, Phela was emphatic on this topic. But down beneath the thin skein of grief there existed a deeper stream, a ripple of suspicion that her mother had never been that woman, had never earned the admiration of her children, and that she had deserved the ugly ending that had come to her.

"Majesty," the envoy from Clan Hartshorn said, clearing his throat.

Fury reddened his cheeks, and Phela could see the tremor of anger on every face. Searching for Aris, the City Guard had invaded all their homes. That insult and intrusion had been enough to enrage the noble clans, and it had only grown worse from there. Queen Lysandra had ordered that search, and none of them knew what the new queen might do.

"On behalf of my lord and master, Baron Hartshorn, official historian of the Crown," the envoy went on, "I must join my voice to those of these others. We mourn the loss of Queen Lysandra and offer our profound condolences. But in the same breath we must object to her final edict. By our estimate at least seven hundred Bajuman slaves have been executed by the City Guard in less than a day, and this . . . this *extermination* shows no signs of slowing. Our beloved capital city of Lartha cannot withstand the economic devastation that would be visited upon us should this edict be fully enforced. The heart of Quandis is dependent upon the blessings of the Four and the successes of the Five Great Clans. In turn, the clans, and the Crown, depend upon the faithful and diligent work of our slaves, and the Bajumen are a large part of that workforce."

The Hartshorn envoy tugged nervously at his graying beard. His brows were thick and bristly, his eyes damp, his formal attire ill-fitting, as if he had aged and thickened in the months or years since he had last had occasion to dress for an audience with the queen.

"Clan Hartshorn beseeches you, Queen Phela—"

"Enough," Phela said quietly, rigid in the High Seat, taking in the entire gathering in a single, sweeping gaze. "You've each had an opportunity to *beseech* me. Kallistrate and Daklan, Ellstur and Burnwell, Hartshorn and the venerable Per Ristolo. That you come to me so swiftly after my mother's passing, and with so little sincerity in your purported grief—"

"Majesty, this is madness," Per Ristolo said, practically choking on his feigned horror at her implication. "So many have been killed. I've even heard talk that two patrols of City Guard have gone missing. This must—"

Queen Phela waved him to silence. She glanced at Myrinne, who sat in the right-hand seat, elevated above the floor but not quite so high as the queen. The edges of Phela's mouth barely twitched, but Myrinne had watched and mimicked her throughout their girlhood together, and she would recognize the smile there. A silent communication passed between the sisters.

Dafna stood by the doors, observing, visible to all but still as a statue unless she was required to speak as the Voice of the Crown. Now she cleared her throat. "The queen is never to be interrupted," she said, without looking at anyone in particular.

Phela wanted to tell Dafna she could speak for herself, but she might need the woman later and had admonished her once already today. And the Voice was effective—the six before her had been silenced with that simple phrase. So instead of chastising Dafna, Phela spread her hands apart, palms up, as if presenting her own beseechment to these envoys.

"Surely your barons must not be as fearful as you suggest, or they would have come to this chamber themselves rather than sending you. They would have come to give their condolences personally, and to beg my indulgence, and to tell me—as you seem to be telling me—that Queen Lysandra's great will and wisdom are called into question by the noble clans of Quandis."

She let her words hang a moment, quite on purpose, but none dared to speak for several seconds for fear of making Per Ristolo's mistake.

"Well?" she asked, privately delighting in the confusion the Voice's command was having on this group.

"Majesty, if I may," the Kallistrate envoy said, her head bowed low. "Clan Kallistrate is already in disarray following the . . . loss of our baron and his family. No one doubts the wisdom of the late queen in naming the Bajumen as abominations and traitors to the Crown. But were she still with us, is it not possible that with the concerns we have voiced, we might have prevailed upon Queen Lysandra to alter her edict?"

A flutter of pleasure warmed Phela's heart. These nobles were doing her work for her.

"The late queen promised to make restitution to the clans for the loss of their slaves," Phela said. "Though I am told there are more than eleven thousand Bajumen on the main island, and I will allow that had my mother been aware of that number, she might never have made such a promise."

It took a moment for the anxiety to strike, and then all the envoys paled. Even Dafna—already so on edge with her unpredictable monarch—looked stricken at this suggestion that the Bajumen might be executed without compensation. Such an act would ruin the noble clans, and surely result in open revolt among them.

Queen Phela leaned forward on the High Seat, regarding the aging Kallistrate woman. "If you could have made such an entreaty, what alternative would you have suggested?"

The Kallistrate envoy glanced round at the others, who only stared back with urgent, hopeful eyes. The new queen had given her an opening.

"Perhaps . . . perhaps those clans who have holdings away from the main island, who have slaves working abroad, might be given time to call those slaves home, and their Bajuman slaves sent to the islands of the Ring to work?"

This time Phela did not dare to look at her sister, for fear that she might grin and give herself away.

"Interesting," she said. "Are you suggesting banishment instead of execution?"

The woman had not truly suggested this, but now her eyes lit up as she realized it might be the perfect solution. The others seemed to be uneasy. For Clan Burnwell and Clan Daklan, this would be an excellent solution, as they had many interests and holdings along the Ring. For Clan Kallistrate it would be difficult, as their slaves would have to be retrained. But they had enough fishing interests that it might work.

Phela could see that the envoys from Clan Ellstur and Clan Hartshorn were displeased.

"Banishment," the Kallistrate envoy said, "if the clans had twenty days or so to make the transition—"

The Hartshorn envoy cleared his throat and gave the Kallistrate a meaningful glance.

"—but what of those who don't have enough slaves on the Ring and beyond to replace the Bajumen?" the woman continued.

"We could simply continue to execute them," the queen said. "The Bajumen cannot be trusted. My mother always believed them to be abominations, but worse, the Crown now knows that the Bajumen conspire against our rule and against our faith in the Four. Their blasphemous insistence upon praying to their 'one true god' and the myth they continue to spread about their ancestors being the First People of Quandis . . . these things have been allowed to stand long enough."

She let the words hang in the air. After a moment, she glanced again at Princess Myrinne. When she surveyed the gathered envoys again, there seemed to be a quiet consensus among them.

"Majesty, if I may?" asked the envoy from Clan Daklan.

"By all means."

The Daklan representative turned to the others, ignoring Per Ristolo entirely. "It may be that my baron and the others with many Outer Ring holdings would consider taking Bajuman slaves in exchange for some of our own non-Bajuman from the Outer Ring. If we didn't have sufficient numbers, then the Crown might offer restitution, as per the late queen's promise."

Queen Phela remained silent until absolute silence reigned in the chamber. The envoys barely breathed. Dafna did not shift an inch from her post by the door. All eyes were upon Phela, and she tilted her head and knitted her brow in feigned deliberation.

"My first decree as queen," she said thoughtfully. "I do believe that had my mother lived to hear these entreaties, in her wisdom she would have agreed. In the name and memory of Queen Lysandra, it shall be done. In twenty days' time, all Bajumen must be gone from the main island. Any who remain upon that date will be ex-

ecuted without further delay. Your barons must work the details of
these transactions among themselves. If there is any disagreement,
any conflict among your houses regarding this edict, it shall be withdrawn and the original execution order reinstated. The Crown has
spoken."

Almost as a single voice, the five envoys from the noble clans
bowed their heads and spoke a single word of assent. "Majesty."

Per Ristolo's features had turned dark and thunderous. "Queen
Phela, your wisdom rivals that of your mother, it is clear. But I must
remind you that Bajumen who join the priesthood are no longer Bajuman at all. They pray to the Four and give themselves over to the
gods completely. Surely you do not mean to—"

Phela stood, towering above them from the platform before the
High Seat. She glared down at him, letting the old priest see the bitterness in her heart. The High Order had indulged her mother's
dangerous whims, had let her taste the magics that had killed her, had
let her madness grow unchecked. She could not say any of those things
aloud, but she would not be lectured by a priest.

"Do not presume to tell me what I *mean,* Per Ristolo."

The old priest bowed his head, the storm of anger still etched on
his features. "Majesty," he said.

"I will consider your plea, Per Ristolo," Queen Phela said.

"That is all we can ask, Majesty."

"Yes. It is."

Per Ristolo glanced up, blinking in surprise at the venom in her
voice. Perhaps confused by it as well. It was clear the audience had
ended, and Dafna the Voice opened the doors for the envoys to file
out past the members of the City Guard who stood sentry in the corridor. When they had all gone, and Dafna had followed them and
closed the doors behind her, Phela and Myrinne came down from
the seats. Myrinne bowed to her, and then stepped closer and kissed
her cheek.

"Tell your love that I have given him what he wanted," Queen Phela said, "and that the Crown expects him to do as he's been bidden."

"Thank you, Majesty," Myrinne said. "Thank you, sister. You are even cleverer than I knew."

Phela did not advise Myrinne to remember the lesson. She suspected her sister would keep it in her mind eternally, because Myrinne was also cleverer than anyone knew. And that was a lesson Phela would keep from today. Because although she loved her sister, she would also keep a close watch over her.

A very close watch.

10

Queen Phela had never truly desired many of the trappings that being queen entailed. Fine clothes, the best food and wine, superlative medical and physical care, servants and slaves, all these were pleasant enough. She would enjoy the food, care, and attention, but they were nothing to do with why she was here.

More troubling to her, even now in only her first week as queen, were the traditions and routines of royalty. She'd had a good taste of this all her life, from almost before she could walk up until the moment her mother's death had been announced. There were scrolls and books aplenty about how royals should conduct themselves, and also whole histories about the duties required of royals, dependent on their gender, placement in the family, and age. There had always been some leeway and movement in these traditions, but there was still much expected of a member of the royal family, and someone with the Blood of the Four running through her veins. For someone with so many servants addressing her every need, and as many slaves as she required, as queen there was a risk that she would become more trapped than ever before by the constraints of a royal existence.

A life with every movement and choice dictated was no life for her. It never had been, and Phela had always intended that upon becoming queen, she would announce a new deviation from the norm. A new royalty.

Yet that was easier thought than done, and she was already feeling constrained. The whole rigmarole of her mother's forthcoming, grand state funeral was bearing on her mind, and while Dafna and other attendants busied themselves with arrangements, Phela found herself dreading the day. She would have to be at the forefront of events, presenting a strong, solid face to the many thousands of attendees. In such tumultuous times as these, there was nothing she wanted less.

As well as the funeral, she would soon be moving into her mother's chambers. She had ordered all furnishings and adornments to those rooms at the heart of the palace to be replaced, and she was already planning some other amendments to the room structures that she would order the Silent to carry out. Shome and her soldiers were not servants or builders, but they would say nothing about the work they performed for their queen. Phela would never be able to relax in her mother's old chambers knowing of the several spying places from where she had once watched. She would not allow herself to imagine strange eyes and ears beyond the walls, watching and listening to her own plans and schemes.

Prior to the move and the funeral, Phela's plans to touch and explore magic drove her on. She'd had the briefest of tastes, and now she wanted more. She understood how effective magic could be in helping her make Quandis the great state it deserved to be. Yet she had seen her mother's rapid demise, and she understood something of its power and the dangers inherent in experiencing its touch.

Her desires were clear, but she would have to be careful and methodical in achieving them.

Before opening her door to the inevitable Guards outside, and

the many people in the palace beyond, she took a moment to herself. Facing the future. Contemplating all that her imminent actions
might summon, and how she would change.

This was what she had always wanted.

She opened the door to the rest of her life.

⸎

"Majesty," Per Ostvik said. Phela heard the surprise in his voice, but
she heard something else there too. Doubt. Perhaps even suspicion.

Not the reverence he should be showing to his new queen.

"Good morning, Per Ostvik," she said, stepping into the arched
stone room. They were low down in the Tower of Bettika, in one of
the many small temple chambers that honeycombed the Temple of
Four.

"I'm honored," Per Ostvik said. He stood from the kneeling
position he'd been in, both hands on his knees, groaning slightly at
the discomfort. With his shaven head and heavy build, it was easy to
forget that this old soldier was advanced in years. Not as old as Per
Ristolo, of course. No one was *that* old.

As the priest stood he glanced behind Phela, clearly looking for
the usual retinue of helpers and advisers who usually accompanied
the queen on her business. Of course, he saw no one.

"I'm here for a private matter," Phela said. "Actually, I'd like you
to accompany me somewhere. We're meeting two other priests."

"A private matter," Per Ostvik said, his voice chilly.

"Something important to me," she said, offering a smile. She
tried to inject it with warmth, but it was difficult. "It was important
to my mother, also."

"Ah," Per Ostvik said. "And where are we going?"

"Deeper," she said. "We can walk together."

Behind her she sensed a shadowy movement, and she knew that
Per Ostvik saw it. His eyes widened, and she almost smiled. *I'm not*

going anywhere completely *alone*. Shome accompanied her, silent and forbidding. If she breathed, Phela could not hear it. Sometimes, she wondered whether the Silent did even that.

"Deeper," Per Ostvik said, nodding. "And I assume the other priests we're meeting are of the High Order?"

"You assume correctly," Phela said.

"And Apex Euphraxia will be present also, of course." The priest glanced aside as he said this, gathering his robes and bending to pull on his soft leather shoes. Testing her.

"She will not," Phela replied.

Per Ostvik did not pause, but his shoulders seemed to slump, as if something he had feared had come to pass.

"Your mother was not ready, and neither are you," the old priest said, standing and looking Phela in the eyes. "You're a fool if you believe otherwise."

Phela bristled at the sudden coolness and lack of respect in his voice. She almost berated him for talking to the queen in such a manner. But she held back, because this was little to do with her being queen, and nothing at all to do with royal duties.

This was all about her.

"With me, Per Ostvik," she said. "Shome will follow on behind.

"Oh . . . and call me a fool again and she'll help you on your way."

On his way to what, she did not say, but the threat was enough to get the old priest moving.

They walked together through the wide base of the Tower of Bettika, heading down narrow stairways and toward the subterranean levels. If Per Ostvik felt surprise that Phela knew the layout of the vast tower so well, he did not betray it. They passed several priests on the way, all of whom stood to one side and dipped their heads to the queen.

Soon they approached their destination, and Phela saw three

other members of the Silent waiting close by as instructed. She had never seen them so tense. Even Shome radiated concern. It was many years since any of the Silent had been inside the Temple of Four, and Phela was more than aware of the antagonism between them and the Phage. There were stories of conflict between the two groups long, long ago, but very little was known of either. Phela herself knew more of the Silent than anyone alive, and as for the eldritch Phage . . . she wasn't even sure they were real anymore. Old stories told of ancient battles, but sightings nowadays were few and far between, and more often than not reported by madmen, drunks, or those ruined by spiza.

Shome's nervous readiness now told Phela more of the Phage than any number of old myths and legends.

"The apex will not take kindly to your soldiers invading the Temple of Four," Ostvik said.

"Your tone is becoming worrisome," Phela said. "I'm your queen, Per Ostvik, and don't forget."

"Majesty," he said, dipping his head slightly as they arrived at a door he must have known only too well. Old and heavy, inlaid with sea glass and ornate metal banding, he would have passed through this opening many times.

"Besides, it's not an invasion. Shome and the Silent are here for my protection, and to carry out my bidding."

"Of course," the old high priest said.

"Of course. Now, open the door."

He opened the door, gesturing for the queen to enter before him. She did, with Shome flowing behind like her shadow. Per Ostvik followed.

Per Gherinne and Per Ristolo were already waiting inside. They were on the far side of the room, a wonderful place of reflections and colored light. A sea-glass spiral was inlaid in the floor between them, and both looked nervous. They stood close together, and Phela had the impression that she'd caught them midconversation.

"Majesty," they said, bowing their heads. Phela smiled and nod-ded. Behind her, Per Ostvik closed the door and she heard the heavy clunk of the lock engaging. Instinct took Shome into a shadowed area to the left, where colored light from the glass and mirrors barely reached her. Phela saw the big Silent's image reflected several times around the room. It gave her comfort.

She glanced down at the pattern in the floor, trying to hide her excitement and nervousness. *I have never been so close!* she thought, even though she wasn't sure that was entirely true. She had at-tempted the journey to the deep places beneath the Temple of Four from Palace Hill, but they had been secretive adventures, ill-judged and fated to fail. Her experiences had frightened her, and although she had never actually decided not to try again, in reality she'd been biding her time for this moment. This moment when she would journey down to those places she sought along the proper routes.

The priests glanced nervously at one another. Per Ristolo looked older than he ever had before. Per Gherinne's silver hair was in disarray, and Phela suspected that the Silent soldier sent to fetch her had woken her. Good. She wanted them frightened and unsettled. What she had to say would certainly disturb them more, and Phela needed complete control of the situation if this was to work.

Her heart beat fast. *Is this what it was like for Mother?* she won-dered. She would never know. But she *did* know that, untouched by spiza, she was far more in control than her mother had ever been. In control, prepared, and aware of what unhindered magic had done to Queen Lysandra. That was why she had three High Order priests here, right from the beginning.

"You know what I want," she said. Her voice sounded strange in the small room, dead and flat, as if the place had no echo or was far larger than it seemed. Maybe the mirrors and glass carried her voice away. Some believed there was another world beyond the mirrors, exactly like their own only reversed. Phela knew that there were more worlds within this world, and one of them was below her feet.

"It's impossible," Per Ristolo said.

"Impossible?" she asked.

"Dangerous. Your mother—"

"My mother was murdered."

The priests' eyes went wide. Per Gherinne gasped in shock, her hand going to her throat. Per Ristolo staggered a little.

"Murdered?" Per Ostvik asked.

"By you," Phela said. "By all of you."

"No. No, Majesty, we served your mother well and with all our hearts, and anything she asked we—"

"Even if it endangered her?" No one replied to that. "Even if you knew that what she asked would poison her, deflate her, and lead to her eventual death?"

"She was being prepared," Per Ostvik said, sad now rather than defiant. "She demanded too much of us, too quickly, and we did our best to keep the process as slow as possible. It takes years for a high priest to get to a stage where he or she is even ready to be taken down, let alone introduced to the echoes of the magic of the Four that persist in the deep places of the world. Many years, and sometimes a priest is *never* deemed ready. We can do all that's necessary from the outside—instruction, education, mental and physical preparation and fitness, contemplation, and meditation. But we cannot change how a person is on the inside. Fear hides deep, like a fish that can never be caught. Doubt sets a seed of rot."

"And what was my mother's fault?" she asked.

"Impatience," Per Ristolo said.

"And she was an addict," Per Ostvik said. "Her addiction to spiza was her great weakness."

"I am not an addict," Phela said.

"But impatient?" Per Ostvik replied. "Majesty, this is not your place. This is not your time. The Blood of the Four runs in your veins, and that is precisely the reason you cannot be——"

"Precisely the reason why I will be taken down!" Phela shouted. "Their blood is my blood, and their magic is my magic. You'll show me *everything*. This one time. Here and now, you'll take me down and reveal to me what you priests have been doing, seeing, finding, hiding down there for generations. Once I know it all, then you will prepare me as you prepare one another. I am *not* impatient. I am cautious, careful. You will be too. But caution and speed are not always opposed, and we *will* do this quickly. I'm open and ready for the magic, and I *will* have it."

"You ask the impossible," Per Ostvik said. "It'll be toxic to you, just as it was to your mother."

"I am not my mother," Phela said, her rage blooming. She had expected resistance, but also reverence. Yet down here, out of sight of everyone, these High Order priests were looking at her like one of their novices.

"Majesty, it's far too dangerous," Per Ristolo said. "Magic is . . . unpredictable."

"I see it in you, Per Ristolo," Phela said. "I smell it. I can almost taste it, and you can't deny that."

"I cannot deny that I have been studying and honoring magic for more decades than you and your mother have been alive," he said. "And still, it haunts and hurts me."

"It also keeps you alive."

Per Ristolo said nothing.

"I do not ask this lightly. I need the magic and the power it affords," she said. Her voice softened, though her determination did not, and she managed to hide her anger for a time. "Quandis suffers from weakness and aimlessness, and with this magic I will ease that suffering. My reasons are sound—you cannot deny it," she said, as if daring them to do exactly that. "My mother . . . I can't pretend to know why she sought magic so quickly and rashly, but her reasons were not my own. My reasons are *righteous,* and you all need to understand that. I accept this is my risk, but it's one that is not up for debate. Our nation is rotting from the inside out, and we *must* do what we can to fix that, so you *must* take me there. I don't know the way, nor the ways of magic, but you do. Take me now, let me see and feel. And then when we resurface, you will prepare me for regular visits."

"No," Per Ostvik said.

Phela glared at the three priests. Though frightened before her, they also presented a united front. Their old eyes were sad, but strong. Their bodies infirm, but set in their ways. Her pleas and demands had not worked. She was disappointed, for sure. But she had also expected this.

She had prepared.

"Shome," she said.

Shome flowed from behind her, a swirl of clothing, a shift of air, and her sword whispered as it swung down into Per Ostvik's head. The Silent stepped back after the rapid assault, and the priests on either side of the old soldier staggered aside in shock.

The assassin's weapon had cleaved Per Ostvik's head in two, the wound traveling down into his torso to just above his chest. Blood and clear fluid flowed across his expression of surprise. He slumped and fell forward, spilling a mess of blood and brains from his ruptured skull. They splashed, then began flowing around the spiral pattern in the floor, following the depressions and lines drawn, carved, and inlaid by skilled craftsmen many generations ago.

Phela's heart quickened at the sight; a modicum of shock, but mostly excitement. She could never go back from this because it was out in the open, before witnesses whose help she needed to survive this day, and the next, if she was going to accomplish all she wanted to do. She would not turn away from what she had done here today.

Per Ostvik gave one final shudder and then he was dead. But

his blood still flowed, and where it touched it had influence on their world.

With a whisper, the floor beneath Phela's feet began to drop away. She backed up, as did the other two priests, as a set of wide spiral steps sunk down around a central stone column. Per Ostvik's body slipped down into the recess and slid a few steps into the darkness, coming to a stop half out of sight around the first tight bend.

"The way down," Phela breathed.

"You . . . you can't . . ." Per Ristolo whispered.

"I think I just showed you I can."

"Or what?" Per Gherinne asked. "You think that scares us? You think death is a fear for us?"

"Oh, not at all," Phela said. "I would never underestimate you. That's why I've made it my business to know things. Such as . . . Per Ostvik has two nieces and a nephew. One nephew and one niece live on Hartshorn Hill. They're both teachers. The nephew has a wife and four children. The niece also has a wife, and they adopted three orphans from the northern lands following the flooding three years ago. They dote upon them. The other niece is a corporal in the City Guard. Ostvik also has two elderly brothers, both retired, both living by the coast with their spouses. There are nine cousins with their own families. Beyond that, the blood relations become more distant, but still traceable. His brothers are both rich, and somewhat antagonistic toward the Crown. But that's not why they will be killed. They'll be killed because they are related by blood to Per Ostvik, and he has displeased me." She glanced at Shome. "Send someone to make it happen."

Shome nodded and left the room, leaving Phela alone with the two priests and the bloodied remnants of their companion.

So easy to issue a score of death sentences, Phela thought. The queen did not feel afraid. She felt *alive.*

"That is why you will do as I say," she said. "Not through fear for yourselves. But because of my promise that if you don't, everyone you love or have ever loved will bear the responsibility of your refusal."

The priests looked terrified, and Phela saw thoughts and fears turning and rolling behind their eyes.

"Your sweet sister, her children, her grandchildren," she said to Per Gherinne. "Your dead brother's family," she said to Per Ristolo.

"You're no queen," Per Ristolo said.

Phela offered a tight smile.

"You'll die," Per Gherinne said. "Magic will destroy you as it destroyed your mother."

"No," Phela said, "it won't."

In their eyes, she saw that they believed that too.

∽

Queen Phela followed the two priests down into the depths beneath the Temple of Four. They had stepped over the body of Per Ostvik, and she had seen how both high priests averted their eyes. She had not. It was good to take ownership of one's deeds, however brutal and unappetizing they were. She would not deny what she had become, nor what she was destined to become soon. She reveled in it.

At the foot of the circular stairwell was another room with a similar pattern inlaid in the floor. The priests followed the pattern, and she followed them, until the floor whispered down into another descent.

Per Gherinne carried a torch, and at the head of the second stairwell Per Ristolo took a lamp from the wall, lit it, and held it toward Phela. Without a word she took it. The old priest grunted.

After the second stairway, Per Gherinne led them into a roughly carved tunnel. Per Ristolo followed, gesturing Phela to bring up the rear.

"I've a story to tell," the ancient priest said.

"I don't want to hear your old tales, Per Ristolo."

"Nevertheless I'll tell it. And if that offends you, have your murderer cut my head in two and spill my brains. I'm sure she's following. I'm sure Your Majesty would not venture somewhere so dark and dangerous alone."

Phela smiled at Per Ristolo's broad back. She had heard no sound from behind, yet she knew that Shome and several other Silent were there. They had spoken about what would happen, and the assassins would be at home in these dark, secret depths.

What might happen when they went deeper and drew closer to the places these priests haunted—the caverns and holes where the dregs of old magic rested—she did not know. That was a problem to confront when it happened, but not one to distract her from her course of action.

"Many years ago, when Lartha was little more than a rough settlement of traders and hunters at the river's edge and the nation of Quandis had no name, there lived a woman called Mephilia Bon. These were simpler times, when people hunted to eat, farmed to live, and war was a waste of energy and resources. Simpler, and more peaceful. Bettika, god of Wind and War, whispered in the air and only dreamed of the conflicts she might preside over in the distant future. But Mephilia Bon came from a nameless island of the Outer Ring with a purpose in mind."

"Let me guess," Phela said. "She wanted to steal magic from the gods and she paid a terrible price."

Per Ristolo coughed something that might have been a laugh, but he did not look back. They were heading along a slowly descending tunnel, turning gently left and right and bearing ever downward. They passed junctions with other tunnels and openings into pitch-black caves where things scuttled and scratched, and Phela had to trust the priests' sense of direction.

"I'm telling the story, Majesty," Per Ristolo said. "In a way, though, you're right. But in another, very wrong. It wasn't Mephilia Bon who paid the price for her transgressions."

They reached a small room with several doors leading off. Per Gherinne paused for a moment, looking left and right. Then she grunted to herself, nodded, and headed down another tunnel. Per Ristolo and Phela followed.

"Mephilia Bon thought herself a whisperer."

Phela drew in a sharp breath. But Per Ristolo kept on talking, no inflection in his voice, no hint that he was trying to goad or lead her into some admission of her own secret pastime.

That word, though . . .

"She spoke to the animals, guiding and cajoling them, supposedly encouraging them to perform tasks for her. True or not, I can't say." The priest coughed another laugh. "Probably she fooled herself. But that didn't stop her from offending Dephine, god of Water and Beasts."

"How did she offend her?"

"It's just a story," Per Gherinne said from up ahead. Her shadow twitched and danced in the flickering torchlight.

"Stories are what we're made of," Per Ristolo said. "This one goes, Mephilia Bon built an altar in a place south of where Lartha now stands, and there she sacrificed six animals to Dephine every hour, every day, for a whole year. Birds, rats, and mice. Spiders, squirrels, and rabbits. Deer, wolves, and any other creature she could find, trap, and slaughter."

"Honoring Dephine," Phela said. "It's done today in some parts."

"Honoring Dephine by building her likeness in dead animals," Per Ristolo said. "Sixty feet high, a stinking mountain of rotting creatures that Mephilia Bon announced to be Dephine's given form. It offended Dephine greatly, this false image of her built from the creatures she loved, honored, cherished. She sent a flood along the river to cleanse the land of Mephilia Bon and her sickly homage."

"I've heard about this," Phela said, her voice a whisper. "The Flood of Floods."

"You've heard the story as told to children," Per Ristolo said. "A storming river, banks swept away, villages and settlements carried down the river and into the sea. Truth is, not only did the flood kill thousands and scour the land for a hundred miles downriver, but it also washed those fifty thousand dead and rotting bodies into its course. Their taint poisoned the river, and many more died from sickness and disease. Dephine was angry. The floods came again and again."

"So an angry god lost her temper," Phela said. "It's just a story."

"One of many such tales," Per Ristolo said. "Tales of fools who upset the balance of things."

"This way," Gherinne said. "We'll reach the first of the safe places soon."

"The safe places?" Phela asked.

Per Gherinne paused and glanced back for the first time since they'd descended the stairwells. Her eyes looked haunted. Maybe angry. Phela would have to remain alert.

"A place that if you tried to pass on your own, you would die."

Phela smiled and nodded. "Like those safe places deep down between Palace Hill and Temple Hill?"

Per Gherinne and the old priest stared at her.

"The lake with the tentacled creature, ready to snatch unwary explorers. The rockfall crawling with ghost spiders. Remnants of the fallen First City."

"Don't know what you're talking about," Per Gherinne said. "Just do as I say when we get there and you'll be fine." She turned away and started walking again before ending her sentence with, "Your Majesty."

"You've seen the hill of Clan Daklan, with its sheer eastern cliffs," Per Ristolo said, and it took a moment before Phela realized he was continuing his story. "Nine thousand years ago Charin, god of Fire and Secrets, cleaved that hill in two when a man named Jerok started carving that god's secrets in stone for all to see. Countless people died."

"Why are you telling me these old tales?"

"Because I fear your ambition will offend *all* the gods. And that one day when the land has recovered from the gods' wrath, survivors will be telling your story in hushed, fearful tones."

"Foolish old man," Phela said. "I offend no one and nothing. There's nothing of the gods left, other than what you keep to yourselves down here."

"There is more than you think."

"Then if that's the case, you preach fear of the Four to keep people away from what you covet. Maybe it's you priests who are the enemies of Quandis, not the Bajumen who have fallen under the blade. Maybe you've been fooling us all along."

"No, Majesty," Per Ristolo said, not at all shocked by his queen's outburst. "We fool no one but ourselves, by following a royal line corrupted by greed."

Phela felt anger simmering in her, but it was tempered by the weight of the world around them. She felt the whole mass of Quandis pressing down upon her, its new queen taking on the mantle of troubles that her mother had passed down. What she was doing here would make her better able to serve Quandis and make it the power she always believed it should be.

She had to believe that.

As Per Gherinne called a halt, Phela gasped. Something . . . came past her. *Through* her. She felt a breeze in and around her body, and it carried a smell and taste that reminded her of that tendril she'd inhaled on the balcony of the Blood Spire. She staggered against a wall, holding herself upright as her heart and mind opened to what she was feeling.

Magic!

Per Ristolo offered a wry smile.

"I'm . . . fine," she said. "Fine."

"We can still head back—"

"I'm *fine*."

He grunted.

Per Gherinne was performing some sort of ritual at a rock face just ahead of them. Water dripped down the rock, and several small, slimy creatures slicked across the wet surface. The priest muttered an invocation that Phela could not hear, performing several complex patterns in the air with her hands, repeated many times as her voice rose and fell.

The rocks before her melted away to nothing, and the slimy creatures dropped to the floor. The priest trod them underfoot as she walked through.

Phela tried to hold in her amazement. She could feel the dregs of magic soaring around and through her, but seeing it used like this for the first time was a shock.

"Was the rock even there at all?" she asked.

"If you think it was," Per Gherinne said.

"What do you mean? It was a false wall that you revealed? Or your words made the rock disappear?"

"Whatever you believe," the priest said. She shook her head as she entered the new chamber. "You know nothing," she muttered, words Phela wasn't certain she was meant to hear. She glanced back before she followed the priests, comforted by the sight of several shadows following them far behind. Shome and the other Silent needed no light to see.

From that point, the journey became something of a dream. Phela followed the priests, trying to concentrate on their words when they spoke, but her senses were taken more and more by the sizzle of power that filled these deep, dark places. It was as if magic was heavier than air, rock, Quandis itself, and its final leftovers from whatever past the land had endured had slumped down here, hiding in the dark and waiting for people to come and find it. Clearly the priests had, over many years. And her mother had also slipped down and drowned in its arcane touch. Now it was her turn, and Phela was determined that, with care, she would be triumphant.

All her life had come to this.

She heard whispers of voices far away or long gone, singing songs of the past. She tasted exotic taints on the air—food she had never tried, wines from places no one knew, the sweat from muscled bodies. She smelled the future and saw herself standing atop Palace Hill with the entirety of Quandis laid out before her, worshipping and honoring her as not only Queen Phela, but the greatest queen the country had ever known. The Eternal Queen. In her mind's eye, day and night flitted past, the Temple of Four crumbled to ruins as she became the tallest part of the land, and hills rose and fell before the endless span of her rule.

Water flowed along the river, and sometimes it turned to blood.

Phela absorbed it all, always remembering who she was and what she had done. That was important. Her sense of self would preserve her, and once she had returned to the surface, the priests would prepare her to slowly, carefully immerse herself in the magic that filled this place.

Deep, dark magic, hiding away no more.

Time passed and Phela found herself poised at the edge of a wide, low cavern. Water filled it, coming to their knees. It was ice cold. She glanced back but there was no sign of Shome, and a sliver of fear stabbed into her heart. Terror flittered at the edges of her perception.

Per Ristolo and Per Gherinne looked older than they ever had before, but they were both smiling at her.

"You wanted this," Per Ristolo said. "Behold, the Four."

"The Four?" Phela asked. She didn't understand. She looked across the chamber, and at its center was a wide raised area, an island in the pool, behind a veil of water cascading from cracks in the ceiling far overhead. The island was only inches above water level. At its four corners, two hundred feet apart, were four enormous stone pedestals. They looked like giant slumped stalagmites.

They had form. Long, almost circular. Unspectacular, and yet . . .

"The tombs of the Four," Per Gherinne said.

"Here?" Phela asked. "No. No, they're not *real*. They're not *here*."

"They're as you see," Per Gherinne said. "Each acts as a foundation to the towers far above, at the corners of the Four Square. Very much here. Very much in the real world."

Neither priest spoke again. They knelt and worshipped, and Phela felt herself dropping to her knees in the cold water, through shock rather than a need to pay homage.

Though at first glance there was nothing special about this place, Phela knew that it was the center of the world.

"I've seen," she said. "Now, just gently to begin with, I must touch."

11

Blane felt the world tilting beneath his feet. He felt punched, winded, and tears began to well in his eyes. From the bare safety of shadows, thirty feet from the edge of the water, he watched Queen Phela kneel, and everything he had ever believed began to crumble around him. Pressure in his chest and the flushing of his cheeks forced his body to remember it needed air, and he made the tiniest gasp for breath. Across the cavernous chamber, one of the Silent stiffened and glanced his way.

Not now, Blane thought. *I can't die now. So close to truth. So close to freedom.*

The Silent tilted her head as if listening for the beating of his heart across the darkened grotto, where darkness and light danced together, and lanterns were supplemented with strange shafts and pools of illumination whose origins were unclear, perhaps uncanny. His heart beat a thunderous rhythm and he pressed his eyes shut, trying to quiet it. He knew that the Silent were only human, but also knew that they were masters at the art of killing.

He opened his eyes expecting her to be there in front of him.

But she had not moved. The Silent was small and thin, her long red-brown hair braided down her back. Flashes of silver came from the thick braid, winking in the torchlight, and it took him a moment to understand these were razors knitted into her hair.

Apparently, though, the braided assassin had heard nothing. The prayers from the pool grew louder and drew her attention, and at last Blane allowed himself to exhale. He felt a rush of wonder as he stared at Queen Phela on her knees between Per Ristolo and Per Gherinne . . . and at the four stone shapes that rose from the corners of the wide platform at the center of the vast chamber. More water trickled down from above, curtains of light rain that cascaded down through the crevices of the city's bedrock, fed by the river or by leaks in Lartha's aging plumbing.

You're thinking of plumbing, he thought, chiding himself. But really he was not. Blane thought not of pipes but of age—the seven or eight thousand years since the founding of Quandis, when the First City had fallen and the city of Lartha had been born anew. Thousands of years of secrets, but they all led here. And the fucking High Order had known all along. They had been keeping the presence of these four tombs to themselves.

Blane pressed a trembling hand over his mouth to keep the cries of anguish and awe inside. The Four did not exist. The god of the Bajumen—the god of his childhood—did not exist. *Magic did not exist.* And yet he had seen the Phage, and the warping of the air that showed the passage of energy when Per Ristolo had used spell-craft. Even then, he had tried to persuade himself that was still of the natural world, the power merely something the rest of the world had not yet interpreted.

But this was different. In those raised tombs, surrounded by the cascading rains of the city's cellars . . . Anselom? Bettika? Charin? Dephine?

Since the first day he'd come to Temple Hill he had done all he could to learn the secret paths and hidden corners, both in Yaris Teeg and in the Temple of Four. Per Gherinne had tracked him down on the day of the slaughter and began to tell him that Per Ristolo had gone to see the queen, but Blane had been below the temple then, exploring for the first time. When at last he reappeared, she'd demanded to know where he had been. He'd told her that he'd been hiding, in fear for his life. Per Gherinne, notorious for the sharpness of her tongue and the withered black thing she called a heart, had shown him sympathy, but she had also reminded him that he had nothing to fear. He was no longer Bajuman.

Her comfort had infuriated him, because it dismissed the murder of his people and all the sins that had come before. Per Gherinne had been kind to him because being a priest erased what she considered the shame of his birth. In the shadow of that moment he had redoubled his efforts, keeping watch over those he knew were members of the High Order, particularly Per Ristolo and Per Gherinne. There were dark looks and conspiratorial whispers, and he began to eavesdrop when he could.

When whispers among the teachers at Yaris Teeg had suggested the queen had made her way up Temple Hill, Blane knew he had to risk everything. So once more he had slipped into the cellar and through the subterranean tunnels that led up the hillside, crept into the Temple of Four, and made his way into the Elders' Corridor. At the end of the corridor he had listened at the door and heard the queen's threats against Per Ristolo and Per Gherinne. Only after they'd gone had he dared to slip into that blue room, with its shifting lights and sea glass mosaics. There he had found the corpse of Per Ostvik in a bloody tumble partway down the spiral staircase, head split, brains spilled.

And then he'd done the most foolish thing of his life. Even knowing a number of Silent were with Queen Phela, he had followed. Courage and idiocy had merged into one, and yet something else tugged him along, some gentle lure, a whisper not in his ears but inside him. Inspiration, he'd told himself, still afraid to really believe that any other influence might linger in the buried places where ruins of the fallen First City were still visible. He'd seen Per Ristolo and Per Gherinne wave away the strange creatures, heard the words they'd chanted to smooth their passage, saw the truth of the wall whose barrier existed only in belief. He shouldn't have been able to duplicate those gestures, those words, that belief. Not without practice. Not without magic.

And yet he had.

The high priests began to undress. The urge to avert his eyes weighed on him, yet he watched Per Ristolo unveil his wrinkled flesh and studied Per Gherinne's sagging bosom and sticklike legs, all the ferocity and authority of his High Order instructors bleeding out with their dignity. There was a certain austere beauty to their ancient bodies, but he knew he would never see them again without imagining this moment.

Together, they undressed the queen. Blane had never seen Phela before, and he had never imagined being this close to the former princess, now monarch. Her skin seemed to reflect the shadows and light of the cavernous chamber. Exquisite in her nakedness, perfect in her lines and curves, her face full of wonder and joy, nevertheless Queen Phela radiated a sense of command. It was as though all of them had merely been making their way into her domain, a home she had lost and to which she had now returned.

Blane felt the animal urge to touch her, what some would have called the Song of Dephine, but it clashed with the Song of Bettika.

The urge to kill.

He resisted both and watched as the two High Order priests bathed themselves and then the queen. They cupped their hands full of water and drank from the pool surrounding the slightly higher level that had the tombs at its corners. They never drew closer, never even passed through the curtains of water that fell from above. Those cascades seemed now to almost be a veil that separated the tombs from those who worshipped what might lie within.

Hello? he thought, directing his thought toward the tombs. *Are you—*

No. He would not. If gods he had never believed in were wielding some influence over him, toying with him in some way, he would not reach out to them. He almost laughed aloud. Even with all this evidence before him, he still had his doubts.

He was pulled from these thoughts as a strange ritual began. Per Ristolo called upon Charin and presented a spark of fire in the palms of his hands. Per Gherinne called upon Bettika and a gust of warm, sweet-scented wind swirled and eddied through the cavern, extinguishing two of the lanterns. Together they called upon Dephine and again cupped the water, pouring it over Phela's head, slicking her hair down. It was Phela herself, instructed by the priests, who searched along the bottom of the pool and found a sharp-edged stone. She slashed at the palm of her left hand, kissed the stone and hurled it past the veil of water, and made a fist and let her blood drip into the pool.

Fire and Secrets. Wind and War. Water and Beasts. Earth and Love.

The Four.

The words chanted by the priests were an ancient tongue, a guttural series of strange syllables that felt somehow familiar to Blane. He recognized it as a language written down in obscure books inside the Temple of Four, but he had never heard it spoken aloud. Still he felt the tug of it, the music in it, though on the surface it sounded so ugly.

"Kneel once more," Per Ristolo said, placing his hand atop Phela's head.

"In obeisance?" said the queen.

"Not at all, Majesty. You kneel so that you don't fall down." Per Ristolo shot a warning glance at his fellow priest that Phela didn't seem to notice, but Blane found curious. Each of them then placed a hand on one of the queen's shoulders as they reverted to that old tongue. They sketched at the air with their fingers and then reached out their arms, heads hung, palms upward.

Blane felt it first inside the cage of his chest. The bones vibrated, his heart clenched, and then all sound vanished from the vast chamber. The sheets of water cascading from above made no noise as they splashed into the pool. A quiet had descended over them unlike anything he'd ever known. Blane could no longer even hear the beating of his own heart.

The pool lit up with eddying currents of light, bright sapphire ripples that spread out from the tombs and their wide platform, and when Blane blinked he could see these ripples also in the air all through the cavern, as if they'd been there all along.

At once, the ripples in the air washed together like waves crashing, washing over the three worshippers in the pool—Queen Phela, Per Ristolo, and Per Gherinne. The queen laid her head back and cried out—the first sound in what felt like forever—her voice heavy with sorrow and yet tinged with the gasping surrender only ever born of ecstasy. Blane shuddered, a thrill of pleasure went up his spine, and though the ripples of light did not touch him, he thought he felt some of that magic in himself.

Then it was over. The High Order priests helped the shaking Queen Phela to her feet. She stumbled between them, and the Silent moved in close as the three of them dressed. In what felt like only moments they were leaving, the priests whispering to their queen, and she keeping her own counsel, except to tell them—breathlessly and flushed—that they would return the next day, and the next. When they tried to dissuade her, she warned them that she would not be denied.

"My birthright," she said. "I feel it even now, in my blood. In *their* blood."

"Your mother—" Per Ristolo began as they all retreated back the way they'd come, through the first of a series of snares and traps and magical defenses meant to keep away all but the High Order themselves.

"You let my mother kill herself," Queen Phela snarled. Her body spasmed, as if in pleasure, and she grabbed the arm of one of the Silent. "She was muddled with spiza, blind with it. I am not so weak."

"You said you would be cautious. Careful."

"You priests will care for me and be my caution, but I cannot wait. Not now. Not after . . ."

The words became muffled after that. Only when they had all left did Blane let himself exhale.

Lanterns still burned. Uncanny lights still glowed, although the sapphire ripples in the pool and air had faded to nothing. He still felt the crackling static of their presence.

Blane knew he should leave, and he was worried. If he could not remember the words and gestures, never mind the precise turns and steps and the hidden passages, he would be trapped down here until the High Order priests returned with the queen, prey for whatever might stalk these silent, mysterious places.

Yet his mind was a sponge for knowledge and information, an ability exercised daily through his studies in Yaris Teeg, both allowed and covert. This place and everything he had seen was what he had been seeking all along. So he *did* remember—every phrase, every gesture, every step.

And not just to escape, but for the ceremony he'd just seen performed . . .

He stepped from his shadowed grotto and walked slowly toward the pool. His heart ached as he gazed at the tombs, and he considered the myths he had been taught about magic, the control of the elements and the summoning of ghosts, premonitions and manipulations. He remembered tales of how magic bound the magician to the land, so the health of one could be tied to the health of the other. So many stories, yet which were true? He had always been a hopeful skeptic, though that had now changed. In that cavern ringing only with the sound of falling water, answers niggled at the back of his brain.

He stared at the tombs through the veil of water, wondering what those ancient, desiccated gods looked like now. Dead for thousands of years, their power still lingered, the remnants of it coalescing here almost as if it had been waiting.

He stepped into the pool and began to disrobe.

BOOK TWO

12

A fortnight had passed since Phela had first gone to the tombs. She had descended at least once each day since then—other than the day of her mother's state funeral, a somber affair that Phela had only wanted over—and followed the rituals set forth by the High Order. Per Ristolo and Per Gherinne watched over her, and with each step in her indoctrination she saw their doubts and fears beginning to slip away. Her mother had gone mad, muddled by spiza, believing that she could expose herself to the full array of the lingering magic of the Four and absorb it without consequence. From the beginning Phela had been more cautious, sipping at it day by day, wary at all times of making the same mistakes as her mother. Lysandra had weakened her mind and body with spiza and ignored the cautions of the priests advising her. Though Phela would not be deterred by their hesitations and doubts, she had still instructed them to advise and watch over her, and when they told her she'd indulged in enough magic for one day, that she risked too much, she listened. She was determined that the magic would not unravel her as it had her mother.

Sitting in her High Seat and gazing upon those gathered in her audience chamber, she wondered if they could also see the flickering blue stars that hung about the room. They were small things, but there were thousands of them, winking in and out as they drifted and eddied like dust motes in shafts of long afternoon light. She felt every breath as it inflated her lungs, felt the patterns in the wood and cloth of her chair, heard the words spoken around her as if each had been whispered into her ears. Heightened by her taste of magic, each moment felt delicious.

"Majesty?"

The single word floated crisply in the air. Queen Phela breathed deeply as she surveyed her audience. Per Ristolo and Per Gherinne stood just a few feet from the dais, the appearance of age so deceptive. She knew what lurked within them now, what they could summon if they had the courage, and her own intimacy with magic had only just begun. With those High Order priests stood a third, Per Stellan, one-eyed and broad, with a wild tangle of red hair that marked her ancestors as outlanders. The others were experts in the rituals of their craft, but Per Stellan had been called in from the Ring at Queen Phela's command. She knew how to wield magic better than any other, or so Per Ristolo claimed. For a moment, the glistening pit where Per Stellan's eye had once been became a distraction. One of those blue stars flickered inside it, as if the magic rested within. Queen Phela felt a flash of jealousy. She wanted that flickering blue star. She craved every last dreg of magic the Four had left behind.

"Majesty, are you all right?" Dafna asked.

Queen Phela snapped her head around to glare at her. "You are my Voice, woman. You cannot speak for me?"

Dafna blanched. "I speak only the words you give me, or the spirit of them if that's what you desire, Majesty."

Phela smiled. Each breath she took felt like a serpent slithering in and out of her lungs. She glanced at the others in the chamber—

the two City Guards by the doors; Commander Kurtness just beside Dafna, standing at attention; her sister, Myrinne, to the queen's left; Shome to her right. There were three other Silent in the chamber. The smallest was Helaine, she of the long red-brown braid, the size of a girl of thirteen but deadly with a blade in either hand. Her reputation had caught even the late Lysandra's attention. Idly, Phela reminded herself that she ought to learn the names of the others. These women were closer to her than her own family now, somehow almost closer than her own skin. They were all bearing witness to the beginnings of her transformation. They were her armor given life. Her weapons. Her fists.

Soon, though, I might not even need them.

The thought made her smile as she looked at each of the envoys the Five Great Clans had sent, but she frowned slightly when she saw that some of the envoys had changed. Queen Phela wondered if new ones had been chosen because the others had been ineffective.

Or maybe I've already had them killed, she thought.

"Sister," Myrinne said.

"Let me ask you a question, *sister,*" Queen Phela said, watching the flickering stars as they swirled in the air. "Do you believe I'm unaware that I am making you all wait? That I care at all about your impatience?"

There was rustling among the noble envoys, but it ceased the moment Phela looked their way. They froze, errant children caught misbehaving.

The queen looked to Dafna. "An edict from the Crown, issued through my Voice."

Dafna nodded quickly, relieved to be getting on with it.

"The royal family is directly descended from the Four. We have the blood of gods in our veins. Thus, as our gods surely intended, the Crown and the Faith are one, and always have been. This is as it was when the Four built Lartha on top of the ruins of the fallen

First City. This is the natural evolution of things. This is the way by which Quandis will reach true greatness once again. From this day forth, Quandis is a holy state, and whoever wears the crown is also the head of the Faith."

Per Gherinne swore quietly. Per Ristolo began to cough, his face reddening, as if he might be having some sort of stroke. Per Stellan kept her expression blank, unreadable, and said nothing. The envoys felt no such compulsion to keep quiet, however. Even Myrinne gasped, and it was this that drew Phela's attention. She turned to her sister, saw the stricken expression that somehow made Myrinne even more beautiful. Shock could do that, Phela knew. So could terror.

"Something, sister?" Queen Phela asked. She watched Myrinne's eyes and wondered if she could be trusted.

"Not from me, Majesty," Princess Myrinne replied, "but you can surely see that there will be voices raised against this."

Phela sat up straighter on her High Seat and cocked her head, feeling the weight of the crown shift. She looked from face to face, beginning with Dafna. The Voice would not meet her gaze.

"I hear murmurings from our good nobles and from the priests who serve our ancestors, the gods, those of *our* blood," Queen Phela said. "But no voices raised in furor. Surely all must recognize the truth of this. Every Quandian knows we are descended from the Four. I have merely decreed that we will follow the natural order of things."

She glared at her sister. "And I am the queen."

"You are," Myrinne said.

"Majesty," Per Ristolo said, clearing his throat and blinking as he caught his breath. "In the full history of Quandis, the Crown and the Faith have always been separate, partners in guiding the lives of our good people—"

"An error I have just rectified," Queen Phela interrupted.

"Surely you'd like some counsel first?" Per Ristolo went on. "If you'd only speak with Apex Euphraxia . . ."

The weight of her gaze quieted him. She did not need to remind him of the fate of Per Ostvik and his family, or even to have one of the Silent move toward him. A pointed glance carried all the warning she would need.

The Daklan envoy stepped forward. "That's enough."

The others seemed split on whether or not to support him. He had the weathered, scarred features of a veteran soldier. His hair was receding, and though he wore the finest fabrics, he reminded her most of one of the filthy, emaciated hounds that wandered the back alleys on the lower hills.

"Enough?" Phela echoed curiously.

"You cannot usurp the apex. You can't seize control of the Faith, especially when Euphraxia's not even here. The Faith is inviolate, our shield from the whims and excesses of the Crown. You can't—"

Commander Kurtness moved swiftly for a man of his size. In two steps he had his sword pressed to the envoy's throat. "You're a good man, Yuris Daklan, but you're speaking to your queen. Men have died at my hand for the sort of disrespect you've shown."

Shome and the other Silent had not moved, and would not unless Phela ordered it or she was in danger.

"Commander Kurtness," said the queen. She studied the whorls in the air as the stars only she could see danced and flickered. "Is Yuris Daklan a good man? Truly?"

Kurtness did not take his eyes off the envoy. "Yes, Majesty. In my eyes, at least."

"Yet you would kill him if I ordered it?"

The commander of the City Guard nodded grimly. "Without hesitation."

"Of course you would. Your flesh was woven with loyalty and courage as the thread. You're precious to the Crown and Faith. Come and kneel before me."

Commander Kurtness had been ready for bloodshed, so he hesitated a moment before stepping away from Yuris Daklan. The exhalation of his unexpressed violence seemed to calm the room as he turned and strode to the dais. He laid his sword on the floor before the High Seat and lowered himself to one knee, bowing his head.

"Now you, Yuris Daklan," said the Queen.

Fury roiled behind the envoy's eyes, and Phela could practically see its tendrils shifting beneath his skin. Yuris Daklan exhaled loudly, glancing around as if seeking support for his little rebellion. None was forthcoming. In fact, the envoy from Clan Ellstur approached the dais and knelt beside Kurtness.

One by one the others followed suit, until at last Yuris Daklan joined them. His fury still raged, and the current of the stars drifting through the room seemed to flow away from him. But he had knelt.

Queen Phela turned to the priests. "Now you."

At her side, she heard Myrinne's breath hitch.

But the three High Order priests were nothing if not wise. Together, they walked toward the dais and joined the others, each on one knee.

"Dafna," the queen said. "You are my Voice. You have heard my edict. Go now, and speak for me."

The Voice bowed her head. "It shall be done," she said and scurried off to perform her duties.

Minutes passed before Queen Phela allowed those on their knees to rise. She wanted them to feel the ache of their obedience, and never to forget it.

⟡

The spiza chimneys in Apex Euphraxia's cellar had been scraped clean. Years of rime had left stains on the stone that even bleach could not remove. Demos knew, because he'd tried. With a heavy cloth tied across his nose and mouth, he'd dedicated himself to this task with uncommon diligence. He didn't care one whit about the end result. If the spiza chimneys sent poison smoke upstairs and killed everyone in the house, he would have been happy. Demos's interest in the spiza chimneys sprang from a unique facet of their construction that he'd discovered while cleaning them.

If you were quiet, and you chose your position well enough— and you knew which chimney opened into which room—it was quite possible to eavesdrop on conversations elsewhere in the house. The conversations were muffled, sometimes incomplete, sometimes frustratingly quiet depending upon where the speaker might be standing in that particular room. But this discovery had made spying on Euphraxia's household a much simpler task.

Not as if it matters anymore.

"I know that expression on your face," Mouse whispered.

Demos shifted. His knees hurt. Though he'd been given other jobs to do, the worst of the scut work, the garbage and grime, he'd kept coming back to the spiza chimneys under the pretense of determination. His neck and shoulders ached from scraping the stone and from bending to push his upper body into this chimney or that, but his knees were the worst, even with the grass mat that Mouse sometimes managed to sneak to him.

"What expression?" he muttered.

"Dejection. You're worried there's no point to spying anymore."

"Is there?" Demos asked. Word had filtered down to even the lowest slaves of the queen's joining of Crown and Faith, and what it meant for Euphraxia. Did Queen Phela even want him to continue spying? He'd sent several short reports out into the city in Tollivar's hands, worried that the boy would never return, and had been surprised every time the little sneak reappeared. Now, what need did the queen have of Demos's spying if she had already usurped Euphraxia's power?

"Give me a turn," Mouse ordered. "Stretch your legs." They'd become allies in recent weeks. Not friends the way they'd been as children, but the memory of that friendship had grown stronger.

Demos slumped away from the chimney with a huff. "This isn't the life I thought I'd have. I'm a sailor. A soldier."

Mouse bumped him with her hip. "That wasn't the life you thought you'd have, either."

He glanced at her. He admired the rise of her cheekbones and the fine line of her jaw, the deep winter blue of those eyes. "What are you talking about?"

Mouse smiled, perhaps the first true smile she'd shown him over these long weeks. A flicker of memory touched his mind. Her as a little girl. The two of them running and laughing together.

"You wanted to be a pirate. Captain Demos, Scourge of the Sea, Master of the Ring!" She chuckled softly, one hand rising to cover her smile as if worried that her usual grim mask had slipped. "Don't you remember?"

Demos leaned closer to her. He breathed in her scent, a combination of rough soap and her own musk that froze him to the spot. Those winter eyes were locked on his. Demos's body remembered every blow she'd given him, every bit of pain she'd caused, but he knew it was the merest fraction of the pain she'd endured through her life of slavery. She was Bajuman, but she never tried to hide the mark on the inside of her left forearm. Mouse resented her lot in life, but she was not ashamed of it. His own slave brand no longer hurt. Just as the flesh had scarred and settled as the days had passed, so too had Demos himself scarred and settled. He needed to escape this place, but his confidence in the world outside—and his place in it—had faded. The brand had done that. It had changed him, jaded him. He'd become the lowest of the low, but at least he was not down there alone.

"Careful," he breathed, not sure if he was speaking to Mouse or to himself. He bumped against her. "Or the Scourge of the Sea'll order you keelhauled."

A child's laugh broke the quiet, loaded moment that followed. Demos and Mouse twisted around to see Tollivar watching them from his usual perch atop a wooden crate at the other end of the spiza chamber. The Bajuman boy moved with stealth that came from instinct—it was how he'd survived to be here with them in the first place—but sometimes it meant he showed up in a room without anyone being aware of his arrival.

"You two going to kiss?" he asked.

Mouse went paler than her normal Bajuman hue. Demos stared at the boy, then at Mouse, and wondered at the answer. Princess Myrinne had his deepest love; she was his intended and his closest friend. This moment of shared intimacy with Mouse felt like a betrayal, but that insight was only coming to him now, after the fact, and he could not be certain what might have happened if Tollivar had not interrupted.

"Let me listen for a while," Mouse said quietly. "You go and keep watch."

Demos nodded quietly. Aching, confused, he began to stand.

Then he heard the voices slithering from the mouth of chimney three. Demos held up a hand to silence Mouse and Tollivar. He recognized the angry tone and cadence that had become typical of Euphraxia of late. But the other voice?

"Who is that?" Demos said quietly, crouching beneath the mouth of the chimney.

Mouse crept over beside him and bent an ear. Knowledge sparkled in her eyes. "Per Gherinne. A hateful woman, that priest. An air of calm around her, but always a spiteful gleam in her eyes."

Demos shook his head. He didn't know Per Gherinne, but she had to be High Order to warrant an audience with the apex, even now, with Euphraxia weakened.

On top of his crate, Tollivar began to swing his legs and to hum softly to himself, the way happy children did. Demos had no idea how the boy could be happy down here in the stinking cellar, hidden away every day, and yet children had that magic in them. He hated to shush the boy, but he pressed a finger to his own lips. Tollivar shot him a grumpy look and crossed his arms, still swinging his legs.

"—am I supposed to trust you?" Euphraxia said, her voice rising with her ire, her words thus easier to discern.

"What choice do you have?" Per Gherinne replied.

"You were there the first day, down below, helping the queen with rituals that are not hers to partake in. She blasphemes. She taints the magic of the gods, and you aided her!"

"The Silent murdered Ostvik before our eyes, and you know what became of his family. She threatened us with the same—"

"Cowards, all of you! What's your own life, the lives of your parents, your sisters, compared to the price of blasphemy? You know the stories and you've seen the ruins. You've read the words on the Wall of the Four."

"Apex, please listen. I *am* with you. The priesthood is fractured now, split in two by the queen's edict. Some are loyal to the Crown and to Per Ristolo, who is abetting her every whim and giving her exactly what she desires. But others feel the same horror and fear that you do. The truth of magic is filtering out into the city in whispers, tales of our rituals, and Phela's claims of seizing her birthright. Even among the novices at Yaris Teeg, priests argue over this, but if I believe nothing else, I believe that magic is sacred. The royals may have the Blood of the Four in their veins, but it's the priests of the High Order who are the true heirs of the gods."

Silence fell, and for a moment Demos pictured Euphraxia staring at the chimney, somehow alerted to those eavesdropping on her. She couldn't know, of course. But the apex and her priests spoke of magic, and though he'd scoffed all his life, Demos could no longer wholly deny its truth.

The apex must have just been deliberating, for now Per Gherinne prodded her.

"I swear to you," the woman said, "I am loyal to the Faith and to your leadership."

Tollivar began to hum again, and the heel of his swinging boot bumped the crate. Demos froze, but Mouse scurried away from the chimney mouth and grabbed his ankles to still him. Tollivar shrugged and smiled. Demos wanted to be angry with him but could not manage it. Mouse glanced over her shoulder, but Demos held up a hand to forestall any questions.

Instead, he listened. When Euphraxia began speaking again, it was much more quietly. Carefully, Demos poked his head into the chimney and listened to the soft echoes of the words above as they filtered down to him. They were words of treason, resistance, and allies they might find among the Five Great Clans. She talked of who might land on the throne if Queen Phela could be toppled from it, whether she might be driven from Lartha, or if it might be best if she died in her sleep one moonless night.

Demos could barely breathe.

His moment had arrived. Now surely he could earn Phela's favor and his own freedom. When Myrinne learned that he'd saved the queen from treachery and murder, she'd insist that her sister free him. Heart pounding, face flushed, lungs tinged with spiza, he withdrew from the chimney mouth and turned to stare at Mouse and Tollivar. The boy's arrival here had been a gift, and Demos's thoughts began to race ahead. He'd send Tollivar out, get a message to a faithful cousin who would pass it to Princess Myrinne, and in the end Demos would make certain that Mouse and Tollivar were freed as well and allowed to leave the city as free people, or stay if they wished. They were Bajuman, but if they helped to save the life of the queen—

"Demos," Mouse whispered.

He smiled, and then noticed that her gaze rested behind him. Tollivar's feet had ceased their swinging.

Demos turned to see Vosto, the praejis, staring openmouthed at the three of them.

"Praejis," Demos began, still on his knees, hands upraised. "This is not what it seems."

Vosto roared as he took a single step and shot a kick at Demos's skull. His boot connected, a blow to the temple, and for a sliver of an instant the world flickered to darkness. Light returned in a flash of pain. Vosto's boot thudded into his side once, twice, until Demos twisted and grabbed at the praejis's leg. Older and smaller, still Vosto had startling strength and speed and a bone-deep cruelty that drove him. When Demos grabbed him around the ankle, he pivoted and dropped his knee hard onto Demos's chest, driving the air from his lungs. Wheezing, snarling, Demos shot a punch at the praejis's groin. Vosto twisted enough to avoid the worst of the blow, but it pained him enough to outrage him further, and his fists began to fall, smashing Demos's skull against the stone floor three or four times, enough to make the lights in his head begin to go out again.

He wondered if he might die.

Then Vosto released a guttural, choking gasp and his weight lifted. Demos shook his head, blinked to clear his eyes, and saw Mouse on the praejis's back.

"Leave him, you fucker! That's enough from you. Enough from you forever and ever and *ever*." Mouse punctuated her words with strength, choking him harder, baring her teeth, winter eyes storming.

Vosto began to turn blue. Vision blurring, Demos struggled onto his knees and then began, shakily, to stand. His hands curled into fists, ready to end this. Whatever happened after tonight, his tenure as Euphraxia's slave had come to an end. Chimney two had a large stone loose, and Demos reached for it, dug his fingers into the crumbling mortar and ripped it free.

As he turned, Vosto pedaled his feet backward with a final burst of strength. His boot caught and he fell, adding momentum as he drove Mouse against the wall. Demos heard the wet crack as her skull met a protruding stone, watched breathless as Vosto landed with her beneath him, stared at the bit of blood and blond hair caught on the stone.

Vosto shook loose of her now limp arms and rolled onto his knees. For a moment he glanced at Mouse, both he and Demos caught in the realization that she was no longer moving. Blood pooled around her head. Her eyes stared, lifeless.

Tollivar's cry broke the silence. He slammed into Vosto, not to attack the praejis but to bump him aside. The boy dropped to his knees beside Mouse, heedless of the pooling blood, and held her face in his hands. He shouted at her, kissed her forehead, pleaded with her to wake up. His grief tore a hole in the world.

Demos felt a stillness akin to death in his own heart. In that stillness, all had gone silent, even the boy's cries. He stepped forward just as Vosto began to turn and brought the heavy chimney stone down once, twice, a third time. Vosto slumped to the floor beside Mouse, and his own blood began to spill out from his shattered skull, one pool touching the other until they seemed one sea of red on that stone floor, one murder instead of two.

When Demos whispered into Tollivar's ear, the boy resisted at first. But he was old enough and smart enough to know that when others came, the two of them would be executed. Just as dead as Mouse.

"She'd want us to run, Tollivar. She'd want me to get you out, to find a way for us both to be free."

This time when he took the boy's hand, Tollivar went willingly. Demos glanced back at Mouse, remembering the laughing child he'd known and the proud woman she'd become, even in slavery. *Good-bye, boy,* she would have said. "Good-bye, girl," he murmured.

Tollivar scrambled up the coal chute, the way he'd first come into Euphraxia's cellar. Demos followed him out into the nighttime streets of Lartha, carrying with him secrets that had the power to save him, or destroy him.

13

Approaching the first islands of the Ring felt nothing like coming home.

Daria stood at the bow of her flagship, the *Nayadine,* and watched the island of Igler's End growing closer. It was not one of the largest islands in that vast, thousand-mile-diameter circle surrounding much of Quandis, but it might have been the most beautiful, and it was home to one of the most important seaports beyond the main island. Igler's End was formed from two volcanoes; one extinct, one partially active. The volcano on the island's southern tip produced a constant stream of smoke and steam, sending colorful gaseous clouds across the island that diffracted sunlight and cast almost constant rainbows. The extinct vent to the north was much smaller, its caldera formed by an eruption that had happened in prehistory. This wide-open crater was now home to a small town linked to the coast by a mile-long path, twisting and climbing from the seaport, rising up staircases and ramps and spotted with signs and proclamations. By the time someone reached the town of Igler's Folly on foot from the port, they had already been regaled with promises of food, drink, and whatever vices they could imagine, and they had a hundred destinations in mind.

Daria had only visited briefly many years before, but she had vivid memories of the island's beauty, and of Igler's Folly's debauchery and decadence.

The island's soil was rich and fertile, and much of it was covered in jungle. Only where mankind had chopped and gouged its way into the land were the trees absent, but even there the island's population ensured that sprays of color remained. Orchid export was one of the main sources of income. Many who lived there had been expelled from Quandis for one reason or another, but ironically most made a better living here than they ever had back home.

Home. What does that even mean?

Daria had never felt a sense of home since finding herself pulled from the sea half dead all those years ago. She supposed where she stood now, on her ship's bow, was as close to home as things got for her nowadays, and she wasn't sad about that. The constant swell and dip of the ocean matched the pulse of her heart and the flow of her blood. Sometimes she thought her heartbeat was synchronized with the surge and tide, and sometimes, in deeper dreams when she was more than human, she thought it might be the other way around.

"Beautiful," Shawr said, appearing by her side.

"You come from here," Daria said. "You *would* think that."

He shrugged. "I left when I was seven, taken to Quandis with my sister to make a life for myself."

"And so you have," Daria said. They stood silently for a while, looking at the distant island and the splay of colors smeared above the steaming volcano. "Is there anyone here for you now?"

"No more," Shawr said. "My parents died. Maybe a few people who might remember a seven-year-old me, but . . ."

"But they won't recognize you now." Daria nodded. That was

good. She could relate, and yet again Shawr made her feel not quite so alone. If he were ten years older, maybe there would have been more than friendship between them. She'd thought it before, and though the idea made her vaguely uncomfortable, she could not shake it.

"It'll be interesting to see the old place again," he said. He smiled, and his voice rose with excitement. "You should see some of the events in the town square: Plays, tournaments, magic shows, puppeteers, duels. There was an old soldier who used to fight fire lizards! And a man who could fit into a food urn."

Daria cringed. "Delightful."

"Once, someone had to smash the urn to let him out." Shawr started laughing. "He'd gotten a cramp. He couldn't move his . . . his arms were . . ." The laughter took over and he bent double over the rail, unable to speak. Daria laughed with him.

The thought of why they were returning to Quandis snapped her back to reality, though. While Shawr dried his eyes and wandered away, she continued staring across the rough sea toward Igler's End, wondering what changes they would find there once they docked.

⌒

Two hours later the *Nayadine* and her accompanying fleet of five ships dropped anchor in Mercel's Bay. The port clung to the northern sweep of the bay, with jetties and docks jutting out into the water, warehouses and official buildings lining the shore, clan flags flying in no discernible pattern. Here, everyone lived and worked together. Being a Ringer usually meant more than which clan or race anyone belonged to, but that bond did not extend to outsiders. Uncertain of the sort of welcome they might expect, Captain Gree had suggested the fleet drop anchor a little way out to begin with, and Daria had agreed. If for any reason they needed to make a fast escape, being moored to the docks was not the best idea.

When the shore party lit blue flares to signify that all was well, a score of boats was lowered from the warships, and hundreds of sailors headed for shore.

"I already feel sick," Shawr said beside Daria.

"Me too," Captain Gree said. "The bay's too flat. And land's flatter."

Daria knew what they meant, but she was admiral, and complaining was unprofessional. They'd been at sea for a long time, and other than landing on a couple of remote islands in their search for pirates, their sea legs had been firm. Now they were about to hit solid ground again, and the sense of constant movement would be taken from them.

Nothing's ever still, Daria thought as they approached a jetty. *Everything's in motion, now more than ever.* She was eager to discover what had changed on Quandis since receiving the message from Demos's mother. Weeks had passed, and that was a long time in love and war. It had been frustrating not being able to dig deeper into the story that enigmatic message had hinted at, but that was why they had stopped here first.

Igler's End was one of the main transit points between Quandis, fifty miles to the south, and the great open oceans to the north. Though inhabited by many people expelled from Quandis for a variety of reasons—political, criminal, religious, and racial—the place also had settlers who'd come of their own free will. Perhaps they were driven by a desire to see more of the world, or a need to be away from the more strictly controlled society on Quandis. Whatever their reasons, Daria knew that there would be people here aware of current events.

Being at sea was what she loved, because she had made a new life for herself there. But at times like this the isolation felt inhibiting.

The boat nudged the jetty, and ropes were tied. The sailors waited for Daria to climb the ladder first. Standing on the warped wooden boards of the jetty, she turned and looked back across the water to her ship.

The ground weaved and waved beneath her feet, and she had to close her eyes. Her stomach rolled. Dizziness made her light-headed. Sunlight scorched her face with no sea breeze to soothe her skin.

"I think I'm going to puke," she said, to a smattering of laughter from the boat bumping the jetty beneath her. The others climbed up, and sailors hung on to each other's shoulders while they waited for their land legs to return.

Almost four hundred sailors had come ashore, leaving crews aboard each ship to oversee restocking and to guard the vessels from unwelcome visitors. The captains would ensure that any who wanted to go ashore and walk up to Igler's Folly would be able to do so. Daria had decided to wait here for a day and a night at least, partly to gather whatever new information she could, partly to restock the ships. They all knew that they might be preparing for a fight as well as a peaceful homecoming, and that would demand a fully prepared crew for each ship, fed and watered, rested and readied.

Daria herself needed the time to digest whatever new intelligence they might gather.

When they left the wooden jetty and felt the dry shift of sand beneath their shoes, the port master was there to welcome them.

"Admiral," he said, his stance casual, eyes cautious. "I'm honored you'd choose to visit us here."

"I'll bet you are," she said. The man raised an eyebrow. He was a skinny fellow, one side of his face blurred with old army tattoos, bald head scarred with a fine network of lines. She'd seen such scars before and knew they were acid burns. He'd been involved in a pirate campaign on Skarroth, one of the westernmost islands of the Ring. He noticed that she noticed, but the look in his eyes did not change. He neither trusted nor welcomed them here. He also had no choice in either.

"What's your name?" Daria asked.

"Chester Burnwell," he said, the name hanging in the air like a challenge.

"I don't care what clan you are," she said. "I don't care what goods you're smuggling in and out of your port, who you trade with, who works for you, or who you work for. My crews are hungry, tired, and thirsty. We're here for a pause and a rest. And all I care about from you is some information."

Chester frowned and looked past Daria, taking in the many sailors and their six fine warships docked out in the bay. Perhaps he'd seen them arrive and feared that whatever life he'd carved for himself here, legal or not, was about to be torn down.

"I'm . . . I'm third cousin to Baron Burnwell's son," the man said.

Daria shrugged. "Like I said, I don't care." She stepped forward and nodded toward where a stone path followed the high-tide mark around the curve of the harbor. Farther along was the first wide staircase leading up toward the dead volcano's crater and the town of Igler's Folly. For now the heavily forested route was hidden behind the buildings lining the coast, but Daria was keen to begin her journey.

"Walk with me," she said. "You can help me find what I want."

"I can?"

They walked. Daria sensed Shawr close by, and when she glanced back, she saw Captain Gree and the other captains leading their sailors in a procession behind her. Fishermen and other boat crews paused as they passed by. Even the sea shushing against the shore sounded quieter, as if holding its breath to see what might come next.

Igler's End had seen many visits from the Quandian navy over the years, but the atmosphere here seemed more expectant than ever.

Or perhaps Daria's mood was making it so.

"I need news from Quandis," she said.

"I don't bother myself with that place anymore," Chester said. He sounded defiant.

"Even though it's home?"

"Home?" He snorted.

"But you must have heard about what's happened there?"

"So the queen's dead." He shrugged as they walked.

Queen Lysandra is dead! Daria thought, the shock sending a cool wave through her body. Things had moved on since the albatross had arrived. Doubtless it had something to do with Baron Kallistrate being executed, but what, she could not tell.

"And what else?" Daria asked.

"I don't know," Chester said. "I keep my head down, see. People and ships come, people and ships go. Some bring what I ask for, many I sell what they need. It's a good life and a decent living, and it's a damn sight more than I ever had on Quandis. So this is home for me now, and I keep my nose out of business that doesn't happen at home. Nothing to me."

"You fought pirates," she said.

"So have you. And?"

She couldn't help but like Chester. He risked heavy repercussions talking the way he was, but she thought he'd sussed her out just as she was sussing him. He'd taken a gamble that punishment was not her game. Speaking his mind endeared him to her, and she wouldn't push for what he didn't know.

"Give me a name, then," she said. "Someone in town I can go to for information about what's happening back in Lartha. The ins and outs, truths gleaned from rumors. One name, and then I'll instruct my quartermasters to run all their resupply business through you."

He paused, standing firm before the admiral and her battle-hardened sailors. "I'll run a fair deal," he said. "I pride myself on that."

"I'm sure," Daria said, knowing they were about to get fleeced. She smiled.

He gave her a name.

⌒

Per Cantolatta came as a great surprise. Not only was it a shock to see a priest in a place like Igler's Folly, bedecked in traditional dress and wearing the chains and sigils that marked her position in the priesthood, but she was also the largest person Daria had ever seen. Over six feet tall, she must have weighed more than five average women, her vast body contained within a hardwood, wheeled frame, long arms bulging around precious bracelets, legs propped up so that her feet did not touch the floor. Her hair was long and unbraided, clean and shining. Her face was fat, eyes piercing, skin clear, and Daria had a feeling the smile was permanent.

They were in a tavern called Done Roamin'. Daria, Shawr, Captain Gree, and a dozen other sailors had entered, the rest of the crews spreading out among Igler's Folly's many eating places, watering holes, and brothels for an evening's entertainment. Daria had ordered a return to the ships by three the following morning to allow a change of crew. It was almost seven in the evening now, and the sailors were in high spirits as they looked forward to a long evening of entertainment, whatever their proclivities.

Per Cantolatta had a place in a wide bay window at the tavern's rear, and it looked to Daria as if she had been stationed there for a long time.

"Your worship," Daria said, bowing slightly.

Per Cantolatta began to quiver and shake, and then a huge laugh burst from her body. It was surprisingly high.

"Worship!" she said. "No more, Admiral. I left the Four behind many years ago."

"But the . . ." Daria indicated the chains and pendants around the huge woman's ample neck.

"I like them," Per Cantolatta said. "They complement my stunning natural beauty." She snorted, and Daria found herself liking this strange woman. She was usually a good judge of character. "Sit down, Admiral . . ."

"Hallarte."

"Hallarte! Of course. Your reputation precedes you. Please, take a seat. Your cabin boy, too."

"I'm not her cabin boy!" Shawr protested.

"You are," Daria said, chuckling at his offended look. "And my steward, valet, aide, adviser, and confidant."

"We all need those," Per Cantolatta said. "Forgive me, boy. It's been a while since I've had to talk proper."

A barman approached and took their orders, and moments later a barmaid appeared carrying a tray of drinks, snacks, and a large, graceful glass horn half filled with water. Daria had seen a spiza pipe before, though this seemed to be carved from solid crystal.

"Hand that over, would you?" Per Cantolatta asked. Daria went to stand, but Shawr was there before her. He had to lean past the woman's timber frame before she could reach the pipe, and she took it from his hands with surprising dexterity. Daria guessed that much about the priest might be misleading.

"So I'll bet you're wondering what a priest like me is doing here in the asshole of the world," she said.

"It's not such a bad place," Shawr said.

"It's really quite beautiful," Daria said.

She didn't just mean the land itself. The atmosphere on this island—it was like nothing she'd felt in a long time. Raucous laughter erupted from somewhere out of sight. Whores drifted from table to table, men and women barely dressed and displaying more of their wares as day fell into evening. Drinkers drank more, warriors told tall tales, and fishermen bemoaned the ones that had gotten away, the fish getting bigger and bigger with each telling. Daria had been in a hundred places like this in Quandis, but something about the

Done Roamin' felt different. There was a sense of freedom about the tavern, even excitement, that was almost exclusive to establishments she'd visited around the Ring. It was as if the people here knew more than most, and part of what they knew was that by leaving perceived civilization behind, they had escaped something confining.

The number of Bajumen present had also come as a surprise. She'd seen the first of them down by the docks, and there were more in the town. They roamed in small groups, but they did not seem self-conscious or fearful. People passed them by without a second glance, but she noticed they didn't try to avoid the glances, either. They were not integrated in other groups, but neither were they spat upon or shouted at. And while a few still seemed downcast, many were wearing brighter, more elaborate clothing than normal for a Bajuman, and these walked with their heads held up. They talked among themselves. Smiled. Some even laughed.

Her heart fluttered at such a sight, and she'd felt the sudden need to embrace them, be with them. But she feared that the sight of her would frighten them away.

Beautiful . . .

"Well, it may be beautiful," Per Cantolatta said as if echoing Daria's thoughts, but also sounding disappointed. "If you *were* wondering why I'm here, I'd recommend you not ask, because I'll tell the truth, and then the two of you might have to decide what to do about it."

Daria raised her hands and shrugged. She was curious, of course, but she had other concerns than this old woman's secrets.

Shawr saw it differently. "What do you mean? The island's always had outlaws come and go. What could you have done that you think would be so horrible we'd put our own troubles aside to deal with yours?"

"I didn't say it was horrible, darling." She tipped him a grotesque wink. "But it is blasphemy."

Daria stiffened, studying Per Cantolatta with new eyes. "You said you'd put the Four behind you. But you're not an atheist, are you?"

"Oh, no. I'm quite faithful."

Shawr sputtered. "You can't mean you're a—"

"Hush," Daria said, fixing him with a dark look. "This isn't your home anymore. And we have enough business of our own without interfering with anyone else's."

The moment lengthened. Shawr seemed uncertain, and Daria understood why. The ex-priest was likely not an ex-priest at all, she'd just swapped her original gods for another.

The woman was a Penter.

Not the first that Daria had encountered. In fact, glancing around the room and seeing the way certain patrons were watching them, she felt sure Per Cantolatta wasn't even the only worshipper of the Pent Angel they'd encountered today. But the enormous woman's faith *was* blasphemy, and it was shocking to meet any Penter so ready to admit what she believed. To risk the arrest and execution that Shawr would apparently have been glad to initiate.

"Admiral," Shawr said now.

Daria made her decision. She'd been a slave once. Spat on, kicked, beaten, and worse. Her people worshipped their own god, not the Four. Why was that any less blasphemous than praying to the Pent Angel?

"We're here on our own business," Daria said to Shawr, and her tone brooked no argument. He looked displeased.

"So what *is* your business?" Per Cantolatta said. She took a suck on the spiza pipe. Water inside bubbled, smoke rose and spiraled up the clear arm, and she drew in a heavy breath. Letting it out slowly, her huge mass seemed to relax more into the wooden frame surrounding her.

"My business is Quandis," Daria said, lowering her voice a little.

"I know some of what's happened there, and I'm informed you can tell me more."

"More," Per Cantolatta said. She leaned sideways, wood creaking, affecting secrecy between the two of them. "I can tell as much as you'll pay to ask."

"I can pay," Daria said.

"Not only money."

"What else?"

Per Cantolatta stroked the pipe for a moment as if musing, but Daria believed she knew exactly what she wanted.

"You're an admiral, so you'll be carrying good wine on your ship. The stuff they brew here is . . ." She pulled a face.

"The best," Daria said. "I have six bottles from Xhenna Pan left, nine years old."

"Nice. Tobacco?"

"Imported from the east."

Shawr stiffened, obviously furious that she'd give a Penter such rewards. Daria ignored him. He was a cabin boy, and she the admiral.

"Which islands?" Per Cantolatta asked.

"Lands so remote they're not yet named," Daria said. "But the finest. You have my word as an officer you'll receive those bottles and a pouch of the tobacco, provided you have information I don't."

Per Cantolatta smiled. "You're not the first Quandian officer to give me your word. Swear it by all the gods there are, but also send a runner now. I'll have my payment today, if you please."

"I swear by all the gods there are," Daria said. She smiled, trying to hide her irritation, and nodded to Shawr. Grimly, he slipped away to instruct one of the crew to return to the ship for the ex-priest's booty. "And it'll be done before you leave this place."

When Shawr had moved off, the woman nodded, smiling. "Then ask away."

Daria looked around the tavern. A few heads turned away, eyes flittered aside, and she knew that even in such a place she would be the center of attention. Though it was already growing into a raucous scene, that didn't mean she should be incautious. This island was away from Quandis, and she could feel the sense of independent community that had grown here over the years. She was the outsider here, and she didn't need to cause trouble if there was no need. She leaned in close to Per Cantolatta.

Captain Gree had been sitting with the other officers who'd come in with them, out of earshot, drinking and laughing and affecting a casual air, although they were in fact keeping a close watch of the room around them. She hoped that was all they'd have to do. Now, noticing the conspiratorial tones at their table, Captain Gree came to sit with them.

"I know of the Kallistrate family," Daria began, acknowledging Gree with a nod. "They're friends of mine."

"An unfortunate affair," Per Cantolatta said.

"I'm not aware of why it happened, though," Daria continued. "All I've had is an unofficial communication informing me of Baron Kallistrate's execution, and an official communiqué from the queen describing strife at home. No firm orders."

"Which queen?" Per Cantolatta asked, and the question confused Daria for a beat. She frowned, shook her head. And then understanding landed.

"I heard that the queen is dead. But surely Aris is king in her place?"

"Dead and gone also." The huge woman took a long drag on her pipe, looking from Daria to the recently returned Shawr, to Captain Gree, then back again. She was obviously enjoying their shock, and the fact that she knew far more than them.

Daria wondered how much there was to know.

Elsewhere in the tavern someone cried out, and Daria's hand almost went to the hilt of her sword, but she'd been in enough tight situations to keep her cool. She sensed Gree tensing to her left, alert and ready for trouble. The shout descended into laughter, and she saw a group of men and women playing a tabletop game in the corner across from them. They were absorbed in the game, content in their small world. Untroubled by what might be occurring beyond. She relaxed just a touch.

"What happened?" Daria asked.

"You understand, the stories I hear are word of mouth," Per Cantolatta said. "Not carried on the wind by gull or albatross, written and immutable. Whispers change from mouth to ear, and more so when those mouths and ears are fleeing or being expelled from Quandis. Bitterness and grief can color a story or change its balance. And so, the nearest to the truth I can perceive is the middle ground taken from all the tales I hear. The common thread."

"I understand," Daria said. She was growing angry. The fat woman was relishing this, but to push her might be the wrong move. She'd likely clam up, not reveal more.

"Which is to say, I can't vouch for a single word of this," the ex-priest continued. "But enough people have told me enough to make it as true as can be."

"Yes, yes. So, Queen Lysandra. Prince Aris . . ."

"Dead. Both of them. The queen from sickness, some say brought on by spiza addiction. Prince Aris murdered by Bajuman whores."

"Murdered?"

"You're surprised at his manner of death, but not who killed him." She smiled.

"The prince's habits were an open secret," Daria said absently. Her mind was spinning, and she was trying to maintain control and keep the news clear and concise. The deaths of queens and princes surely had hidden depths, but until she knew for sure what they were, she could not afford to speculate.

That didn't mean that an ex-priest could not.

"Of course, other rumors suggest that Aris was murdered by the new queen."

"You're saying Phela murdered her brother?" Daria asked, shocked at the accusation.

"I've said no such thing, only that there are rumors. They're royals, my love. There are always rumors."

Per Cantolatta shivered in her frame, sending waves across her body. The pipe bubbled and spat smoke, and Daria caught a scent of spiza. She had never used it and forbade its use on any of her ships. She did not like the taint. Yet here in Done Roamin' it marked the air and merged with the smells of spilled beer, orchids, sweat, and sex.

"What of the Kallistrates?"

"Queen Lysandra accused Linos Kallistrate of treachery, of being a Penter, and had him executed."

The news hung in the air. There were Penters here in the room, including right in front of them. If Kallistrate's execution made Per Cantolatta nervous, she didn't show it. Penters could be desperate and zealous, and thus dangerous, but in Daria's experience they lived away from the main island—such as here—and were mostly in hiding, or at least keeping their faith to themselves. But now one had been found not only on the main island but in Lartha, the baron of a Great Clan? And not just any baron, but one so close—if the rumors were to be trusted—to the Crown?

It didn't add up. And coupled with Aris's untimely demise . . . she couldn't put it all together, but she was sure something was missing here. For now, though, she moved on—the sooner she could be free of this tavern, the sooner she could clear her head and make some decisions.

"And the baron's family?" she asked, thinking, *Not Demos. Don't let Demos be dead.* He was the nearest thing to a great friend she had. Other than Shawr, perhaps, although the boy was more of a dedicated, loyal companion. He was also her subordinate, and that created a distance between them.

Demos was a friend to the bone.

"Sold into slavery," Per Cantolatta said. "All of them, though rumor has it the son Cyrus died also. And not only the Kallistrates have suffered. The purge has spread to other noble families, although the information out of Quandis since Phela took the throne is more confused. Dead queens and princes are big news. The slaughter of their subjects—"

"Slaughter?" Daria asked. More heads turned at her raised voice, both sailors and residents of Igler's Folly. She did not care anymore. Her concerns must surely be theirs, too, and Per Cantolatta had said nothing about her words being secret.

"You've seen the number of Bajumen on the island?" Per Cantolatta asked.

Daria nodded, not trusting herself to speak.

"They've been banished from Quandis. All of them. At least, all those left alive after the purge. When Aris was murdered, the ailing queen ordered the whole race wiped out. It was Phela who commuted the order to banishment, after her mother's death."

Daria was reeling. Shawr looked as shocked as her, and Gree's face was set in a grim mask. *He already sees war in our future,* she thought, and though initially alarming, the idea of rebellion seemed inevitable. If it had just been the Bajumen being killed or banished, perhaps not, but executing and terrorizing the nobility would have unsettled the whole city. She tried to keep the news from hurting her. Yes, she'd been Bajuman at birth, but she had lived her adult life as a sailor, a warrior, a woman of means and substance. But when she closed her eyes at night, awake and dreaming, she still felt the fury and spite of those days, those beatings, being treated as less than a beast, sometimes as nothing at all. Of believing for so long that Bajumen were lesser creatures, no matter how much resentment roiled inside her.

"Some say seven hundred Bajumen died in the first day," Per Cantolatta said, and Daria flinched. The ex-priest looked serious for the first time since she'd started speaking. "Some say over a thousand. A slaughter born of ignorance and madness. Why anyone listened to the insane old bitch . . ." She shook her head and took another draw on her pipe.

"What of the Bajuman priests?" Daria asked. She felt every eye on her, all the attention of those she knew in the tavern, and those she did not. She felt them knowing her secret—sensing it in her question and how she asked it, and in the silent fear for her brother. Again, she didn't care. She knew that Blane had become a priest, and even though she had never seen him since being dropped from the cliff, her blood demanded she know what had happened to her brother.

"Those who join the priesthood are no longer Bajuman," Per Cantolatta said. It sounded like she was reading from a sheet, but she looked serious.

"They're still there, then," Daria said. Per Cantolatta frowned. Daria looked away.

One of her sailors arrived with a tray of fresh drinks, and Daria was pleased for the interruption. She drank some wine, eyes closed to allow her to think.

"Of course, there's more," Per Cantolatta said. "News that's mere whispers. So quiet I can barely call it news."

"Tell me anyway," Daria said. "We need to know everything."

Per Cantolatta shrugged, sending shivers around her body and creaking the joints of her heavy wooden frame. "If I spread mere rumors, I'm perpetuating false news. That's dangerous for me. I'm a woman known for the veracity of her information. I don't need to make things up, because I know things. This, though . . . these recent days, so much has happened and is still happening that my channels are . . . unclear."

"What do you want?" Captain Gree asked. Quiet up to now,

Daria welcomed his intrusion. His voice was calm and soft, but carried an unmistakable strength.

But Per Cantolatta did not look at the captain. She looked at Shawr.

"An hour with the boy."

"What?" Shawr said. "Wait . . . *what?*"

"No," Daria said, and she meant it. Wine and tobacco were fine, but she would not trade Shawr with this woman. She wouldn't trade any person. When you had suffered slavery yourself, the idea that a person was merely an object was so abhorrent that she once again thought about reaching for her sword.

Per Cantolatta looked disappointed, but then she smiled and shrugged again. "It was worth a try."

"What else?" Daria demanded, no longer playing games. The woman would tell her, or she would learn what it meant to insult a Quandis officer.

Per Cantolatta seemed to consider the unvoiced threat before finally saying, "Whispers arrived late last night, with several members of a family serving on Hartshorn Hill. They fled Quandis in fear for the land and its future. They claim that two days ago, Queen Phela declared Quandis a holy state, Crown and Faith combined. Those who protested were immediately marked as Penters and will either be executed or sold into slavery. Many are going to flee. Some are talking of resistance."

"She did it herself," Daria whispered, as everything came together in her mind with an almost audible click. Her words carried above the hubbub, and Per Cantolatta grew serious again as she nodded.

"If these rumors are true, that would be my guess also. Phela devised a coup. I've no real love for Euphraxia and the Faith, not after . . ." She blinked, as if reliving something terrible. "But the land has lived well enough these past decades. Queen Lysandra was just and fair, until close to the end. There's no telling what sort of ruler Quandis has now." She shrugged.

Daria sat up straight and glanced at Shawr and Gree.

"We need to go," Gree said.

"Not yet," Daria said. "We stay here for a while. Let the crews rest and recuperate, restock the ships. And while we're here, you, I, and the other captains will run scenarios and plan for each one."

"Are you sure?" Per Cantolatta asked, and Daria turned back to her. But she was looking at Shawr.

"Thanks for your interest but . . . no thanks," Shawr said. He stood, nodded politely, then was the first of them to leave the tavern.

"Oh well," the huge woman said.

"Thank you for your time," Daria said, standing to leave.

"One thing," Per Cantolatta said. "Don't bring the fight to the Ring." She looked around the tavern, and Daria saw the first hint of sadness in her eyes. "We've made something good here. And there are other islands on the Ring where good things are happening, too, though many on the main island would have you believe otherwise. Now that the Bajumen have been banished, have you seen their attitude? Their faces? By the Four, when's the last time you actually saw a Bajuman's face? Some of them even seem happy. Wouldn't surprise me if they'll even be allowed in here, given a year or two."

There's one in here now, Daria thought. "I'm not sure there's even going to be a fight," she said.

Per Cantolatta only looked at her. Neither of them needed to say how naive those words had been.

Daria left, and Gree and the other officers were waiting outside. Shawr was nowhere to be seen.

"What now?" Gree asked.

"Now we find another tavern," Daria said. "We drink and talk."

And plan, she thought.

We plan for revolution.

༧

Looking up at the stars, Daria was amazed that they had not changed when so much in Quandis had. A steady breeze blew across the island, indifferent to her worries. The smell of the jungle, the scent of gases from the active volcano, the feel of grass beneath her back, none of them cared about what she had heard, nor the deception she had carried with her for so long.

They're killing my people, she thought. For the first time in a long while the Bajuman in her rose up, fearful and furious.

She'd had too much bad wine, and then Gree had bought a bottle of brandy and they'd toasted fallen comrades and absent friends into the early hours. With every toast she saw Blane more clearly. She imagined how he might look now, as an adult, and as a priest. While those around her prayed to the Four, she silently sent a plea to Lameria to keep Blane safe. The guilt over never contacting him was constant, but she'd made her peace with that over the years. Now, though, the urge to ensure his safety was almost overriding everything else.

Even duty.

"There you are," Shawr said. "Been looking for you. The crews are heading back down to the port to switch off. The others want a taste of local wine and local whores." Shawr sounded as drunk as she felt. He laid down beside her and sighed deeply.

Daria had taken herself away from the taverns and brothels and restaurants, down toward the edge of the town where it overlooked the sea. A small park with tall, spindly trees and lush undergrowth was built on several layers across the rim of the shattered volcano, and, down below, moonlight glinted off the bay and made shadows of the six grand navy ships docked there. It was beautiful, and private, and it gave her a place to think.

She'd thought too much. Shawr's arrival was welcome.

"It feels like everything's changing," Shawr said.

"It might be," she agreed. "It will be."

Shawr propped himself up on one elbow. He shoved her in the side, hard. "And Admiral Hallarte will lead the way!"

Daria chuckled. Then she felt his hand still on her, just beneath her right breast. He leaned down, across her, shutting out the moon and stars. His wild hair was a halo about his head.

She felt his lips on hers, and his hand moved up over her breast. Daria shoved Shawr aside, hard, and sat up.

"What the fuck do you think you're doing?"

Shawr rolled back and knelt, three feet from her. He swayed slightly, but he was looking right at her.

"I thought we . . . I wanted . . ."

"You want what, exactly?" Daria said, fury rising in her, bubbling up amid the queasy wave of stale wine and strong, bad brandy. "You want me? You can't hold your drink and now you presume what, that you'll fuck me? Your *admiral*?"

"No, I—"

"No, you forget yourself. I may have offered you a certain latitude, but I see that was a mistake." She shook her head. "And here I thought I was the one with all the secrets, sailing the sea of lies, because that's the way Lameria—"

She saw Shawr's frown, even in the darkness. "Lameria?"

"Yes, Lameria. What of it?" Daria said, challenging him with a withering glare. "Shawr. My boy, my friend, you presumptuous little bastard. My past isn't my present. I lived as a slave before I became a Hallarte. But I *am* Hallarte. An officer . . . your admiral . . . and you think you can put your hands on me like you have the right? Like you own me?"

"You're . . . you can't be—"

"Amazing *that's* what you focus on," Daria said, shaking her head once more before grinning. "It's a mask, boy. This life of mine, it's a mask. But maybe it's time for the mask to fall away."

Shawr scrambled to his feet and backed away. "You can't be Bajuman. I kissed you."

He backed away farther, heading for the entrance to the park.

And for the first time that night, a moment of panic raced through her.

"Say nothing, Shawr. I'll tell them in my own time. Everything's changing. Everything." She regretted drinking so much. She wished she could think straight, analyze everything she'd been told tonight, all that she and Gree and the officers had discussed. "Say a word and I'll have you keelhauled for trying to force yourself on me."

She wished Shawr had never come. And yet, she was also glad. She felt as if she was seeing clearly for the first time in years. Now her secret was out. She'd always known that to tell one person would be to tell the world. That was how deep, dark secrets worked. And while she would have wished for a better circumstance, she wouldn't have taken it back even if she could.

"I need to go," he said, and he hurried from the park, footsteps disappearing into the distance.

Daria stood and walked to the wall. She looked over the railing and down the steep slope toward the port. A little while later a shadow appeared on the sloping path below her, still running, and she watched Shawr until he disappeared around a fold in the hillside.

Though a weight had been partially lifted, Daria knew that she had to venture down to the port to see if another, heavier weight was about to be applied.

She could not run from this.

Everything had changed.

⟡

Daria saw them turning her way as she approached. She knew what Shawr had done. One hand resting on the hilt of her sword, she did not break her stride. Pride carried her on, and a deep conviction that she was as good as any of them. She'd proven it time and again over the years, serving side by side with many of these men and women, gaining promotion, enjoying and welcoming their respect and admiration.

"There she is," Shawr said. He sounded even more drunk than before. Drunk on bitterness, perhaps. She wondered what would have happened if she'd let him carry on kissing her.

The sailors and officers who had come ashore and spent time on Igler's End milled on the dockside, many of them swaying, a few bloodied from drunken fights with locals or each other. They were silent, watching her approach.

The others from the ships had already reached the large jetty, eager to have their own time ashore. They, too, watched.

How so much can change so quickly, she thought, and she wondered what was happening in Lartha right then. She imagined terror stalking the streets and fear hiding in shadows. She hoped that Blane was well. She wished that she'd seen him one last time.

Daria Hallarte, not a true Hallarte yet still a proud user of that name, knew that she might die this night.

"There she is," Shawr said again. "Bajuman bitch!"

Apparently her threats had seemed hollow to him, or his humiliation at being rejected—and by a Bajuman—had overpowered his fear.

She was disappointed . . . and yet she wasn't surprised.

"Strong words, considering you tried to have sex with me," she said.

Shawr scoffed. "As if I'd ever knowingly touch one of your kind. Though if I had, it'd be no crime. The law wasn't made to protect the likes of you!"

"Admiral," Captain Gree said as she approached. He was standing close to Shawr, with one hand hooked into his belt, close to his sword. "Shawr has made a strong accusation. I don't believe him."

"Believe him," Daria said. "But also believe that he's a cowardly little fucker who put his hands and his tongue where they weren't invited—"

Gree turned to glare at Shawr, and so did some of the others. The boy flushed with humiliation, but he did not look away.

"—but yes, the bit you're talking about?" Daria went on. "That much is true. I'm Bajuman. I always have been and, here, I always will be." She pressed her closed fist to her chest. Kept her head up. Stared at them all as they stared at her, and at least half of them averted their eyes. She faced hundreds of men and women in the bright moonlight, and she had never felt so proud, nor so afraid. She realized with a start that it was fear of rejection more than fear of death that set her pulse racing.

"I've seen you bare armed a hundred times," Gree said. "Your scars—"

"From coral, as I've always said. You know the tale. I nearly drowned—"

"You should have, filth," someone said.

"—the coral raked my skin, stripped my brand. The sea changed my eyes. Others made assumptions about my identity before I could even regain consciousness. I simply chose to accept those claims. Not to argue the gift of a new life."

"Scum." Another voice.

It was Shawr who made the first move. He took Gree by surprise, darting away from the captain's grasp, drawing a blade from his boot, and by the time he reached Daria his teeth were bared in an animal snarl.

Like the filthy dog he was.

Daria stepped to one side and smacked him across the ear with her flat hand. He howled and stumbled, but also twisted with a deadly grace, knocking her hand aside and stabbing at the softness of her armpit, where the right cut would bleed her out. His knife never touched her. Instead, Shawr staggered, head lolling, and stared down at the tip of Captain Gree's sword, slick with blood where it had punched through his chest.

Captain Gree turned and let Shawr slide from his sword. The steward tumbled from the dock into the sea.

"Stabbed him in the fuckin' back," someone snarled.

Gree spun to snarl back. "That I did! A mutineer deserves no quarter. We're going to sort this out among us, but we'll do it orderly, and anyone who takes up arms against a superior officer gets the same as Shawr."

Daria stared at where Shawr had fallen. She'd believed him to be her friend, and now he was dead and gone. She'd kept her blade sheathed, willing to accept whatever came of her deception. But now she wondered if Gree might not be alone in his loyalty.

"I hid it from you all," she said. "I was the very thing you were all brought up to hate and despise. Your families and your society told you to loathe and look down upon me. Spit at me if I dared catch your eye. Kill me if I offended you."

"Deceiver!" someone shouted. A woman stepped forward, a deck-hand from the *Breath of Tikra,* but someone else shoved her aside.

"Let her speak!" the other sailor said. "She deserves that."

"She deserves nothing! Bajuman filth, I can't believe I shared my ship—"

"Lying bitch needs a keelhauling."

"She's commanded us for years, led us from one victory to another—"

"Betrayal—"

"Warrior—"

"Give her to the—"

"Quiet!" Captain Gree shouted. He was out there alone, standing between the milling group of Quandian sailors and the Bajuman admiral they had all followed for so long. He turned a full circle, never pausing with his back to anyone as he spoke.

"I'm taught to spit on Bajuman," he said. "They're lower than low. I'm brought up to despise what this woman is. But I can't find it in myself to do it. Can you? Our *admiral*? She's the finest officer I've ever known, and the thing I'm meant to hate. The two don't sit together, and it's shaking everything I thought I knew."

He turned his bloodied sword toward Daria, but she kept hers at her side. He'd just stopped a mutiny. But she wasn't going to let her guard down while the rest of the crew stood on the dock just behind him.

"We can't pretend there's not a cloud of mystery around Phela's taking the throne," Gree went on. "Mother dead. Brother dead. All the Bajumen are banished. Nobles have been executed, flung low, sold into slavery. Now she's cast aside all the traditions of our history to claim herself as head of the Faith. If she's willing to do all that, there's no telling what Queen Phela will do next." Gree fixed Daria with a hard stare. "I judge people by their actions, not their station. I'll judge Phela that way, and I'll do the same for the admiral. Whatever she was at birth, I know what she is *now*."

He paused a few steps before Daria and lowered his sword, planting its point in the ground before him.

"You still have my sword, Admiral Hallarte," he said. "And my respect. And Four damn it, my love."

A few sailors cheered. Then a few more. People started stepping forward, some of them jostled or jostling. Punches were thrown, some shouts were raised, but by the time Daria's heart had beaten out a minute, three-quarters of her fleet had gathered around Gree, and they were cheering her name.

She tried to hold back the tears, but in the end she had to let them flow. She had lost someone she had thought was a friend.

And yet she had gained not just most of her crew, but also her very self back.

⁓

Of over a thousand sailors in Admiral Hallarte's fleet of six ships, under two hundred chose to leave her command. None offered violence, although once or twice leading up to sunrise Daria feared that conflict might erupt. She guessed that in the end, even most of those who left were juggling their decision, and questioning inbred beliefs when set against the woman they had known and respected for so long.

She gave them a ship. She could have left them stranded on Igler's End, but that would have left her short crewed across six vessels, rather than fully crewed across five. Where they were going, that would not be a good idea. Sailing into a potential battle, she wanted her crews and ships to be at their prime.

Gree feared that those she'd let leave might end up fighting against them, but Daria thought not. She *hoped* not.

Confused, saddened, and also relieved at the weight of guilt that had been lifted from her shoulders, Daria proudly stood at the bow of the *Nayadine* as it left port, four other battleships following them out.

And then she saw something incredible. In the rosy light of dawn, several smaller vessels accompanied them. Then several more. Sailing ships, fishing boats, all seaworthy but none of them even a twentieth the size of the *Nayadine,* as they came closer she saw who was sailing them.

Bajumen. Dozens of them, perhaps hundreds. Following her navy.

Following *her.*

"I saw some of them listening," Gree said. He was standing beside her at the rail, and sensitive though she was, Daria could detect nothing different in his voice, nor how he conversed with her. If anything, he seemed even more respectful.

"At the dockside?" she asked.

Gree nodded. "Behind you, so you couldn't see, but they were hiding among the fishing nets and cages. Only a few of them, but they must have gone back up into the town and spread the word." He started chuckling. "A Bajuman." He laughed some more. "A Bajuman is in command of a Quandian fleet."

"And look at that," Daria said. More vessels sailed with them now, stringing out in a line all the way back into the bay. There must have been thirty small boats following in their wake. "They've only just got here, and now they're leaving again."

"Maybe they're fools," Gree said.

"Maybe we are."

He did not respond to that. Soon, they would all know the answer.

14

In the middle of the night, Yaris Teeg breathed with its own life. A life of wood and stone and iron nails, the creak and shift of wind and earth upon the structures built by ordinary people. Blane lay in bed and listened to those familiar night sounds, the living voice of Yaris Teeg, so soft that the other nighttime noises seemed loud in comparison. His fellow novices breathed deeply in sleep. Conavar snored, as she did nearly every night. The tiny feet of rats or mice scritch-scratched inside the walls, and balls of dust and grit skittered along the floor, carried by the draft that came from nowhere and everywhere at once.

Peaceful and quiet, somehow both solid and vulnerable, the darkness enveloped them all.

Blane licked his lips to wet them. The air inside Yaris Teeg never used to seem dry to him, but now he always felt parched. He opened his eyes and stared at the ceiling, still unused to the way light lingered for him now. A fortnight earlier, the room would have been so dark he would barely have been able to make out the beams in the ceiling. Now he could see the grain in the wood, the cobwebs in the corners, and the sparking blue static in the air. For better or worse he could smell the stink of the other novices on their mats and the blankets they slumbered beneath. Tomorrow was wash day, and Blane could not wait.

He'd only tasted magic thus far. Breathed it in, carefully mimicking the things he'd seen Queen Phela doing each time she'd gone down to learn. Every night he threw himself into a series of risks, both in shadowing Phela and the High Order priests who now served her—not to mention the Silent who guarded her—and in touching the magic itself, without anyone there to help him if things went awry.

But what other choice did he have?

It prickled his skin. Dried his mouth all hours of the day. Made him alert, even paranoid. He felt it growing in him as if he had planted a seed inside his flesh and nurtured it, but magic clearly took root faster than any tree or crop.

Blane inhaled, felt it flow, and thought, *No wonder they guard it so carefully, this power. And this is only a tiny portion!* While they walked the world, the Four would have been capable of anything. Of course. They were gods, or perceived as gods. His doubts still prickling, he was not sure the distinction made any real difference.

He rolled silently off his mat and crept from the bedchamber. In the corridor the shadows whispered, and he turned to see a shape stepping quietly in his wake. It ought to have panicked him, but instead Blane smiled and padded farther down the hall until he reached the stone staircase that led to the cellar and the tunnels beyond. There, two steps down, he turned and waited until the shape appeared.

In the dark, with only a thin veil of light from wall sconces back in the corridor, Gemmy's eyes gleamed.

"You're up late," he whispered as she took the first step.

Gemmy flinched, surprised to find that he'd stopped. In that light he must have seemed almost a ghost to her.

"You've been making a habit of being up late," she said. "Going places I'd wager you're forbidden to go."

Blane saw the flush in her face, the skittish way her eyes moved. "And you've been pretending to sleep. You're very good at it."

"Where are you going?" she whispered, glancing over her shoulder, seemingly just as anxious as he was that they might be discovered. Blane took that as a good sign.

Blane moved up so that only a single step separated them. She stood a few inches higher than him and he had to look up at her, though their bodies were close enough that when next he inhaled, he tasted the warmth of her exhalation, caught the scent of her. That breath came alive in him, the magic he'd tasted turning it into something more, a sampling of her that he found intoxicating.

And so Charin, god of Secrets, lets me delve into hers.

For a moment he could only shiver, trying not to meet her gaze, afraid of the intimacy. When Blane had begun this deception, he had seen the other novices as his enemies, just as he'd viewed all priests that way. And yet . . .

"Do you trust me?" he asked.

Gemmy smiled with a fragility unlike her. "What do I say to that? You've been sneaking off in the middle of the night for who knows how long."

"Do you trust me?"

She stared into his eyes, glanced away. "I trust you." With a puff of breath she met his gaze again. "Maybe more than that. But I'm afraid now. Can't you see that? With all this talk of magic, the way our teachers—ordinary priests and High Order alike—the way they glare at one another, the suspicion and hostility simmering here now that the queen has taken control of the Faith . . ."

"What?"

"It isn't supposed to be like this. I came to the priesthood seeking something, hoping to become something better. Whatever is to come now, it isn't what I envisioned."

Blane took her hand. Even as he did so, he felt the complications that would arise, the entanglement. Yet he held her hand tightly against his chest anyway, almost glad for such mundane problems when compared to his expanding consciousness.

"Not what I envisioned, either," he said. "But power is never what it seems on the surface."

"The Faith is not supposed to be like this," she breathed, and he could almost hear her pulse quicken.

"I can't tell you why I'm awake in the middle of the night, Gemmy," he said. "Not without putting you in danger. Secrets keep people safe. You can trust me, though, and trust that I wish you only health and happiness."

Gemmy placed one hand on his cheek. He felt the skin of her palm, the calluses of her fingers, rough from their hours of work. The stubble on his chin rasped beneath her touch.

"Is that all you wish for me?" she asked.

Gemmy slipped down to join him on his step. She wrapped her arms around him, pressed herself against him, and her lips brushed his. Gently at first, and then hungrily. He felt their dryness, felt the slick texture of her tongue, inhaled the complicated mélange of scents from her skin, her sex, her robe, and then his hands were inside her robe and racing over the hard muscles and soft curves of her. Her fingers dragged open his own robe.

She whispered his name. When he braced his back against the wall and lifted her onto him, they both whimpered. Breathless, they crashed into each other, tasted sweat and fear and abandon, and for a brief time all questions of trust were forgotten. It was only afterward, shuddering and spent and with Gemmy astride him, that those questions returned.

"I'm not . . ." Gemmy faltered. Smiled. Ground down on him a bit, shivering as he did with the echoes of their lovemaking. With a quiet laugh, she grabbed his chin and stared into his eyes, adopting a more serious mien. "I'm not in love with you or anything like that. I just needed this . . . connection."

"You needed a friend," Blane said softly.

He gave a gentle thrust and she bit her lip. He kissed that lip, then her throat, and at last they both seemed to breathe more freely. Gemmy put a hand on his chest and pushed backward, rising to sit a couple of steps above him, arranging her robe and closing her legs.

"We've broken our vows," she said, studying him.

Blane shrugged. "We've been vow breakers since our first day. Friends since our second, in spite of our differences."

She pondered that for a moment before she nodded and stood. "Put your cock away and go on about your secrets, friend. But be careful. A little bit of trust is a dangerous thing on Temple Hill lately."

With that, she turned and vanished back into the corridor.

Blane let out a breath and stood, arranged himself, and descended into the cellar. He went into the tunnels, and then up through the subterranean path that would take him to the Temple of Four. Into that ocean-blue room. Down the hidden spiral stairs. Deeper, and then deeper still, past traps that ought to have killed him and illusions meant to deceive him. Into the presence of the Four, the tombs of dead gods, to breathe the magic that still bled from their ancient corpses.

But with every step, he could still taste Gemmy on his lips.

ᨆ

Blane felt as if the Chamber of Tombs kept watch over him with a wary eye, as if taking his measure. The place had no name that he'd heard spoken, but in his mind he'd christened it that way—the Chamber of Tombs—although the phrase felt insufficient. This was no chamber, not even a cavern, but the honeycombed ruin of the First City, the place that had stood in Lartha's place before Lartha had even been built. There were columns down here, halfway-crumbled walls, stone edifices that appeared to have been bridges once upon a time. And yet the ruins he saw around him could not be mentally reconstructed into anything resembling a city, as if all the remnants of that ancient place had been collected into this cavern by some desperate curator, while all other evidence of a long-ago society had been scrubbed away.

The Chamber of Tombs breathed. It helped him to remain calm and centered, to remind himself of magic's dangers. The core of him, from balls to heart, clawed at the dirt with savage eagerness, wanting the power it felt crackling in the air around him. The urge to take as much magic as he could drink in, to revel in the inferno that these sparks could become, tempted him with every moment he spent in the Chamber of Tombs. He'd seen so many lives lost to spiza, but the taste of magic made him tremble more than any spiza addict.

Yet he did not succumb. Instead he simply breathed, relishing the moments, taking his time. Blane had seen Phela rushing. He had heard the warnings of the High Order, so he deliberately moved more slowly in his rituals than the queen did in her own. She had skilled priests around her, true magicians there to save her if anything went horribly awry. Blane had only echoes, the winking sparks of magic in the air, the impossible lights in corners, the water sluicing down through the rock of the land from the city high above, and the tombs of four beings or gods who had been dead for millennia.

On his knees in the pool, still in front of the veil of water, never daring to go any nearer to the tombs, he stripped to the waist and cupped his hands in the clear blueness. He stared at the intense color for a moment, then drank deeply. He drank again, and a third time, and then splashed the water over his face, anointing himself. Searching within, he found a calm oasis, a place where the seed of magic had been nurtured these past weeks. He began to murmur the words of the Fourth Rite, which he'd seen Queen Phela intoning the night before.

"You are certainly not what I expected."

The voice made Blane twist around. He tried to rise too quickly, and his feet slipped on the slick bottom of the pool, causing him to splash backward onto his arse. Gentle laughter came from the shadows and for a heartbeat he thought the gods themselves were talking to him. But only for a moment, and he soon realized how foolish such a thought was. Magic muddled minds, just like spiza.

The woman stepped into the flickering light, striated patterns of darkness across her body. Blane swore under his breath.

"Not the most graceful, are you, slave?"

Blane scrambled up, at least as far as his knees. "I'm a priest. A novice."

She waved a hand in the air as if the assertion might be smoke she could disperse. "Ah, of course you are. So we'll pretend you're not Bajuman. It's a courtesy I've never quite managed to turn into reality. But then again, you're not quite a novice either, are you? Unless my High Order have changed their teachings dramatically and failed to inform their apex."

Blane only lowered his gaze, unsure how to reply. He had seen Euphraxia before, of course, but never spoken with her or been this close. A dozen threads spun themselves out in his thoughts. Would he be imprisoned? Cast out of both the Faith and the main island, just another Bajuman to be banished? Or would she have him executed for what he knew?

Then another question brushed his mind.

What was she doing down here by herself?

Euphraxia took another step toward him, entering the edge of the pool. Ripples formed around her ankles as she stood staring down at him.

"I'm speaking to you, novice."

"Yes, Apex." What else could he say?

"I heard you whispering just now. I heard the words of a ritual you can't possibly have been taught, unless some renegade faction within the Faith is working to turn more priests into magicians without my approval. And I can think of only one reason anyone might do such a thing."

Blane blinked, the logic coalescing slowly.

"No, Apex. There's no—"

"Treachery."

"Apex, I swear to you. No one knows I'm here but you."

Euphraxia knelt before him in the pool, water soaking into the fine fabric of her robe, so different from the rough things the rest of the priesthood wore. Her eyes were dark and gleaming with cruel intellect.

"If only I could believe you. Once I might have, but I've had spies in my own house. Murder, novice. I've had *murder* in my own house."

"I don't know anything about—"

"Yet even if I did believe you, I'd have no choice. You see, nobody knows I'm here either."

Blane's throat had been dry before, but now it seemed to shrink. What was she saying? How did this make any sense?

"No choice," he echoed.

The apex clicked her tongue. "None."

She lifted a hand. The fingers twirled and danced and her lips moved with words so quiet that even there, so close, with so little other sound to compete with her voice, Blane could not hear more than a syllable or two. Yet he knew the contortions of her fingers, had heard those syllables before, and a chill went through him. A cold resignation. He swore inwardly, pressed his eyes closed, and when he opened them he saw the figures that had manifested in the cavern around them. The Phage. There were four of them, moving like swift mist with no weight of their own. They had weapons at their hips, swords and daggers that seemed nothing but gray smoke, until they touched them. The Phage themselves seemed to vanish where the light touched them and appear fully formed only where shadows ought to have hidden them, as if they were the opposite of ordinary flesh and bone. And perhaps they were.

"Please, Apex," Blane said, holding his hands out to her. "I can . . ."

But what could he say to her that would change what was about to happen? The truth would condemn him faster than any lie. Sorrow crushed him as he understood that his people would never be free.

The magic prickled his skin, crackled in the air all through the cavern, let him smell the anger and the curiosity and the bitterness of the woman before him. None of that would save him. It had all been a waste, a pantomime of false hope.

"Kill him," Euphraxia said. "Take the body so deep even the Four couldn't find it."

The Phage slipped toward him in a shimmering flow.

"Please don't," Blane whispered, talking to them now—to the dead—for he knew the apex had no mercy.

As if those words had unfrozen his limbs, he scrambled backward in the water, splashing deeper into the pool around the tombs. Water sluiced across his back and he realized he stood beneath the falling curtain of rain, piercing the liquid veil that separated the tombs on their wide raised area from the rest of the cavern.

The Phage came on faster. Inside his skull he heard a low keening as if they screamed, but only the most ancient part of him could hear it. Their mouths were wide and their hands reached out, fingers grasping air, lunging for his throat. Euphraxia might as well have vanished for all she mattered to him now.

"No!" he screamed, and he shot his hands out to defend himself.

He felt tides within him, an ebb and flow of power, and was surprised when the water leaped up into a clear blue wall, rushing upward from the pool to shield him. The Phage collided with it and the water flowed against them, shoving them backward half a dozen steps before they blinked out of reality and then back in again, closer to Blane than before.

Blane stood straighter and took a step away from the veil.

"What did you just do?" Euphraxia asked, striding into his peripheral vision to his left. "Did Dephine bless you? Did she protect you?"

The apex thought the damned gods had taken an interest in him. Maybe that would help him, maybe she would also take an interest and spare him if he let her believe that. But Blane had hidden himself and lowered his gaze and bent his back for the wealthy and privileged long enough. He'd *felt* the water rise, *felt* the connection between himself and the fabric of the world around him.

He had made that happen. Not any god, true or not.

"I protected *myself*," he said, and he reached out and muttered a string of words as he brought the shield of water up from the pool again. He smashed it against the Phage, knowing that to surprise them and push them back had been a trick that would work only once. But there were other elements and rituals he'd read or seen practiced by the High Order and the queen. He'd never have believed himself capable, but now he had seen the power at his disposal, and he felt it surge within him.

Yet there was still so much he didn't know. The magic was there, but could he actually wield it against the Phage? They screamed inside his skull again, crying out from the void of death. Blane looked at the one he could tell was Bajuman. "I'm doing this for you," he said to it. "For all of us."

Did the Phage warrior hesitate? Perhaps. But the others careened toward him again, shifting through and past the water he brought up in his defense. They drew their weapons and the blades and spikes grew solid. Blane shouted for them to stop, tried to call the wind against them, felt the bones of his spine and the stone beneath his feet tremble with the awakening of magic he did not yet know—

"Enough!" Euphraxia barked.

The Phage ignored her and tore at his robes, dragging him up out of the water, feet dangling beneath him. One lifted its ghostly hand holding a glimmering blade.

Euphraxia clapped her small hands. The sound blew through the cavern with such force that the water and air and the fabric of the Phage themselves rippled with it. They dropped Blane, darted away from him, and stood at wary attention as Blane crashed into the pool. Both fuming and yet resigned, ready to die, he rose to his feet again.

But the Phage did not attack.

The apex walked toward Blane, eyes narrowed as she examined him.

"You're an odd one," said the woman who'd ordered his death only moments before. "How is it you know what you do? You've learned a bit of magic, exposed yourself to the breath of the Four, and yet you don't appear to have gone mad. No drool, no ruined eyes, no blood or magic seeping from your orifices—not the ones I can see—"

"Nor the ones you can't see," Blane said, watching her, twitching his gaze over to glance at the Phage, waiting for her curiosity to end in his death.

"Smart, too, or so it seems. Strong-willed. Most Bajumen are broken things."

"Broken at birth by people like you," he replied, surprising himself with the freedom of his tongue. With death so near, why not speak his mind? He'd already decided the time for pretense had ended.

"You haven't answered me. How have you learned—"

"Magic? I know a bit. What I've learned I gleaned as Per Ristolo and the others introduce the queen to the rituals every night. I follow. They're teaching her—"

"Ah," the apex said, inhaling deeply. "It begins to make sense, now. They teach her and don't know they're teaching you as well."

"Something like that," Blane said.

Euphraxia approached him, hands at her sides. "You could be useful to me, novice. There is a rift in the Faith."

"I'm aware."

"I have no doubt you are. Have you chosen a side?"

"I'm Bajuman."

"You're a priest of the Faith. You've left all affiliations behind."

"And you, Apex? Did you leave all your old affiliations behind, all those years ago when you first joined the priesthood?"

"You *are* smart." Euphraxia smiled. "You've heard, then, that Queen Phela rescinded her mother's edict. She saved the lives of eleven thousand Bajumen."

"Only to banish them. Drive them from their homes. Send them off into the world with nothing to their names, to live or die as fate would decree."

"So you *have* chosen a side."

"I'm Bajuman. That is my side."

"But you'd agree we share certain interests?"

"In the immediate future, without a doubt," Blane admitted. "We'd both like to see Phela dead or imprisoned, or banished herself. Past that, I can make no promises. My aims may not be the same as yours."

"You say this knowing that I could kill you where you stand. I'm not sure if that's brave or idiotic, but for the moment it's enough. I think you'll be useful to me. As long as you are, you'll have my support. For now, continue as you've been. Learn what you can. Harsh times are coming, perhaps even war. If and when that happens, I'll summon you into my service."

"That's it? You trust me to just go on my way? What if I go straight to Per Santoger?"

The apex laughed. "You won't do that."

"I won't?"

"If you do, I'll kill you, and all the novices in your class." With a wave from the apex, the Phage vanished. The casual display of power chilled Blane to the core, and excited him at the same time.

"Go now," Euphraxia said, turning her back on him and kneeling in the pool, bowing her head toward the tombs of the gods. "They whisper to me and I must have silence if I am to hear them and whisper in return."

Blane didn't hesitate, although he yearned to hear the whispers between the apex and whatever responded. He knew he had already tempted his fortune enough tonight. He left the Chamber of Tombs and headed back toward the surface.

Everything had changed, but it would take time for him to discover whether that change would help him fulfill his ambitions or destroy them completely. His body still trembled with the aftereffects of the magic he'd conjured, the excitement of it and the prickling static left behind by his tapping of the sparking, glittering energy of that power.

Quietly, secretly, he had just chosen sides in a war not his own.

⁓

Demos did not feel safe, no matter what the tavern keeper said. He sat on the floor in a pantry at the back of the tavern amid cobwebs and shelves of dry goods and canned fruits and drying vegetables. There were sticky spots on the floor, spilled grains, squashed spiders, a rotten shirazi pepper, and a broad scattering of little brown dots that looked suspiciously like mouse turds. No sign of mice as yet, but he thought perhaps when the hour turned a bit later, they would appear.

The walls were thin. A general tumult punctuated by moments of uproarious laughter reached him, and part of him felt warmed. It was good to hear laughter again, to know that despite the chaos and murder and the rising oppression in Quandis, people could still find things to make them forget their troubles. Footsteps creaked overhead where there were rooms for let, some of them with long-term occupants and others filled an hour at a time. Demos had never been inside the Snake's Tail Tavern before, but he'd known of it most of his life. He'd never crossed the threshold because he was the son of Baron Kallistrate, and surely would be baron himself one day. His father had schooled him on the lessons of avoiding the appearance of impropriety. The irony sickened him.

The Snake's Tail was perched on the edge of the river Susk, right at the base of Palace Hill and in the shadow of Scholar's Bridge, the oldest and most ornate of the seventy-seven bridges in Lartha. Scholar's Bridge connected Palace Hill to Hartshorn Hill, where the historians and educators of the kingdom made their home. Demos had always held a great deal of respect for Clan Hartshorn. He wondered what they made of Phela now.

He shifted position. The mat upon which he sat had its share of stains whose history he preferred never to discover. Uncomfortable and filthy, it had seen nothing but better days, and he had a feeling he knew what the tavern keeper used it for, there in the dry pantry.

Come on, Tollivar, he thought.

The boy had been gone four hours at least, and there was little Demos could do to combat his boredom and anxiety. Out in the tavern there would be many who knew his face. He'd spent two nights in a barn, and now here he was. He might've visited a dozen homes, but there was no way to know the allegiances of his former allies and friends. And even if he could be certain, they had servants and cousins and neighbors. Here at the base of Palace Hill, at the very least, Myrinne would not have to go far. That was *if* Tollivar could deliver on his promises, if the kitchen slave who fed the strays behind the palace truly was the Bajuman boy's cousin, through some inter-breeding no one would dare admit. But Demos had learned to trust the boy. He'd learned also that he knew nothing about the inner world of Quandian slaves, their cultures and relationships, and even less when the topic narrowed itself down to Bajumen. He was at the mercy of this boy whose presence he'd have ignored not long ago.

Because you're a fool, he told himself.

There was no part of him that wished to argue the point.

A creak and scuff came from beyond the pantry door and Demos froze. Footsteps approached and he picked up the long kitchen knife he'd taken while passing through. As quietly as possible, he shifted forward off the mat, crouched on one knee in the slash of light that came through the gap between door and frame.

The door opened. His grip tightened. He expected to see Tolli-var but was taking no chances, and indeed it was not Tollivar but a smiling, beautiful serving girl, a mass of curly hair bouncing as she turned away from the man she'd led to the pantry by the hand. Demos saw it all clearly in that first instant—the playful gleam in her eyes, the way she shushed her would-be lover, the dirty mat upon which he'd been sitting, available for anyone who might want it . . .

Framed in the lamplight from the dingy kitchen, the girl looked fragile and beautiful. She was laughing and so sweet that it took Demos an extra second to see that the lucky bastard she tugged by the hand wore the uniform of the City Guard.

"Fucking hells," Demos rasped.

The serving girl let out a little gasp and froze in place. The Guardsman's lustful grin turned to a scowl at the interruption, but Demos saw the moment when irritation turned to recognition. The man's eyes narrowed and he took a step backward. A moment's hesitation, that was all, and then he'd shout an alarm and there would be others, and Demos would be enslaved again, or dead.

The girl squeaked as Demos lunged, shoved her aside, and thrust the kitchen knife through the Guardsman's throat. He felt the dull, dirty blade punch through skin and muscle and then blood sluiced along its length and showered to the floor. He left the knife where it had lodged and spun toward the girl. She drew a deep breath to scream and he was on her, one hand over her mouth. She clawed at his arms and punched him in the temple hard enough that his grip slipped for a moment, and she managed half a shout before he struck her silent. She crashed into shelves full of grain sacks and jarred fruits and fell to her knees, torn bags spilling grain down on top of her.

She took a breath. Demos put a finger to his lips.

"Shush. Don't die for this."

The warning stilled her. Before she could think it over, he dragged the dead Guardsman away from the door and closed her inside. The ruckus had been loud but the laughter and boisterous conversation in the tavern was louder. Still he had no idea how much time he might have, and he needed to be somewhere else when the next person entered the kitchen. The tavern keeper had been willing to help, but a dead Guardsman on his floor would almost certainly make him reconsider.

He glanced at the kitchen knife jutting from the man's throat, then at the sword that hung in its scabbard at his hip. Demos opted for the sword, unbelted it and then fastened it around his own waist, so the scabbard hung on his left hip. As he rushed for the back door, he paused a moment. There had to be some way for him to leave a message for Tollivar so the boy could find him.

But then the serving girl began to shout, not as terrified of Demos as he'd hoped. He had run out of time.

The door latch stuck a moment, but he muscled it open, knocking rust away and stumbling out into the half-moon night. In the shadows behind the tavern, garbage and broken tables and chairs had been stacked high. The smell rushed into his nose but he ignored it, making for the trees that lined the road, already focused on the darkness beneath the Scholar's Bridge. Perhaps there he could find a little boat and escape along the river.

At this moment, escape was the only thing he could focus on. He would return for Myrinne at some point, and for his mother, but it wouldn't be long before the City Guard found their dead man and began tearing every house apart searching for his killer. Demos had no doubt that Queen Phela would give them a long leash.

His thoughts churned. If he stayed, they'd catch him for sure, maybe kill him on the spot. If he fled, at least he might figure a way out of this. It might also allow him time to get a message to Myrinne, even if only to warn her about Euphraxia's plan for rebellion. With that information, the queen might still spare him.

A path led through a copse of trees on the hillside. He raced toward the deeper shadows there and nearly stumbled when he spotted two figures emerging from the trees. Out in the yellow gloom of the half-moon night, he was exposed, with no chance of going unnoticed. He drew his stolen sword, hoping he would not have to bloody it.

Then he saw the way the smaller figure hurried, and how the taller one glanced back the way they'd come as if worried they might be pursued. He saw the determination in her stride and knew. He ran to her.

Myrinne met him there under the half-moon. Tollivar urged them in hushed tones to move swiftly, but still Demos took her in his arms and she kissed him. Wanted for murder, an escaped slave, his face known throughout the city . . . still, he had never felt so free.

15

The port town of Suskmouth had seen its share of ships over the years, but never anything like the strange flotilla that sailed into its harbor that morning. On the deck of her flagship, Daria watched through her telescope as fishermen stopped in the midst of unloading their morning haul to stare at the naval ships and the motley array of boats that accompanied them. Children playing on the docks ceased their games and skirmishes and ran the length of the longest pier to gaze in wonder. On either side of the mouth of the river, men and women began to gather. Daria knew that what they saw must have felt ominous to them, and it was no surprise when she spotted the full complement of Suskmouth's army garrison taking up positions along the dock and harbor wall. Hidden away behind the fortifications, gun crews would be zeroing their aim.

Good, she thought. It was important that they see her coming.

The ship swayed in the harbor, and the anchor chain rattled as it unspooled. The crew scampered among the masts, lowering the sails.

"Ready to go ashore, Admiral?" Captain Gree asked, striding along the deck toward her.

Daria closed the telescope and held it in her left hand. Three sailors had followed in Captain Gree's wake and now stood at attention behind him. The one woman among them stood a head taller than any of the men, as dark as cooled lava, an outlander from one of the volcanic islands on the eastern edge of the Ring. Her name was Sujita, and aside from Demos Kallistrate, Daria had never served with a better fighter, or one more loyal. It helped her to know that sailors like Sujita had stayed with her, despite her revelation. Others had refused to serve under her command, but in truth Daria had expected many more to abandon her. If Sujita had stayed, it wasn't just out of loyalty to her admiral. It meant she believed in the fight, and that was heartening.

"These are the three you've chosen?" she asked.

"You said three who could fight but were smart enough to know when to keep their mouths shut," Captain Gree said. "Hard to find that combination in sailors."

Daria studied the three of them again. Sujita, a man called Lorizo whom she knew was a devil with a sword in his hand, and a third who seemed too young for this mission.

"I don't know you," she said, pausing in her inspection to study him a bit closer.

"Name's Hudnall, sir. Honored, sir."

Captain Gree smiled. "Hudnall's been cooking for us since the last time we left port. The young man's got a gift when it comes to turning tasteless ingredients into something palatable. Last week I saw him scrap with Bospur in the mess hall. Trust me. He can more than handle himself."

"That true, Hudnall?" Daria asked.

The sailor—no more than eighteen—stood a bit straighter, unwilling to meet her gaze. "True enough, Admiral. I don't like a scrap, but I ain't ever lost one."

"Good enough for me," Daria said. She walked to the railing and looked out at the fishing boats and skiffs, some of which should never have made it this far from the Ring, all of them filled with Bajuman slaves ready and willing to fight. "And this? Putting together an army that's half composed of rabble most sailors never notice unless they want a chamber pot emptied or a secret fuck that no one will ever speak of? You're willing to fight alongside Bajumen?"

None of them spoke, not even Captain Gree. The ship creaked, a pulley clanged against the foremast, and the shouts of the crews going about their duties filled the air.

Daria turned to face Gree and his three handpicked sailors. Her personal guard to go ashore, these three, and it haunted her that there weren't more she knew well, more she trusted. Demos would have been her first choice, her right hand, but he was not here. *And what will he think,* she wondered, *when he learns what you are? Will it be the same as with Shawr? Will he shun you?*

"Nothing to say?" she prodded.

"We're with you, Admiral Hallarte," Sujita said. "Yesterday, today, and tomorrow."

Daria exhaled. She studied Lorizo, who only nodded, one hand resting on the pommel of his sword. That left only the boy, Hudnall, who muttered something quietly.

"Speak up!" Captain Gree snapped.

Hudnall raised his eyes and stared at Daria. "Permission to speak freely, Admiral?"

"By all means. If we're all going to be getting to know one another better, you'll all need to speak your minds when we're alone, and keep quiet when we're not."

Hudnall glanced at the deck and gave a little shrug. "I'm a quarter Bajuman myself."

Gree, Lorizo, and Sujita all turned to gaze at him in surprise.

"A quarter," Daria repeated.

"My mother's mother," Hudnall said quietly. "Always been

ashamed of it." He glanced out at the dozens of little boats around them, then met her eyes again. "Until now, Admiral. I'm with you, whatever it takes."

Lorizo grinned. "I'm a fucking heathen, Admiral. No Penter, mind you, just a common everyday atheist. The priests up on Temple Hill might be full of shit, but at least for the most part they seem to want what's best for Quandis. Our new queen, though . . . if she's killing nobles and slaughtering or banishing a whole race, taking over the fucking Faith by force . . . well, I was never too fond of the idea of monarchy to begin with."

Sujita burst into laughter so infectious that even Daria couldn't help smiling.

"What do you find so amusing?" Lorizo sniffed.

"Haven't heard you say more than three words at a time since I met you. I wasn't sure you knew that many of them," the towering woman said.

Captain Gree took a step forward and clicked his heels together, standing at attention. "If they'll do, Admiral, it's time for you to go ashore. Dinghy's waiting."

"Let's do it, then," Daria said, smile fading. "Time to see whose side the Suskmouth garrison will be on."

The admiral led the way, with this new contingent of her loyalists falling in behind her. Ever since her revelation she'd been wary of the crew, wondering what might be going on aboard the other four ships under her command. Thus far there had been no mutiny, no desertion, but they were at the main island of Quandis now, with the capital a day's hard ride inland. If any of them were having second thoughts, she would know soon enough.

"Captain," she said as she reached the thick rope ladder that led down to the dinghy. Hesitating a moment, she reached inside her jacket to withdraw a small envelope bearing her seal in blue wax. When Daria spoke again, she lowered her voice and put her back to the others, so that only Captain Gree might hear. "Do we have a runner left in the fleet who has half a brain?"

Visibly stifling his curiosity, the captain nodded. "Fissel on the *Royal Dawn*. Quick and quiet as a mouse, smarter than average, too ugly for anyone's eyes to linger overlong upon his face."

Daria handed him the envelope. "Get this to Fissel. Your hand to his, Captain. Have him deliver it to Yaris Teeg, to a novice priest named Blane and to no one else."

"It shall be done."

"No one else," Daria repeated.

Then she started down the rope ladder. Her shore team had already piled into the dinghy. Her sword and other weapons were heavy at her hip, but the weight felt satisfying. Whatever happened now, there would be no going back.

Sujita pushed off and Lorizo began to row. It felt as if time had begun to speed up. The waves rocked them and the morning sun burned its way across the sky. Up and down the harbor were the little boats of the Bajumen who had fled this island only weeks ago, and now they were returning to the place from which they'd been forced, and the lives that had been torn away from them. Daria might not look like one of them anymore, but not since she had been beaten half to death and chucked into the water had she felt so much like a Bajuman.

At the pier they were met by half a dozen rough fishermen, an officious little man who claimed to speak for the mayor of Suskmouth, and roughly forty soldiers garrisoned in the town. There'd be another force on the other side of the river's mouth, in the old fort that perched there and from which they could control the boom that blocked boats from entering the river without authorization. There would be cannons at the ready behind the low stone walls, too. She wasn't exactly worried—she'd left her forces with instructions to ready their own guns. The five battleships could blast and flatten Suskmouth's seafront in a matter of minutes, if the need arose.

Daria waited until the first of the faded fishing boats pulled up behind her dinghy. She caught the eye of the old Ring islander piloting that boat and an aging but formidable-looking Bajuman. She nodded to the two men and they did the same in return. Only then did Daria step off onto the floating dock and start up to the pier with Hudnall, Sujita, Lorizo, and three Bajumen from that fishing boat, walking up the ramp behind her.

On the pier, the fishermen backed away, leaving the mayor's bootlick and the soldiers to greet them. The garrison's lieutenant stepped forward, one hand on the hilt of a dagger in her belt, casually, as if this was her natural pose. Then, as if only now remembering protocol, she snapped to attention and saluted.

"Raise the boom, Lieutenant," Daria said.

"Admiral Hallarte. Welcome back to Suskmouth." She glanced at the Bajumen in confusion. "Have you . . . have you returned to answer Queen Phela's summons for assistance?"

Daria smiled. To her left, Lorizo shifted slightly, his hand only inches from the grip of his sword.

"In a sense, I have," she replied. "But you seem nervous, Lieutenant. Are you distracted by the presence of Bajumen? Surely not, given these very same thousands passed through Suskmouth only recently and were given your kind assistance in departing. Now, again I ask you . . . raise the boom."

The lieutenant had shaved the left side of her head and tattooed it with images of sea monsters from the Outer Ring. In Lartha, she'd have been stripped of her rank and set to digging ditches, but here she was in command.

"I'm not distracted by them, Admiral," she said, "though I'm forced to wonder about their return so soon after their banishment. You know the queen has ordered that any Bajumen remaining on the main island are to be executed."

Here came the moment, then.

Daria rose to her full height, made sure she wore no trace of a smile. "The sea and the gods and the grip of death changed me, Lieutenant, but I'm Bajuman myself. My eyes don't give me away, but once they were the same winter blue as the rest of my people."

A ripple of angry muttering swept the garrison soldiers and the fishermen. The mayor's bootlick recoiled so completely that he stumbled and bumped into a soldier, who rudely brushed him aside. Someone in the crowd called her a deceitful whore, but most of those murmurs were more of shock than condemnation.

Most.

Daria saw a flurry of movement to her left. A short, stocky soldier knelt and brought up the small crossbow from his belt, aiming past her left shoulder toward the Bajuman behind her. She reacted quickly, plucking a throwing star from her belt and letting it fly in the same movement. It whistled through the air and struck the soldier in the throat.

His eyes went wide. He coughed, gagged, and when he tugged the razor-sharp blade from his flesh, blood began to spurt.

Two more soldiers stepped forward and aimed their crossbows, but Sujita was already moving, darting forward and piercing one soldier through the face with her sword. The other ducked down and back, switching his aim to Sujita.

Daria felt the air swish past her ear as a short spear flew and found its mark in the soldier's gut. He went down, and Hudnall darted past her ready to finish the job.

"Wait!" Daria said. Sword in her hand, she knew that Lorizo and the three Bajumen were also crouched and ready to fight. Mere seconds had passed, but already three soldiers were down, two dead or dying, the other badly wounded. "Wait," she said again, and she looked the lieutenant in the eye.

"Stand fast!" the lieutenant shouted.

"Is nobody going to do anything?" the mayor's man cried. "She's standing right there! She's just told you she's Bajuman and she's brought them all back. The queen—"

A huge soldier covered the politician's whole face with one giant hand and shoved him backward. The man's arms pinwheeled and others got out of the way, and if he hadn't fallen and bounced his skull off the pier, he'd have gone off the side and into the drink.

"He's not wrong," another soldier said, sneering as he glanced at the lieutenant. "Fucking Bajuman trash and we're meant to salute her? Cut off her head and Her Majesty'll pin a medal on your chest."

The lieutenant glanced at her fallen men. She studied the trio of sailors around Daria, looked at the Bajumen there on the pier with them, and then out at the warships and the long line of motley vessels that had brought the banished slaves back home.

"No question about it, Admiral," the lieutenant said. "Forgive my impulsive troops, but you've put me in a bad spot. I should lock you in irons, deliver you to Lartha. Or just save the time and kill you right here."

"You can try," Daria replied.

The lieutenant shifted nervously. "What are you doing here, Admiral, if you're not coming to help the queen put down the unrest in the capital?"

Daria liked the monster tattoos on her scalp and the way her remaining hair hung in a jagged curtain on the other side. She liked the glint of mischief in the woman's eyes.

She did not want to kill her.

"Queen Phela has declared herself leader of the Faith," Daria said. "She's silencing all those who would oppose her with intimidation, death, or imprisonment. She's executed members of the nobility and others and is defying generations of tradition and understanding. We've come to—"

"Traitorous Bajuman bitch!" shouted the soldier who'd wanted her head. He rushed forward, drawing a dagger from his belt.

Daria rolled her eyes as she prepared to defend herself, but before she needed to do more, the lieutenant tripped the soldier, giving him a shove to help him along the way, and the man went tumbling off the pier. He struck the ramp on the way down and cried out in pain, then splashed into the water.

"Anyone else wanting to act without my orders?" the lieutenant shouted, turning her back on Daria to face her troops. She plucked a dropped crossbow from the ground, checked its draw, walked to the edge of the harbor, and shot the soldier she'd just sent splashing into the water. The bolt hit him in the eye.

"*Anyone* else? I fucking dare you."

No one dared.

The lieutenant turned back to Daria. Though anger had surged in her voice, her breathing was still calm and slow, and Daria guessed her heartbeat had hardly risen at all.

"So what's your intention?" she asked.

Tension sang in the air, but Daria kept her composure.

"I have five naval ships and their crews with me," she said, "as well as a thousand banished Bajumen returned to fight. I see plenty of differences among your troops—dark and light skins, soldiers from Quandis and the Ring, and even a few with ancestors from beyond. But these aren't differences that matter. Because we're all the same in wanting freedom, and a ruler who respects their position rather than misusing it. Queen Phela's mother went mad, and it seems to have infected the daughter as well. Quandis is in turmoil. We've come not to extinguish the sparks of rebellion against Phela, but to feed the flames."

The lieutenant's mischievous eyes gleamed as she grinned at Daria. "Hells, Admiral . . . why didn't you just say so?" Then the lieutenant turned to her garrison, a few of them grumbling, but most of them mumbling and nodding their heads in agreement. "Martyn!" she shouted at a potbellied sergeant.

"Yes, Lieutenant?"

"Raise the boom."

⁀◡

With Myrinne's hand in his, Demos could almost believe that any-thing might be a good idea. When she kissed him and he inhaled her scent, when he tangled his fingers in her hair, he felt courage and hope flood into his heart. He stood taller, and the bruises and aches from his enslavement diminished. But even blinded by her confi-dence, he still thought she might be about to get all three of them killed.

They'd spent most of the night in a grist mill at the base of Palace Hill, just on the other side of Scholar's Bridge from the tav-ern where Demos had stabbed a member of the City Guard in the throat. Every fiber of his being screamed to flee the city, to get into the river somehow and keep floating till he reached Suskmouth. In his current state, a branded slave and a fugitive, Admiral Hallarte would never take him back into the fleet, but he knew that the pirate captains were always hiring, and half of them bore brands themselves. That was a joke now, a very small one that he made with himself, though as a boy he'd dreamed of being a pirate. The reality seemed more like a nightmare.

Myrinne had told him about his mother's death. Ailing since his father's execution and Cyrus's death, though comfortable with Clan Daklan, she had simply faded away. Grief had taken her. For Demos the news had not come as a shock, because in truth he had been expecting it every day. But he'd cried in Myrinne's arms nevertheless. So much taken from him, so many people he loved.

At least now he was trying to make amends.

"My love," Demos said as gently as possible, "this seems like a terrible idea."

Myrinne tugged his hand and they kept walking. Outside the walls of the palace itself, Palace Hill teemed with life. Courtiers and rich merchants who were not members of one of the Five

Great Clans had built up the hill with grandly designed homes that were stacked—sometimes literally—on top of one another. Nobles from foreign lands lived in the shadow of the palace, there to keep good relations with the Crown of Quandis and to negotiate trade agreements. Among the homes and inns were a multitude of shops of all sorts, from dressmakers and milliners to jewelers and bakers. Myrinne and Demos walked hand in hand, her in the sort of veil sometimes worn by maidens from religious families and him in the hooded robe of a Kolbarite diplomat, stolen from the man's carriage as his driver helped him inside after some morning jaunt or another.

Tollivar had promised to meet them at their destination. How he intended to make his way up Palace Hill unnoticed, Demos didn't know. Once it would have been a simple task for a Bajuman child to move unseen, but now his presence would shock any who spotted him. In weeks, the world had changed. At the Temple of Four he'd be safe, but anywhere else in the city, he'd be killed by the first City Guard he encountered.

The day had turned cloudy, the temperature falling as the morning progressed. In a narrow street near the top of the hill, they passed a tailor's shop and the studio of a portrait artist whose mother had once painted a portrait of the late Queen Lysandra's father, King Bejin, or so said the sign in the studio's window. A few steps past the artist's studio, near the end of the quaint little street, Demos paused and turned to her.

"You can't keep ignoring me."

Myrinne tucked a lock of hair behind her ear. He could make out the shape of her face behind the sky-blue lace veil. "I love you," she said, "but you've got to trust me. This is the only way."

He moved closer to her. "We should be fleeing," he whispered.

"We can't."

"Why not?"

Myrinne squeezed his hands in hers, fixed her gaze on his. "My sister is ruining this city. The rest of the nation will follow. She must be stopped."

"By us?"

"I don't know the answer to that. Not yet. I know I was the first to suggest we flee together, but if there's any chance of us getting out of Lartha alive and together, we've got to buy ourselves time. That means you standing in front of the queen and telling her what you've learned. I don't trust her word, but I trust her fury. We need that fury directed elsewhere."

Demos sighed. "I see the logic. Though I'm afraid she's no longer the sort who follows any rational logic."

Myrinne did not bother to lift her veil before she kissed him. The lace kept their lips from touching, but the rough scrape of the fabric made him shiver. It had been far too long since he'd traced the lines of her body with his hands. Queen Phela might have him executed eventually, but in that moment he prayed to Anselom that he would make love to Myrinne one more time before he died.

Carriage wheels clattered and a horse chuffed behind them, and the two of them shifted out of its path. Demos turned his back to it, hoping it wasn't the Kolbarite diplomat's carriage. That would be just his luck, being stopped because of his stolen robe instead of his noble name or the murder of a Guardsman.

But the carriage rolled on. Demos grinned at Myrinne and they fell in behind it, marching in its wake as if part of some entourage. The carriage rattled along to the end of the road and then headed downhill. Demos and Myrinne turned uphill, and now there was no more hiding. A sprinkle of rain began to fall, and the chilly wind whipped along the much broader road. The small guardhouse beside the palace gate contained one Guardswoman. Four other Guards were visible, though two of them were focused on the ragtag camp of the queen's subjects who always seemed to be clustered to the left of the gates—dozens of the queen's subjects who had come to make some entreaty or other, to beg her help or forgiveness.

Which is precisely what I'm here to do, Demos thought.

A child in a jacket comically large on him darted from the gathered citizens. He wore a fisherman's cap pulled down over his face, hiding his hair entirely. As the rain picked up and the boy rushed toward them, Demos realized this was Tollivar. He grinned, though he was not at all surprised that the sneaky little bastard had made it all the way to the gate undiscovered.

A rugged-faced Guardsman in a faded uniform came forward to challenge them, not yet reaching for his sword but very evidently willing. Demos used his left hand to cover the brand on his right.

"Get in line with the others," he snapped, gesturing toward the huddled group.

Myrinne removed her veil, letting it dangle from her fingers, down at her side. "Open the gates, Sergeant."

She never stopped moving, striding right up to the seasoned Guardsman. The two who were overseeing the supplicants paid no attention, but the woman came out of the guardhouse and she and the others took positions in front of the gate, hands very clearly on the pommels of their swords.

Swords.

Fuck. Demos had forgotten all about the Guardsman's sword dangling in its scabbard from the belt around his waist. He felt his face flush but kept his head tilted downward, hiding as best he could beneath his stolen hood.

"Princess Myrinne?" the aging Guardsman said.

"I'm glad you recognize me. It will make this moment much easier. Open the gates."

"For you, of course," he replied. "But you know better than anyone what the queen's law states regarding entry into the palace."

Too much to hope, Demos thought. *It was always going to come to this.*

He threw back his hood and drew aside the cloak to reveal the sword at his side. The Guardsman swore and drew his own blade.

"Kallistrate," the man snarled, full of hatred but no surprise. And why should they be surprised, when by now the whole city must know of his escape from the apex's home?

Demos calmly raised his hands. "Sergeant, I don't think either of us wants to die today, but I promise you that if you come anywhere near me or the princess, you'll lose your head. I'm not confident I can kill five of you, but I know you'll die first." He gestured to the larger of the two Guards by the gates. "Then him. Probably at least one more. I suppose it'll be up to the rest of you which one."

"Quiet, you fool," Myrinne snapped at him.

Demos frowned at her, telling himself she'd meant it lovingly. "I haven't even drawn my sword."

The other two by the gates had drawn theirs, though, and the two watching over the gathered citizens had finally noticed the trouble and were making their way over.

Myrinne reached out for Tollivar and pulled the boy to her. She ripped off his hat to reveal his blond hair, and those winter eyes.

"What are you doing, Princess?" the sergeant asked, unsure now, almost mystified.

"Returning home with my fiancé and a new friend."

"A Bajuman child," one of the Guards muttered. "What do we—"

The sergeant seemed to realize that with his sword held a certain way, it might seem as if he meant harm to the princess. Uncertainty etched his brow.

"Demos Kallistrate is an escaped slave wanted for murdering the praejis of the house of Apex Euphraxia. There was another murder last night, in a downhill tavern," the sergeant said. "There's a witness who described the killer. We believe . . . your fiancé is the man. And that sword at his hip tells enough of the story that I'm convinced."

Myrinne gave Tollivar a little shove. The boy stumbled against

Demos, who had to catch him. Weaponless, Myrinne approached the Guardsman, her greater height forcing him to look up at her.

"I've seen you at this gate a thousand times, Sergeant, but I don't know your name."

Off-balance, eyes shifting to glance at Demos, the sergeant steadied his grip on his sword. "Rokai, Princess."

"Sergeant Rokai. I want to be very clear." She glanced past him at the other Guardsmen. Many supplicants had stood and shuffled closer, but not so close that a sword might find them if a fight broke out. "I am the daughter of Lysandra, the granddaughter of Bejin, the sister of Queen Phela, who is waiting to hear the words my fiancé, Demos Kallistrate, is prepared to speak. The queen is head of the Faith now, so the apex will have to take up the question of Demos's supposed enslavement with her. Whatever crimes you may accuse him of, it is up to the queen to determine his guilt or innocence, is it not?"

Frustrated, the sergeant glanced at the ground, as if the answer might await him between the cobblestones.

"She's got you there," Demos said.

Tollivar elbowed him in the gut. Demos huffed but said nothing more.

"Is it not?" Myrinne repeated.

"It is," the sergeant allowed.

"Then we will let her decide, after she's heard what he has to say."

Sergeant Rokai shook his head. "Princess, I'm sorry. I cannot—"

Myrinne reached back, lightning-quick, and drew the sword from the scabbard at Demos's side. He tried to reach for her, but she turned on the astonished sergeant. The Guardsman tried to defend himself, but Myrinne was too swift. She twisted, easily parried, and plunged the sword into the side of his neck, where his armor could not protect him.

"Gods, Myr, what are you doing?" Demos shouted, his words lost in the cries of the waiting people and Guardsmen.

"We're going to die," Tollivar whispered.

Myrinne did not take so much as a backward step. Instead, she brandished the bloody sword toward the other Guardsmen as their sergeant lay dying on the ground.

"Sergeant Rokai disobeyed a direct command from a princess of the Crown," she said. "I am Myrinne of Quandis. The Blood of the Four runs in my veins. This man and this boy are under my protection. I tell you now, and for the last time, to open that fucking door."

They opened the door.

16

As both Queen of Quandis and Head of the Faith, Phela could never betray any doubts about what she was doing, nor any sense of weakness or uncertainty. The Faith had split in two almost immediately upon her proclamation that the Crown now ruled over the priesthood. Word had traveled quickly down into the ranks, from High Order member to ordinary priest to novice, from Temple of Four to Yaris Teeg. Per Stellan had been her greatest source of information about the war of loyalty tearing the priesthood apart. The one-eyed woman came from the Ring. She'd spent time with pirates and Penters and atheists and kept her faith firm. Per Stellan believed in Phela's claim, that the Blood of the Four ran in her veins and gave her dominion over the Temple of Four. She agreed with Phela's aims to use magic to make the land truly great once more—forging peace with foreign lands, forcing trade agreements, expanding their influence, all with the heavy threat of magic underpinning everything that Queen Phela did or said. So the queen knew that factions had formed and friends had become enemies, and she knew which of the High Order priests were with her and against her.

Strife and chaos had erupted, but Phela cared nothing for such disruptions. If anything, she welcomed them as she worked to consolidate her own powers. She was firm in her actions and aims, focused in her aspirations and where they would take her. In the end, Quandis would be the better for it.

Her doubts and uncertainties were only dreams.

Yet they were dreams that she could feel and hear, taste and smell, and she knew that if she were to address them with the apex, or Per Ristolo, or even Dafna the Voice, they would tell her things she did not wish to know. If she ventured down to the Wall of the Four—that buried place she had visited many times, but which she had studied far less than she should have—she would find answers to the doubts presenting themselves to her now. In sleep. In dreams.

In her dreams, Lartha had been laid waste, its seven great hills cracked by violent upheavals, buildings fallen or burned to the ground. The Blood Spire was shattered halfway up, its upper section crumbled to nothing and scattered around Palace Hill like shards of frozen blood. The scent of decay hung over the once-great city, as if its whole population had huddled in their basements and died. A terrific wind swept in from the north and slowly, slowly settled a film of glimmering ice across the ruins, hiding her city from view. Perhaps after the wind would come snow, burying the sad remains beneath an eon-long winter. Water washed through the city's lower extremes, carrying with it the detritus of a dying land—upturned boats, bloated cattle corpses, splintered timbers from shattered buildings, uprooted trees, all mixed into a sad stew.

In the city, behind the shadows and beneath the places where the dead rotted into history, shades of things unknown and unknowable stirred, promising a revelation of utter horror.

It was always then that Phela woke. Sweating and cursing, grasping on to the new day and clinging on for dear life.

Five times she had suffered these nightmares, each time during sleep following a descent to the tombs. She mentioned them to no one. She kept them to herself because she was Queen of Quandis and Head of the Faith, the strongest and most important person in the land, and soon she would have access to the full magic of the Four, and she would become the Eternal Queen. The dreams were merely a way for her mind to expand and comprehend the enormity of what was happening to her. They were what she could do to this world, should she wish it so.

She would never wish that upon Lartha and Quandis. Everything she did was for the good of the land and its people, and she knew that her mother would be proud.

"You look tired, Majesty."

Her sister's voice startled Phela from her thoughts. She snapped up a wineglass and took a long swig, covering her expression and allowing herself time to gather her senses. Sparks of light danced in her vision. She heard the breath of mice, the sound of a gull's wings somewhere over the city, and she smelled street food from a mile away, and the closer, more animal stink of betrayal.

"Kallistrate," she said, before turning around and laying eyes upon Demos Kallistrate and her sister, Myrinne.

"Are you sure you're not sick?" Myrinne asked.

"Sick?" Phela asked. "I've never been better." She looked them up and down. Demos had dried blood beneath his fingernails, and a spatter across his cheek. She'd expected the slave brand on his hand, but the sight of it was still startling somehow, a stain on all nobility, not merely his own. He wore a Kolbarite's robe, evidently stolen, and a sword hung from his belt. The blood on Myrinne's hand was fresher.

"That's not your blood," Queen Phela said, nodding at Myrinne's hand. "It's a commoner's."

"Are we alone?" Myrinne asked, ignoring Phela's comment. That annoyed Phela for a beat, but then she shrugged the annoyance aside. Myrinne could act familiar for a little while longer.

"Alone," Queen Phela confirmed. "But I must ask, how did the two of you get here?"

Myrinne looked around the room as if she had never seen it before. Phela saw something different in her sister's eyes, a weight of some new experience, a strength that carried a hint of sadness alongside. Myrinne took in the paintings and sculptures hung and placed around the chamber. It was a place of history that kings and queens traditionally used for private contemplation and introspection, watched over by ancestors, afforded wisdom by likenesses of some of the great men and women from Quandis's long history. Phela had taken to coming here once each day in the certain knowledge that she was adding a huge new chapter to the land's story, and the people staring at her with painted or stony eyes would be proud of what she was about to achieve. Or if not proud, then at least respectful.

"Your Guards are easy to blind with a royal's needs," Myrinne said, staring at Phela at last. "You do look different."

"I am," Phela said. "I'm ruling Quandis as it always should have been ruled."

"And how is that?" Demos asked.

Queen Phela looked him up and down and ignored his question.

"He's come with news," Myrinne said. "He's fulfilled the task you set him, listened for news from the house of the apex."

"Good," Phela said. "It seems, however, that you don't require my intervention to afford your release."

"I had to escape," Demos said. "I heard too much."

"Too much of what?"

He shifted his weight from foot to foot, as if nervous. She could sense worry coming off him in waves and wondered what he had been through in the house of Euphraxia.

"If I tell you, you'll keep your bargain? Free me and allow—?"

"You dare bargain with the queen?" Phela asked. Her voice was loud, edged with a magical power that she felt surging through her system, sparkling in her brain, sharpening her senses. She heard a heavy rattle, and the soft hush of falling grit as ancient sculptures vibrated and shook on their pedestals.

Demos took a step back, eyes wide. To her credit Myrinne did not, but Phela saw the fear growing in her sister's eyes.

And what do they see in mine? she wondered.

"Majesty," Demos said, lowering his head. "I would not dream of bargaining."

"But the arrangement stands," Myrinne said. "He spies for you, you let him free."

"He seems to be free already."

"You know what I mean, sister. Demos and I could never have any sense of liberty in and around Lartha unless he is pronounced a free man."

Queen Phela shrugged. This was becoming tiresome, and she needed to hear what Demos had to say. She had the feeling, the *certainty,* that it would impact current events. She already believed Euphraxia to be preparing to stand against her. This might be confirmation.

"Tell me what you heard," she said.

"Majesty, I heard the apex plotting and planning against you with a priest of the High Order," Demos said.

Phela's heart darkened. "Which priest?"

"I don't know her, but I heard Euphraxia use her name. Per Gherinne."

Anger flared in the queen's breast. Per Gherinne, who'd presented herself as so loyal alongside Per Ristolo and Per Stellan, who knew what would become of herself and her brother and his family, and others of their blood. The bitch had betrayed her queen.

So Per Stellan didn't know everything. She'd come from the Ring, of course, so she couldn't have been expected to, but still it rankled Phela. As Demos continued relaying what he had overheard, she felt her rage growing and the fire of magic burning deep within her belly.

By the time he had finished she was ready to catch aflame.

She shivered, fury singing through her muscles and bones. She felt a power deep within her, but Phela was sensible enough to rein that power in. She nursed it, soothing it with inner murmurs like a mother singing her child down from tears to sleep. She didn't need it yet and it would be best to wait until it was fully formed, readily absorbed, before revealing its full presence.

Besides, she was queen. There were powers other than magic at her disposal.

"Shome," she said, and the Silent slipped from the shadows at the corner of the room. Phela heard Myrinne's and Demos's soft gasps of surprise as the tall warrior drifted to Phela's side. "Go and fetch Commander Kurtness and Dafna to me," Phela said. "And raise your warriors. All of them. We'll be careful and canny, but the Silent are going to war, and the City Guard with you."

Struggling to keep her voice modulated and even, Phela closed her eyes. "The Temple of Four will fall, and anyone there who plots against me will pay for their treachery. And you." She opened her eyes again and pointed at Demos. "You were once a warrior for Quandis, and you will be again. You'll lead a platoon of the City Guard in the initial attack and bring me Euphraxia's head."

"The apex?"

"That's the price of your freedom, Demos Kallistrate," Phela said. "The head of the bitch who goes against me. Now leave, all of you." Shome moved quickly from the room, but Myrinne and Demos remained.

"Sister, this surely can't be the way."

"Go!" Phela shouted. Across the room, the bust of a forgotten Quandian cracked in two and fell to the floor. A painting nearby burst into flame. Shadows seethed and settled again, and stars bloomed and faded all across the room. Breathing heavily, Queen Phela watched as Myrinne and her lover hurried from the room, confused and scared, and left her alone.

Alone but for the magic that roared within her. *And it will roar even louder,* she thought. All *of it. The time for caution and care has passed, and every shred of magic must now be mine.* While the Silent and her forces attacked the Temple of Four and put down the simmering insurrection, she would follow the more treacherous path to the subterranean tombs from beneath Palace Hill. She had gone that way before but been turned back by impassable tunnels and uncrossable voids. Now, though, she knew she had the power to pass and cross.

War above would allow her to fulfill her ambitions below. In a way, Euphraxia's betrayal would feed her queen's success.

"Per Gherinne," she said. She would instruct the woman to prepare the ritual to channel all of the magic into her. "Per Gherinne!" Louder.

And then she began to scream for the traitorous high priest.

∽

Blane tried to appear normal when nothing in his life would ever be normal again. His conversation with Apex Euphraxia colored every thought, every move he made, and every decision he was destined to take. And deep down inside, empowering his mind and swelling his heart, was the magic he had touched and used.

He was not the man he used to be, yet for now he had to keep up appearances.

It was wash day among the novices. Blane no longer felt like a novice, yet Yaris Teeg was now the place where he felt most at home. The washroom was large and humid, and most of the novice priests had stripped down to their undergarments as they worked. Usually this would mean nothing for any of them—their vows were strict, their dedication to the priesthood solid. Today, things were different.

While Blane scrubbed bedding, Gemmy hung wet clothing on a long line across the room. He knew that she knew he was watching. Her vest clung to her breasts, loose undershorts molding to her body as she stretched. She kept glancing at him, a curious look on her face. She did not dare speak.

Blane tried many times to look away. His own growing interest was becoming difficult to conceal, and Per Santoger would punish him severely for such a transgression. He returned Gemmy's smile, but not in a suggestive way. With everything that had happened to him over the past days, he found it ironic that it was a woman possessing his thoughts.

"Something is different about you," she whispered as she carried a pile of dirty robes past him. Blane picked up some clothing and followed her toward the bank of washing baths set against the wall. He glanced around, but no one seemed to have noticed their brief exchange. Per Santoger was there, but he appeared distracted, standing at the door and looking out into Yaris Teeg's courtyard.

"Don't you feel different too?" he asked Gemmy. He felt a rush of guilt at diverting the fact of his change onto their brief, lustful liaison.

She smiled, glanced away. He saw a flush on her cheeks. Not coyness. Excitement, perhaps. Yet again he had to concentrate to avoid his own interest rising. *I'm in turmoil!* he thought, but in some ways his life and direction had never been so clear. He could allow himself this pleasure, at least.

"A little," she said. "Only in a good way."

Nothing could come of their dalliance. She had made it explicit to him that there had been no romance in her intent. Even if they had feelings for each other that extended beyond friendship, they were priests, sworn to the Faith. They would one day pledge themselves to one tower or another. They'd made vows.

Then again, Euphraxia had broken many vows and she was the

apex. And Blane's plans for the future did not include remaining faithful to the Four. What would Gemmy think when he flexed the new power he had begun to acquire, when he had mastered the magic he siphoned from the tombs of the Four and used it to free the Bajumen? What difference would their vows make then?

The question made him study her a little longer, made him think of her a bit differently. There were possibilities he had never before considered, and he wished to ponder them.

Blane worked the washing down into the warm soapy water, and with every push from his hands he remembered that curtain of water rising up and flushing across the Phage when he'd encountered the apex. He could also hear Gemmy's breathing close beside him, and he had flash memories of their lovemaking, her grinding down on him as he thrust up, forbidden congress that had felt so right. His pondering of the future became a revelry in the past.

"I see you want to feel different again," Gemmy said, glancing down at his evident interest. She stared at him, serious now, and whispered, "I'm ready."

"Gemmy—"

"In the drying room, behind the blanket pile."

"Blane!" Per Santoger was looking across the steamy room at him. The old man seemed alert and anxious, and Blane knew immediately that this was not to do with him and Gemmy. This was nothing so trivial.

Has Euphraxia changed her mind? he wondered. *Does she want me dead after all?*

Blane gathered himself, drawing in all he had learned of magic, and felt his strength growing. Perhaps here in this wet place he could call on Dephine once more.

"Blane!" Per Santoger called again. "A messenger, for you." The old priest kept glancing out into the courtyard where Blane could not see.

"Messenger?" Gemmy's eyebrows raised. Novices were never contacted by their families and friends outside, even less so if they were Bajuman.

Blane shrugged, unsure himself, and walked past Gemmy. He crossed the big washroom, the other novices watching him go, silent and curious. Per Santoger left the room as he approached, and exiting into the coolness of the courtyard beyond, Blane saw a man standing inside the gates. They had been closed behind him, as they had each day since the City Guards had come for the Bajuman priests. Another change in the order of things that now seemed normal.

The man was breathing hard, coated in a sheen of sweat. He wore the uniform of a sailor of the Quandian navy.

"He says he's here for you, and you alone," Per Santoger said, clearly not happy with any of this.

"My name's Fissel, from the naval ship *Royal Dawn,* under command of Admiral Hallarte," Fissel said, still catching his breath. "I've run from Suskmouth with a message for the novice priest Blane."

"I'm Blane."

"Then this message is yours, direct from the admiral herself." He walked across the courtyard and held out a bamboo tube the length of his forearm, a traditional scroll holder used on navy ships to keep paper dry.

"Admiral?" Blane asked. He was confused. He looked to Per Santoger, but the old priest merely shrugged, seeming angry at the intrusion rather than curious.

"Take it, then," Per Santoger said. "The poor man's run thirty miles to drop it in your hand."

"I don't understand," Blane said.

"And you never will unless you read the gods-damned thing!"

Blane was shocked by the priest's swearing, as was Fissel. But he knew very well what distracted Per Santoger. He must have gotten wind of the queen, the tombs, her lust for magic, and her murder of Per Ostvik. The Faith was tearing itself apart, the old man was witnessing change before his eyes, and now something else strange had happened.

Blane could not help thinking that this mysterious message must be connected in some way to that change.

He took the bamboo tube, nodding his thanks. He could see no distaste in Fissel's expression in handing such a message to a Bajuman.

Blane turned and walked to the far side of the courtyard. He expected the priest to call him back, but he was given his privacy, and when he glanced back, he saw Per Santoger guiding the sailor to the mess building where he could find food and drink. Beyond, crowded in the washroom doorway, half a dozen pale faces watched him, Gemmy among them.

Blane cracked the wax seal and pulled the tied scroll of paper from the bamboo tube. It was only one sheet, the message short.

From the very first words, Blane's world lurched and changed more than it ever had before.

> *Blane, my dear brother,*
>
> *It's time to tell you the truth of my fate, my nondeath, my survival, and the life I have led since that fall from the cliff. There is so much to tell, but for now I have so little time, so I must keep this message brief.*
>
> *I was picked up by pirates, and then saved by the Quandian navy. They believed me the last-surviving Hallarte from a pirate raid on Tan Kushir and took me into their care. The sea bleached my eyes, sharp coral scoured my Bajuman brand, and I became a sailor in the navy. From there, over the years and through many promotions, I am now admiral of my own fleet. A fearsome naval warrior. Who would have thought it, brother?*
>
> *You might not believe me, and so . . .*

Mother sang as she dressed you in the morning, while I dressed myself. Older than you, I was able to do so.

You liked the stale knobs of bread from street vendors. I liked apple cores. Mother liked neither, but we thought that was only so that we could both eat.

Mother called you her little puppy, while I was her kitten.

I hope you believe me. I hope you can forgive me. I have been following your life and making sure you are well, though from a distance that is difficult. I'm glad you chose the priesthood. I think I would have done the same if fate hadn't cast me down a different path.

A time of conflict is coming, Blane, and that's why I've chosen to contact you now. I will be in Lartha soon. Perhaps amid the inevitable turmoil we can meet. I dream of it.

Your loving sister,
Daria

Blane's whole world turned, spun, blurred, and pulsed around him, its center. He had never felt the focus of anything, but now he saw himself as the core about which everything else orbited—the novices, the tombs of the Four, Queen Phela and her deceptions and murderous ambitions, Per Ristolo and the high priests . . . and now his dead sister, living again.

He was the center, but everyone and everything around him told lies.

He stumbled to the tall courtyard wall and sat on the edge of a well, leaning against a timber upright before dizziness spilled him to the ground.

Daria was alive. No longer the living sister in his memory, or the dead girl floating in the endless, cruel ocean of his imagination, she claimed now to be an admiral in the Quandian fleet.

An admiral!

He looked across the courtyard to where Fissel had disappeared into the dining building. He had so many questions for that messenger, yet none that he could ask in front of Per Santoger. Would the old priest let him quiz the sailor on his own? He doubted it. Influences from outside were kept to a strict minimum for the novices, because it was the Four within that they sought.

Blane squeezed his eyes shut, and for just a moment he wished himself back to before he had joined the priesthood, when his mother had still been among the living. Things had been simple, then. He'd been a Bajuman slave and nothing more.

But now Daria was back, and nothing would ever be simple again.

He had been a Bajuman forever, and despite the protestations and teachings of the priesthood, he still was, heart and soul. That was the whole reason for his being here. His plans were succeeding beyond his wildest dreams. Soon, he would have the power he had always dreamed of, and the ability to free every Bajuman from the slavery they had been subjected to for generations. But that didn't include Daria.

Daria had not been Bajuman since the day she had died.

To Blane, that was a betrayal. She had denied her heritage to take the easier path. She fought for Quandis, the oppressors of all Bajumen. She had forgotten her family.

Daria, you left me alone all this time, he thought, and even though it was a selfish idea, he could not think anything else. She had escaped her heritage, left it behind, and forged a life for herself beyond.

Beyond *him.*

⌒

Queen Phela had been through these tunnels before, but those were vastly different times. She was only Phela then, a young woman with ambitions, not the queen, and certainly not a woman bristling with newly acquired magic. She had felt her way through the darkness, alone, scared but excited. Now she had Per Stellan, Per Gherinne, and Per Ristolo with her, as well as her faithful Shome and the diminutive Helaine to guard her way. Back then she'd had no idea what she was doing, but now she had a very definite aim in mind.

There was no more need of Whispering. Phela was ready to shout.

As soon as they'd entered the first of the tunnels beneath Palace Hill, Per Gherinne had fallen silent. She'd been there when Per Ostvik died, she knew how determined and merciless Phela was, and yet she had betrayed her queen. Bold as this had been, what astonished Phela the most was that Per Gherinne had been courageous or idiotic enough to continue to pretend to be loyal. Once she had chosen to side with Euphraxia, she ought to have gathered up her brother and the rest of her family and fled the city. Fled the main island. Fled beyond the Outer Ring to somewhere so far that she could never be found. Yet here she was, still pretending to follow her queen.

Per Stellan said nothing. Keenly observant, even lacking an eye, she knew when to be quiet and just watch. Queen Phela could sense that Per Stellan knew something was amiss in their small band, but the other priests didn't seem to notice at all.

Other than Per Gherinne. She had seemed unsettled. Abruptly, she dared to give voice to her unease.

"I must beseech you, Majesty—"

"You've been beseeching me for the past hour," Phela said.

"And yet I don't feel I've communicated the enormity of what you're asking us to do."

"I'm not *asking* you, Per Gherinne."

"Magic wielded clumsily can cause great cataclysms," Per Gherinne said, seemingly unaware of the treacherous ground she was on. "The Covenant of the Four is quite plain about that, and the evidence is available for all to see. There have been—"

"Yes, I know, I know. Earthquakes that Charin sent to cleave Daklan Hill in two. Dephine's Flood of Floods."

"I've told her all this," Per Ristolo muttered as he walked.

Per Stellan paused to face the other two priests. "There are larger considerations," she said gravely.

Per Gherinne ignored them both, forging ahead. "You've been told, Majesty, and yet you don't quite understand."

"I understand everything," Queen Phela said. Her raised voice echoed around the chamber they had stepped into. It was a rough cavern, naturally formed but with evidence of human hand in the tunnels that led off from it. "I understand your fear over magic you can't really control, but I carry the Blood of the Four, and I *will* control it. I understand your cowardice in facing the remnants of gods you claim to worship. Yet I face them, down there in the cavern of tombs, and they bless me each and every day."

Per Gherinne glared at her with unshielded contempt.

"What I don't understand," Phela went on, "is your betrayal. After my demonstration with Per Ostvik, the idea that you'd run to Euphraxia with your tail between your legs like some shivering cur, eager for her master's love . . ."

Even in the strange light of the caverns, Phela could see Per Gherinne turn pale.

"Per Gherinne, you didn't . . ." Per Ristolo whispered. The woman had been his student once, and the corners of his eyes crinkled with grief at this revelation.

Per Stellan wisely took a step backward, away from her fellow priests. "You fool."

"Shome," Phela said. The Silent moved by her side, one hand on the great curved sword at her belt, the other still holding the flaming torch that lit their way.

Per Gherinne barely had time to utter a plea for mercy before

Shome impaled her with her sword and Helaine slit her throat. A moment later the two of them stepped away and Per Gherinne's body toppled wetly to the stone floor.

Queen Phela saw Per Ristolo's tears and Per Stellan's grim acceptance. The priests knelt to say a prayer by the corpse. Phela wanted to tell them to back away, to leave the dead woman unblessed, but she found she cared very little what they did now, as long as they did it quickly.

"Come along," she said.

Per Ristolo stood, and he looked stronger than before. Stronger than she had ever seen him, as if new purpose had been born within him.

"There is more to the Covenant than anyone alive knows," he said. He nodded toward the narrow passageway leading from the cavern. "I know some of what lies on that route to the tombs, and I suspect you do too. But no one knows all of it. If you'd spent enough time at the Wall of the Four, like every priest training to be part of the High Order does for at least two years of their lives, you'd understand that much of what is missing from the Covenant is likely more important than that which still exists."

"How can you know that?" Phela asked. "All of you in the High Order are tainted by foolishness."

Per Stellan bent her head respectfully. "Per Ristolo is correct, my queen. The missing wall panels tell a story. No one knows the true end of the First City and its people, but there are hints throughout Quandis. It's a story of pain, and threat, and a deep, dark power that existed before the Four. Before the First People. You've heard legends of the Gods Unnumbered?"

"I've spent my life in the Archives of the Crown. I've read a thousand tales of those ancient things, and every one of them is little more than an allusion to something in the shadows. The Gods Unnumbered are stories to frighten children, to keep them out of sewers and away from dark alleys."

"Yet there are so many, aren't there? That's a lot of writing dedicated to just scaring children," Per Stellan said.

"What's your point?"

"The Faith has never been so certain," Per Ristolo said. "The Gods Unnumbered may have walked our world at the dawn of time, just as the legends say. Before Quandis and before the First City. They may still exist."

"Exist where?" Phela asked.

Per Ristolo shrugged. "Far away, perhaps. Across the oceans, on frozen islands or lands of fire and lava. Or maybe deeper. Way down deep, past those things you believe are here to protect access to the tombs. I had a teacher once, more than a century ago, who believed that the deep things are not there to keep those above from coming below, but to keep those even farther below from coming above."

They stood silently for a moment, the only sound the steady spitting and hissing of Shome's blazing torch. Then Phela coughed a loud, hard laugh, leaning back and guffawing at the cavern ceiling. Many-legged shapes scuttled out of sight, startled by the sound. Echoes twisted away through tunnels they would soon be traveling.

"Trust you priests to make up such stories," she said. She shook her head. "You really are fools, all of you. So obsessed with your religion that you fail to see what's right in front of you. You fail to see the Four! But they're down there. The Gods Unnumbered may haunt your dreams, but the magic of the Four is real and vibrant, still ablaze with power. I've been close, I've felt them, and soon I'll see them. I don't need stupid nighttime stories to scare me from my destiny, Per Ristolo. So lead the way. My time for caution, for kowtowing to your fears and superstitions, is over. My final ritual awaits, and next time I walk into the sunlight, I'll be the greatest queen there's ever been. The Eternal Queen."

"Majesty," he said, glancing down at the pool of blood spreading from beneath Per Gherinne's corpse. "I dare not defy you, but please be certain. You risk us all. You risk Quandis, if you cannot contain the power."

"I risk nothing. I will be eternal," she said again. "I promise you, Per Ristolo. And you, Per Stellan. All will be well. I will raise you up. The High Order will begin anew, with the two of you at its head."

"And it's you we'll be praying to," Per Stellan said, gazing at her with that one eye, the other a black pit of scars and shadows. "It may work, Majesty. And I will stay with you and do all I can to aid you in this. But do not forget the last time a sorcerer tried to become the Fifth."

Queen Phela felt a sickness in her gut. This reminder felt like a reprimand, words spoken warily but with the impact of a slap to the face.

"You dare compare me to the Pent Angel?" Phela whispered.

"I express a concern," the priest replied. "You cannot deny the comparison is apt, for the moment. Only time and your own self-control will reveal if it remains so."

Shome and Helaine shifted toward Per Stellan without being asked, eyeing her with deadly expectation. The priest saw them but did not seem frightened or even uneasy. Queen Phela waved the Silent assassins away.

"One thing I will say for you, woman," Phela said. "I will never doubt that you mean what you say."

Per Stellan inclined her head respectfully.

Phela glanced at Per Ristolo to see if he'd dare to voice any further hesitations. Something crossed his face, but the thoughts remained unspoken. Phela let him wallow in those thoughts, and the priest turned and headed into the narrow tunnel. She followed, with Per Stellan and the two Silent behind them.

They left Per Gherinne's corpse cooling in the cavern, blood pooling. Perhaps the ghast spiders would eat her, or perhaps something worse. *The Gods Unnumbered,* she thought, smiling in the darkness. *Such foolishness.*

They followed a twisting route that descended deep beneath Palace Hill, and then started rising again as it ventured beneath Temple Hill. She remembered this way, though when she had come before she'd carried a small oil lamp, and the way had not been so well lit. This time she could see more detail in the tunnel walls, evidence of old tool marks and carvings in forgotten languages. If either of the high priests knew what these words said, neither of them betrayed their knowledge.

Shome had moved in front of Per Ristolo and now led the group. The other Silent brought up the rear. As they approached the huge underground chamber, even Shome slowed down and glanced back at her queen.

"Let me," Phela said. "I've been here before, but I'm better prepared this time."

The darkness ahead of them was thick, the sense of space intimidating, and even the two torches combined could only light a small expanse. Four natural stone bridges headed away from their side of the cavern, spanning a dizzyingly deep ravine. The vastness was staggering, but it was the feeling of something within that darkness that set even Phela's nerves jangling. Last time she was here she had been alone, but she had not known what to expect. Now, she remembered.

From far, far below, she heard the gentle splash of something breaking the surface of an underground lake.

"This one," she said, choosing one of the four bridges. It was the one with old, rusted rings hammered into the stone, and rotted ropes spanning between some of them. The way she had come before.

"Dhakur is there," Per Ristolo said. "We can't cross. Dhakur is there."

"Dhakur, the beast of the lake?" Phela asked. She fisted her hand, then opened it, and a mist of water condensed from the air and wetted her skin.

"Hear that?" Per Stellan said. "Per Ristolo is right."

"Neither of you is right," Phela said, and she walked out onto the bridge.

Her heart hammered, but she breathed deeply and held her fear, her surety guiding her. The darkness grew heavier, even though Shome followed her, as if the weight of nothing was growing even thicker. She took the torch from Shome and breathed into the flames, letting her senses expand, feeling the rush of magic flooding her veins. The fire grew brighter and wider, small flickering embers drifting up and out from the torch to enlarge the circle of light around them. The dark flinched back.

Phela passed the place where she had once turned back, and that was when she heard the sound of something brushing against rock far below.

She looked down. The limbs were long, thin, and there were dozens of them. They twisted at the air, bending, rising, as if holding on to darkness to haul themselves up. They were coming for the bridge, and moments later the first of them wrapped over the stone structure just twenty steps ahead of her. It was a pale, flexible appendage, and its color grew darker as it seemed to tighten around the stone. This was Dhakur.

"Behind!" Per Ristolo said. "Dhakur is behind us as well!"

Phela glanced back to see the small Silent Helaine wielding her sword, crouched and ready to hack at the three limbs twisting and dancing on either side of the bridge.

"Wait," Phela said. "Don't hurt it."

"Dhakur can't be *hurt*!" Per Ristolo scoffed.

Phela smiled at him, then closed her eyes.

Dephine came to her, god of Water and Beasts, and Phela channeled the power and grace she felt from that god, feeling magic flow through and out of her mind and thoughts, veering down into the chasm and connecting her, briefly, with an intelligence so alien and profound that she staggered. If Shome had not caught her, Phela would have met eternity deep down with the thing that was Dhakur.

The touch was brief, but in that instant Phela understood Dhakur's confusion. There was no pleading, no negotiation, but rather an understanding in Phela that their momentary touching of minds might give her a chance.

She opened her eyes, looked at her companions, and said, "Run."

Phela drove the priests on ahead. Without them, she'd never complete the necessary rituals. They ran across the stone bridge, Shome ahead of her queen with the expanded torch held out in front. The sound of cracking rock echoed around the chamber, and as they reached the far side Phela felt movement beneath her feet. Her final few steps were sickening, the very land rocking underneath her, and as she leaped she felt everything beneath her opening up and falling away.

Shome and the two priests made the opening on the far side of the vast cavern. Phela had no choice but to leap, reaching out her arms to Shome, who grabbed her and dragged her to safety.

Behind, the stone bridge crumbled and fell, and Helaine went with it. Even plummeting to a terrible, unimaginable doom, the diminutive Silent kept her voiceless vow.

Thousands of tons of stonework crashed down into darkness. It was some time before they heard the first splashes.

"Nothing can hurt Dhakur," Per Ristolo whispered.

Phela could find no words. Still reeling from her touch on that alien mind, she nodded at Shome to lead the way. The four of them continued in silence.

༄

On their underground journey from Palace Hill to Temple Hill they encountered three more obstacles designed to prevent easy passage, and each time Phela moved them aside or neutralized them. One was a glimmering passageway filled with the webbing of hundreds of deadly ghost spiders, which she purged with a blazing burst of fire, channeling the great god Charin. It was so powerful that the stone itself cracked and glowed afterward, and the carbonized remains of spiders disintegrated beneath their feet as they passed by. The second was an illusion: a wall of blood mirroring their faces. Phela tumbled a fall of splintered stone along the passage that shredded the image and opened up the path beyond.

The third obstacle might have been the greatest, and the one about which Phela had most doubt. The chasm was too wide to ford, and so deep that she believed it might not have a bottom at all. By her estimation they were at the foot of Temple Hill, and the idea that such a place existed beneath that most holy part of Lartha would have been enough to drive much of the population mad.

While Per Ristolo held the torch, Shome heaved a heavy rock and hurled it out into the darkness. It quickly disappeared beneath them, and the four people—queen, Silent, two unwilling High Order priests—listened for the impact with breath held.

None came. No splash, no crack of rock upon rock. Phela wondered how far down the bottom would have to be to prevent the echo of the rock's impact reaching them. A mile? Two?

She didn't have much time to contemplate it, for rising from the abyss came a darkness so profound that Phela thought she might be able to grab hold of it. The torch's effect was minimal, however much she used magic to boost the flame. Darkness threatened to smother them all. She thought of the Gods Unnumbered, and for just a moment their existence did not seem quite so easily dismissed as a story to frighten children.

Per Ristolo began praying to the Four, but Phela grabbed his arm and spun him around, holding him so close to the edge that even she doubted her own intent, just for a beat.

"You pray to *me*!" she shouted, and her voice echoed deep and long, as if taken up by other things and mimicked endlessly into the night. The old priest's eyes went wide at such blasphemy, and his voice fell silent.

"So now we go back," Per Stellan said.

"Back?" Phela asked. "No. Forward."

"Across that?"

"Of course."

"But . . ."

Phela stood at the very edge of the ledge and looked down into nothing. One shove from any of them would have sent her plummeting, but she knew that she was safe. She knew that now the two High Order priests respected and feared her enough. As for Shome . . . she had served Phela since the first time she'd asked her to. Of course she had. The Silent served the queen, and Phela had been bearing the mantle of queen since before her mother raved into death.

"Across," Phela said. She summoned the magic within, and it was a strange relationship, as if the magic was its own thing and would translate what she required with no need of explanation. Charin again, this time the Charin of Secrets. And then she knew. She did not have to imagine the bridge across the gulf—it simply was. Clear, only slightly more solid than the darkness, there was no sign that it had appeared, yet still she took her first step out across the void. Her trust was complete, even when she heard a small, startled sound from Shome. Perhaps the first noise she had ever heard from the Silent's mouth.

Phela's foot landed on something solid and she continued walking, out across the abyss and toward the far side that was still out of sight.

"Bring the torch," she said. She heard the high priests following her and knew that Shome would be behind them.

They crossed, and upon entering a new network of tunnels she at last smelled something familiar.

Magic on the air.

The tombs were close, and her destiny was closer still.

17

Somehow on their march from the palace down toward the foot of Temple Hill, Demos Kallistrate—warrior, sailor, prisoner, slave, and now warrior again—found himself in joint command of the assault upon the Temple of Four.

Commander Kurtness of the City Guard had once been a friend of the Kallistrate family. That friendship had withered and died as Linos Kallistrate's corpse was rotting, but the respect he held for Demos as a fighter was still evident, and it emerged once again as they made their way through the Larthan streets toward their target.

"How do you see this going?" Kurtness asked.

"In two phases," Demos said. "First, a detachment I sent ahead from the apex's house will launch a diversionary assault on the main temple gates."

"Which will mean climbing Temple Hill, a steep haul," Kurtness said.

"True. A climb that will not go unnoticed by those allied to Euphraxia and the priesthood. They'll be ready when the detachment arrives at the gates. And that bitch Euphraxia will believe that is our main assault."

Demos and a small contingent from the City Guard had already visited Euphraxia's official residence close to the foot of Palace Hill. As expected, the apex had not been home, but while her staff was lined up against a wall, shivering in terror, Demos had led a thorough search of the place. Some of the slaves had been surprised to see Demos of the spiza basements now dressed in a Guard uniform too small for him and wielding a secondhand sword. He'd considered liberating them, but that was not his mission. Also, it would have been frowned upon by the other Guards. But maybe he didn't need to physically free them. He felt the slaves' eyes burning into him as he left them behind, and he sensed their thoughts. *If he can get out, why can't we?*

You can—you just need to want it enough to risk your lives.

In a damp but clean room in one of the basements, Demos had found the body of the praejis, laid out for burial. In another, where he had spent many hours scrubbing and scraping at a chimney, the remnants of a fire still glowed a deep, angry orange. Among the ashes, bones.

Mouse. Thrown into a chimney and burned without ceremony. She had beaten him, hated him, and been his friend, many years ago and again so recently. Such a friend that he undoubtedly owed her his life.

He'd stood staring at the ashes and bones until a Guard tapped him on the shoulder and confirmed what he already knew. "The apex isn't here."

All the way out of Euphraxia's house and its extravagant grounds, Demos had craved finding the apex and burying his sword in her wretched, hypocritical body.

"Their Phage will be ready for us," Kurtness said now, startling Demos from his grim recollections.

"If they even exist," Demos said.

"You doubt them?"

"They feel like a . . . story. To frighten children." He shrugged.

"Then I'm a child," Kurtness said. "There are already rumors . . ."

"What rumors?"

The soldiers pushed through a crowded market square, fifty City Guards and an unknown number of Silent accompanying them. Demos caught sight of the women warriors now and then, moving with the Guards yet not part of them. He was surprised that the Silent had not moved out to undertake their own missions. Perhaps that would happen soon, or maybe they really would join forces.

"When Queen Lysandra called for the Bajuman extermination, a detachment was sent to the Temple of Four," Kurtness said. "They've not been seen again, and the temple's gates have been closed ever since."

"You must have investigated."

"Of course. But the old priests and novices who were there at the time knew nothing."

"Of course not," Demos said. He frowned, walking on in silence. Uncertainty about what they were doing here, and his part in it, nipped at his heels.

Queen Phela's orders were clear—track down and kill any members of the Faith who were allied with Euphraxia against her. It was Demos's word that had inspired the queen's rage and her orders for an assault, and the result of that word would be, eventually, his freedom to flee Lartha with Myrinne. That was all he wanted. There was nothing else. Lartha and Quandis could shake themselves apart for all he cared, so long as the one he loved was by his side. Home was where Myrinne was, and if that ended up being one of the islands of the Ring, or even beyond, then he would accept that with good grace, and even grow to love it. He had been out at sea for many years under Admiral Hallarte's command. He knew that as well as wild, violent places beyond the Ring, there was also beauty.

Yet Phela's manner troubled him. The idea of murdering priests did not sit well with him, even though it was under the orders of the queen. Euphraxia, on the other hand . . .

He would be happy to put that bitch to the sword. His bones ached, his muscles were torn, and his wounds and bruises were still caked in blood from the beatings she had put him through. If turning against her was his last act serving Quandis, he would leave a happy man.

"So with a detachment acting as a diversion at the main temple, we go in through Yaris Teeg," Kurtness said.

"Of course," Demos said. "The novices won't fight. We gather them and the priests, give them the ultimatum."

"And kill those who ally themselves with the apex."

People were hurrying out of their way. Demos saw a Silent dart by to his left, flitting behind a row of market stalls, hardly slowing even though she dodged through a huddled, harried crowd.

"You seem comfortable with killing unarmed people," Demos said.

"In service of the queen, of course."

Even this queen? he thought but dared not say. The pardon Phela promised covered his past crimes and treasons, not any new ones.

They passed through the market square and entered the maze of streets and alleys that led up a gradually steepening slope to the foot of Temple Hill. Soon, Yaris Teeg was visible across an area of raised planters, crops of various types nurtured from the ground by the novice priests. The City Guard soldiers knew their orders, and the dozen Silent who marched with them would fight their own fight.

Demos called a halt. He looked up at the hill's summit, where the grand and massive Temple of Four poked its towers at the blue sky. Sunlight gleamed from the towers, but part of the view was hazed by a slowly drifting cloud of smoke. Its source was not visible, but seemed to be somewhere close to the main entrance into the temple.

"Perfect timing," Commander Kurtness said, and with a signal from him, their assault on Yaris Teeg and the great mass of Temple Hill began.

Still shaken, Blane barely heard Per Santoger as the teacher came across the courtyard toward him. From the look in his eyes, the priest must have called to him several times before he finally looked up.

"My apologies," Blane said. "My mind was elsewhere."

"Yes, I see," Per Santoger said. "In the admiral's message, no doubt. What is it that has upset you so?"

"A sister I once thought was dead is alive," Blane said.

Per Santoger frowned. "Admiral Hallarte sent you such a message?"

Blane frowned. His senses were heightened by magic, and now he could hear the surreptitious padding of feet, smell the sweat of many, and taste violence on the air.

"Something's coming," Blane said, looking at the closed courtyard gates.

Per Santoger cocked his head and listened to noises from beyond the walls. His confusion changed to sadness. "I feared it would come to this," he said.

From beyond the wall came a shouted order, sharp and high. Over the gate and stonework appeared several grappling hooks, snagging and pulling tight.

"Queen Phela makes her move." With one final, baleful glance at Blane, Per Santoger hurried to the center of the courtyard. He scratched at the air with clawed hands, calling the Phage to him.

Blane looked up the steep hillside toward the grand Temple of Four, its spires piercing the sky, and saw that smoke was rising around them.

When he looked back at the gate, six Phage had materialized around Per Santoger. The robed specters stood ready for battle. The air sparked with a powerful static, and the promise of violence.

"Go and hide, Blane. You and the others are not ready for this," Per Santoger said.

A swirl of conflicting motivations twined inside Blane. He knew what he wanted for his people, and that meant Phela had to fall. For now, his interests aligned with the pact he'd made with Euphraxia, but he knew that would not last much longer. Too, his sister was on her way, doubtless with expectations of her own.

And Per Santoger wanted him to run. If he ignored the old man, if he stayed and fought, he felt certain that he'd unleash the magic he'd acquired. Per Santoger would learn his secret.

But Blane no longer cared. He was done with hiding who and what he was.

His time was now.

◡

Demos ran across the open garden area with the fifty other City Guards. They moved quietly, yet the Silent were quieter. The warrior women reached the wall before the first of the Guards, and as grappling irons were heaved up and over the gates and walls, the Silent were already climbing.

Demos grabbed a rope and pulled himself up. A few weeks before he would have completed the climb in moments with only a small amount of effort, but his body was weakened by abuse and malnutrition, and he had to grit his teeth and concentrate to avoid failing at this first obstacle. He had been tasked with killing Euphraxia for the queen, and he had to focus every ounce of his strength and determination to succeed. His and Myrinne's future depended on it.

To his left and right, other soldiers climbed faster than he did, reaching the head of the wall or gate and dropping down the other side. Several Silent had already flowed over the wall, and from beyond he could hear the noises of combat—clashing swords, muffled shouts, and the unmistakable sound of steel cleaving flesh.

Demos reached the top of the wall just beside the gate and its wide stone posts. He caught his breath for a moment, resting over the wall on his stomach and looking down into the wide courtyard beyond.

His caught breath fled as shock and fear winded him.

"Phage," he whispered, because there could be no other explanation for what he saw. They seemed to stand, but they moved as if in flight, shimmering in and out of sight, translucent wraiths with solid swords in their hands.

The first few Guards had been cut down and were bleeding across the cobbles. One was crawling, trying to reach her dropped sword even though her severed hand still gripped it a dozen paces from her stump. Another was holding in his guts as he whispered to the sky.

Toward the rear of the courtyard stood an old priest. Beside him stood a young novice who looked like a Bajuman. A doorway opened and several more novices streamed out, all of them carrying long pikes with cruel spikes on their tips.

"Come on, Kallistrate," Kurtness said along the wall from Demos. He was standing, hefting a small crossbow and taking aim. He fired, the bolt passing through one of the shapes and ricocheting off a building. "Earn your fucking freedom." He leaped from the wall, landed in a roll, and was up and attacking a Phage with three other soldiers.

Demos drew his sword and jumped, bending his knees and rolling sideways as he landed. Standing, he found himself face to face with an indistinct figure. It was robed, partially transparent, long hair escaping the hood and drifting in defiance of the still air, limbs moving with grace and speed, and in each hand it carried a short, thick sword. The weapons looked less opaque. When one swished in an arc toward his head and Demos parried, the impact jarred through his hand and up his arm.

He took a step back and the Phage came for him, swinging both swords in a whirlwind of steel that hissed and whistled at the air. Demos struggled not to trip over his own feet, letting his mind settle and allowing instinct to take over. He was confident in his abilities, though troubled by his current weakness. He pushed that doubt aside, though—anxiety in a sword fight would get him killed. Allowing his natural talents to steer the fight, to defend, and to go on the offensive was the only way to win.

If there *was* a way to win against a spirit beast such as this.

He ducked two more lashes of the Phage's swords and stepped forward, swinging his own long blade into his enemy's legs. It howled, the noise strangely distant as if from across some invisible divide, and took a step back.

Demos glanced at his sword. It was stained with shadowy, swirling things like fluid worms that quickly faded and then vanished from the polished blade.

He didn't have much time to wonder at it, as the Phage stepped sideways and came again, seemingly uninjured and not at all affected by his blade passing through its legs.

Not fair, Demos thought, and then he was joined in battle by one of the Silent. The woman stepped in front of him and shoved him back, and he bridled at being cast aside. He hefted his sword and went to step into the fray once again, but what he heard and saw next froze him to the spot.

The Phage roared. It was a high, ululating scream that tore

through to Demos's core, scratching at his ears like nails on stone, reverberating through his spine and ribs, and the fury and rage on the creature's face was almost enough to drive him to his knees with a sense of hollow, empty hopelessness.

He thought, *We're all going to die.*

The Silent darted forward and lashed out with her sword.

Still screaming, the Phage embraced her with its ghostly arms and turned sharply, throwing her back against the courtyard wall she had just jumped from. She struck stone with a sickening thump, but instantly dropped, rolled, and attacked the Phage once more.

Swords clashed. Blood splashed from a wound across the Silent's shoulder. The Phage staggered to the left and fell to its knees, then jumped up again without any apparent effort, fending off more swordplay from the Silent and burying one of its blades in the woman's right thigh.

She hissed in pain, and Demos darted in from behind. He plunged his sword into the Phage's chest, feeling little give as the blade passed through and almost impaled the Silent on its tip.

The Phage turned to face him. Demos held on to the sword and tugged it out, shaking shadowy dregs away and stepping back.

"How the fuck do you die?" he said. As the Phage came at him one more time, the Silent took a giant leap on her one good leg and slashed her sword through its neck.

The spirit screeched again, even louder and more unbearable than its first furious cry, fingernails across Demos's skull. It dropped its remaining sword and reached for its throat, even as its head tilted from its shoulders and rolled across the ground.

The scream continued. Demos went to his knees, hands over his ears, trying to scurry away as the being settled onto the cobbles and melted down to an argument of shadows and sunlight.

The Silent tugged the sword from her thigh, but Demos could already see that the wound was infected with something deadly. The Silent saw too. Trails snaked away from the ugly wound, a network of darkness beneath her skin that seemed to follow veins both large and small. The blood that flowed was speckled with blots that expanded and turned her blood from red to black.

She looked up at Demos, blinked, took a few unsteady steps toward another enemy, then dropped down dead.

Demos snatched up his sword, shedding his shock to take stock of the situation. "Take their heads!" he shouted.

A dozen Guards were down, and two more fell as he watched, slashed open by Phage swords, wounds and blood darkening with the toxic shadows those things spread.

Thus far failing to smash the gates, more Guards poured over the wall, and while the Silent engaged the Phage, the Guards skirted around the edges of the courtyard. Demos went with them. Commander Kurtness was at their forefront, and he was the first to reach the small group of novices. They had spread out around a doorway leading into the first buildings of Yaris Teeg, holding a loose protective formation as if to keep the soldiers out. They were almost naked, shivering, yet determined.

"This doesn't need to happen!" someone shouted. It was the old priest, still standing at the rear of the courtyard with the Bajuman novice beside him. The novice caught Demos's eye, and Demos saw something in him that he didn't like. A defiance he had never seen in a Bajuman before. A confidence, as if he knew a dangerous secret he was eager to share.

"State your allegiance to the queen," Kurtness said. The fighting had paused for a moment. "Let us pass into the temple, and then perhaps the violence might end."

"This is sacrilege," one of the novices said.

"Gemmy!" the Bajuman warned.

"This is holy ground!" the woman called Gemmy said. "We serve the Four first and foremost, and what your queen is trying to do—"

Kurtness and three other Guards stepped toward the six novices, swords held up. The novices prodded forward with their pikes.

Kurtness laughed. "I serve the queen, first and foremost," he said, and he lashed out with his sword.

One of the novices fell, pike splintered and chest opened to the ribs. The others cried out and backed away, all but the one called Gemmy. She hefted her pike and threw it at Kurtness.

He knocked it aside and darted toward the novice.

"No!" the Bajuman priest roared.

Demos felt something in the air. The fighting had started again across the courtyard—shouts, grunts, the clash of swords, the screech of Phage, the thud of bodies hitting the ground—but now there was something more. The ground seemed to be shaking beneath his feet. The air vibrated, as if with the echoes of the Phage's awful screams. The sun shimmered high above them, sending waves of heat across the courtyard that stretched his skin and dried his eyes.

"What's this?" Demos muttered.

Kurtness grabbed Gemmy by the robe, lifted her from her feet, and prepared to run her through with his sword.

The Bajuman shouted again. "*No!*"

The ground around Commander Kurtness erupted. Cobbles burst from their beds, thudding upward into his groin, chest, face. He dropped the novice and she fell back. The others dragged Gemmy to safety as Kurtness was battered and pelted with heavy stones from all directions, every one of them leaving its mark. Several City Guard rushed in and dragged him back, and only then did the stones stop flying. The moment they did, though, a single figure dashed across the courtyard toward Demos, sword out. He turned, ready to kill the madman loping toward him, until the man lifted his head and Demos saw his face and recognized him immediately.

"Fissel!"

The sailor had once fought by his side as a part of Daria's crew. Now Fissel reached him and turned, sword in hand, ready to fight at his side again.

"What are you doing here?" Demos demanded, though he was glad to see his comrade.

"Fighting first, story time later," Fissel replied.

But the fighting had entered a lull. As if at a silent signal, the Phage pulled back to the edges of the courtyard, leaving the City Guards and Silent standing among the dead and dying.

The old priest stared aghast, not at the carnage being wrought around him, nor at the inexplicable eruption, but at the Bajuman standing by his side.

"Blane!" the priest shouted. "What have you done?"

But the man called Blane was not listening. He had taken the woman, Gemmy, in his arms and looked her over, checking for injuries.

Demos nudged Fissel, and the two of them stepped back toward the closed gate and wall. The air thrummed with a strange energy, a potential that vibrated in Demos's bones and ached in the roots of his teeth.

"Back!" he shouted, but even as the Silent and few remaining Guards obeyed his panicked command, he saw Euphraxia emerge from a door at the courtyard's far corner. Shock etched upon her face, her gaze instantly shifted to the Bajuman.

She smiled.

"Good, Blane," she called across the courtyard. "Good!"

Everything came into sharp clarity for Demos with those words: forty paces away stood the woman he needed to kill. His need was rational, because it was what Phela wanted, and Euphraxia's death would mean his and Myrinne's freedom from this mad, degenerating place. Yet it was also emotional, because this was the woman who had so enjoyed his fall from grace and encouraged his beatings and tortures at the hands of poor, dead Mouse.

Killing Euphraxia would end this part of his life and launch him into a fresh, new beginning.

As Demos took a step forward, though, the whole courtyard erupted into a maelstrom of smashed stones and crackling heat, swirling up in a widening spiral that swept up a Silent and tore her to shreds, blood, flesh, and bone adding to the chaos.

"Run!" someone shouted, and Demos hated the cowardice in that voice. Yet he knew that was their only option. The Bajuman, Blane, was the center of this, and although there was nothing visible, Demos could sense the waves of energy radiating out from him. He didn't understand what was happening, but survival instinct needed no understanding. Clearly he wasn't the only one confused, as Demos noticed the old priest beside Blane had taken a step back, watching with his mouth agape.

The only one who seemed okay with everything was still framed in the darkened doorway: Euphraxia, beaming with delight.

She caught Demos's eye, and rather than a look of anger at his escape, her grin widened. In it he saw a promise of worse pains to come, and he knew that Euphraxia believed she had already won.

Not yet, he thought.

Demos and Fissel turned and ran for the walls. Other Guards and a few of the Silent went for the closed gates, and the maelstrom closed in on them and snatched them up, smashing bodies against stone and wood. Blane's focus on them allowed Demos, Fissel, several Silent, and the bruised and bleeding Kurtness to climb the walls. It was difficult, finding hand- and footholds in sheer masonry, but fear drove Demos on. Fear . . . and rage at the grin Euphraxia had sent his way.

It's far from over! he thought, reaching up and grabbing one of the grappling hooks, hauling himself up onto the head of the wall, and glancing back only once.

The courtyard was a swirling tornado of dust and stones, blood and bodies, dropped weapons and smashed buildings. Through the storm he could make out those who had done this to them, novices, priests, and apex alike, holy people who had defeated the Silent and the City Guard. The Phage were still there, little more than shimmers on the air, but the magic of the High Order had turned out to be even deadlier. His mind reeled at the power that crackled in the air, at the presence of magic he'd never truly believed in, but there was no time to assess reality now. Feelings of awe and wonder would have to wait until the fight was done. If he survived.

Demos dropped from the wall and landed hard. Fissel came next, and then Kurtness, who landed beside them, staggering. The commander touched a bloody welt on his forehead, but he still looked strong, hardened by combat. With a nod from Kurtness they ran, not looking back.

As they sprinted down the street, Demos knew that a balance of power had shifted. What they had witnessed in the past five minutes would be spoken about across Quandis for years to come.

He hoped they would live that long.

Behind them a loud boom echoed, and he risked one last look. The gates of Yaris Teeg had burst open, and a dozen raised planter beds across the gardens broke apart and became part of the storm.

With no destination in mind, Demos ran for his life.

ᴄ⌒ᴅ

Blane had never been looked at like this before. With disgust, yes, and hatred, and sometimes a sort of hidden pity from people who didn't hate Bajumen but could not bring themselves to like them. Even Gemmy, who had overcome her hatred for Bajumen to become his friend and then his lover, seemed frightened of him. He'd saved her life and then held her close, but now she stepped back from him, gaze uncertain.

"This is what you've been hiding?" she asked quietly, looking around at the scattered dead.

He could only nod.

Gemmy looked toward Per Santoger, as if their teacher had the answers to the questions swirling in her mind. But it was Apex Euphraxia who walked past her and stopped just a few feet away from Blane, staring at him with what he thought must be fear.

When she spoke, he realized it wasn't fear at all. It was respect.

"I've never dreamed that anyone could harness the magic as quickly and fully as you have," the apex said. "And a Bajuman, at that."

He didn't mind her mention of his race. He was proud.

"And perhaps there's something in that," she mused.

Around them, the courtyard of Yaris Teeg was a battlefield, but one whose battle had been distinctly one-sided. It was difficult to see how many dead were there, smashed apart as they were. It was grisly and sickening, but Blane felt a strange distance from what he had done. It was as if he was viewing painted images of a story of his deeds, not the true aftermath. He was all there, yet something protected him against the effects of his deeds.

Perhaps it was magic. If so, he welcomed its protection.

Though Gemmy held back, the other novices gathered around. Along with Per Santoger, they looked at him with a sort of awe. And with fear. He welcomed both, except from Gemmy. Blane didn't want her to be afraid. He wanted to go to her, tell her that this was what he'd always wanted, this strange and dreadful power that might enable him to save his people at last.

Before he could move, Euphraxia grabbed his arm. "Come with me," she said. "And you, Per Santoger." He looked to Gemmy, who simply nodded—there was no denying the apex. So Blane looked away and walked with Euphraxia into a doorway leading from the courtyard. With most of the destruction out of sight, he could almost pretend none of it had happened.

"They'll be coming back," Per Santoger said.

"Eventually," Euphraxia said. "But that's not my main fear. Phela will be going for the tombs, I have no doubt."

"She's been down there more than I have," Blane said. "And she has High Order priests aiding her in the rituals."

"We have to stop her. If she fulfills her ambitions, then her power will be . . ."

"Greater than mine?" Blane asked.

Euphraxia smiled at him, as if speaking to a child. "Yours is nothing," she said. She frowned, glancing up the hill at the silhouette of the Temple of Four, far above them. "They'll have attacked the main temple as well, though I'm sure they'll have been repelled for now. I must go to the temple and descend into the tombs—"

"Apex, I'll go with you," Per Santoger said. "We'll take all the High Order priests who have at least a touch of magic and we'll fight her at the temple, or beneath it. Perhaps combined we can combat any threat the queen presents."

"Perhaps," Euphraxia said. "And I agree. We must go to the Temple of Four and take the battle to her. But while Phela desires magic, she will also use her forces to take control of Lartha. All those opposing her will be killed, and that includes any priests or novices." She looked at Blane. "I'm not a good person, Blane. I can't pretend to be that."

"Apex . . ." Per Santoger breathed.

She ignored his brief expression of surprise. "But I'm nowhere near as bad as I fear Phela can be."

"Apex, my sister . . ." Blane said. He trailed off. It felt so unreal, the message he'd received, that he wondered whether it had all been a dream. He pulled the crumpled paper from his pocket and unrolled it. Not a dream, then. He held it out to Euphraxia and saw her eyes widen as she read the message.

"Admiral Daria Hallarte," Euphraxia said in wonder, staring at the paper as if it could not be real. She looked up at him. "Admiral Hallarte is your sister. A Bajuman . . ."

Blane nodded. "I can go to meet her. Tell her what has happened here."

"Yes—do that," Euphraxia said. "We can only hope that Admiral Hallarte's loyalties will be on the side of Quandis, not its mad queen." She raised one corner of her mouth into an almost-smile. "It seems that after centuries of being unseen, the Bajumen are about to make their mark."

His heart swelled. That was everything he had always wanted.

Inside, like a living thing, the heat of magic pulsed in time with his heartbeat. Perhaps with Daria's help, he might be able to complete what he had begun and become the true Kij'tal. Not a myth, but a real savior for his people. A new legend.

18

In the labyrinth beneath the city of her birth, the city she had always been meant to rule, Phela felt her heart swell with wonder. Since her earliest days she had Whispered through the walls of the palace, had pressed her ear to cracks and listened to intimate secrets with the hope of unraveling the mysteries of her world and of the people she encountered each day. Yet even that Phela, with all her years of puzzle solving and stealth and the keen mind her mother had helped to hone, would never have been able to navigate her way through the traps and ruins and switchbacks of the tunnels deep beneath the Palace. The High Order priests had done their work admirably, centuries ago, making it much simpler to reach the tombs from Temple Hill than from the palace. They'd placed obstacles and diversions and snares and frustrations in the way, so that anyone would be turned back.

Anyone but *her*.

Phela had High Order priests with her, but even Per Ristolo was not old enough to remember how to solve this perilous maze alone. He and Per Stellan had their little magics and certain wisdoms and memories, but Phela breathed magic. Unlike members of the High Order, she had pledged herself wholly to each of the Four, not only one, and she could feel their presence in a way the others seemed unable to. Though the priests helped, the Four called only to her, luring her onward through the maze as if they desired her among them nearly as much as she wished to be there.

"Do you still believe I've gone too quickly?" she asked, swollen with pride and joy. "Do you still doubt that the Blood of the Four flows within me, that I am destined to inherit their power?"

They stood in the golden glow of impossible light that shone from cracks in the ceiling overhead, with no source she could identify. Per Ristolo and Per Stellan stepped up behind her to take in the same view, and she heard the old man's wheezing breath. Magic had kept him alive, but after two hundred years, his body had worn down. Behind the two High Order priests, Shome lingered in the shadows.

"You want an honest answer?" Per Stellan said, her ruined eye socket seeming to stare even more balefully than her remaining eye.

Phela gazed down at the ruin below her. A stone tower, built by the First People before the gods came to this land, had fallen on its side, collapsed into the world. Water flowed in a stream that passed on either side of it and through its throat, spilling out of windows from which the First People had once gazed upon the Seven Hills. She wondered what Lartha had looked like then, what it had been called in their language, and how those people would have appeared to her. Other wreckage of ancient architecture lay there, including a stone bridge, broken in half. The last tunnel had led here, to this ledge, overlooking the ruined tower and bridge. Stone slabs had been laid like stairs down to the broken bridge. Fifty yards from its end, water spilled from the ceiling in the silver curtain she had come to know in these past weeks. Beyond the falling water sat the familiar shapes of the tombs of the Four on their large square dais, though she had never seen them from this angle before. No one living had stood upon this ridge, until now.

The queen turned to smile at Per Stellan. "Go on, priest. Tell me *your* truth."

The woman of the Ring nodded slowly, meeting her gaze without fear. "You have a natural affinity for magic. Your mother had it as well, though she could not hold the reins of it, muddled with spiza as she was. You've done well thus far. I've sworn loyalty to you, and I'll keep that vow, but what you're asking us to do is lunacy. The magic of the gods still emanates from their tombs and seethes within their remains. These rituals will open a channel within you so that magic will flow into you directly and without any hope of controlling it. I don't know whether you will receive it all—it's possible there is no end to the power that still simmers within the Four—but you will *not* be able to contain it. They were sorcerers, ancient even before they were gods, and there were *four* of them. You are but one."

Phela sneered by reflex alone. She wanted to strike the woman down. Had she not needed Per Stellan she might have had Shome kill her on the spot. But she wasn't so naive that the words didn't resonate within her, a bell tolling in her skull, and once struck, no bell could be unstruck. And because of that, Phela, Queen of Quandis and Head of the Faith, hesitated. Magic prickled her skin, and everywhere she looked she saw the sparkling blue stars, the glittering energy that bound the world together. Coupled with this seemingly impossible new realm, the hesitation should have frayed her nerves, and it did a little. But it also gave her a strange new confidence. If she could still feel doubt, then she had not gone mad.

She had not become her mother.

"Per Ristolo?" she asked, turning to the ancient priest. "Do you feel the same?"

He still stood at the ridge, gazing down at the ruins and the falling water and the tombs with a serene expression on his face.

"Not anymore," he replied, turning to smile at her. "I had my doubts, but they have been erased."

Per Stellan stiffened. "Magic unbound, uncontrolled, destroyed the First City."

"Legends—" Per Ristolo began.

"Legends that lay in ruins around us!" Per Stellan growled, throwing her arms wide to take in the broken bridge, the fallen tower.

Phela felt a ripple of anger, but Per Ristolo reached his fellow priest before she could. The old man put his hand on Per Stellan's shoulder and gazed into her one eye.

"You did not come down here to stop now."

"I came down here because my queen commanded it. And you, Per Ristolo, came down here because Her Majesty threatened to kill everyone you've ever loved."

"Nonsense," Per Ristolo said. "If what you fear comes to pass, they will die anyway. I came because this is their best hope for survival, and for ours. And . . . confess, sister, you came because a part of you wonders what will happen. A part of you yearns to know if the age of the Four can begin anew."

Per Stellan hung her head. In the shadows, Shome started forward, but Queen Phela gestured for her to be still. After a moment, Per Stellan exhaled and met Per Ristolo's gaze.

"I confess I am afraid," the woman said.

Queen Phela took her hand. Kissed her cheek. "Fear is wisdom, priest. Have courage. The Four are with us. With *me*. I can feel it in my blood."

This was the only truth, pure and real. The lure of the gods, the song that seemed to hum in Phela's heart, grew louder. They knew she was coming, and that the future was about to begin.

∽

They stood in thigh-deep water so suffused with magic that it felt more like cold fire crackling on Phela's skin. It swirled and eddied with its own strange currents, the color and visual texture of blue silk. Queen Phela luxuriated in that feeling, letting the magic wash over her, breathing it in and reaching out to cloak herself in the sparkling air. Per Ristolo and Per Stellan stood on either side of her and she could see the emotions playing across their faces, terror one moment and ecstasy the next.

"Kneel," Per Ristolo said. "Kneel, my queen, before Dephine and Charin, before Bettika and Anselom. Let the Four bless you."

Phela surrendered to this moment and sank to her knees, the water rising to her throat. Her linen trousers clung to her legs while her long cloak floated up around her like the wings of a falcon. Per Stellan put a hand on her scalp and began to intone the words of a ritual that had become familiar to her by now, but then the words changed. The ritual altered. The charge in the air and the crackling in the water seemed to sheathe her. Queen Phela felt the small hairs on her arms bristle. When she inhaled, she felt weightless, as if not the water but magic itself now buoyed her, so that her flesh and bones were no longer subject to the clutch of the world.

"Bettika," Per Ristolo said, putting his hand over Per Stellan's, and the ritual continued. The words flowed. The ancient priest threw his head back and when Phela looked, she saw that tears streamed down his face. "Dephine."

"Anselom," Per Stellan said. "Charin."

Queen Phela laid her head back. "I open myself to you. My blood is yours. Your blood is mine."

More than an hour they had stood in the water in the midst of the tombs. More than an hour to reach this moment, to cleanse herself and to pay obeisance to each of the Four in turn, and now to all Four at once. With no little astonishment, the queen realized that she too had begun to weep and to shudder with an ecstasy unlike any she'd felt from the touch of another. She cried out in joy. A flutter of movement drew her attention from the corner of her eye and she saw Shome moving forward as if concerned she might be in danger. The assassin had come within the curtain of falling water but no farther, unwilling to move into the midst of the tombs, to be among the Four so intimately. She had steeled herself to face any danger without flinching, but this had made even the Silent give pause.

"Bettika," Queen Phela said, beginning to name them as the priests had.

The magic rushed into her with such ferocity that she cried out again, this time with no pleasure at all. She coughed once, tried to breathe, but felt her nose begin to bleed and tasted that copper tang on her lips.

"Dephine," she went on with a gasp.

This time the magic stabbed her deep in her breast, a jolt of pain that penetrated and then spread like a flood of agony within her chest. Phela tried to cry out again, only to have water plunge down her throat. Her eyes snapped open—she hadn't even known that she'd closed them—and she found herself beneath the surface of that glowing, silken, crackling pool.

With a roar, she planted her legs and thrust herself up and out of the water. No longer on her knees, but still bleeding from her nose and now from her eyes and ears as well. She wiped at them, and then felt the warm trickle along her inner thigh and she knew she'd begun to bleed from between her legs as well. The magic raged inside her, churning her guts and rushing through her veins, thundering in her heart as if two lions had gone to war in her chest.

Vision blurring, she turned to Per Stellan. Reached for her. Hands around her throat. "What have you done?"

Per Ristolo clasped the queen's short hair and hauled her backward, breaking her hold on his sister priest. Holding her by her hair, he forced Phela to look at him, to focus on him.

"Majesty, listen to me. We've made a terrible mistake—"

Queen Phela punched him in the temple, knocking him into the water before standing over him, her emotions, like the magic of the two gods, battling within her.

Shome appeared as if from nothing, standing over the priest and ready to kill if her queen commanded it.

"Stop!" Per Stellan shouted. "Listen to him. I know you can feel it, Queen Phela. The magic is not balanced. Without harmony, it will tear you apart. Per Ristolo wants this for you, he wants to bring the magic into the world, to see Quandis become a kingdom that encompasses the entire world, from dark horizon to dark horizon and beyond. And I . . . gods help me, I want it, too! But you have to believe us."

Phela gasped, trying to slow her breathing and quiet the war within her. Again she wiped at the blood dripping from her eyes and nose. It seemed to be slowing, and that calmed her. Perhaps she would not die this very moment.

"What then?" She pointed at Per Ristolo, who remained crouched in the water, afraid to rise fully in case Shome might carve out his heart. As if she needed the Silent to do her killing anymore. "You said we've made a mistake."

Per Ristolo's eyes gleamed with the light of faith. "We were foolish to attempt this *here*. You wanted to be close to the tombs, to be among the Four, and I understood that. But with the water so deep it is impossible to precisely determine the point of harmony. The axis."

Queen Phela narrowed her eyes. She glanced around the vast chamber, surveyed the tombs, and then she tilted her head back and stared upward. The water rose in tendrils around her as if it would reach out toward the ceiling of that great subterranean cathedral. A sudden wind appeared, dancing with those tendrils of water, and she knew what she'd felt had been the magics of Dephine and Bettika, and that they desired what she desired. She *knew* it.

"The axis," she echoed.

"Yes," Per Stellan said. "In the courtyard of the Temple of the Four, the point of harmony in the precise center, where the lines of power from the four towers meet."

Queen Phela reached for Per Ristolo's hand, helping him to rise fully to his feet. "We should have thought of it before."

"It's not like we had a precedent, Majesty," Per Stellan said.

Ever brazen, Phela thought. Before she could show the priest her displeasure, Per Ristolo said, "If there is any hope of succeeding in this, it will be at the temple. I . . ."

"What? Speak!"

"I worry now, after seeing you bleed. After the pain you've just been through. I fear even you, even one of the Blood . . ."

He did not complete his statement. There was no need.

"I bleed, yes, but I bleed the Blood of the Four, and what is left in me is still strong. No, I have other concerns," Queen Phela said. "The Temple of Four is full of traitors and blasphemers, your brothers and sisters who refused to recognize my authority as head of the Faith. Euphraxia will have marshaled them by now. We have allies among them, but we must kill all those who stand in the way if we are to complete this ceremony."

The High Order priests, these who had become her servants, knew better than to argue.

Phela glanced at Shome. "The others are in place?"

Shome nodded, and the queen smiled in return.

"Excellent," Phela said. "Then we ascend once more, this time along a more familiar route. Those in the temple will not expect us to rise from beneath them."

"And if they are willing to kneel to you?" Per Stellan said. "If they do not fight back?"

Queen Phela smiled. "Perhaps you had better spend your time on the way back up praying that they do."

❧

Demos stormed across the bridge that separated Temple Hill from Palace Hill, every inch of his back prickling with the anticipation of a blade, his skull singing with the expectation of a cudgel. As far as the rank and file of the City Guard knew, his father had been a Penter and a traitor. None but Commander Kurtness knew that he'd escaped slavery—the rest likely assumed he'd been freed—but they all knew he had been a slave. A nobleman, son of a baron, heir to one of the Five Great Clans, a warrior honored for his service to the Crown . . . all of that, yes, but fallen. His honor erased. For those who didn't know, one glimpse of the slave brand on the back of his hand would be enough to reveal him. The skin remained tight where the mark had been burned into his flesh, but even when all remaining discomfort had vanished, it would still burn him. He felt as if the brand was some kind of beacon, drawing attention, declaring itself.

Slave or not, Queen Phela had commanded him to go and attack the temple with the City Guard and he had done as she'd instructed, even wearing a Guard uniform. Many had been killed before they'd been driven back, and now that his mission had failed, he expected repercussions. Had Phela given her loyalists orders to take his life should he fail?

Or had she given them those orders regardless of his success?

He marched toward the far side of the bridge, waiting for the death blow. They could mark him with any scar they liked. Now that he had freed himself, he would never be enslaved again. A knife in the back would be better. At least then he would have died free.

"What are we doing?" Fissel rasped low, nudging closer to him in the cluster of City Guards.

Demos glanced over his shoulder, but Commander Kurtness seemed almost to have forgotten his presence. Kurtness barked at his men, looked up at the palace, and then back toward the temple, and hurried them onward.

"Quiet until we can speak alone," Demos whispered to Fissel. "On your life."

The sailor tugged at his blood-spattered beard and fidgeted with his hands. They'd taken away his sword, unwilling to trust a sailor of the queen because they'd found him inside the Temple of Four. Fissel had spoken only the truth, that Admiral Hallarte had sent him with a message for one of the novice priests, but this had made Commander Kurtness more suspicious than ever. Why a priest? What had the message contained?

Fissel claimed not to know the answers to those questions, and perhaps he did not, but Kurtness clearly did not believe him. Demos had taken up his cause, insisting that Fissel was loyal to Admiral Hallarte and thus to the Crown, and that he must be speaking the truth. Kurtness had let him live, but planned to put him in a cell until he could be questioned further. The commander had always struck Demos as a fair man, and he seemed more than a little conflicted over the chaos reigning in Lartha today, but he would follow the queen's orders no matter what. That much was clear, and it made him very dangerous to Demos and Fissel at this moment.

The sky churned with dark clouds, and a cold wind blasted between the city's hills, sweeping in and around them, rushing above and below the bridges, whipping at flags and bending trees. Rain had just begun to fall, lightly at first but with the promise of much more to come.

"There they are!" one of the Guards shouted. Their pace quickened, a dozen men and women hurrying across the bridge.

At the far end, where the bridge met Palace Hill, a detachment of City Guards awaited them. Four clusters of perhaps forty each, standing in orderly rows. Demos had seen such formations many times before and he knew what he was looking at—assault units ready to be deployed. Fissel began to speak again and Demos hushed him with a single glance; this was not the time for questions to be spoken aloud. With each of the four units were two Silent assassins, swathed in gray, their posture making their intentions clear. They were no longer meant to hide in shadows. The queen had sent them out into the capital to kill.

"Commander!" called a sergeant as he stepped out from the nearest formation. Demos recognized the sergeant as Konnell, the friend who'd snuck Myrinne in to see him when he'd first been arrested. Apparently the young City Guardsman had been promoted. "All Guard units are in position, awaiting the signal, sir," Konnell reported.

Kurtness, still nursing bloody wounds and bruises, joined Sergeant Konnell.

"Take two units back to the Temple of Four," the commander ordered.

"Right away, sir."

"Send the other two units to Yaris Teeg. Be aware, they have Phage on their side. And a priest who commands . . . magic."

"Magic?" Konnell asked.

"Dangerous. Powerful. But it must be confronted. Some of the priests will hide in the tunnels, but do not pursue them there. Seal the entrances and set a watch. Queen Phela's edict is in effect from this moment. Accept every surrender, but execute anyone who refuses to swear fealty to her."

Sergeant Konnell's face went pale. "Anyone, Commander? What of the apex?"

"Especially the apex," Kurtness snarled. "If you can get close enough, kill her on sight. The queen will give an island to the Guard who brings her Euphraxia's head."

Demos felt his gut roil as he watched some of the Guards roar their assent. To their credit, some also seemed uneasy, but none of them were willing to disobey. In moments the four units were passing them, rushing back along the bridge the way they'd come, and it was clear this had been part of the plan all along. If the initial assault failed, it would be enough to distract the priests who were loyal to the apex and allow them to think themselves triumphant. But now Sergeant Konnell took four times as many Guards with him as had been part of the first attack. The priests would never stand against them for very long, not even with magic on their side. The Phage might even the odds, but the Silent were a counterbalance.

The priests would either surrender, or they would be massacred.

Fissel tapped Demos's shoulder. "Look there."

In the distance, smoke rose from two hills, the ancestral homes of Clan Hartshorn and Clan Daklan. Nearer still, they could see fire blazing from a block of merchants' homes just a few hundred yards away, on the road back up toward the palace.

"Apparently they did not await the signal," Commander Kurtness said grimly. "Let's move. We're to join the sweep of the courtiers' district. Every household must kneel." He looked pointedly at Demos and Fissel. "Every soldier and sailor must take up the sword for the queen, whose orders have been conveyed through me."

"There is a chain of command," Fissel argued.

"And the queen is atop that chain. Her word supersedes any other," Kurtness said. He patted one of his Guards on the back and then gave the woman a shove to get them all moving. "Don't be afraid to get your blades bloodied. You won't make it through the night without killing, so get it through your heads now."

They began to troop past Demos and Fissel, these ten men and women who'd been among Kurtness's most trusted Guards. The commander took a step nearer to Demos and locked eyes with him.

"You have something to say, Kallistrate?"

"I'm not going with you. Neither is Fissel."

"I've given you an order."

Demos smiled and cocked his head. "Queen Phela ordered me to accompany you on the assault at Yaris Teeg and then to return to her, and to Princess Myrinne. You've just said that the word of the queen supersedes any other. Unless you believe that you're an exception, I'm sure you'll agree that my duty is to obey her instructions."

Commander Kurtness glanced at Fissel, eyes narrowed. He might have argued, but just then the bells in the Bone Spire began to ring. White and fluted, like an enormous musical instrument, it stabbed the air above the palace, half the height of the Blood Spire but far more beloved because of its bells. *That changes today,* Demos thought, because he saw the way the Guards around him stiffened. The Bone Spire would not be beloved anymore.

"I take it that's the signal your Guards were supposed to be waiting for?" he said.

"Go," Kurtness said. "But you don't go alone." He grabbed the shoulder of one of his soldiers, a monster of a man, arrogant but skilled, and not half as dumb as he looked. "Cofflin will see that you return to the palace."

Cofflin knew better than to argue, though he seemed disappointed as Commander Kurtness led the others away at a run, the bells still pealing. The wind picked up, and with each gust the sound of the bells grew louder and softer. Cofflin wiped rain from his eyes and shot a pointed look at Demos and Fissel.

"Let's move. Faster the better," the ugly Guard said. "Don't be stupid and we'll all get where we're meant to be tonight." He grinned at Demos. "Some of us to warmer beds than others, I'd wager."

Cofflin indicated that Demos should lead the way, with Fissel between them, and they started up the hill, into the shadow of the palace and the pouring rain.

At the first blind corner, still half a mile from the palace, Fissel sprinted away. Cofflin shouted furiously and ran in pursuit. Demos cut the large man down before he'd taken his third step. Fissel hurried back to him, the two of them staring for a moment at the blood mixing with the rain that sluiced around the cobblestones in the road.

"Free to talk now?" Fissel joked, as he bent to retrieve Cofflin's sword for himself.

Demos started walking, still toward the palace. "Say it quickly, old friend. Myrinne awaits and decisions must be made."

Fissel began talking, and with every word Demos felt his heart lighten. It did not entirely surprise him to learn that Admiral Hallarte had brought a fleet that even now made its way up the river Susk, but the news kindled a powerful hope within him. Today was a dark day in Lartha, and the people would be both terrified and revolted by Phela's actions against the Temple of Four and the apex. And even though the common folk probably hadn't harbored any thoughts of rebellion before this, if Daria truly meant to make war upon the queen, to take the city from the Crown, she would certainly find willing allies among the furious and the oppressed.

"I never dreamed it would come to this," Demos said, quickening his pace.

"There's more. A bit of a shock, really," Fissel noted. "It's about the admiral."

Demos slid against a wall, peering around a corner. The gates of the palace were guarded, of course, but he'd been sent out with Commander Kurtness and he wore the cloak of the City Guard. Myrinne would be waiting for his return just inside the gates as they'd agreed, unless Phela had ordered her confined to her chambers.

"What about her?" Demos asked as he moved around the corner and started toward the gates.

"She's Bajuman."

"That's not funny."

Fissel grabbed his arm. "I'm not laughing."

Demos faltered. Then he saw in the other sailor's eyes that he was not jesting, not at all. A shudder went through Demos and for a moment he felt a familiar revulsion. Then he thought of Mouse and Tollivar and his own childhood, the Bajumen executed and banished these past weeks, and the woman he'd fought beside, the woman he'd followed. Daria Hallarte was one of his dearest friends. More than that, she'd been his leader. In every battle he'd fought under her command, he'd hoped for her approval. And though the initial shock had torn through him with speed, this news changed none of that.

"Her eyes . . ." he began.

Fissel held up both hands. "Don't ask me. I haven't got the whole story, but I promise you it's true."

"And the fleet still follows her," Demos said in wonder.

"Most of us. Not to mention thousands of Bajumen in a parade of little boats that shouldn't even have made it through the waters of the Ring. But they follow nevertheless."

Demos imagined a string of small boats full of rebellious Bajuman slaves following a fleet of warships led by a Bajuman admiral. Laughter bubbled up inside him and he had to let it out. His smile grew so wide that it hurt his face, but he hung his head, trying to force himself to breathe and to quiet his laughter.

"What's so gods-damned funny?" Fissel asked, staring at him with such concern in his eyes that it caused a fresh wave of laughter.

"All of it," Demos said, catching his breath. He wiped at his eyes. "It's lunacy, my friend. The world is upside down."

"It doesn't matter to you that she's Bajuman?"

That sobered him. "People are being slaughtered all over the city because they won't kneel to a queen who will kill anyone who doesn't cheer her every cruel whim. Today I find that nothing matters more than that." He turned his hand so the brand was clearly visible, reminding Fissel that he bore the mark. "As for following a slave . . . who am I to argue?"

He put one hand on the pommel of his sword and started for the gates. "I wish Daria hadn't kept her secret from me and I look forward to seeing her again. I believe in her mission. But my only concern is finding Myrinne and getting away from here. I've dreamed of a life with her since we were children, and I won't abandon that dream now."

"That seems the coward's way out."

Demos spun on Fissel. "I don't care what you think. You have never been a slave. You have never seen your father torn apart in front of you or had your family murdered for a lie. You can do what you want, but don't think for one *second* you can judge me."

They stared at each other for a moment before Fissel nodded, and they moved once more toward the palace. As the rain pelted them and the sky grew darker, a wagon raced through the square in front of the palace gates with a wild-looking bearded man at the reins. Two City Guards on horseback pursued him as objects tumbled out of the back of the wagon, lanterns and pottery and clothing. Small hands appeared, hurling things . . . a family attempting to escape execution, using their worldly possessions to defend themselves. Demos quickened his pace, thinking to aid them, but Fissel took his arm and he remembered what he'd just said. Hundreds would die in Lartha today. Perhaps thousands. But Demos's duty was to Myrinne.

The hooves of the Guards' horses clattered on wet cobblestones. Demos wondered how long the family had spent packing and realized that they'd planned to evacuate the city long before the City Guard had begun their house-to-house sweep. Maybe he had underestimated the unrest in Lartha. The people were terrified and ready to flee. Or to fight.

The palace gates lay ahead. There were no supplicants to the throne lined up now. The usual Guards were there, now with reinforcements. The small guardhouse could not have held the nine men and women who were standing sentry, and their number made Demos's spine stiffen. Could he and Fissel kill this many?

Certainly not, which meant they had no choice but to talk their way inside. Myrinne would be waiting on the other side of the gate, ready to command them if she could choose the right moment to intervene, if she knew when he would be there.

If, if, if . . .

"This seems poorly planned on your part," Fissel said quietly as the nine gate Guards saw them coming and began to react.

If those Guards had been dogs, they'd have begun to bark at the approach of two soldiers they did not recognize. Instead they tapped one another and put hands on their swords. One woman drew her blade. Demos could not argue with Fissel's criticism.

When a small, hooded figure moved out from the shadow of the northern palace wall, they all ignored it at first. A peasant who'd been hoping to make an entreaty to the queen and was unafraid of the rain, or so Demos thought. So he imagined they all must have thought. But when that small, slim figure marched toward him and Fissel, the gate Guards stared in suspicion. Two of them broke away from the gate and began to follow the hooded one, who quickened his pace.

Fissel began to draw his sword.

"No," Demos said. "He's a friend."

For he'd seen inside that hood and he knew the pale face within. "Tollivar," he said quietly, just loud enough for the boy to hear him above the rain. "You were supposed to wait for us."

"No more time for waiting," the boy said, walking right past them. "Follow me, Demos. You and your friend. And if those bastards at the gate follow, you'll have to kill them."

What is this now? Demos thought, but he followed, and Fissel did the same.

Over his shoulder, he looked at the guards and called out, "We'll see what he's up to. Commander Kurtness sends orders to stay to your posts. It's begun now, and no doubt there will be those who try to rush the gate to reach the queen."

The two Guards who'd set after them looked unsettled and uncertain. They faltered a couple of steps and then consulted quietly before starting back toward the gate, glancing around as if afraid that at any moment the populace might attack the palace. Demos was now beginning to think this a very rational fear.

Tollivar led them half a block west to a small alley of shops, most of which had been shuttered. Several still had people rushing in and out, but word had spread quickly and they knew the City Guard and soldiers were on the way. One woman saw Demos in his cloak and screamed. She toppled the cart of fruits and vegetables she'd been trying to drag inside her shop and fled within, screaming for someone, perhaps her husband. The cloak had helped them before, but now Demos thought it would work against them. As Tollivar quickened the pace, Demos reached up to unclasp the cloak. When he glanced up again, the boy was gone.

"Here," Fissel said, seeing his confusion.

They glanced around. A handful of worried faces were watching them, so there was no chance of slipping away unnoticed, but Demos saw no other option and followed Fissel into a small theater. He glanced back at the doorway, but it seemed none of those out in the alley were brave enough to follow.

In the darkness of the foyer, with the sound of the rain outside the door, Tollivar stood between curtains that draped the entrance into the theater proper. A hand touched the boy's shoulder and he stood aside, and then she emerged from behind him.

"Myrinne," Demos said, hurrying to her, the clasp of his cloak forgotten. Her eyes gleamed in the darkness, alight with determination. "You were meant to wait in the palace. What—"

"The palace isn't safe now, not even for a princess. The time's come for us to leave," she said, glancing warily at Fissel.

"He's a friend," Demos said, introducing him. "We've fought together before."

Myrinne nodded. "Tollivar heard whispers on the street, out among the peasants, of a fleet coming up the Susk to challenge Phela."

"We know. Daria Hallarte's in command."

A smile touched his princess's lips. "Well then, by all means, let's go and greet her."

Demos removed the cloak of the City Guard. They were leaving Lartha behind at last, chasing their dream of the future, and he preferred not to be killed by his own allies in a case of mistaken identity.

All we have to do is live until tomorrow, he thought.

Myrinne took his hand and led him deeper into the theater. An old man, perhaps the owner, bowed to the princess as they passed by, and then he retreated backstage.

They made their way into a cellar with Fissel and Tollivar in tow, then into a tunnel, down a set of stone steps, and by the time they surfaced half an hour later, they were nearly at the bottom of Palace Hill and only blocks from the river. In the gray storm light, with the rain pouring down, they made their way to a boathouse. It was clear that Myrinne had been here before and was prepared for this day.

The boat wasn't much, but the hull didn't leak and the oars were strong, and Demos and Fissel had been rowing all their lives. They'd make it to the fleet.

They had to.

⁓

Blane felt Daria's approach as if it were midwinter and his soul yearned for spring, knowing it was coming but impatient for its arrival. He was angry with her, nurtured an ember of fury in his heart, and yet he'd read the words she'd written over and over. Daria.

This was Daria. His sister was still alive. His rage existed alongside the joy of that thought, and the urgent ambition that had propelled him for years. His sister had returned, and she had returned with an army. Apex Euphraxia wanted him to broker an alliance, and perhaps that would serve Blane for now, but if the queen could be overthrown, and if Blane might seize even more of the magic he had watched Phela wielding—had wielded himself—then he knew he would no longer need the apex. His dream of freedom for the Bajumen would be made true.

Pleasure rippled through him, though he wasn't sure if it was the thought of freedom or the the magic inside him. The falling rain merged with the sparkling blue in the air, and he smiled. This was the fabric of the world, and he felt as if he could almost touch it, unravel it, weave it into whatever pattern he wished. Once he had believed in no gods at all, but now he could almost imagine what it might feel like to be a god himself. A Bajuman god. The idea made him laugh before he caught himself short.

Don't be a fool, he thought. *You're only a man with a little taste of the miraculous.*

And yet, Blane was growing to like the idea of the miraculous. It seemed like a miracle that Daria was still alive, and even more of a miracle that he found himself here, with this power and an alliance with the apex of the Faith, engaged in two wars against the queen— one war for the people, and one for the magic of gods.

He ran alongside the river, leaving Temple Hill behind. His heart felt tethered not to the Temple of Four but to Yaris Teeg, and he wondered how Gemmy fared. He could remember the way her lips tasted and the way her skin felt beneath the roughness of his hands. Blane hoped to see her again, and he hoped if that day came, they would find themselves on the same side.

Across the river he saw smoke rising from a dozen places in the city. Despite the rain, two fires burned so furiously that their glow could be seen against the gray sky. If there were screams, the river drowned them out.

At the Market Bridge he saw merchants lowering boats toward the water. There would be more soon. Most would not think to flee, assuming their past loyalties would not be called into question, that the City Guard would treat them with decency and a sense of justice. But there would be those among them who would have heard whispers about the behavior of the queen and taken them seriously, and some of those would no doubt try to escape the city. Some would attempt to leave by the roads, but the smart ones would take to the river.

Which made things difficult, because Blane needed a boat. He peered across the river through the rain and decided that a nearby merchant's boat would do perfectly well. Whispering a prayer to Dephine, he reached out to touch the magic that fell with the rain, flowed with the river. Nothing more than a shadow on the riverbank, he stepped into the water and waded up to his knees.

Then he heard a voice off to one side, words carried by the wind. He looked upriver and he saw another boat, this one nearer to him. Four passengers, one of them tall and dark-haired and rowing powerfully, not content to let the current carry them toward the sea.

This'll do even better, Blane thought, and he spoke his prayer a little louder. His eyes closed to slits and he breathed deeply. As he let out that breath, he felt the magic of the gods flow through his heart. From his lips. From the tips of his fingers. The water around the boat rose up and carried it toward the riverbank in a wave. The rower swept his oars, stabbing comically at the water while the rest of them tried to hang on. Another man and a woman tumbled into the river a dozen feet from the bank. Flailing, a young boy leaped after them. Only the rower held on as the wave delivered him and his boat to the riverbank, shoving it ashore.

Wild-eyed with shock, the rower stood and drew his sword while his passengers swam toward the bank. The boat rocked beneath the rower's boots as he stared at Blane, and then the man's eyes widened.

"I know you," the man said, stepping from the boat onto the riverbank, sword held firmly as the others dragged themselves from the water behind them.

Blane muttered the beginning of a prayer to Charin and fire blossomed in the palms of his hands, but then he realized that he recognized the other man as well.

"Oh, this is a gift," he said. "The Four have blessed me. You were there at the temple, helping the City Guard murder my friends. You're one of Phela's dogs."

"I have no love for Phela," the man said, eyeing the fire in Blane's hands warily. "Nor any loyalty to her. She had my father murdered, and my mother and brother died because of her. Clan Kallistrate has been torn apart, and that was only the beginning."

Demos Kallistrate, Blane thought, remembering the name. *Cast down into slavery.*

"Yet you fought for her," he said. "You *killed* for her."

The woman who'd been on board his boat pulled herself out of the water behind him, followed by the boy. Demos held up a hand to prevent them from coming any closer, as if distance mattered for Blane's powers. The woman ignored him and drew her sword, apparently more than willing to die at Kallistrate's side. Soaking wet, her hair plastered to her cheeks, she looked somehow familiar, but Blane could not place her.

"Yes, I did. And you killed for Euphraxia," Demos said. "She's as corrupt as the queen."

Blane heard shouting and looked across the river. The merchants had gotten their boat into the water, reminding him that there would be others. He wanted to reach Daria as quickly as possible, before he could get lost in the midst of an exodus.

"Step aside, Kallistrate," he said. "I have need of your boat. If you're running from the city, you might die today, but it doesn't have to be at my hand."

"You're High Order," the woman said. "With that kind of magic . . . how can you desert the Faith now? If you hate my . . . if you hate the queen, the priesthood needs you. The *Four* need you."

"The *Bajumen* need me, and that's all that matters."

Blane let the fire burn higher in his hand. It rose into a spiral, whipped by the wind, a tornado of flames in his palm. He felt as if he could paint the sky with it and knew he could kill them all.

"Stop, please," the boy said, stepping past the woman, and for the first time Blane saw that he was Bajuman.

He faltered. *No,* he thought. He wouldn't kill this boy. Enough Bajuman blood had been shed, and more would surely be spilled in the process of trying to bring freedom to them all.

But he had to get to Daria, and they had what he needed . . .

The fire in his hand dimmed, but only a bit. "Get out of the way. I must have that boat."

Then the other man rose from the water, staggering, and drew his sword as he stepped forward. "Enough talk. You can't have the fucking boat. Let's see what your gods-damned magic can do."

Blane could only stare at him. "You . . . you're Fissel. The messenger my sister sent."

Fissel lowered his sword as if all the strength had gone from his arm. "Blane?"

Demos Kallistrate did not lower his sword, but he did begin to laugh. "Wait," he said, glancing at Fissel. "You're telling me this asshole is Daria's brother?"

"You know Daria?"

"I served under her," Demos said. "She's who we're going to see."

The fire went out in Blane's hand.

Everything was different after that.

19

Before any skirmish or full-blown battle, Daria was used to having Shawr close at hand to help her prepare. Not just laying out her weapons and uniform, helping her dress, checking the clasps on her armor, and tightening the straps and belts that kept her weapons close to her body, but also acting as her sounding board, confidant, and, sometimes, the voice of reason and calm. Daria had never faced a conflict with fear in her heart, because for her every new day was another day of a life she should never have had. The real Daria had died upon hitting the sea below those cliffs, and this new version was a blessing from Lameria. Yet the absence of fear did not mean she had not contended with doubts and worries. Shawr had always been there to help with those.

He was dead now. He'd loved her in secret, and then he'd hated her. The memory of his sneering disdain echoed bitterly in her thoughts and Daria felt his absence keenly. But as her fleet moved up the river Susk and toward Lartha, it was not Shawr who occupied her thoughts. With the greatest battle of her life facing her, all she could think of was the face of a small boy, and how that boy might look now, as a man.

I'm going to see you soon, brother, she thought, and although so much heaviness weighed on her mind, she could not help smiling.

"Admiral?" Gree asked. "Your orders?" She could hear the concern in his voice.

"Yes, Captain," she said. "Send the runners on ahead to scope out the land. Though we're rowing upriver, I can't help thinking we're rushing into this."

"I'm not sure delaying would benefit us at all," Gree said. "You heard what that lieutenant said. Things are moving on apace in Lartha, and any element of surprise we have, we must use."

Daria nodded and looked around the table at her ships' captains. None of them disagreed, and they had all signed their names to the battle plan she had drawn up. She appreciated the trust in that, but also knew that the truth was obvious to them all, both from experience and from the complex situation they were about to immerse themselves in—no battle plan ever survived the first clash of swords.

"No sign of Fissel?" she asked.

Gree shook his head.

"Tell me when he returns," she said. "Anything else?" She looked around the table at the men and women facing her. Grim but confident, she sensed no trace of doubt in her leadership, only in their situation. They were sailing to a possible war against their queen. No sane person would not be troubled by that.

No one spoke up.

"There is one more thing," Daria said. She stood, smiled, and felt a surprising heat behind her eyes. She was not normally an emotional woman. This was not a normal time. "Thank you. For everything that has happened, and all that's to come. We've fought some real battles together, and we have always been bound by trust. I'm . . . honored that still remains, and it feels stronger and more precious to me now than ever before. I know that we're facing genuine uncertainties today, but I'm *convinced* we're doing the right thing. We're standing true to our convictions, and I firmly believe that we are upholding our duty to Quandis, first and fore-most. I love this land as much as you all. I love its people, Quandians and Bajumen alike. And I love you, for . . ." She did not finish her sentence. She didn't need to.

"Captain!" a sailor said, knocking at the open wardroom door. "A small boat's approaching, and Fissel's onboard."

"Thank you," Daria said. She turned to her officers. "Captain Gree, with me. The rest of you, dismissed. Make final preparations for the liberation of Lartha." Gree left first, and she followed him out of the wardroom and up onto the deck.

The wind blew rain into her face, stinging her skin and nar-rowing her eyes. She was nervous. Had Fissel delivered the message to Blane? More importantly, had he returned with a reply? Many scenarios were swirling in her head—Blane could not be found, he was allied with the queen, he was lost in the chaos of what Lartha had become . . .

He was dead.

He hated her for what she had done.

She actually wasn't sure which of the last two would hit her harder. Daria's heart thumped and her skin tingled with anticipa-tion at whatever news Fissel might bring.

"Stand to!" she heard from amidships. "Who goes there?"

She saw a group of sailors at the gunwale aiming crossbows down at a boat that was out of sight. Beneath the shush of the wind, she heard the boat nudging against the *Nayadine,* and Fissel's voice as he offered a response.

"Seaman Fissel from the *Royal Dawn,*" he called up. "With me I have Princess Myrinne, seeking to ask Admiral Hallarte for sanctu-ary. Demos Kallistrate, next in line for the Kallistrate baronhood. A Bajuman boy, Tollivar. And Blane, brother of Admiral Hallarte."

Her heart pounded and she could not stop the smile that touched her lips. *He's here! Not a message . . . he's come to me in the flesh!*

"Let them onboard," Captain Gree said. He glanced back at Daria, and it might have been the first time she'd seen anything like disapproval in his eyes. She tried to vanquish her smile, but could not. Instead, she offered him a small shrug. Yes, she should have told the captain, but this had been a personal affair. She had feared her revelation might be met with anger and resentment, that Blane might never forgive her. Yet here he was, and with him somehow was the sister of the mad queen, her old friend and comrade in arms, and a Bajuman boy!

Daria waited away from the railing while the passengers from the boat came aboard. Crossbows had been lowered, but she could still sense her sailors' alertness and caution. The princess came first, Captain Gree bowing his head in welcome, Princess Myrinne hugging her robes tight against the wind and rain. Daria was surprised to see that the royal wore a sword, and she wondered what was going on in Lartha that warranted this unexpected appearance. She glanced behind the princess to see a young Bajuman boy come next, wide-eyed and fascinated.

Then Demos, her old friend whom she'd started her journey back to Quandis to save. He stood at attention and saluted, and Daria returned the salute halfheartedly. Demos reached to shake her hand and she clapped him on the shoulder, told him how glad she was to have him back. How sorry she was about his family. The words were sincere—Demos meant a great deal to her; he'd been her brother-in-arms—but Blane truly was her brother, and the anticipation of his arrival distracted her from what ought to have been a more enthusiastic reunion.

"I wasn't sure if you'd come back," she said, squeezing Demos's shoulder. "Once you'd learned my story."

"Yes, you were. If all of these sea dogs are standing by you, surely you knew I would do no less." He released her hand, almost but not quite returning to attention. Then he showed her the back of his right hand, and she blinked in surprise at the slave brand burned into the skin. "Besides, I'm seeing things quite a bit differently these days."

Daria knew he'd been enslaved, but still the brand was a shock. "Was it hellish?"

Demos narrowed his eyes. "Nothing I'd ever complain to a Bajuman about, Admiral." He leaned in slightly and spoke more quietly. "You could've told me, you know? I'd have kept your secret."

Daria nodded as if such loyalty was a foregone conclusion, when only two days before she could never have imagined the truth would have ended in anything but disaster.

"Apparently you've kept a great many secrets," Demos added.

He looked back down into the boat, then at Daria once more, and then he stepped aside to make way for a tall, strong man who mounted the top of the rope ladder, ignoring the helping hands offered to him. The young man in his priestly robes had begun to scan the faces onboard even before he set foot on deck.

When he locked eyes with her, Daria's chest tightened and shame warmed her cheeks. She wondered what he saw, whether he recognized her, and whether the flood of childhood memories he was experiencing was similar to her own, as warm and comforting.

"Blane," she said, and he blinked several times upon hearing the name from her lips.

"Sister."

One word, but she had longed to hear it forever. Daria's whole world narrowed and her focus shifted from her crews, her command, her duty, to lock solely onto her long-lost brother.

She held out her hands and beckoned him forward, terrified that Blane would turn his back on her and walk the other way. In his eyes she saw grim uncertainty and realized Blane also thought he might still reject her. He had every right. He'd come to this ship, true, but accompanying Demos and the princess. There were stories within stories, and she desired to hear them all, but right then the only tale she needed was the one between the two of them. To make sure there still *was* a story between the two of them.

That was all that mattered.

Abruptly the hesitation vanished from his face. He shook his head with a quiet laugh, then stepped in close and embraced her, his hands clasping behind her back, his forehead resting on hers. This close she could see how tired he looked, how ill, and yet there was something in his eyes that caused a shiver of fear. A strength. A power.

"Daria," he whispered, voice barely higher than the wind.

"Blane," she said again, enjoying the name on her lips. "I'm so sorry."

"Sorry?"

"For . . . everything. For letting my life carry me away from you. For not finding you sooner." She pulled him closer and pressed her cheek to his, closing her eyes and shutting out the rest of the world, just for a while. He hugged back.

"You only did what I would have done," he said into her ear. "You escaped. Took a chance. And"—he pulled back, looked her up and down, then around at the majestic battleship—"you seem to have done quite well for yourself."

Daria laughed, a short, sharp bark that she couldn't hold back.

"Admiral," Captain Gree said. "We need to be moving."

She blinked, letting the reality around them back into her thoughts. Officers and sailors had awkwardly glanced away to give them privacy, and Daria appreciated that discomfort. Now, though, she focused on Captain Gree again, and on the task ahead.

"Of course," she said. "Give the order, Captain."

"Admiral," Demos said, coming close. "There's so much to talk about." He glanced back and forth between her and Blane.

"I'm sure," she said. "Demos, this is Blane, my brother."

"Oh, we've met," Demos said. The words were spoken with humor, but her old friend also looked afraid. He was bruised and battered, thin and wasted within his City Guard uniform, and in a way he and Blane looked similarly bedraggled. Once more she wondered just what had been happening in Lartha.

"They know about you?" Blane asked, looking around at the crew members who had been watching the small boat's arrival and the reunion that followed.

"They know, and we fight side by side regardless," she said. "Considering your arrival, that's fortunate, don't you think?"

Blane shrugged. "I would have made them understand."

"You would?"

His eyes flickered from her, and he lowered his head. For an instant she thought he was reverting to the usual stance of a Bajuman, looking down in case he accidentally caught someone's eye, and she touched his chin to tilt his face up again. But then she saw that he was looking down at his hands. He turned them palms up, then over again, fisted and then fingers splayed, and he seemed fascinated.

Daria saw Demos watching, and there was definitely fear in his eyes.

"Demos?" she asked.

"As I said, my friend, there's so much to talk about, and it can't wait. You need to hear it all before any attack is launched." He glanced around at the other four ships' captains, who were waiting to board dinghies back to their vessels. "We should include them."

Daria nodded at Gree, and her captain passed the order.

"You've returned to a terrible time," Demos said. "It began with my father . . ."

"I know," she said. "It was your mother who first warned me what was transpiring here. She sent an albatross. She set all this in motion," Daria went on, gesturing to the assault force assembled on the river.

"Queen Lysandra's fault," he said. "And now Phela, that raving mad bitch, she's taken the throne and she's even worse than her mother."

Princess Myrinne had held back half a dozen steps during Daria's reunions with her two brothers—one by birth and the other by war—but now the royal stepped forward, tall and commanding, eyes flaring with determination, and for the first time Daria saw how it was that Demos had fallen so completely in love with her.

"Admiral, perhaps this discussion is better conducted in private," the princess said.

"Of course," Daria nodded. "A war council, then, and quickly."

She glanced at Blane. He was still staring at his hands, as if amazed or aghast at what they could do, and it made her wonder. But she and her brother would have to wait. Before family, there was duty. Before stories of the past, there was war.

❦

Standing in the pouring rain and the scything wind in the open square within the Temple of Four, the great towers to the gods rising around her, Phela felt as if her old self had become a stranger. Hundreds of gargoyles looked down upon her as sickness roiled in her stomach and her bones ached. Her muscles felt fluid and weak, and every time she blinked she worried that she would not be able to open her eyes again. Blood dried on her skin, but she liked its cooling feel. It meant that she was alive.

It was not only emergence into the storm that made her feel born afresh. It was her heightened sense of self, of her surroundings, of life. While pains and sickness bit in and made her feel so wretched and wonder whether her ambitions in magic had driven her too far and fast, a deeper part of her reveled in what she had done, and in what she was becoming.

I will be the Eternal Queen, she thought, *rich in power, forged by*

magic, and Quandis will last for a thousand years with me on its throne.
Even so, sickness spun and throbbed as if it was a living, breathing
thing. She leaned forward and gagged, and the spittle dripping from
her lips was alive with sparking things.

"Majesty," Per Ristolo said, "please let me help you." The old
priest was in awe of what they had already done, his wrinkled face
given a youthful hue by his fascination. Behind him, Per Stellan
looked on in disapproval, robes blowing about her form. But Phela
could see the excitement in her, too. In all their preparations and
rituals with fellow priests over the years, she knew they had never
seen anything like her. They had never believed.

Perhaps that was their problem.

Per Ristolo held her beneath the arms and then lifted, supporting
her weight as he guided her toward the center of the Four Square.
Phela shivered as the wind cut through her damp clothing, and the
sounds and smells of war suddenly became more prevalent. Bettika,
god of Wind and War, watched from her eyes and smiled.

"Shome," Phela said. "I need to speak with Shome."

"You need to preserve your strength for the final ritual," Per Ristolo said. She knew what he was thinking. She was his queen, true,
but now she was also his project. The priest was as eager as she was
to discover just how much she could take before breaking.

All of it, she'd said to them down by the tombs of the Four. *I
want all of it. Not just those few fleeting tendrils of magic that you
priests gather, haul in, keep like wisps on the air. I want it all, and I will
not break!*

"Shome . . ." she gasped, and the Silent was by her side. She
seemed taller than before, or perhaps Phela was stooped with the
sickness, crushed by the weight of what she bore. For the first time
she saw an expression other than calm understanding on the Silent's
tattooed face. Shome looked afraid.

"You're my right hand," Phela said. "You'll be with me forever,
my guide and my guard. My protector."

Rain running across her scarred features, Shome nodded once.

"It'll be over soon, and everything will be new. Everything will be *better*! For now, remain by my side."

There was no doubt in Shome's eyes, yet Phela would not have blamed her if she wondered just when it would all be over, and whether something grand and new could really rise out of what was happening here. And not just here, but throughout Lartha, and Quandis.

For while weakness and sickness battled inside Phela with the magic that promised so much, outside, throughout the Temple of Four and beyond, war raged.

Smoke rose beyond the Four Square walls, crests of fire blooming from timber and thatch roofs. In the far corner of the square, close to the foot of Charin Tower, several bodies were huddled against the wall, fresh blood spattered across skin both dark and pale. Phela could make out the robes of priests and cloaks of her Guard. She felt no flicker of regret. Anyone in the Guard knew their lives were owed to the Crown. Anyone speaking out against her was to be put to the sword, and she anticipated that throughout the priesthood there would be a great many martyrs today. Let them martyr themselves for whatever cause pleased them, Crown or Faith. Tomorrow, when the rest of the nation saw what she had become, they would be forgotten.

Who needs martyrs when they can have a new goddess?

Around the square stood several Silent and a score of City Guards, all of them facing the towers and surrounding walls, watching the doorways and arches for any attack from beyond. They had secured the Four Square, killed any who stood in their path, though many of the buildings no doubt still housed priests who were even now plotting against her. Phela was not worried. The warriors who fought in her name were alert, confident, strong, and dedicated to their queen. They would deal with whatever rebellion remained. But she was also sure that if any of them did falter, she had the power to defend herself.

Soon she would have *all* the power, and any skirmishes or squabbles remaining undecided would come to an end.

From beyond the walls, farther down Temple Hill and out of sight, she heard the sounds of combat. Even over the storm she could hear the clash of steel, shouts, and screams. Perhaps the magic enhanced her senses, and the flickering blue lights, those starry motes in her eyes, connected her to the elements more intimately than before. Regardless, she could hear the dying screams of those who opposed her, and some who fought for her, and she cared not at all. They were symptoms of change, the inevitable results of her deviating from a norm that had been holding Quandis down, and back, for generations.

Now that she had been imbued so deeply with magic, she had trouble understanding why such power had been rationed for so long. The High Order had much to answer for. They had not even been keeping the magic for themselves but had been guarding it jealously, ensuring that it fell into no one's hands.

Had guarded the people from the very thing that could have helped them.

Well, no more.

"Per Ristolo," she said. "I'm ready."

"Majesty . . ." Per Stellan said. The priest remained a dozen steps from her queen. Still *she doubts!* Phela felt anger boiling, but she had to hold it back.

"Per Stellan, this *will* happen," Phela said. "I called you in from the Ring because I believed in the depth of your Faith. Now you can witness, play a part, and share in the results. Or you can be against me." She nodded toward the bodies in the corner. "And you can see what happens to people who stand against me."

"I'm neither for, nor against," Per Stellan said. "I am simply loyal to the Four."

"As am I," Phela said. "As am I. Now, the ritual. When can it begin?"

"Soon," Per Ristolo said. "You are where you need to be, Majesty, at the perfect point of balance between the four towers and the tombs far below."

"So this is the spot? You're certain?"

The priest blinked, nervous and uncertain. "This has . . ."

"Never been done," Per Stellan finished for him. "And I remind you, Majesty, for good reason. Any fault, any error, and the magic might be unleashed in an unhindered storm that could destroy all of Quandis."

"'Might'?" Phela said. "'Could'? Where is your courage, priest?"

"This isn't about courage," Per Stellan said. "It's about knowing what's right, and knowing what's wrong."

I had hopes for her, but Per Stellan will have to go, Phela thought. *I need her for the ritual, but afterward . . .*

"Enough talk," Phela said. "Enough fear, enough caution. Begin." Per Ristolo nodded, let go of her arms, and called over those few priests still faithful to the Crown who had remained at the edges of the large square. He started issuing orders. Gather this, fetch that, prepare this, honor that . . . Phela listened but hardly heard. She did her best to hold down the sickness, withhold any whimpers of pain that throbbed through her. When she was a princess, Whispering through the palace and absorbing information and news, patience had been a virtue. Now her time for patience had gone, but she knew she only had a small while to wait.

"Majesty!" a voice called. From the corner of the square Sergeant Konnell and two other City Guards were dragging a robed figure. He was moaning as he came, feet dragging across the stone slabs and leaving thin trails of blood to wash away behind.

"I ordered no prisoners!" Phela said. She knew that this clampdown had to be hard and harsh, a display of power that put down any resistance to her rule once and for all. Prisoners were always a problem. Demos Kallistrate had already proved that, though she'd put his inconvenience to good use.

"Per Solis!" Per Stellan said.

Per Ristolo stopped what he was doing and looked over as the Guards dropped the man close to Phela's feet.

"What's this?" she asked.

"He came to the front gate alone," Sergeant Konnell said. "He says he has information."

"Not . . . not information," Per Solis said. "A promise."

"A promise of what?" Phela asked.

"Failure."

The priest hadn't been beaten, so far as Phela could tell, but he had been dragged, perhaps all the way up from Yaris Teeg. She was aware that the first assault on the novice temple had been a failure, resulting in the loss of many City Guards and Silent, and that an enemy none of the survivors recognized had fought against them. That was unfortunate, because it meant that Euphraxia still lived. Phela was expecting that dog Demos Kallistrate to come crawling back to her at any moment, him and her weak sister, begging forgiveness and pleading with her to let them go. Love blinded them to the reality of this moment.

At first she'd assumed the mysterious enemy to be the Phage, but now she believed it had been sheer magic. Many of the High Order priests dabbled, but Per Ristolo had insisted that none of them could wield it that effectively.

But perhaps this one? Per Solis? She readied herself for a trap, expecting him to leap up at any moment and attempt to sweep them all from the Four Square with a scream, or a look, or a dismissive wave of his hand. But Per Solis looked ready to die.

"Explain," Phela said.

"Your armies rise against you," Per Solis said. He struggled to his elbows, staring at Per Stellan and Per Ristolo as he spoke. Blood and rainwater ran into his eyes, but he did not blink. "You're all going to die."

"You're mistaken," Phela said.

"No," Per Solis said. "Admiral Hallarte sails up the Susk even now, her armada behind her, and she brings countless banished Bajumen with her. Allied against *you*, Majesty. Standing against *you*. But it's not too late to stop all this madness. Surrender your throne, Majesty. Give up this insanity. This *blasphemy*. Do the right thing. Too many have died."

Phela controlled her surprise, yet Per Solis saw that, and smiled.

She did not appreciate his amusement at her expense. "The madness is in those who would dare to stand against me," she said. "But that means nothing. Others may die, but soon I will have such power that I will *never* die."

Per Solis's smile dropped. He looked to Per Stellan, who stared down at her feet. Then he looked at Per Ristolo, who glared right back.

"You can't," Per Solis said. "You mustn't . . ."

"Shome," Phela said. The Silent drew her sword and ran him through, spiking him to the stone beneath. He gasped, still raised on his elbows, and then slumped to the ground. Phela was aware of the two priests looking away, but she did not.

She staggered slightly as a pain thudded deep in her chest, mimicking the beating of her heart. Per Ristolo was there to hold her arm.

"Sergeant Konnell," Phela said.

He bent his head. "Yes, Majesty."

"You're in luck. You're now Captain Konnell. Take a force of City Guards down to the Susk River Gates, and send some expeditionary squads along the river to set an ambush. If Admiral Hallarte and her forces reach that far, prepare to stop them."

"If they reach that far, Majesty?" the newly promoted captain asked.

"I'm hoping I'll be able to halt them beforehand," Phela said. "What do you think, Per Ristolo? A first great test?"

The ancient priest nodded like an excited dog.

"Good," Phela said, breathing deeply, shutting out the pain. "Good. Then let's get the ritual under way."

Phela closed her eyes, smelled smoke and spilled innards, heard footsteps marching away, and tried to swallow down the sickness that still threatened. *I honor the Four,* she thought, *and pray they will grace me with their knowledge, for the good of all Quandis.*

༄

Daria stood at the bow of the *Nayadine* and watched Lartha growing closer. Parts of the city were already in flames. Using her telescope, she could see that Kallistrate Hill was blazing, and some of the other great hills also sprouted their own fires. Palace Hill seemed quiet and untouched, which was hardly a surprise. But even that wouldn't last. Already, the merchants and diplomats and wealthy families who lived in the shadow of the palace would be panicking, trying to flee their homes, perhaps the city itself. Or they'd be hiding, praying to the Four that this would pass.

And it would. Daria would see to that.

Her heart ached at the sight of the city she loved in flames.

"Row!" she shouted behind her. "Row *faster*! That is your home on fire! Your families in danger. Row for them. Row for Quandis!"

The timekeeper increased his tempo on the great drum, and the two hundred sailors rowing the massive battleship sped up, digging deeper, shouting a song of war as they stretched forward and heaved back. The oars were long and light, their paddles made of shaped whalebone, but even with a hundred on each side of the ship on two levels, their passage was slow. The wind gusted with true ferocity, but it would have been impossible to navigate the big ships along the narrow river using sails. Even now she worried about running aground, or striking one of the many smaller vessels hurrying out of their path. Hitting a wooden dock, or a sunken ship, or striking chained or spiked barriers that might have been hurriedly put in place. As far as she knew, nothing as large as her warship had sailed up the Susk before, certainly not as far as the capital city.

But these were extraordinary times, and they called for extreme measures.

Soon she would have to make a decision about docking and continuing their journey on foot. But the *Nayadine* and the other four ships that remained in her fleet carried fourscore cannons each, as well as deck-bound, giant crossbows capable of firing over two miles, flame mortars, and enough munitions to hunker down for a potential long siege.

She looked at the eastern shore of the Susk, little more than a hundred feet away. She'd detailed shore parties to accompany the ships as protection against attack from the banks, and she could see that they were still running to keep up with the vessels. It only felt like they were rowing at a crawl. With ships so large, once a speed was reached, their momentum carried them onward.

The detachments on each shore were composed of Bajumen, soldiers from the Suskmouth garrison led by their tattooed lieutenant—a hard woman who went by the chosen name of Skin—along with Princess Myrinne and Demos Kallistrate.

And with Daria on board the great ship *Nayadine,* her brother. So changed. So different. Yet in some ways—perhaps only seen by her—so much the same boy she had left behind all those years ago.

"Strange allies we have, sister," Blane said.

He'd come up beside her, quiet as a whisper. Daria smiled thinly. Once they'd had a bond that none could sever, but there had been no outside interference then. Other than their mother, the siblings had no one to care for them but each other. Now here they were, fighting alongside the daughters and sons of nobles and heroes, a princess of the Crown, and a flotilla of other Bajumen who looked at Daria as a hero. Yet beneath it all, that old bond remained. Frayed it might have been, but intact nevertheless. Somehow.

"Strange indeed," she said. And that was all.

There was so much to say that it felt like too much. For now it was enough to simply exist in each other's company once more. The time would come for reminiscing and recriminations. For now, battle was at hand.

"Demos spoke of magic," Daria said finally. "He said Phela's after it, and that's what all this is about. I've heard tales of magic, but they were just stories handed down from the past, from parents to children. I mean . . . magic?"

Blane looked at her and she saw struggle, both a deeper wisdom and something dark and unknowable.

"It's all true. All of it," he said. "Phela will already be able to do extraordinary things. But if she gets what she wants, she'll be even more powerful than you can imagine."

"Should I be worried?"

Blane laughed. It was a heavier laugh than she remembered, and she missed the high chuckle from their younger days. The Blane she remembered had been unconcerned with grown-up things, and still young enough to not have had humor and delight bled from him by the demands and disadvantages of being a Bajuman. His laugh now carried such knowledge, and something besides.

"Sister, I don't know you anymore, but I still feel I do."

Daria felt hurt at that, even though it was true. "How so?"

"Your confidence. You always knew more than me, Daria, or believed you did."

"It was never like that," she said softly.

"No, no," Blane said. "You were a good sister, but I was always a little boy in your eyes."

"Not anymore," she said.

"Not anymore." Blane looked toward the city in the distance with something like hunger in his eyes. "As for whether you should be worried? Don't for a second think that commanding a force like this will give you an edge. Not if Queen Phela gets the sum of all magic, which is what she wants. You might be an admiral and have a thousand men and women beneath you, all armed to the teeth and ready for a fight. You might have these ships, with their cannons and whatever other weapons they contain. You're confident and accomplished and . . . proud, I can see that in you. I'm sure you've fought enemies that would make most Larthans piss their pants the moment they set eyes on them. But magic, Daria . . . magic is unlike anything you've ever known."

He clenched his fists and looked down at them, and Daria was startled to see sparks igniting and dying beneath his fingernails. She gasped and took a step back, blinking, trying to focus her eyes. Too much staring into the distance, perhaps. Too much sun.

"Blane?"

"Demos Kallistrate has seen what I can do," Blane said. He unclenched his fists, blew on them. "I might be able to help, to begin with, at least. But if Phela completes the final rituals, her potential will be . . ." He shivered, eyes closed, face pointing to the sky. "She doesn't deserve it," he whispered, almost to himself. "Not a dreg of what she's got. It's all me, Daria. I'm the one who deserves it all." He opened his eyes again and glared at his sister. "Because I'm Bajuman."

"As am I."

"Really?" A thin line of blood dribbled from his nose. He seemed unaware.

"Of course I am. Blane, what's happened to you?" She knew his face, his voice, and yet now that they'd met once more, Daria was beginning to feel that she was growing to know her brother less than ever before.

"While you were making a career for yourself fighting for the enemy, I've been striving to help our people. With magic. I'm almost there, Daria." He grinned. "Almost ready."

Magic? Confused, perturbed, she was about to probe deeper when Captain Gree hurried up to the foredeck. Blane didn't seem to notice and continued.

"Our people have been waiting for a myth. A fairy tale. A savior who will never come—"

"The Kij'tal," Daria said. "You don't believe in the savior?"

Blane shot her a dark look. "No supernatural savior is coming to help us, sister." He raised his hands, and those sparks danced along his fingers again. "So I intend to be the savior the Bajumen have been waiting for all this time."

Daria stared at him. "Brother . . ."

"Admiral!" Gree called. "Our advance forces on the eastern shore have come under fire from a keep. We can circle around it, but it'll take time."

She swore loudly.

"And we'll lose sight of the shore force," Daria said. Her tactic had been to reach the city wall en masse. The more fragmented her force became, the more difficult it might be to break into the city and restore order. She still had no real idea how much of a fight they were facing, despite reports from Demos and Blane. There would be City Guard and regular army units standing against them, but from her experience at Suskmouth, she also hoped that some of those units could be persuaded to join her *against* the queen. She knew nothing for certain, though, and she wanted to be as prepared, and as strong, as possible. She opened her telescope and looked along the shore. The keep was large, more like a massive curved wall starting by the waterside and extending inland. She could just make out soldiers atop the wall firing crossbows down at her ground troops, hidden within a mass of low buildings behind a row of jetties and moored boats.

"We can't get bogged down in a battle still three miles from the city," Gree said. "Cannons?"

"Prepare them," Daria said. "One gauging shot from each ship, then open up with ten starboard cannons. And send a signal ashore—tell Lieutenant Skin to pull back when she sees our red signal flag raised."

"Too much time," Blane said.

"What are you now, a military commander?"

"Not at all," he said. "That's you, sister. I'm a Bajuman, but one with power. Let me." He closed his eyes and gripped the railing. Daria watched for a moment, then snorted and turned back to Captain Gree.

"Captain, our cannon fire has to be pinpoint accurate, I don't want to risk—"

Gree's eyes opened wide as he looked over Daria's shoulder. "Admiral . . ."

Daria turned back to her brother. Blane was muttering, eyes closed, hands gripping the railing, and as she heard the name Charin—god of Fire and Secrets—smoke and steam began to rise from the blackening timber beneath Blane's hands.

"Blane!" she said, darting closer to pull him away. She didn't know what was happening and feared that he might burn. The flames, the scorching, the smell of singed wood, what was it? She reached for him . . . then held back.

Magic, he had said.

She could feel heat pulsing from him, and for a heartbreaking moment it took her back to their childhood, when he was sick in his cot and she and her mother took turns wiping him down with damp cloths. They'd had no money for medicine, not even from the street sellers who sometimes sold their weakest and faulty mixes to Bajumen. So they'd sat with him, terrified that the infection was burning him up from the inside out, and only time and Lameria had ensured that he'd pulled through.

Now he was hotter than he'd ever been.

"Blane?"

"Watch, sister," he whispered. "Watch, Admiral, and see what I have become." Daria swore she saw a flicker of flame at the corners of his eyes.

Between the ship and shore, the air started to waver with heat haze, pulses of bright light bursting out and sizzling across the surface of the rain-swept river. Daria felt the heat where she was, stretching the skin on her face and drying her eyes. She blinked, held up her hands, and watched aghast as a spitting, blazing ball of fire grew and expanded before them.

Was Blane doing this? Her little brother? Gasps of surprise and fear sounded from crew members behind her, but she had no comforting words for them, and nothing to say that made sense.

"Charin, help me," Blane said, and the ball of fire grew more violent and terrifying by the second, rolling away from them at a diagonal across the surface of the Susk, steam erupting behind it and leaving a misty trail in its wake. Waves burst up and out where the fireball touched the water, great steaming geysers firing superhot water skyward that dispersed in the air and left circular rainbows in sheets of rain falling in its wake.

The fireball powered across the river and her fear turned to anticipation. Moments later the fire struck the river's shore adjacent to the stone keep.

She did not need her telescope to see the destruction it wrought.

Several boats burst into flame, the violence of the fireball's arrival flinging them into the air, breaking them apart, scattering a thousand blazing shards across the river and against the tall stone walls beyond. Towers of steam thrust skyward, and the fireball's forward motion continued, powering into the keep and spreading across its front façade, rolling up and over the wall's highest levels and dropping down behind like a wave crashing against a jetty. As the fireball came apart and its impact splashed across the whole length of the keep, Daria hoped that her own forces had pulled back in time. Some of the buildings along the riverfront burst aflame, and a boiling explosion bloomed skyward, throwing debris far out over the river.

She watched amazed, shocked, terrified, and delighted. To have such power on her side! She had seen some strange sights during her years at sea, especially in those wild, exotic lands many hundreds of miles beyond the Ring, but never anything like this. Rumors of magic had been proven true, its source the last place she had ever expected it to be.

Her brother.

She turned to Blane. He was grasping onto the railing, blood streaming from his mouth and nose, hands held out and still smoking, hairs on his arms singed to blackened spots. Even through such a horrible visage, he managed a grin.

"You see, sister?" he said. "You see?" Then his eyes rolled back in his head and he slumped down to the deck.

"Blane!" Daria rushed to him. *Kij'tal!* she thought. Holding out her hands ready to help him, she was reminded once more of that time as a child when he had almost died.

Even now, he was still too hot to touch.

&

Demos could see how eager Myrinne was to fight.

Tollivar huddled between them. They remained on top of a small slope, hidden among trees in a parkland while they watched the combined Bajuman, naval, and army force completing the attack on the keep.

Flames roared high all along the heavy stone structure, and even from this far away Demos could feel the heat and smell the burning. Several buildings between them and the scene of destruction had spontaneously burst into flame, and the sound and stink of fire filled the air.

They'd watched awestruck as the ball of fire rolled from Admiral Hallarte's lead ship and struck the keep. *Blane,* Demos had said. He'd seen the Bajuman conjuring a whirlwind of destruction in Yaris Teeg, and he had only just escaped with his life. Now that they were allies of a sort, the novice priest was no less terrifying in what he could do, nor in his ambition.

"Quandis will change today," Myrinne said, watching the end of the battle with tears in her eyes. "It already has changed."

"Civil war has a way of forcing change," Demos said.

"Not because of that," she said. She looked around at the soldiers and Bajumen who remained with them. She knew well enough that they were there to protect her, the princess and potential future queen of Quandis. "Or not just because of that. Because of *who* fights. Bajumen together with sailors from the navy, and soldiers from the army. It's Quandis they fight for. The good of the land where they live. All other differences, real and perceived, are set aside. *That* is the change. If one person dies today, or fifty thousand, it's the uniting of people behind the common good that will lead us out of the darkness."

"We're only just entering the darkness," Demos said, but Myrinne did not reply. She was looking beyond the blazing ruin of the keep, past the celebrating rebel forces, and at Lartha in the distance. Flames and smoke rose from the city, and she was right, a change was at hand.

"We should go," she said. "The city needs us. Quandis needs me."

Demos knew she spoke the truth. The kingdom did need her, and in this moment it needed him as well. She could be the greatest queen Quandis ever had. But he wanted her for himself, wanted a life with *Myrinne,* not *Queen* Myrinne, who would need to give all of herself to the Crown. And that's who she was now—things had changed in mere hours. When Tollivar had reunited them in the theater, she'd said it was time to leave Lartha, and Demos had hoped. But now they were in the midst of the war for Quandis, and the kingdom would need a new monarch. A just, courageous leader. A true queen. As blood flowed and fires burned, he sensed the future opening up before them with a grim inevitability. One hope had died, but he wondered if another one might be rising from its ashes.

Yet as he gripped Myrinne's hand tight in his, and as she squeezed back, he feared that he had already lost her.

20

Though shocked by Blane's display of destructive magic, Daria had gathered her senses, issuing orders upon their approach to the greatest city in the known world. Blane sat leaning against a bulkhead, bloodied rags pressed to his mouth and nose, head nodding, and she feared he might be dying. Having found him again after so long, she might be losing her dear brother.

But she could not let one man's pain distract her, even if it was Blane's. War was here, and war was always about more than a single person.

Lartha lay before them. The river Susk snaked toward the city's boundary wall half a mile distant, winding through the chaos of low buildings that smothered the ground outside the wall. Here lived visitors from other lands, slaves given their freedom, and many other people either not connected to any of the clans, or not wealthy enough to live within the city. Now those buildings and streets were quiet, the people either fled or were hiding low and deep from the battle that was to come. Daria expected to find some of Phela's troops lying in wait among these buildings, but she also expected her ground forces would take care of them. She knew that many of the returned Bajumen would relish the chance at revenge, and that made them a powerful part of her army.

Her attention focused on the city wall, and more important, the two towers protecting the river.

She'd once been on a tour of these towers, conducted by Commander Kurtness of the City Guard for a selection of Quandis's top military personnel. Its intention had been to display how well protected Lartha was from outside attack, following concerns about the resurgent pirate threat presented by Kharod the Red. These defensive towers had stood on either side of the river, punctuating the tall wall where the river passed through, for generations, but until quite recently they had been little more than hollow sculptures portraying the Quandian skill at architecture. Now, though, they were true fortifications.

Daria remembered the giant crossbows with blue-fire-filled tips, cannons primed and pointed permanently downriver, over a hundred firing points in each tower for archers, oil bladders ready to burst onto the water's surface and set it on fire, and a dozen kill holes in each tower aimed across the river, ready to unleash a hail of blazing death upon any vessel that dared approach uninvited. There was also a sunken boom connected by heavy chains to a series of counterweighted cogs and wheels. The only human strength required to raise it was a hand on a sword, slicing two thick ropes that would release the weights and raise the boom.

She had never believed that she would be on the receiving end of these towers' daunting array of defenses, but she believed they would make it through . . . as long as the boom had yet to be raised. Though she vowed to herself that even that would not keep her out forever.

"Ground forces are in position," Captain Gree said.

"Good," Daria said. The *Nayadine* was the lead ship, and they continued rowing upriver. There was no point in waiting. Beyond the high city wall was the rest of the city, laid out over scores of square miles, the seven great hills and the wide valleys between them home to a million Quandians and their rulers. And that city was in chaos. Even this far away she could smell the taint of burning flesh on the breeze. They all could. She could see the seriousness in her crew's eyes.

"Why haven't they raised the boom yet?" Gree asked.

"They'll be waiting for us," she said. "Might be they plan to raise it under the *Nayadine,* trap the ship, perhaps even slice it in two and sink it, turning us into a barrier to prevent any of the others from progressing farther. Doesn't matter. If they manage to stop the ship, we'll take the fight to the banks of the Susk."

Gree nodded grimly. "Shall I give the order?"

"Now," Daria said. As Gree turned away to instruct his bugler, Daria knelt close to her brother. "Blane, it's going to get noisy. Do you want to go below?"

He looked up at her, but it took a few seconds for him to focus, his eyes watery and blank. Blood smeared his face, and a drop sat in the corner of one eye. Blood vessels had burst and turned the whites of his eyes a garish pink.

"I'm afraid," he said.

"Stay close to me," she said.

"Not the battle," he said. "Not the war. I'm afraid of . . . me."

The words chilled Daria. But then the bugler sounded the signal, and she knew that the time to worry about her brother was not now. "Just stay with me, Blane, and I'll look after you."

She stood on the forecastle as the great ship started to swing to the left. Her stomach dipped and lurched as the anchor was dropped and the two hundred great oars stowed, and the hull dug into the river and surged left, sending huge waves out toward the shores. Behind them the other four ships were doing the same, the *Royal*

Dawn shifting its bow toward the opposite bank. Staggered as they were along the river, it gave their gunsmen what she hoped were clear firing solutions.

As she heard the heavy clanking of firing ports dropping open along the *Nayadine*'s starboard side, the first puffs of smoke bloomed along Lartha's city wall.

"Incoming!" someone shouted, and the sound of cannon fire boomed along the river.

Cannon shot roared past above them, ripping through sails, splintering heavy timber crossposts, and one mast took a direct hit, shards and splinters of wood blasting outward and falling in a deadly shower. Several shots struck the ship lower down, smashing part of the superstructure in a hail of shattered wood and blood. Voices cried out and then fell silent. Daria felt the ship shudder from impacts lower down, and she hoped the repair crews were already jumping into action.

She remained standing and looking ahead. She knew how vital it was to her crew's morale to see her unswayed and unafraid, though she expected to be struck by a cannonball and blasted into meat and mulch at any moment. It helped her be stoic knowing if it happened, it would be over before she was even aware of it.

"Fire!" she heard Captain Gree shout, and the next explosions came from much closer. The whole ship juddered as forty cannons fired from their respective starboards, a rippling series of explosions that were over in the space between heartbeats. Smoke billowed out, the stench of gunpowder filled the air, and Daria felt the curious sense of joy that overcame her at the beginning of every battle.

This is me! she thought. *This is why I'm alive!* It was delight that stopped short of bloodlust, but the excitement she felt when the cannon shot smashed along the city wall could not be denied.

A series of pounding impacts struck the wall to the right of the river, starting at the tower and stretching hundreds of feet along the structure. A few of the shots were low down, shattering jolts that pulverized stone and timber, but many more were higher up, close to the crenellated head of the wall. Her crew's targeting had been perfect, and a whole section of the upper wall disintegrated into clouds of dust, blasted stone, and smoke.

It was half a mile away, but she still fancied she could hear the screams of the dying.

From behind her ship came the thundering reports of the rest of her fleet firing their cannons, and she heard the deep hissing of the ordnance whisking past the *Nayadine* on its way toward the wall. One volley landed short, blowing apart low buildings close to the wall's foot. Another struck the wall on the left of the river low down, punching holes in the stonework but doing little to disturb the forces arrayed along its head.

"Tighten up that aim," she said under her breath, knowing there was no way all the gunners could hear her.

The enemy returned fire, and several more volleys splashed into the river around the fleet or smashed holes in their hulls, superstructure, or rigging. So far, though, she hadn't lost a ship.

Daria scanned the defenses through her telescope, resting her view on the starboard tower. Twice as high as the wall, it bustled with activity.

"Captain, incoming from the towers," she said.

As if reacting to her words, both large towers sprouted plumes of smoke as their own weaponry entered into the fray. Daria could actually track the massive crossbow bolts as they arced through the air toward them, one splashing down into the river a hundred feet to the *Nayadine*'s port side and expending its blue-fire charge beneath the water in a glimmering display, the other ripping through their rigging and impacting the *Royal Dawn* four hundred feet behind them. The bolt smashed through the decking, buried itself in the ship, and then ignited with a bright white pulse that flashed across the river. She saw several shapes blazing white as they jumped into the river, then turned back to the battle.

"Bugler, *Nayadine*'s fire to concentrate on port tower, *Royal Dawn*'s on the starboard tower. The other two ships continue to hit the wall." The bugler sounded his orders, a complex signal that would be picked up by captains and gunmasters of all five ships, and moments later the next volleys blasted outward.

The tower targeted by the *Nayadine* sprouted gray-white growths of shattered stone and smoke, and a great slab of wall tumbled away and splashed into the water. Daria saw broken bodies falling with it. The river's fish would have a feast before this day was out.

Cannons continued to fire from along the wall, the enemy now assessing their range and dropping shot directly onto the attacking ships. The deck shuddered beneath Daria's feet, both from *Nayadine*'s cannons, and the impact of enemy fire. She heard men and women screaming. She saw three sailors cut in half by one of the heavy cross-bows, one of them still clawing at the deck as the massive bolt burrowed into the ship and burst into flames.

"Get that fire put out!" Captain Gree shouted. "Keep firing! Drag cannons from starboard to replace any damaged on our port side, we can't lose any firepower, not now."

Daria shifted her gaze to the shore on either side. She knew that their ground forces were hunkered down waiting to attack, closer to the walls yet not close enough to risk injury or death from the bar-rage. Demos and Myrinne were on the shore on the right, and Daria felt a pang of concern for them both. Their war council had included a brief conversation about what would come afterward, when Phela had been defeated. All involved had presumed that Myrinne would take the throne, to keep the Blood of the Four in possession of the Crown. Daria had no interest in ruling Quandis and the last thing the nation needed was more turmoil. A member of the royal family on the throne would calm the public's fears. It made sense to all of them, and yet Demos had seemed deeply troubled. He'd said nothing, but it was clear that his own plans for the future had not included being married to a queen.

For Daria's part, she had argued against Myrinne going ashore with Demos and the other warriors. Their future queen should not have been involved in the heart of a brutal battle—she should have been left ashore far from the city proper. Yet Myrinne had hefted her sword and insisted, as if responsibility for her sister's actions lay with her, and Demos had assured them all that she was more than capable with the blade. It wasn't as if Daria could have prevented her from fighting—not if they hoped to have a good relationship when all was said and done. Instead, she'd shaken hands with the princess and instructed her to do her best not to die. Myrinne had laughed, but Daria hadn't been joking. Now they would see.

"Be well, Demos," Daria said quietly.

She scanned the buildings scattered between them and the base of the wall, seeing nothing but knowing that her own troops were there, well hidden and ready to charge at a moment's notice. The Bajumen were there, too. She had seen the passion in Blane's eyes when he'd seen their people armed and ready to fight. She only wished she could feel that same passion. She envied him his ambition and was troubled by how numbed she had become to their people's struggle. They inspired her now, but not because she felt any real connection to them.

An explosion among the buildings caught her attention. Debris was blasted skyward, lifted on a column of mud and rubble, and she saw several tumbling bodies in the mass. She frowned and lowered the telescope as more explosions blasted across the plain.

"Captain, are those misfires from us?"

"No, Admiral. I'd say our ground troops have been spotted. Look—the walls!" He pointed and Daria immediately saw the plumes of cannon fire as some of the enemy's weapons shifted aim, now firing down into the buildings before them rather than at the ships.

"We can't charge," she said. "If we do, we'll have to stop firing, and we'll lose our advantage. Keep shooting. Double the rate, Captain! We've got to neutralize those cannons before they kill everyone."

Captain Gree relayed the order and the bugler sounded his signal.

"We could pull the troops back?" Gree suggested.

"No," Daria said. "No withdrawal." If they lost that ground now, there'd be almost no way to gain it back before Lartha's defenses could rally against them. She saw several more explosions, more buildings blown apart, and she turned to her brother, grim-faced. "Blane?"

He was still sitting with his back pressed against a bulkhead, unable to see the battle, hardly looking at anything. He was shaking, bleeding, the rags he'd been using to wipe his face now soaked with blood.

"Blane!"

He looked up at her.

"Can you do it again? That fire? We need your help."

"You . . . need my help?"

"*I* need it, Blane. Our people need it."

More thuds of cannon fire, more screams, the splintering of wood, a cracking, pained roar as the *Nayadine*'s aft mast fell majestically into the river, rigging torn and whipping through the air as ropes unwhirled, and the ship's cannons let off another volley that whistled through the air and impacted on stone, wood, flesh. Dust hazed the air. Fires erupted and were fought on three out of five of Daria's ships. Blood smeared the deck, and several bodies were floating away downriver. In the height of battle she felt complete control, but that control allowed her to see details that she knew she would remember forever. She owned a sad, deep store of such memories.

"It burns . . ." Blane said. "In my head . . . my guts . . . it burns . . ."

"Water," Daria said.

"Water," he said, nodding. "Water!" He held out his hands as if to take a drink, but Daria clasped his hands and pulled him to his feet. He staggered, fell into her. She held him tight and talked into his ear.

"Whatever you have, whatever you've done, now we need you most."

"You need me, Daria," he said again.

"I do."

"I'm afraid. I'm not sure whether I've gone too far, and maybe . . ."

"Water, Blane."

A shot struck the deck twenty feet from them, punching a hole, planks spinning and wood splintering as the cannonball ricocheted off across the river. Blane tensed in her grasp, then seemed to relax again.

Something changed. His burning skin cooled, and when he pulled back, his eyes were more watery than ever, his face indistinct as if seen through tears. Daria wiped her eyes, but she was not crying. Neither was Blane.

He was smiling.

"Oh . . . water," he said, and he turned from Daria and staggered to the ship's bow.

Daria went to go with him, but Gree grasped her arm and held her back. "Leave him be," the captain said. "You have to keep control of the battle. Our shore troops are awaiting your orders, our captains are eager to move on, and you have to be here to make sure it all works. Whatever he's going to do . . ." The captain shuddered. "Whether it'll help or not, he'll do it on his own."

It was an improper way for a captain to talk to an admiral, but just the thing Daria needed to hear from a friend. Gree knew that sisterly concerns had no place in the height of battle, and she knew that he was right.

Fortunately, Blane appeared stronger than he had since their re-union just a couple of hours before. *He would do what was needed.*

"The eastern tower!" someone shouted. More voices took up the call, then cheers rose from all through the ship.

The tower on the eastern shore seemed almost to be bulging, pulsing, spewing showers of stone out into the water, clouds of dust, and then a startling flare of blazing white flame that rose skyward and scorched across the river's surface, raising geysers of steam in its wake. The tower crumbled in terrible slow motion, and while it was the first sign of the victory she sought, Daria could not help think-ing of the hundreds of soldiers within. Quandian soldiers, fighting Quandian soldiers because of the capricious whims of this new, mad monarch, now being burned, crushed, and blown to pieces.

A larger explosion blasted debris out over a wide area, the ex-panding bloom of smoke and fire so large that it seemed to hardly move at all.

"Concentrate all fire on the western tower and wall," Daria said. "Send a signal to shore telling them to prepare to move. But await my signal. And get these ships moving again, Captain. Sails up, rowers in."

While the bugler sent his signal, Daria turned to watch Blane. But then she saw movement past him, and her heart sank.

Between the destroyed tower and the one still standing, the heavy chain boom was rising from the water, strung from one side of the river to the other and thirty feet high. Even from half a mile away she could make out its thick links and swathes of riverweed hanging from it.

"We'll have to blast it before we get there," she said. "But we can't wait—we've already slowed down enough and we need momentum. If we're going to take the city, we won't get another chance at this."

"I agree," said Gree. "But when we've moving head-on, two-thirds of our guns won't be able to get an adequate angle of fire."

"Then let's make the most of it while we're straightening up."

As the rowing drummer started sounding his slow beat, a flurry of cannon fire drowned out the noise, but only briefly. And the drummer never lost his rhythm. The city wall spat smoke, dust, and stone, and the remaining tower took the brunt of the fleet's fire. But it gave back as much as it took, pumping its massive fiery crossbow bolts into the ships and the river around them. One bolt whisked by so close over Daria's head that she felt the breeze of its passing, and it took out their central mast before veering off course and smashing into a dock a hundred feet away, setting it aflame.

"Here comes the oil," Gree said. He growled. "I was hoping we'd finish them before that." She nodded in agreement—if there was one thing a sailor feared it was fire onboard the ship.

Between the fallen tower and the one still fighting, a slick of blazing oil spewed into the river beneath the raised chain boom. The current caught it and started dragging it downriver, directly toward Daria's ships. The river was slow moving here, but she guessed it was only a few minutes before the burning oil reached them.

There was nothing for it, though—they would have to sail the ships right through it, and deal with the burning, sticky oil when the time came.

"Get the beaters ready on all ships," Daria said.

"Your brother . . ." Gree said.

Blane was standing tall and straight at the bow, seemingly un-aware of the chaos around him—the cannons blasted away below, the geysers of splashing water where enemy ordnance fell short, the thundering impact of cannonballs against wood, the smoke and dust and screams of pain and rage. He was taller than Daria had ever seen him, as if whatever he'd taken into himself—whatever strange magic he had somehow become a part of—was making him larger in this world, stretching him, expanding him until he was ready to burst.

He held his hands out, and somehow they were leaking water. *Perhaps he's been splashed,* Daria thought. But the water was tinged pink with blood, and when it fell to the deck it seemed to move too slowly, out of sync with the frantic events surrounding them.

She felt a heavy thud through her feet. Experienced sailor that she was, she knew that was not an impact or cannon shot. It was something striking the hull, and as she rushed to the railing to look over, she saw the first wave raising itself up out of the river.

The wall of water lifted up before them, forming an arc around the *Nayadine*'s bow. Ten feet high, thirty, then fifty, the water held there in defiance of all natural laws.

"Gods save us," Gree whispered. He'd come to stand beside Daria, and he held her arm, giving comfort as well as taking it.

"I think perhaps they might," Daria said.

Blane pulsed, jerking every bone in his body and thrusting his hands forward, and the wall of water started to move upriver. It roared, smashing along both shores and destroying moored boats, docks, shore buildings. It carried the detritus with it, and by the time it approached the river defenses, it was seventy feet high, a boiling mass of water, broken vessels, smashed buildings, and mud.

It scooped up the drifting slicks of blazing oil and then smashed itself into the two towers . . . and the boom slung between them.

The sound was staggering, and the impact shook the ground. Giant ripples powered back down the river, traveling unnaturally fast and jarring against the ships as the water smashed the fallen tower into a million pieces and washed into the standing tower through firing vents and holes already blasted by cannon fire. The wave fell beyond the line of the wall, roaring upriver and diminishing as it went, vanishing deeper into the city of Lartha.

Daria stared wide-eyed at the destruction the wave had wrought. The chain boom was gone, washed away out of sight. The standing tower was still and silent, glistening with reflected sunlight. Water left behind poured from every opening. Surely no one could have been left alive in there?

She waited for only a few moments before embracing the victory and seeking to advance it further still.

"Send the signal to shore," Daria said to the bugler. "Charge!"

·ᅇ·

"Stay close to me," Demos said.

"I can look after myself."

"I don't doubt it! But have you been to war? Have you seen men and women gutted and slaughtered before your eyes? This is different from anything you've experienced before, Myrinne. There are no rules here. In fact, maybe you should—"

"Don't even suggest it!" Myrinne said. Demos saw her anger and hurt. In truth he believed that she'd be safest with him, not left behind in some building, even if they did leave a guard with her. Lartha was in chaos today, and it was only going to get worse. The queen who would rise from this chaos would be best born from blood. A wise queen, having witnessed the violence and death that had led to her ascension.

"As for you," he said to Tollivar, but the boy was even more stubborn than the woman he loved.

"No one tells me what to do," the Bajuman boy said. "I might not be good with a sword, but I'm a *master* at sneaking around unseen."

"Come on then, master," Demos said. "The order's been given. This is our time."

In the wide streets all around them sailors, army soldiers, and Bajumen were charging toward the blasted city walls. He saw the lieutenant Daria had placed her trust in, Skin, dashing back and forth as she directed her forces toward the pockmarked city wall. Demos led a small squad of sailors from Daria's own ship, some of whom he'd served with before, and he felt a rush of optimism and positivity for the first time since the day his father had been arrested. Everything was going to pieces around them. Lartha was aflame and in turmoil. Yet be believed they were in the right, and the right path led them ever onward.

A barrage of cannon fire from the river thudded through the ground and air, and as they ran forward between the buildings scattered across the river plain, the long city wall ahead of them erupted once again in a series of explosions along several hundred feet. The gunfire had been perfect, landing shots all along the wall's upper section. He only hoped they'd knocked the majority of cannons out of action.

"I hope they stop firing soon," Myrinne said.

"That was the last barrage," Demos said. "Daria knows we're charging. She'll hold fire unless there's a threat we can't counter from the ground."

"Such as?" she asked.

"Any big ordnance they might have missed," Demos said, and he didn't like to think of what might be awaiting their troops as they approached the wall. However much the cannon barrage had damaged the defensive positions—as well as Blane's wave—they were still charging against one of the strongest and most entrenched defensive lines in the land.

"Blane worries me," Myrinne said. She was hardly even breathing hard, though they ran at full pelt. Demos's recent mistreatment must have weakened him, because he was already finding their pace difficult. *Time to stop running soon,* he thought. *Of course, then there'll be fighting . . .*

"Whatever power he has . . ." Demos trailed off.

"He has magic," Myrinne said. "A novice priest. A Bajuman!" Tollivar glanced at her, but she did not seem to notice. "It's Phela's addiction to magic we're fighting against now, and it was our mother's before her that started all this."

"When she killed my father," Demos said.

"Blane is helping us for now, but what then?"

A door opened ahead of them. Demos tensed, gripping his sword, expecting an ambush by City Guards hidden away in these buildings beneath the wall. But he saw only several frightened faces, and at the sight of the rushing soldiers they ducked back inside and dropped the heavy door lock closed.

"I don't know," Demos said. "It's not something to worry about now. Is it?"

Myrinne didn't reply. He looked along the shore at the ruins of the two river towers, one completely demolished and still sparking with the remnants of blue fire, the other a shell, holed and damaged, hollowed and silenced by the incredible wave that had smashed into and through it only a few moments before.

"This won't be the end of it," Myrinne said.

"It will for us. When we leave."

A shout from ahead cut off any reply Myrinne might have been about to give. Lieutenant Skin was gathering troops to her, hidden behind a long, low building that might have been a storage hall for the many ships that docked along the river just a couple hundred feet to their left. The wall was close now, and from here Demos could see the destruction that had been wrought upon it by Daria's fleet's big guns. Rubble was strewn around the wall's base. Holes were punched into its façade, some small, others huge where great sections had caved in or fallen away. Dust drifted in the air, and even the heavy rain did little to wash it down. The top of the wall was an uneven topography of broken stone and blasted walkways, with a few bodies visible here and there, several cannons pointing at the sky or falling into wounds in the huge structure, and fires burning in several places, spitting in the rain. He scanned left and right but could see no signs of life.

"Three squads that way, toward the doors," Skin said, pointing along the wall to where two big wooden gates hung on broken hinges. "Two squads to the steps in the wall, there and there." She pointed out sets of zigzagging steps that climbed the wall, its front façade sloping up and back. There were several such staircases, but only a couple remained passable. "Archers down here, covering the attack. Crossbows closer to the wall, sniping anyone who dares look over the top."

"What about the kill holes?" Demos said. At regular intervals along the wall were gatherings of firing holes, some narrow enough for arrows, others wider and meant for small cannons or blazing oils. Many had been destroyed and opened up, like giant creatures with their guts exposed. But a few remained, and they stared like the ominous eyes of a predator awaiting its prey.

"Bajumen!" Skin shouted. "The kill holes. Anyone and anything behind them is your enemy. No prisoners here. No surrender. Are you with me?"

A roar went up. Demos couldn't help smiling, especially when Tollivar joined in. Lieutenant Skin was a fearsome woman, with a shaved head and tattoos, but her charisma made her a natural leader.

"Lieutenant, one more volley?" Demos asked.

"We're very close," she said, glancing past the building at the wall. It was less than three hundred feet distant, silent and smoking and yet looming tall and dangerous.

"Which is why they won't be expecting it," Demos said. "Admiral Hallarte and her crews are very accurate, and they know where we are."

Skin frowned, and then grinned. "One more volley. Send the signal!"

Behind the lieutenant, a sailor raised a blue, triangular flag and swept it back and forth three times. The signal was picked up behind them and carried back, and a few heartbeats later Demos saw smoke plume from Daria's flagship. The boom came next, the heavy whistle of ordnance flying overhead, and then the earsplitting impact of cannonballs smashing into the city wall one more time. Stone exploded, shattered, fell, and even before the dust started to settle they were running, weaving past the last of the buildings and crossing the open space at the wall's foot, dodging falling blocks, the force splitting into squads to attack where Skin had pointed out.

Demos saw the squads approach and enter through the smashed doors, and there was no sign of resistance. *And we're in the city,* he thought. *Lartha is invaded.* It had been centuries since Quandis's capital city had been successfully attacked, and he felt a pang of some undefinable emotion. Sadness? Guilt? He wasn't sure.

"There!" Myrinne said. "On top of the wall!" Shapes had appeared along the damaged pinnacle, and a hail of arrows scratched at the air and sailed down toward them.

Demos, Myrinne, and Tollivar crouched low to present smaller targets, with the two adults slipping the small shields from their backs and protecting their heads and chests. Tollivar didn't carry a shield, and they huddled him between them. Arrows snapped and spat down around them. There were grunts and cries as a few found their mark, and then from behind Demos heard the familiar whip and whisk of archers and crossbow bearers returning fire. It was devastating in its accuracy. All across the head of the wall shapes jerked and fell, and the second volley from the defenders was vastly reduced in scope and aim. Battered by the ships' guns, shocked at the speed of the attackers' advance, they were firing blind. Demos had observed the fighters on both sides. The soldiers and City Guard were well trained, but most of them hadn't been in real combat in a very long time—if ever—whereas the warriors who were part of Admiral Hallarte's fleet had been fighting pirates and other enemies of the kingdom for years.

The sailors might be outnumbered, but the queen's protectors were badly outmatched.

They stood and charged again, closing on the wall, and Demos was already picking his route up one of the external staircases. He led Tollivar and Myrinne and started climbing behind a group of Bajumen, glancing back and down with an elevated view of the battlefield. A few of their forces had fallen, but most had made it to the wall and were climbing or pouring through the ruined gates farther along.

A shout from up ahead brought them to a standstill. Fluid flowed down the wall onto the staircase ahead, and Demos smelled the sharp tang of lamp fuel.

"Stay back!" he said. He glanced around, up and down the staircase, marking routes of retreat should the oil be lit. But he hoped that would not happen. "You!" he said, pointing at a crossbowman. "To me." The man hurried up a few steps to Demos, loading his weapon as he came and gazing up. The opening from which the oil was being poured was twenty feet above and ahead of them.

"I can't get the angle!" the man said.

Demos slipped off his belt and tugged at the cord around Tollivar's waist, knotted them both together, then pushed one end through the equipment strapping on the man's chest. The man smiled.

"Ready?" Demos said.

"Just hold tight."

Demos tied a slipknot in the cord, then took the weight as the man leaned back and out from the steps. He aimed his crossbow upward, setting his feet apart, and Demos concentrated on holding him still and steady. Past the man he could see the river and Daria's ships now moving toward the city once again, driven by a combination of wind and manpower, edging ever closer to the ruined towers and their entry to the city. He wasn't sure he'd ever seen vessels so grand and intimidating on the Susk. Even with signs of battle damage visible on each of the ships, they presented a mighty sight.

The clunk of the crossbow firing startled him, and from above he heard a grunt.

"Run!" he said, and the attackers waiting on the staircase hurried over the area affected by oil, watching their footing and glancing up nervously, all of them awaiting the burning torch to come sailing down. The crossbowman reloaded in a matter of seconds, and he was aiming again as Myrinne and Tollivar passed the oil.

Demos hauled the man in and they both hurried on, now taking the rear.

After two more staircases, they reached a ragged opening blasted into the wall by cannon fire. Others had already entered this way, and he saw the bodies of three defenders and several Bajumen nursing sword wounds.

Demos paused, staring at the face of one of the defenders, so familiar and yet unknown. Who was he, this City Guardsman? Why did Demos know him?

"Konnell," whispered a voice.

Startled, Demos turned to see that Myrinne had appeared behind him. With a crestfallen look she gazed down upon the dead Guard, and now Demos remembered him. The man who had helped her sneak into his cell when the Kallistrate family had first been arrested. A loyal member of the City Guard and Myrinne's friend.

"Myr," he said, taking her arm, whispering into her ear. "We have to keep moving."

"He was a good man," she said, sheathing her sword. She knelt and took dead Konnell's hand as Tollivar looked on, wide-eyed. "He was a friend to me. Always so kind."

"I'm sorry," Demos said urgently, "but we're liable to see other good people dead today, other friends. We might have to kill them ourselves. This is what—"

Myrinne stood and turned to face him in one swift motion. "Don't you think I know that?" She pointed a finger toward the Blood Spire and the Bone Spire in the distance, jutting into the sky above the palace. "People we both know and love are dying right now. If I have to put a sword through my own sister to put a stop to it, I'll do it. But I'll mourn her when it's over, Demos. I'll mourn them all."

With that she strode off, drawing her sword, ready to fight again. Demos and Tollivar stared after her a moment, and Demos was now certain he'd just lost a battle. All he wanted was to take Myrinne and flee Quandis forever, to put their family names and responsibilities behind them, but the woman who'd just marched away from them was not merely a princess, she was a leader.

"Let's go!" Demos said. He and Tollivar ran, catching up with Myrinne in a shadowy corridor and passing through a wider area strewn with more bodies. From ahead he heard the clash of swords. "With me."

The hallway opened onto a series of stone staircases and galleries built against the rear of the tall wall, scattered with broken blocks, grit, and dust, and here the fight was entered into again. City Guards stood their ground, facing up against people who had until recently been their comrades. A few pairs circled each other, hesitating to enter the fray. Killing at a distance was easy, but fighting hand to hand with someone who might have been a friend was much more difficult, even for professional soldiers.

He used the hesitation to glance beyond the galleries, toward Lartha proper. Demos could hear shouts and screams, not only from the soldiers in combat but from farther away. He could see streets thronged with people, many carrying backpacks or pushing carts loaded with possessions. Fires had sprung up all over, and a couple of the hills were ablaze. He looked toward Kallistrate Hill—his home, his heritage—and his heart almost broke at the sight of so many buildings aflame, so much of his history rising in boiling, stinking smoke.

Farther away, higher up, Temple Hill sparked and pulsed with a strange, pale blue glow, as if lightning were striking the hill again and again and bleeding down into the ground.

"Demos!" Tollivar called.

Demos spun, bringing his sword up just in time, and parried the blow from a short, squat City Guard. The man feinted left, dropped right, and thrust the sword in toward his gut. Demos swept the blade aside and brought his back foot forward, stamping down on the man's shin, stabbing his own sword behind his back and into the side of the man's chest. The Guard gasped and then sucked air through the bubbling wound in his side as Demos turned again, using all his weight to swing his sword around and slam it into the man's neck. His head tilted and fell, bouncing three times before disappearing down into the street.

Myrinne was fighting a man who seemed almost twice her size, but his girth was more fat than muscle, and she danced around him and stabbed at his gut, his chest, his thighs, moving with a grace that might have been beautiful if it were not so deadly.

The man went to his knees, grasping a slashed thigh that spurted blood. He was out of the fight, but Myrinne finished him with a slice across the throat.

"This way!" Demos said. "We need to keep pace with the ships."

To his left, the bow of the *Nayadine* was already shoving past the remains of the river towers. The waterway was scattered with debris from the towers' destruction—burning structural timbers, smashed furniture and staircases, bodies—and the sight of the ship sailing past the towers and entering the city was both grand and chilling. Demos spied Daria on the foredeck along with Blane and Captain Gree, and waiting along the gunwales were archers, and soldiers preparing to disembark at any moment. There was no saying just how far up the Susk the ships would be able to travel, and a rapid disembarkation would be essential.

He glanced right, along the wall and down at the wide thoroughfare leading along the river valley and between the first two great hills of Clan Kallistrate and Clan Daklan. The road was filled with Bajumen and rebel soldiers, and resistance appeared to be intermittent at best.

It seemed that Daria's lightning strike upon the city's defenses had proven successful. But Demos could not entertain any sense of victory. It was too early, and breaking into Lartha had seemed too easy to be entirely down to their planning and luck.

Myrinne was staring along the valley between the first two hills and at Temple Hill in the distance. Its four great towers rose high above the city, stark against black storm clouds, which flashed and sparked with lightning. The towers' shadows danced left and right, sweeping back and forth across the lower slopes like dark tentacles searching for a grip.

"What has she done?" Myrinne asked.

Waves were washing down the river Susk and breaking against the *Nayadine,* as if from a disturbance out of sight upriver. The ground shook, a series of deep vibrations that smashed windows, slid tiles from rooftops, and cracked pavements.

As Demos watched, a tower halfway down Temple Hill leaned and fell.

"Come on!" Myrinne said. "We can't slow. We have to hurry! Whatever she's done, whatever more she's going to do, she has to be stopped now!"

"Maybe she's already done too much," Demos said, but Myrinne did not reply. There was not much she could say to that.

They sprinted down staircases to the ground, stepping over a few hardy defenders who'd put up a brave fight. Several dead Bajumen lay on the ground as well, thrown from the wall by the more experienced City Guard, and Demos felt a pang of sadness at the sight. Even now, the Bajumen were being killed. At least this time they were doing some killing in return.

They ran through the streets, the squads keeping a tight formation, and soon met up with Lieutenant Skin and her squads. Hundreds of sailors, Bajumen, and soldiers from Skin's Suskmouth battalion hurried through Lartha. When they met resistance, they fought hard, and the determined attackers quickly overcame the few pockets of defiant City Guards. None of them surrendered. Demos wondered what Phela had offered them to fight, or what punishment she had promised if they did not.

He wondered if her threats were worse than the death they found at the end of his sword.

From their left came a heavy grinding sound, and peering between buildings Demos saw the *Nayadine* run aground close to the shore. Sailors were already throwing grappling ropes onto the docks and sliding across, and he took a squad to the river to offer cover in case they were attacked while coming ashore.

Daria met him on the wide wooden dockside, Blane beside her. He was bleeding, pale, weak-looking, but his eyes were locked on Temple Hill and whatever was happening there.

"We'll maintain momentum," Daria said. "The Temple of Four seems to be our target. I'm leaving half the crews to defend the ships, and I'll send runners to pinpoint targets for the guns. We might have run aground, but these ships are still the best weapons we have."

"Target the temple," Myrinne said. Her words caused a stunned hush among the others.

"No," Blane said. "Try and destroy her and it'll make no difference. It might even make her more powerful. She'll be bloated with the magic by now, seeping with it. Cannonballs won't harm her. Soldiers won't get close enough to stab or fire an arrow."

"What, then?" Daria asked. "What do you suggest we use to stop her?"

"Me," Blane said.

A chill went down Demos's spine when the novice spoke. He'd already seen the amazing, terrible things Blane could do. He wondered what more he might have in store.

"Get me up there and I can fight her," Blane said. "My people will take me, sister. *Our* people. While your army protects us all the way."

Daria smiled. She looked at Demos. "It sounds like a plan."

"Then let's go," Demos said. "While we've still got the upper hand."

If we ever really had it, he thought.

But they started moving through the city anyway, toward Temple Hill. Toward what Demos could only think was the oldest, darkest magic. *And if that's what we face, there's no telling what winning means.*

21

Demos stumbled as Temple Hill shook beneath him. He went down on one knee and Tollivar appeared instantly. With Myrinne finding her own purpose, the Bajuman boy had become his greatest asset somehow, his most loyal friend. They'd avoided murder together, lost Mouse together, and maybe that had forged their bond, but Demos thought perhaps there must be more to it, that these moments now, fighting side by side for a higher cause, were the ones that were the most important.

"Are you all right?" the boy asked.

Once upon a time, Demos would have scoffed at the question, but he knew the boy meant well. The hill continued to shake. Off to their right, ravines had opened where none had been before, splits in the face of the hill where much-rumored tunnels had once allowed the priests to travel uphill from Yaris Teeg. The novices' temple itself had half collapsed. In the distance, Demos could see young priests working in the ruin, but they were trying to save their fellows and were none of his concern.

At the top of the hill, where the winds and rain raged in the

Temple of Four, where the towers of the gods shook and swayed . . . that was his concern. The sailors and warriors and Bajumen following Daria climbed upward as quickly as they could, and for a moment Demos watched them continue on without him.

Myrinne jostled through several warriors and stood by him, somehow managing a smile as the world shook and cold rain pelted down. Her clothes were soaked, her braid dripping.

"That was graceful," she said.

Demos rose to his feet, one hand on the pommel of his sword. "I'm nothing if not agile."

"Let's go!" Tollivar said excitedly.

Demos nodded and they started upward again. The hill shook and they all staggered. Myrinne grabbed Tollivar to keep the boy from falling. Demos gritted his teeth and focused on their objective, focused on ending Phela's mad reign and Euphraxia's time as the apex, all in the same day. A few more deaths in a day full of killing, and it would be all over.

He glanced at the boy. Tollivar had a leather-sheathed dagger hanging from his belt, and like his own sword, that blade had seen its share of blood today. The boy looked tired and thin and very, very young in that moment, and Demos hesitated. Then a phalanx of sailors and other warriors bustled past them. Daria and her officers were ahead of them all, followed by the strong men who took turns carrying the weakened Blane. Demos should have been with them. Daria had always been able to rely on him and he'd been proud of that. He'd gone into a thousand battles at her side, but now he was a shell of himself. Moreover, he wasn't sure he *wanted* to battle anymore. All he wanted to do was see an end to this. To put Lartha behind him and find a new beginning somewhere, in a place whose people had not stood by and watched his father executed. It was that which drove him.

"Come on!" he said, urging Myrinne and Tollivar to quicken

their pace. "We're no good to them if the battle is over before we get there."

Instead of running, though, her hand clasped his wrist and he felt her strength as she tugged him back. Myrinne called to Tollivar as she guided Demos to one side, away from the others who were marching up Temple Hill.

"What's wrong?" he asked, because he knew the look in her eyes. They'd known each other all their lives, and that look worried him.

"We're not going with Daria," Myrinne said.

"What are you saying?" Tollivar asked. "Do you defend your sister?"

"Of course not," Myrinne said, eyes narrowing as rivulets of rain streamed down her face. "But I've been thinking on this, and there is more to saving Lartha, more to saving Quandis itself, than defeating Phela."

"What do you mean?"

Myrinne tugged his arm, dragged him up beside her so that they were facing the same direction and then she pointed. To the bridge. To Palace Hill. To the palace itself, with its walls and spires. Then she turned to face him, so close that even in the rain he could feel the warmth of her breath.

"In the Archives of the Crown are the written histories and the artifacts of our people. Quandis is—"

Demos put his free hand on her shoulder. "You can't be serious."

The hard flint of her eyes gave him his answer.

"There's a bust in an alcove near the queen's chambers. I know you've seen it. Growing up, Aris and Phela and I always called it King Nothing because the ancient records from that era were lost in antiquity. Our history cannot be allowed to die again. Look around you. The city is shaking itself apart."

"We'll stop it," Demos said. "We—"

"And if we can't?"

Demos started to argue again, but Myrinne shifted her grip to his hand, squeezing it tightly. "Quandis is more than the here and now, just as we are. Think about it."

And he did. He exhaled and hung his head. "The crown itself."

"We can't just leave it there. If the palace falls—"

Her words were interrupted by a boom of thunder that shook the sky. Lightning crashed down on Palace Hill and one of the structures outside the walls burst into flames. A home collapsed and slid, crashing into another. In the midst of the storm, they could see the damage already unfolding. Demos glanced at the bridge, but for the moment it remained intact.

"The crown," he said again. The relic had been used for centuries for the coronations of new rulers, all descended from the same family line, all with the Blood of the Four in their veins. But in its way the relic had just as much importance as that blood. Its symbolism carried unmeasurable weight among the subjects of the queen.

"Yes," Myrinne said. "The crown, and all the histories of times we know and some we don't, they must survive. We'll move them to the fleet, get them aboard Daria's flagship."

Demos glanced again at the bridge, saw the cracks forming in the stone supports and the way the hill seemed to buck against it, as if the land itself wanted to destroy that crossing.

"Gods-damn it," he whispered, and then he kissed Myrinne, trying not to think about the Crown and her plans for the future, trying only to see as far as the end of this day and not even willing to consider tomorrow.

He reached up and held Myrinne's face in his, his nose inches from hers. "We'll do all we can. If the palace is too dangerous, if the city keeps tearing itself apart—"

"Then we run," she agreed. "I'm not losing you again."

Demos smiled. If he noticed the smile fade from Myrinne's lips as he turned away, if he noticed her sadness, he told himself he'd imagined it. He shouted to a trio of sailors he knew, hailed them over, and explained to them what must be done. They were hesitant, determined to follow Daria, but these were intelligent fighters, two women and a man who'd pledged their lives to protecting Quandis almost before they'd left childhood behind.

"You know Daria would agree if we had the time to catch her and ask her," Demos said.

They did know.

Demos glanced around for Tollivar, but the boy had already moved to Myrinne's side, waiting expectantly.

"She dies," Tollivar said, tilting his head to indicate the top of Temple Hill. "Whatever else happens, Euphraxia has to die. For Mouse."

"Before the next sunrise," Demos said. "You have my word."

Together, the six of them ran for the bridge. Ran for the palace. Ran for the crown.

⌒

Queen Phela stood on the nexus point in the temple courtyard, the Towers of the Four rising all around her, and the magic thrummed deep inside her. It flowed through her the way the wind blew through the Bone Spire, creating a new music, something no one alive had ever heard before. The pain in her gut ceased. The flow of blood from her nose and eyes halted, and every breath she drew made her shudder in ecstatic awakening. Rain pelted her and the wind scoured the stones around her feet, but she felt aware of them only in the way a sleeper hears the voices of the waking, as if she lived in a dream. The tangible world had a certain texture, but magic wove a fabric of its own. It slid over and through her as smoothly as the finest silk.

This purity was what she had waited for. The Four knew her and they loved her. Their blood flowed in her and she would not be denied.

Per Ristolo stood on one side of her, with Per Stellan on the other. Their hands were on her body, touching her forehead and her shoulders, her abdomen and the small of her back, blessings on her throat and her eyes. They spoke, and Queen Phela echoed their words unconsciously, as if they had mesmerized her, when in truth it was the Four who had mesmerized them all. Somewhere nearby one of the other priests could be heard sobbing over the fallen. Through everything, Phela could smell the blood of the novices and priests her Silent and the City Guard had murdered. The City Guard who'd come to join her here were even now watching over the priests who had smartly surrendered. In between the words of the ritual, Per Stellan sniffled like a difficult child who'd been disciplined. Phela knew the priest wanted this, but still the woman wept for her brothers and sisters of the Faith who had betrayed the queen and suffered for it.

It doesn't matter, Queen Phela wanted to tell her. *Can't you feel it? Everything is going to change now. All will bow. The nonbelievers will embrace the Faith with their whole hearts when they see that a true god walks the world.*

And it wasn't just Quandis that would benefit. The Eternal Queen would lead her people to conquer all the lands across the oceans, until there existed no place that could call itself anything else but Quandis or worship anything but the Four.

The Five.

With the magic of Anselom, Queen Phela exhaled and the stones beneath her feet shifted. The entirety of Temple Hill began to tremble. With the magic of Bettika, she made the wind dance and then cast it outward to circle the Temple of Four, so that it grew still—so very still—there at the nexus of the towers. With the magic of Dephine, she diverted the rain so that it no longer touched her, and she sent the puddles of water at her feet slithering away like serpents across the trembling stones. With the magic of Charin, she felt the fire blossom at her fingertips and wreath itself along her forearms until Per Ristolo bent to whisper into her ear, "Not now, Majesty. We're almost done."

Burn him, a voice said in her mind, but Queen Phela resisted. Ristolo worshipped her. He was good and faithful, her true friend, and she would make him apex this very day.

Again she inhaled. Exhaled. Found the magic of the Four at peace within her, working in harmony, and she knew these two servants of the Faith had been correct to bring her to the nexus. The magic filled her, racing through her veins. Her lips still formed the words of the ritual and the song still reverberated through her bones, only louder now. She sensed the grass in the parks and open spaces on Temple Hill, the strong current of the river at its base, and the fear of dogs and cattle up and down the hill as they curled on the ground or bolted in an effort to save themselves. She felt the earth crack down near Yaris Teeg where a tunnel collapsed. And yet instead of frightening her, the deepening quake of the ground only meant that the magic in her simmered and seethed and reached out more. Queen Phela wondered about the secret thoughts of those around her, and if she could see into their hearts. The magic felt much sharper than she'd imagined. With it she might invent love where none existed, sow hatred where it served her. With this magic she might enslave the spirits of the dead.

Where did it end, this power?

Did it end at all?

With a smile she gazed up at the sky. Thunder rolled overhead. Veins of blue-white lightning stabbed the clouds, fire in the air, such that the girl she'd once been might have thought the gods were at war in that storm. But Queen Phela knew the Four were here in Lartha, buried deep beneath the city.

And the Fifth now stood upon this hill.

She laughed out loud and the thunder echoed back. The rain

turned to snow because she willed it—she loved the pure beauty and silent hush of snow as it fell.

The hum in her bones grew louder. So loud that it might almost have been pain.

But there could be no pain for her. Not for the daughter of the Four. The Eternal Queen.

Unbidden, a stream of acid bile rose up the back of her throat. She raised a hand to her lips, trying to stop it, then surrendered to the vile taste of it in her mouth. The queen spat onto the snow-speckled stones of the courtyard.

"Majesty?" Per Ristolo said, and Phela heard him. His voice penetrated her reverie.

"Finish your work," she said, and the entire temple heaved underfoot. Her two High Order servants stumbled and Per Stellan fell to one knee, but Queen Phela rode the bucking earth as if she were one with it.

A fresh trickle ran from her left nostril. Queen Phela reached up to wipe it away and her fingers came away black instead of blood-red. But the black ichor dripping from her nose did not alarm her as much as the sight of her hand and forearm. Her skin was pale, and so dry that it had begun to flake and crack. Her bones sang, and now they thrummed with pain.

"No," she whispered. Then she repeated it, louder, stiffening her spine and standing firm. "No."

Taking a deep breath, entirely focused, she let the magic slithering in and out of her begin to reach toward the Towers of the Four. She could feel the gods far below in their tombs, and now the magic that flowed in her flowed back into them, a crackling loop of power that pulsed and grew and raged within her.

"Yes. *Yes!*"

Fire raced along her arms, but she pulled it into her palms, made it dance along her fingers. The bile choked her again and once more she spat into the gathering snow. *I will hold it,* she thought. *I will have it all.*

Smiling so widely that she felt the corners of her mouth split, she turned to gaze lovingly at Per Ristolo. Only then did she realize that he was screaming her name. He was pointing past her . . . beyond her. Queen Phela had been lost in the magic, but now she looked to see what had so terrified her priest, turning just in time for a spray of hot blood to scythe across her face and arms and chest.

Per Stellan fell to her knees with blood gouting from a hole in her throat. A ghostly Phage warrior stood behind her, a translucent spirit sword in his hand.

The tangible world roared around her. The fugue of magic dispelled, and she saw them charging now, more than twenty Phage warriors. They screamed as they whipped through the air toward her. Shome and the other Silent rushed to fill the space between the dead priest and their queen. Swords clashed. Snow fell through the Phage as if they weren't there at all, and yet their blades held substance. One of the Silent died quietly, her blood painting the snow red.

The City Guard closed in to protect the queen as a wave of priests emerged from doors and archways into the courtyard. They fought with staffs and blades and fought poorly. They died quickly, even against the least of the City Guards. But there were others, High Order priests who had refused to kneel when she'd proclaimed herself Head of the Faith, and now Queen Phela saw them here, seven all told.

With Apex Euphraxia leading them.

"You should have been satisfied to be the queen!" Euphraxia cried. "Your duty is to your people and your gods, not to yourself. You blaspheme, Phela. For that you will die!"

She reached into the sky and called down the lightning. It lanced from the clouds toward Phela, but the queen waved it away.

It slammed into the walls and smashed blocks that had been there a thousand years. Euphraxia spoke ancient words and reached out, and this time the courtyard opened beneath a Silent and two City Guards, and as they fell into the gap Euphraxia slapped her hands together and the gap crashed shut, powdering bone and pulping flesh.

Queen Phela could not breathe. She tasted bile and black blood. Her bones hummed that song of pain. Per Ristolo stepped up beside her and began to carve the air with his own meager magic. She saw the magic so close to her, and she wanted it. So she took it from him, stepping toward him and grabbing his throat as she dragged the magic out of him. His eyes went wide and he gazed at her with such sadness that she almost regretted it.

"Majesty . . ." he began, as his age caught up to him. Years withered him in an instant, centuries that turned his skin to paper and his flesh to dust. When he fell forward onto the stones of the courtyard, there was little left of Per Ristolo but bones and memories.

Gone. Her High Order had left her, and now the magic made her scream with pain and ecstasy. She reached out and tried to draw more from the towers, feeling out with her spirit into the tombs far below and worshipping the Four in her heart . . . but only pain came back. Searing, stabbing pain as she moved away from the nexus.

"No," she whispered. "It's mine."

Mustering her strength, steeling herself, Queen Phela ignored the agonies haunting her body, and the black tears that poured from her eyes. Instead she focused on the snow and the wind, and she reached out and froze half a dozen priests where they stood, turning the blood to ice in their veins. A pair of Phage rushed at her. Phela laughed through her pain once more as she slipped sideways, standing both in the world of life and the world of death. She felt for the puppet strings the High Order priests used to command the Phage and seized those strings for herself. She could have used the

Phage to kill Euphraxia, though the apex would surely have fought her, but instead she turned the two ghost warriors on each other.

Across the courtyard blades sang and clashed. Warriors and priests shouted and bled, fought and died.

And the magic screamed.

Euphraxia bore fire in her hands as she strode through the midst of the battle, the fight raging around her. Queen Phela stared at that fire and then at her own hands, and she felt a dreadful envy. Euphraxia had just a touch of magic, but she also had a gift for wielding it. Phela wanted both—the control, sure, but the power perhaps even more. She craved every last dreg. It was wasted on the apex. Because though Eupraxia had spent an impossibly long lifetime perfecting her magic, Phela could feel the limits of the other woman's ability, as if her soul were only large enough to contain enough to fill a pond. Phela could drink down the entire ocean.

"Mine," Queen Phela said.

"Never." And then Apex Euphraxia barked a command and, as one, the remaining Phage flew at the queen. Euphraxia touched the ground with one hand and the trembling ceased for just a moment, and then a fissure opened in the courtyard, the crack rushing toward the place where Phela stood. In the same moment, Euphraxia seemed to snatch at the wind with her free hand and Phela felt the breath stolen from her lungs. Blackness crept around the edges of her vision. Gasping, suffocating, she fell to her knees as the fissure collapsed the stones around her.

Pain stabbed her. Carved her. Kept her mind singing with the certainty of her destiny as the Four molded their new sister. Queen Phela felt the gods inside her skin, and she reached out and wrested the wind away from Euphraxia. She took the ground back. Bettika and Anselom were *her* kin, not Euphraxia's. Charin's magic and Dephine's power were *hers*.

A spike of pain made her scream and throw her arms wide.

Only when she looked down and saw the point of a spirit sword jutting from her shoulder did she realize this was not the gods or magic, but rather a Phage having stabbed her through the back. The dead priest withdrew its sword, and Phela staggered a few feet away.

Leaking inky blood, bones singing with power and pain, she spun on the Phage who'd stabbed her and whispered, "You dare attack the Eternal Queen?"

She reached out and touched the Phage, slick and cool against her skin. The sword vanished from its hand and what fell to the ground was a withered husk, the corpse it would have been had it been buried in the ground instead of turned into this restless shade. The effort made her cry out with a fresh wave of pain, but she shuddered as if in pleasure instead. Perhaps this, she thought, was how gods were made. This was her metamorphosis. Now that she understood that she reveled in it, screeching her pain at the sky as she would have her deepest ecstasy.

With a roar she turned on the others who dared attack her. Queen Phela saw the paltry magic of her enemies, felt the way Euphraxia dared to wield the wind, and it enraged her. She whispered to Bettika in the shadow of her tower, and Euphraxia's eyes went wide as she felt the power of gods seized from her. Phela swept her off her feet in a single gust, hurled her two hundred feet in the air, higher even than the Towers of the Four, and then she drove Euphraxia down again, not content to let her fall. The apex hit the stone courtyard, flailing for control of the magic that would never be hers again.

The sound of her impact and the shattering of her bones echoed through the Temple of Four and made even the Phage hesitate.

In that moment, when all the rest were holding their breath, Queen Phela cried her sweet agony to the Four. Fire rolled out from her hands and coiled with the wind, a burning maelstrom that swept across the courtyard and incinerated priests and City Guard and even

several Silent. Wounded yet buoyed, Queen Phela barely heard the
tiny voice in the back of her mind that spoke up, telling her Shome
remained there with her. It was that final shred of loyalty that forced
her to pull the magic back and keep from leveling the entire hill.

She fell to her knees and vomited onto the stones, wondering
how she could feel so hollow and yet so completely full at the same
time. Wiping that black fluid from her mouth and nose and eyes,
Phela managed to lift her head, still on her knees, and she stared at
the death around her. The whole of Temple Hill quaked beneath
her, and the wind rushed back in, no longer in her control. Snow
turned back to rain, hissing as each droplet hit the charred embers
of the dead.

Shome stood, slowly. She'd thrown herself onto her belly to avoid
the flames. Four other Silent remained. There were half a dozen
City Guard, most of them burned but alive despite their wounds.
Queen Phela saw several priests kneeling by the dead, bowing their
heads and praying. Per Santoger was among them and she felt a new
spark of hatred for this old man who had dared to defy her.

The surviving Silent should have closed in around her, then, for
her protection. Yet not even Shome dared come close to the queen.
Phela took note, but did not chide them—she did not *need* them
now. She strode across the broken stones, skirting around the edges
of a section that had collapsed into the temple below, and marched
toward Per Santoger. Every step made her shudder. The hum of her
bones had grown so loud inside her skull that she thought they might
be cracking, but she knew this was all a part of becoming a god.

As Queen Phela approached, the old man lifted a hand as if to
defend himself. Phela only smiled, whispered a prayer, and drew all
the magic from him—all that he'd worked his life to acquire, worshipping on his knees. Per Ristolo had been much older and losing
his magic had killed him. Per Santoger did not die, but he wept as he
collapsed to the ground, his body racked with seizures.

Thunder boomed so loudly that windows shattered in the towers. The wind swept through the courtyard, tearing at the embers and the bones of those Phela had burned. Temple Hill shook itself harder and a new fissure opened in the ground. The Tower of Dephine cracked and a portion of its western corner crashed down into the courtyard. Queen Phela glanced toward the wall. From this height, with the walls around her, she could see nothing of the rest of Lartha save for the Blood and Bone Spires. Both were swaying, and as she watched, the tip of the Bone Spire broke away, tumbling out of sight.

"No," she whispered. "No."

The queen exhaled as she tried to draw the magic back inside her. She felt her connection to the Four even as the pain continued to carve her insides. She turned to stagger back toward the nexus, only to see that the fissure had split it in two.

This is mine, she thought. *The magic is mine and I* will *control it.*

The trembling of the ground did seem to ease a little, and the wind to quiet slightly. But only slightly.

For the first time, Queen Phela began to worry about what it meant to be a god.

More importantly, she began to wonder what had killed the Four.

22

Though most of the City Guard had been dispersed throughout Lartha, locked in battle with the rebel forces or slaughtering priests, there were still four at the gates of the palace when Demos and Myrinne arrived with their allies. They'd forgone any effort to hide themselves. In the chaos and the pouring rain, with fires and the near constant tremors in the earth, with windows shattering and fissures in the streets and cracks in walls, nobody paid attention to six people rushing uphill. Nobody but the four City Guards who seemed just as terrified of the thundering skies and the quaking earth as the people in the streets.

Demos would have just killed them, but Myrinne grabbed his shoulder at the last moment and once again put herself between him and the palace.

"You know my face?" she barked at the sentries.

They did. The four men and women were meant to shout warnings to those within the palace and to fight off invaders, but this day confusion and fear reigned. One woman spied the sailors with them and the Bajuman boy, and it was clear on her face that she knew they ought not to open the gates, but when she began to speak up, her sergeant silenced her with a raised hand.

"Princess Myrinne," the hollow-eyed, ashen-faced sergeant said. "Welcome home. I hope there is still a home for any of us after this day."

He gestured and one of the Guardsmen went into the booth to signal those within. A moment later the doors began to open, dragging loudly across the stone entryway. The doorframe had cracked and the doors sat at an odd angle now. But it moved enough to let their group through. The Guards glanced around in fear of being observed, knowing their lives might be forfeit even though they were only admitting a member of the royal family, the next in line for the Crown. Perhaps, Demos thought, they hoped that Myrinne might be able to save the city before all was lost.

I'll admit that I hope so too.

"Close the doors behind us," Demos said as he passed the Guards. "And hush, now. Not a word of our presence to any who haven't seen us with their eyes. Quandis may stand another thousand years, but only if the princess is successful within these walls."

The sergeant, watching as the sailors rushed through the gates and Tollivar went by, nodded. He touched two fingers to his forehead in a salute to Princess Myrinne and then turned his back on them. When Demos raced through the gates, they were dragged closed. The Guards on the other side could pretend they'd never passed this way at all.

On an ordinary day there would have been at least half a dozen guards on the inside as well, but this was no ordinary day. There were two, one male and one female, there to watch over the comings and goings through the gate, and they looked like children masquerading as City Guards. Demos was impressed with them nevertheless. Stone grit showered down from the ceilings as the whole of Palace Hill shook. Cracks had split the floor, and a chandelier in the entry hall had fallen and shattered across the red-veined marble. The palace roared beneath and around them, rumbling and shifting. Smoke billowed from an ornate stairwell forty feet ahead. Something was aflame, and yet these two young Guards had remained at their post.

The girl came forward, drawing her sword at the sight of the sailors. Her hand trembled as she challenged them. "Not another step," she said, voice quavering.

"Kira, it's the princess," the other said, his hand nowhere near his sword.

The girl faltered. She couldn't have been more than fifteen.

Demos stepped toward them. "Kira—"

She darted toward him, lunging with her sword aimed for his heart. But the other Guard shoved her aside before the blade could land its strike. Kira stumbled and went to her knees, then turned and sneered at her companion.

"Coward!" she snapped. "Traitor."

Princess Myrinne took her sword away. "You're brave, I'll give you that. But those loyal to the Crown would do well to ask themselves not who wears it now, but who'll be wearing it tomorrow."

Then she kicked the girl hard in the temple. Kira hit the ground, shifting and moaning but not rising. Demos gave her fellow Guard an apologetic shrug, then turned to Tollivar and the sailors. "Let's not die here, shall we?"

Myrinne led the way. Tollivar's eyes were wide at the opulence all around them. Despite the growing damage, despite the chunk of ceiling that crashed down just after they'd rushed along a corridor, despite the cracked doorway they had to break down to pass, the boy had never seen anything so beautiful and so lavish in all his life, not even in the homes of nobles.

"It's incredible—" the boy said.

"I'd have made a good king," rasped Yarn, one of the sailors who'd accompanied them. A brave man, better with his fists than with a sword or with the rigging of a ship, he laughed at his own words. "I'd never have opened the doors to anyone."

"Not me," Tollivar said. "I'd have opened the doors to everyone. What a waste."

Demos smiled. "The boy shames us all."

A pair of servants appeared in the corridor ahead, terrified. Myrinne ordered them to stand aside and then to find safety if they could, and they scurried away. In that way they continued through the palace, with echoes of thunder rolling through the corridors and servants and royal ministers hiding beneath archways and heavy tables, some of them crying out to their princess, asking her what they ought to do, asking if they were going to die and whether the Four had forsaken them all. Myrinne answered their cries at first, but eventually she simply went silent.

They raced up a curving staircase and down a wide corridor toward the Archives of the Crown. Windows lined the corridor to one side, and all but one were shattered. Halfway along, the floor had cracked so badly that they had to leap over it one by one, and Tollivar barely made the jump. As Demos leaped across, the whole palace seemed to shift and he landed in a sprawl, careened into a wall, and tumbled onto broken glass. Small shards jutted from the legs of his trousers as he stood, cursing. Blood trickled down his legs, but he ignored it, glad it was the worst of the damage.

Then they were at the archives' doors and Myrinne pounded on the thick, banded wood.

"Step aside, Princess, and we'll break it open," Yarn promised. He glanced at the other sailors with them, Alita and Lien, and the women nodded and prepared to smash through into the archives.

"No," Myrinne said. Again she pounded on the door. "Samnee! It's Princess Myrinne. Let me in!"

Demos glanced at Tollivar and saw only faith in his eyes, but for his own part he felt doubtful. The rain sweeping through the broken windows had begun to turn to sleet, and the chill in the air was unmistakable. Myrinne kept pounding on the door, shouting for the archivist.

The floor shifted, buckled, and Lien had to hurl Alita aside to avoid falling through the crack that opened there. From somewhere below, in the cellars, voices were screaming. People were trapped. Demos wished he could rescue them, but his duty was here.

"Princess," he said, "Samnee does not answer. She's not here."

Myrinne hammered at the door. "She's here. She's the archivist. She'd never have left the books to themselves, nor the crown unattended."

Which made the sailors freeze. Yarn stared at her. "The crown is here? The true crown? The relic?"

"In a vault beneath the *Illuminated History*. We've got to get it out, but Samnee—"

For just a moment, a single breath, the world stopped its shaking. In that same moment, Demos heard the lock tumble. They all looked up as the archives door swung open. Just beyond it stood the archivist herself. Samnee backed away from the door, retreating into the Archives of the Crown, where a thousand books had been hurled from their places, shelves had toppled and busts had shattered, and sleet swept through broken windows. The spiral stairs had broken away from the wall and crashed to the floor, a makeshift bridge across a chasm that had opened there.

But Demos's focus was on the item Samnee held in her hands. The old woman gazed down at it with tears in her eyes, refusing to look at them as they pushed across the threshold and into the archives. Iron and gold, crude and yet perfect, woven metal with four raised points each with a single jewel to represent one of the Four, this was the crown. The true crown, which had been wrought before the gods had died, placed on the head of the first king when the cataclysm had come to the First City, after the First People had been overthrown.

Samnee raised her chin and stared Myrinne defiantly in the eye. "I love your sister as if she were my own. You were an excellent student, brilliant and intuitive, but I could not help the fondness that grew for the sneaky little girl who stole the knowledge that was forbidden to her. Any book I refused to give her, she had to have. I found it beautiful. Charming. And she was the princess, after all. Only now do I see what it has cost her, and what it has cost each of us. Take it, Myrinne. Gods forgive me, you must have it."

When Myrinne reached out for it, the archivist nearly collapsed in her arms. Together they held the crown. For the first time Demos noticed that the altar upon which the *Illuminated History* had sat had broken apart. The stone vault beneath it lay open.

"Come with us," Myrinne said to the old woman. "Come to safety."

Samnee shook her head as if she were a toddler rather than withered and stooped with the dignity of age. "The histories are here."

"Not for long," Demos told her. "We've come for those as well. Princess Myrinne knows that to save Quandis, her history must survive."

As the ground shook beneath them, the archivist sobbed and held Myrinne more tightly. She thanked them all between breaths, then held Myrinne's face in her hands. "I loved the wrong princess."

"Then love me now," Myrinne said.

Samnee nodded, stood straighter perhaps than she had in years, and began to bark at Tollivar and the sailors, shouting for them to gather certain books, told them where to find crates, which artifacts to pack. In moments she had begun to shout orders at Demos and even at the princess. The crown went into a silken bag and then into a rougher cloth sack and a box with the *Illuminated History*, its cover now torn and some of its pages wet. They moved quickly. Yarn climbed the supports to the second level, damning the fallen stairs, and dropped books down to Alita. A high shelf toppled forward and had Tollivar not shouted, Lien would have been crushed beneath it. Despite the horror that kept their hearts pounding, and in spite of the battle raging in the streets and across the hills and upon the river, a lightness had touched this small band who had such faith in the mission they'd undertaken.

That lightness had not touched Demos's heart, though. His thoughts were only on the crown in its crate, in its harsh cloth sack, in its silken bag. On what that crudely wrought, bejeweled metal meant for his future.

When they'd packed the most vital volumes, things that could never be found elsewhere, Samnee still insisted on staying with the rest of the archives. Myrinne tried to dissuade her, but the woman would not be moved. The books in this vast chamber had not only been her trust, they'd been her life, and she would not leave them.

"Come back to me when it's over," Samnee said, touching Princess Myrinne's face again the way a mother might. "Come back to me when you are queen and we will restore the archives together."

"I shall," Myrinne said, nodding. "I swear it."

The dread in Demos's chest blossomed then, spread through him so completely it nearly stopped his heart. He waited, though, until they were all laden with crates and had said hasty farewells to Samnee, who did not bother to close the door of the archives behind them as they began to hurry back along the wide, cracked, glass-strewn corridor. The floor shook and the gap in the floor had grown larger, but they managed to pass the crates across, one to the other. Yarn hurled Tollivar across the gap and Demos jumped last of all, landing surely this time.

Lightning struck just behind them, stabbing through the window as if aiming for it, and the stone floor blackened and buckled into a smoking ruin. The shaking underfoot had seemed to calm a bit, but Demos shouted at them not to tarry. The others might think the rumble had abated, but to him it seemed as if the instability had only gone deeper underground, far beneath the hills, and that frightened him even more. He wondered for a moment if it were possible for the entire world to split apart.

The others had gone ahead, reached the curving stairs, and Demos caught up to Myrinne.

"Keep moving," he said.

"I was waiting—"

A shout cut off her reply. Demos and Myrinne were on the stairs, but Tollivar and the three sailors had reached the bottom just as a cluster of City Guards had rushed into the space that awaited them. Tall windows beside the stairs let the rain in and Demos had to blink the drops away to see the small figure that led those Guards: young Kira, whom they'd spared. It seemed she'd made her choice about who ought to be queen tomorrow, and Myrinne had not been her answer.

"Princess!" one of the Guards shouted. "Order these treasonous pigs to stand down or—"

"I order *you* to stand down!" Myrinne replied. "In the absence of my sister, I command you!"

A dozen members of the City Guard were there, all fully grown save for the girl, but it was she who shouted indictments against the princess, rousing the others to approach with swords raised. Slowly, the sailors put their crates down.

Alita had always been quiet. Adept as a sailor, skilled as a warrior, lean and muscled and brutal without being cruel. It was she now who stepped forward and almost nonchalantly killed the Guard nearest to her, and then swords clashed. Boots crashed into chests and kicked at knees. Two City Guards cornered Lien and cut her down, only for Yarn to slay both of them with a ferocity Demos had never seen in the man. Tollivar blocked a sword with the crate in his arms and it burst asunder, sending him sprawling to collect the items he'd lost even as a Guard pursued him. Demos reached the Guard first, dropping his wooden crate and drawing his sword before the box hit the floor.

Even as he cut the Guard down, even as he saw Alita drive her sword through Kira's skull, Demos felt the way the whole palace seemed to settle and quiet, like a ship becalmed upon a glass sea. Even the rain lessened. Even the wind died outside. And yet he knew.

Demos grabbed Tollivar by the arm, dragging the boy with him as he turned toward Myrinne and shouted her name, cried out for all of them to take shelter.

But there was no shelter from the hill beneath them.

Like an ancient beast waking, the world itself shrugged and the palace cracked down to its cellars. The outer wall collapsed as Demos hurled Tollivar toward Myrinne. He saw a part of the ceiling crash down on Yarn with a sound that would echo in his mind even into his own grave—which was almost certainly not far off. And then something struck him in the head and Demos felt weightless a moment before the world went dark.

⁓

Demos heard his name. Blinked his eyes. Groaned as Tollivar and Alita shifted a fragment of the marble stairs off his chest. The architecture had saved him, the curve of the stone preventing it from crushing him. Blood matted his hair and felt warm on his face, but he felt strong enough to help them shove it away. With the ground still trembling, he struggled to his feet in the full force of the storm. No ceiling stopped the wind and rain now, no walls shut it out, and the respite they'd felt earlier was well past them now. He glanced over and saw that the entirety of the corner of the palace that had held the Archives of the Crown was only a smoking ruin. He spared a thought for loyal Samnee, who must surely be dead, then turned the other way and saw that the corridor from which the Guards had come had been sealed off by collapsing masonry.

Myrinne dragged a crate over toward the others. She'd recovered three in total. Whatever portions of the history of Quandis had been in the others had been buried, for now. Perhaps forever, if the world did not stop shaking. He knew then that she had been right.

"The crown," he said as he rushed to her.

His princess tapped one crate and nodded. That, at least, was safe.

The way behind and the way ahead were both blocked, but the outer wall of the palace had collapsed entirely. Through the storm Demos could see other buildings in ruin down the hill, including on Kallistrate Hill and Hartshorn Hill, where familiar towers no longer marked the horizon. Above them the Bone Spire was no more, but the Blood Spire remained, defiantly spearing the sky.

Together, they picked their way across the rubble—Demos, Myrinne, Tollivar, and Alita—carrying what remained of Quandis in their arms. Saving what they could, knowing it might not matter.

Knowing they might be carrying the crown to a doomed kingdom.

⌒

"I don't want to lose you so soon after finding you again," Daria said.

"You're not losing me," Blane said, but she could not be sure. She had never seen anyone looking so sick, yet he was also brimming with the strange energy that magic brought, pained and wretched, strong and aware. Each step up Temple Hill toward the Temple of Four at its top brought tears of pain to his eyes.

"You're bleeding," Daria said at his side. She held his arm and helped him walk.

"Everyone bleeds," Blane said. "It's weakness leaving the body. It will make me stronger."

Bajumen marched around them. Some already bore wounds that would scar, providing them physical evidence of this tragic, triumphant day. Many more who had come with Daria now lay dead, but she knew that each death was earned, and every one of them prayed to Lameria that every Bajuman lost today would make the world a better place for those left behind.

Perhaps Blane might make that so.

From above, sounds of war rolled down from the main Temple of Four up on the hill. Snow was melting beneath the constant rains, and light still sparked and arced above the temple, from the wide courtyard hidden from sight by the rise in the slope and the temple's walls. One of the towers had cracked, a great wall slumping down to the ground and landing with an impact that had shaken the hill. Fires raged, walls shook, buildings farther down the hill shook themselves to pieces with the violence of what was happening above and out of sight.

They all knew what it was. Phela, their queen, using whatever magic she had drawn or stolen from the Four to make this land her own.

"Magic is fighting in me, sister," Blane said, "but I'll win." He sounded sad, but his voice was strong, emerging from a face stained with wet and drying blood. His eyes glimmered with terror and delight. Even so, she saw the boy she had known and loved—and feared the man he had become.

"Good. Fight back," she said.

She kept hold of Blane's arm and walked with him, at once just a brother and a sister in the midst of this battle for Quandis's greatest city, but also the very epicenter of that battle. For while they were being driven to a final confrontation just ahead of them, without them, there would be no fight. And although Phela might not know it, she and Blane were the focus of how the world would look tomorrow. It was a great weight of responsibility that weighed heavy on Daria's shoulders, but she had borne such weight before.

And Blane had been preparing for such a burden his entire life.

"For our people," he said. "For the Bajumen."

"We fight for even more," Daria said. "I've seen what you can do, brother, and though I don't understand it, I love you all the more for it. We were born slaves. We each found our own way up from bondage. Now we fight not just for ourselves or our people, but for the whole kingdom."

A great, booming detonation punched through the air, shaking the ground, smashing windows, and startling a flock of birds aloft. Daria felt the thump in her chest and gut. Ahead and above, the top section of the damaged tower was crumbling and falling, disintegrating as it fell and scattering debris across a wide area. Stone blocks, shrapnel, and dust showered down around them, and her forces ducked for cover.

As the rumbles of destruction went on, Daria looked around at the devastation. Blane was caked in wet dust, wide-eyed and staring right at her.

"You're our only chance," Daria said, snapping him out of his shock. "Come on. I don't think we have much time."

They hurried uphill. Lieutenant Skin had led her troops at the fringes of their advance, closing on the temple from two directions in a pincer movement. Daria's own troops had moved upward in six lines, winnowing between buildings, confronting resistance wherever they found it and dispatching it quickly and efficiently.

The Bajumen had poured around them, without discipline and many of them carrying no real weapons. Sharpened stakes, digging tools, kitchen knives, blocks of wood, they took whatever they could find, hundreds of them surging up the hillside like an avenging tide. They had swept everything before them, and now they were closing on the Temple of Four.

The gates were open. No one guarded them, but several bodies were splayed against the wall.

Daria didn't hesitate and signaled that they should advance. There was little time for caution. The air was alight with terrible change, and if magic had a smell, she could smell it in the rain; if magic had a taste, it settled on her tongue.

She and Blane remained close together. She carried a deep pain and had ever since they had been reunited on the *Nayadine* only hours before. It wasn't physical, but rather a pang of regret and nostalgia, and many times she'd simply wanted to stop and stare at the man he had become, remember their childhood, and try to re-create the love that had been between them. But aside from the precarious situation they were in, she had been too long out of Blane's life, and now wasn't the time to expect him to simply move past that. She wasn't sure if that was even possible at this point.

And she worried there might never be a time, now.

They passed through the main gates and into the outer compound of the Temple of Four. Several dead priests lay scattered across the area, and Daria recognized sword wounds in their chests and stomachs. Some of them were novices. Blane ran to them, examined them briefly, and then moved on.

Skin's forces approached from two different directions.

"The outer parts of the temple are deserted—other than the dead, that is," she said.

Daria nodded. No one needed to say where to go next.

"She'll have set guards," the sailor Lorizo said.

"Maybe," Daria said. "But that's why we are armed. Besides, it sounds like she's still fighting a battle in there, and I don't know if she'll be in a position to counter our rush. Things are moving quickly, and we must too. Lieutenant, you force through to the courtyard to the north. We'll approach from the east."

"And us?" a Bajuman asked. He had a cut across his nose and carried a City Guard's sword. He still looked at Daria's feet as he spoke, but she had hope he would find his pride today, if he survived. She hoped they all would.

"Tell the Bajumen to charge," Daria said. "I hate to be blunt, but you're not soldiers and you don't know formations and tactics. But you *do* have passion, and if you can marshal it, that will be your greatest weapon."

"No," the man said. He looked at Blane, and although what he saw must have shocked him, he grinned. "Our greatest weapon is revenge."

The rebel forces charged. From the outer compound they entered the temple buildings, and Daria ensured that she stayed close to Blane. She'd seen how he could defend himself in a terrible, shocking way, but there was also a vulnerability apparent in her brother, almost an innocence. He knew what he carried, and he craved more, but at the same time it was crushing him. While they fought this battle outside, his conflict raged within. She wanted to be there whether he lost or won.

They surged through the buildings, meeting little resistance. She heard sounds of combat from elsewhere, but she was confident that her troops were holding their own against whatever City Guards remained active in the temple. They moved ever forward.

They found more dead priests. It looked as though some of them had been executed, their bodies in positions of repose while their decapitated heads were kicked into a corner. A few had been killed while resisting, but Daria found their deaths sad however they had died. Murdered for beliefs, and for not supporting their new mad monarch.

As they drew closer to the vast inner courtyard, Blane bolted ahead. Cursing, Daria raced to catch up with him, and so it was they were among the first to break cover and emerge onto the Four Square.

Where Phela and her forces were waiting for them.

The queen stood at the center of the courtyard, her clothing streaked with blood, the air around her simmering with heat haze even though the rain still fell. To her right side crouched Per Santoger, the big, old priest Daria had met once or twice before at grand social occasions. He looked diminished now, cowering down like a dog before a brutal master. He saw them enter the courtyard and his slack-jawed, wide-eyed expression did not change. Daria saw no hope in his eyes. Only a vacant, calm acceptance.

Bodies lay all around, but the one that caught Daria's attention was dressed in religious finery, blood spattered and broken, and the air around it crackled with weak energy, arcs of white light leaping between raindrops and steaming the blended water and blood on the ground. Apex Euphraxia was dead.

The ground around Phela was cracked. The energy in the air was cloying, heavy.

The queen did not even have to tell her soldiers to attack.

As they came, Daria counted four Silent and six City Guards including Commander Kurtness, carrying injuries yet loyal to his queen to the last.

Because this was their last stand, surely? There was no way these few ragged defenders could triumph, even though four Silent stood among them.

Was there?

Daria ran with Blane, but both of them slowed as they saw the Silent assassin who came for them. She was a tall warrior, bald-headed, tattooed, and Daria knew of her.

"Careful," she said to Blane. "This is Shome. Deadliest of them all."

Blane smiled, and something about that smile made Shome hesitate. The assassin paused thirty feet away and then approached more slowly, warily.

"Admiral!" someone shouted, and as Daria turned and ducked she cursed her momentary lack of alertness. A blade whispered by just above her head, and she knew that a second later it would have taken her head. She stabbed out with her own sword, kicking out the legs of the City Guard attacking her and dropping him on his back. The man fell forward and she followed him down, pinning him to the ground. He shouted and screamed, spitting blood at her as he struggled, but she paid the histrionics no mind. Her sword's tip scraped against stone as he tried to pull away. She shifted her weight and twisted the sword. The cracking of bones, the flowing of darker blood, and the life went from the man's eyes.

Standing and whirling to take on a new attacker, instead Daria's eyes were drawn to the center of the courtyard, where Phela watched the attack with a curious calmness. The ground around her had been turned and disturbed, paving stones cracked and pointing skyward with sharp fingers, yet the piece of courtyard she stood on remained solid and untouched. There was still snow on her shoulders. Her eyes glimmered as if from a fire inside. She looked wrong, as if the angle of her limbs was altered, the weight of her unsettled.

Daria caught her eye, and Queen Phela smiled.

She doesn't think we have a chance, Daria thought. *Which means she doesn't know about Blane.*

Out of the corner of her eye, Daria saw Shome creeping toward them, like a predator unwilling to frighten off her skittish prey. Blane stood and waited, and even the rain seemed to avoid him, though it poured down on the assassin.

Across the courtyard dozens of Bajumen charged the remaining City Guard defenders. They entered into battle, the more experienced soldiers keeping their composure, issuing calm and careful death to the Bajuman hordes. Many fell, but there were more to take their place.

And more after that, revenge driving them on.

At the same time, Lieutenant Skin and her soldiers finally stormed into the courtyard, archers unleashing a hail of arrows at the queen. With a wave of Phela's hand they burst into flame and disintegrated in the air around her.

Shome charged at that moment, sprinting toward Blane with her sword poised to strike. Daria stepped in front of her brother, her own sword drawn. She stood no chance against the captain of the Silent, but she would not let Blane die so easily.

Her brother must have felt the same way about her chances. A gust of wind swept her up like an ocean wave and brushed her aside, leaving the path between Shome and Blane open.

Blane raised his hands, and the greatest of the Silent ignited in a moving inferno. Clothing ablaze, face melting, limbs blackening and cracking, still Shome swung her sword, trying to kill him. Somehow she had sensed the threat in him, and now here it was.

She fell at Blane's feet, her body bursting into cinders. The fire burned so brightly around her remains that even the driving rain could not put it out.

The whole time, Shome made no sound.

The same could not be said for Phela, as the queen screamed in rage.

Where Shome had died, the ground exploded upward in a hail of shattered stone and fire, enveloping the dead warrior and blasting her burning remains skyward in a boiling geyser. Parts of her fell back to the ground. Other parts were smashed and burned to nothing.

Phela screamed again.

Where Skin and her soldiers had entered the courtyard, the whole section of wall crumbled as if crushed down by a heavy, invisible weight from above. Several soldiers went down beneath the falling stone, and others tripped and slipped, a few falling victim to two Silent who rushed into their midst, taking advantage of the confusion.

"My time is *now*!" the queen shouted. Beside her, old Per Santoger started crawling away.

Blane went to his knees and lowered his head, and for a moment

Daria thought he'd been wounded. She stood by his side, sword ready. But then she saw that he did not need her help, and when she heard his whisper, she understood. "I am the Kij'tal."

He was preparing himself, and she stepped back and away, giving her brother space and praying to Lameria, the god she knew, that he could defeat this bearer of magic from the gods she did not.

It was as if a heavy fist punched her directly in the face. Blinded, stunned, Daria fell back and dropped her sword. Up and down seemed to lose meaning, and while the ground pounded at her back with tremor after tremor, it might have been her body being slammed against a vibrating stone ceiling, or a wall. The breath was snatched from her body. Her lungs and chest burned. Her vision was pale, little more than a shimmering miasma with bursts of bright fire blooming across it, and she felt pulses of heat singeing her hair, stretching her skin. Struggling to make sense of what had happened, she brought her hands in and pressed them to her face, terrified at what she might find.

Eyes, nose, mouth. Some blood, but not too much damage. Cupping her hands over her nose, she took in several slow breaths, then sat up and looked around.

The wide Four Square was almost unrecognizable. The ground had been churned and stirred, and several pools of smoking, molten rock glowed, spat, and steamed as rain hit them. Around their edges were the torn remnants of dead people, flesh blackened and still burning in places with a low purple light. Another tower was on the verge of tumbling, great blocks and tiles falling away and their impacts adding to the cacophony.

Some survivors remained. They pulled themselves from the rubble, battered and bloodied and looking around in an effort to make out what had happened.

Unscathed, Blane was walking through the destruction. He

seemed more certain than before, stronger than she had ever seen him, and as he approached the center of the courtyard—the place where the ground remained stable, and the destruction seemed minimal—Daria went to call after him. To warn him about Phela.

But Blane did not need warning.

Queen Phela was across the other side of the square, pulling herself upright against one of the few walls that remained standing. Even from this far away Daria could make out the blood coating her features, a red mask from which two wild, stunned eyes stared. The air around her flexed and shimmered, her limbs shook, and when she opened her mouth to scream, she vomited a torrent of black blood.

Why would she even want this power if it works to destroy her?

Blane took his place at the center of the Four Square. He stood up tall and straight, staring at Phela as if daring her to challenge his place.

Phela was trying to rein in her powers. Daria could see the struggle within her, body shaking, limbs shivering as if each was held by a different entity and pulled, shaken, tugged in four different directions.

"It's mine," Blane said. Daria heard that very clearly, and in her heart of hearts she knew that was the end of Blane her brother, and the beginning of someone so much worse.

"It's mine!" Phela screeched.

Blane raised one hand and pointed at Phela as if to answer when, with a deep, almost calming sigh, half of the courtyard slumped, and then fell into darkness. Blane went with it.

Daria scrambled back toward the tumbled courtyard walls, seeing others doing the same. Though a million tons of rock fell, from the black pit before her came nothing but the echo of Blane's wretched, furious cry.

23

Queen Phela felt as if she must be flying.

Her legs moved, but her feet had gone numb. The hill heaved beneath her, turning her thoughts back in time to when she was nine years old, the day she'd watched a horse die in the palace stable, the ancient beast shuddering and huffing as its heart beat out the final hour of its life. Was this, then, the final hour of Lartha? The final hour in the long history of Quandis? The quick end to the short reign of the Eternal Queen?

Had she brought about this moment?

No. Of course not. The wind gusted at her back, and the rain washed her clean. The hill undulated like the high seas beneath her and she stumbled and rose and staggered and ran, half falling and half flying—yes, flying, for what was beyond the power of the gods?—down the hill. The music in her bones had dimmed, the song of magic somehow distant from her now, and yet the magic itself poured from her. Black blood ran fresh from her eyes, or perhaps it was merely tears this time. Merely tears, at last.

A spike of pain jolted her heart and she staggered, shuffled, tripped, and fell tumbling down the hill. Arms and face scraped, she pushed back to her feet. *Not flying at all,* she thought, and she allowed herself a glance at her boots. She could see them, knew her feet were there, but had only the barest sensation of them. Her left hand, too, seemed almost a ghost of itself, solid and there, where it had always been, but somehow also divorced from her. The fingertips had split and bled, appearing charred as if from flames. She curled her left hand into a fist and held it against her as she began careening down the hill again.

Charin, she thought. *I pray you give me your blessing.*

But her fingers were scorched and she could feel a searing at the base of her skull, as if her spine were some kind of explosive fuse and even now burned and sparked. Charin had forsaken her. Once, Phela would have wept, but she was Queen Phela now and so instead she raged. The Four had become Five, whether they accepted it or not. Anselom and Bettika, Charin and Dephine . . . they would have to share their worship with Phela, the Eternal Queen. They would have to share with her the way she had already forced them to share their magic. They would have to share . . .

But not their tombs. She would not share that with them. Phela had no intention of dying. With this magic, she would live forever. She would give Quandis the dedication and beauty and discipline it deserved, make her enemies weep and surrender, and then love her.

She *knew* this in her heart . . . even as she fled from the temple.

The rain had formed torrents sluicing down the hill and turned worn footpaths to mud. Her boot slipped and she fell, struck her head on the ground, slid and rolled and crashed into the post of a fence along the trail. Ribs cracked.

Moments vanished as if erased. One second she lay on the path in the mud and the next she found herself standing. Crying out to Anselom and Bettika, to earth and water, she reached down into the ground and seized control of it, summoned up the dirt and rock so that it opened and grasped at the fence, dragged it down into a new furrow in the hill, shattered it to splinters and then buried it. This time the gods did not deny her, and with a wave of her arm and another whispered prayer she swept all of the sluicing storm water aside. For a moment it felt invigorating and she shuddered with the pleasure of it, but then the reflexive pain shot through her and she screamed. Pain racked her bones. Nausea bent her double and she vomited black and red, and in the midst of the steaming pile she retched onto the ground were bulbous bits of what she knew must have been pieces of her.

Queen Phela told herself they didn't matter, those bits. This was merely metamorphosis, a transformation to godhood.

She glanced up and saw the bridge to the palace. Its moorings had cracked. Part of the span had split and fallen away, but a band of it remained. It shook and swayed, but Phela rushed toward it so swiftly that it seemed to her the world had frozen and only she remained able to move. Her vision dimmed and went to black, and when she blinked, she found herself crossing the rain-slicked spit of stone that still linked hill to hill. Three feet wide, with a two-hundred-foot drop onto stone and hill and rushing river below, it twisted snakelike as if to evade her step, but somehow she managed. Her heart soared. Her vision went dark again, and when she blinked, she was already on Palace Hill, staggering upward, moving toward home.

Phela seemingly flowed past fires and smoking craters, and when she lifted her gaze, she saw only a sliver where the Bone Spire had stood. The Blood Spire, though . . . the Blood Spire stood tall, stabbing at the sky. It swayed like the tallest of trees in the storm, but it would never fall. Queen Phela knew that. It was thrust deep into the ground, sunken into the heart of the city. The Blood Spire's very presence shouted the supremacy of the Crown, declared the royal family's claim to the Blood of the Four, reminded the people what they worshipped, what they served.

The crown, Phela thought, and a brightness filled her. She grinned and felt her lips split further, tasting the sickly black blood. The kings and queens of Quandis had not worn the true crown for a thousand years or more, preserving its sanctity.

That will change after today.

Numb, she staggered uphill, still holding her left arm against her side. She glanced at her right arm and saw that it bled. The skin had opened in several places, not sliced but split from inside, and that blackness seeped from the holes. *Metamorphosis,* she thought again, and she felt jubilation. For a moment she thought of her mother and wished she could share this moment with her, wished Lysandra might embrace her as she had when Phela had been a small child. A smile touched her lips, one that the stabbing pain, the searing beneath her skin, the screaming pain of the music in her bones could not erase. She thought of Myrinne, a memory floating up in her mind of her little sister laughing, only just having learned to walk, chasing her through their mother's chambers.

Myrinne, she thought. Mother was dead—she vaguely recalled her part in that, but brushed it away—but her little sister, who had once gazed at her with such perfect, uncomplicated love . . . Myrinne still lived. Phela wanted to share this jubilation with her.

With the wind, she eased the weight of her own body against the earth, helped push herself up the hill. The rain seemed to make way for her, parting like curtains without Queen Phela even attempting to command it. The magic hummed and pulsed around her. The song in her bones shrieked, but somehow she heard voices over it and glanced up to see people in the street. There were warriors wearing navy uniforms and noblemen with swords and a brutish woman with a bruised and swollen face and a handful of merchants who pointed and shouted.

Queen Phela expected their worship. Instead, she felt the rage and disgust that emanated from them, saw the loathing on their faces. They moved across broken cobblestones to surround her. A mother cradled a dead boy, his body crushed and limbs broken, beside a row house whose façade had collapsed. A scorched dog dragged a useless limb as it licked the dead child's face.

They all screamed for the head of their queen, championed her murder.

Phela staggered to a halt, gasping for ragged, painful breaths. She spat a lungful of black bile onto the broken street. With a sneer, she prayed to the Four. With their magic, with their fire and their wind and their power over the stones of the street, Queen Phela killed every last one of the traitors, even the dog. The effort ripped her flesh further, tore at her insides, and as she marched on toward the palace, more determined than ever, she felt herself slipping into darkness again.

She thought of the darkness the Bajuman had fallen into and shuddered.

When she blinked, the queen found herself standing in front of the palace. Fires burned from the windows of the south wing. The gates had collapsed into the ground and even as she watched, the city trembled and the rubble shifted and separated and even more of the face of the palace spilled into the gaping hole, tumbling into the caverns below. Queen Phela heard sobbing somewhere nearby, but it seemed so distant, and once again she felt as if she had slipped into a kind of dream. The rest of the world existed for her only across the wonderful distance at which sleepers could hold reality.

The east wing of the palace had vanished. Only a ruin remained, and it smoked as the rain poured down upon it. The Archives of the Crown had been there. The history of her family, of the bloodline, of the Crown, had been in that chamber, along with twenty thousand volumes of science and exploration and drama and whimsy. This loss pained her somehow even more than the loss of the great relic, the ancient crown itself, for the Crown was her future but the books in the archives were her precious past. She thought of Samnee, and the laughing little child Myrinne had been, and she thought of wretched Aris and how much his approval had once meant to her.

She thought of the mother whose death she had hastened, and this time she couldn't shake it off. Her own mother, whom she had killed.

The blackness enveloped her again. When she blinked, she found herself halfway around the gaping hole in the ground, scrambling over the wreckage of what had been the palace gates. The queen blinked again, and the darkness came with pain this time, like a dozen knives in her back and neck and gut. She opened her eyes to find herself on her knees at the bottom of the stairs, inside the gullet of the Blood Spire. The skin of her arms had split further. Her abdomen pulsed, pregnant with pain, as the magic clawed at her.

Woke her.

She began to climb, and with each step she felt stronger, the magic lifting her, burning away the frailty of flesh and blood. Her tongue slid out and found the ichor on her ruined lips delicious. Her teeth shifted as she worked her jaw, and she let her tongue press against them. Several were so loose that they tipped from their sockets and she spat them onto the stairs as she climbed. As she evolved.

Queen Phela breathed deeply, feeling the power growing within her. The stairwell bloomed with blue light, not only from the billions of tiny incandescences that floated in the air, but from the glow now pulsing in the punctures and splits in her skin.

She blinked and the blackness swam in. Blinked and it swam out, and she found herself not climbing the hundreds of steps up the throat of the Blood Spire but running them. Sprinting them effortlessly, as if muscle no longer mattered. As if breath no longer mattered. To her, they did not. The queen opened her mouth, and the song of her bones burst forth. She made no effort to summon that noise or put voice to it. No, this was the voice of the magic suffusing her.

Phela laughed. How foolish she'd been to think she needed that relic of a crown. How foolish to grieve for Samnee. How foolish to desire the company of her weak, fleshbound sister.

She blinked. Black. Blinked and saw the final, familiar curve of the stairs just above her. The walls of the spiral stairwell were cracked. Red dust sifted down from those fissures and fell like snow upon the steps. The Blood Spire swayed and she careened into the wall, pressed her palm out to stop herself, and sliced the skin open. Only light came from that wound, and Phela laughed as she let the swaying momentum carry her the last ten steps to the door, which hung open already, the frame shattered by the twisting of the architecture around it.

In the windswept rain, with the spire shuddering, Queen Phela wheeled across the balcony to the cracked stone railing. Whole sections had broken off and slipped away, but she leaned against a portion that seemed to have withstood it all. Out across the storm-dark hills whole areas stood intact, somehow untouched, but they were the exception. Every last bridge had fallen. The hills of the Five Great Clans were scarred with wide new ravines, the wreckage of houses, and fires so hungry even the rain could not douse them. With the storm raging it was impossible to see the full grandeur of Quandis now, even from the balcony of the Blood Spire, so Phela could not know how far the damage ranged any better than she could guess how long the ground would continue to roar. Were the seas themselves shaking? Had the islands of the Ring begun to tear themselves apart and float away?

Sorrow twined with joy inside her. Thousands of her people had died, were dying now, rattling their last breaths or being crushed beneath rubble as towers collapsed or the earth itself swallowed them.

They did not need a queen. Not now.

They needed a god.

But that was okay. She would be that god.

She spread her arms wide, though her left fist had withered to a gnarled claw, and she laughed. How they would love her now. How they would worship her. Queen Phela—the god Phela—cried out the names of the Four who were her kin, cried out for Dephine and Bettika, Anselom and Charin. She could feel them now in their tombs, could feel the seething power there and the way it flowed up through her and back down again, connecting them forever. With prayers not to them but to herself, urging herself on, she reached out as if to grasp the storm in her own hands, reached down as if to twist the rock and dirt beneath the streets, to wield it all. The song in her bones reached a pitch inside her skull that made her open her mouth and scream with such ferocity that it shredded her throat to silence. She felt her bones twist and crack, felt her rib cage shatter, and staggered forward to catch herself on the railing.

The wind seemed to hesitate, the trembling to pause, and then it all roared back as if she'd never touched it, as if she had never communed with the gods.

As if she had no magic at all.

Phela glanced down, saw that she'd landed on one knee. Bones had torn through her chest and her thigh, stabbing so sharply that they'd ripped through clothing as well. She could no longer feel them. The sight made no sense to her. The storm made no sense, nor did the loss. With that gnarled hand she reached painfully to touch her head, sure the crown should be resting there. A strange, impossible silence enveloped her and she thought she heard, as if from a great distance, the sweet, innocent laughter of her little sister. Phela wondered if she herself had ever laughed like that. She wished that she could remember.

She glanced out across a city tearing itself apart and she thought, at last, that perhaps the magic of the gods had not been a gift, but a curse. An infection.

And never truly hers.

A crack resounded across the sky, a sound like the world breaking, but it was only the Blood Spire as it splintered and began to fall. Phela tried to hold on to the railing, but she slid and tumbled as the spire broke and toppled.

For the second time, Queen Phela felt as if she must be flying.

She kept hoping for the blackness to return, but she remained awake and aware all the way down.

∽

In the presence of gods, the rest of the world fell silent.

Blane did not understand how he could have fallen so far. There was no passage of time in his perception from launching his final attack upon Phela in the temple's courtyard, to opening his eyes down here. Yet he must have fallen so far down, and then risen from the rubble, descended farther, through tunnels and caverns and underground spaces and to this place where his whole life had been leading him.

And he was not the only one. He saw movement to his left, two shadows emerging from the dark mouth of a tunnel. One of them was Gemmy, caked in mud and blood and coming for him.

Standing in the cavern of the tombs, he felt distant from everyone else.

Blane blinked dust and water from his eyes and felt a surge of something dragging him almost physically across the cavern floor. He crawled, scrabbling like a huge spider, his limbs acting of their own accord to carry him toward the tombs.

"Blane," a weak voice said, and it was Gemmy calling him back. To help her, maybe, or to draw him away from the tombs.

He didn't heed it. He *couldn't*. No one would hold him back now. This was everything he wanted, and had always wanted. Gemmy should know that, and if he had time he'd have paused to tell her, *This is the beginning of the Bajuman age.* He didn't want to risk not completing what he had begun. Too many people depended upon him, and he felt a stab of pain and guilt for every Bajuman who had died today. If he'd worked harder at gaining this magic . . . if he had believed some more . . .

He splashed across the spreading and deepening pool of water, and toward the tombs of four gods he had never believed in. He couldn't doubt them now. Now with the power he had surging inside, and the greater power he had yet to find.

And Blane felt suddenly *good*. Gone were the pains in his gut and chest, and the terrible throbbing inside his head as if his brain were about to burst. He still bled from countless wounds, but they were from his long fall, not from damage wrought by the magic. He felt ready to wield it again, only a thousand times more effective.

No longer a man, he was ready to wield magic like a god. Ready to be the savior for whom the Bajuman had waited so long. Ready to be the Kij'tal.

"Blane," a voice called again. He paused, stood in the waist-high water, and looked back toward the cavern wall. Gemmy stood there, nursing a broken arm and staring after him, her expression hidden by dust and distance. But the voice was not hers. "Blane, you must not . . ." Per Santoger was staggering toward him. The old priest's robes had been ripped off in the fall, and his dark, leathery skin was torn and ridged with caked dust. He was a strange old creature, and Blane grinned. How he had survived the long fall was a mystery that only magic could explain.

"You're wrong," Blane said. "I must! You'll see. They're calling me. They know and welcome me, and they're calling me!"

"You saw what it did to the queen, and her mother before her."

It drove them mad, Blane thought, but he did not feel mad. He looked down at his hands, and they were not the hands of a madman. He leaned over, still, and looked at his reflection in the water. Stirred by movement, if that was the face of a madman staring back, he could not see it well enough to know.

He turned and splashed toward the tombs, passing through the water curtain that still fell, entering their space, and he didn't stop until he had climbed the dais and stood among them. The four tombs lay around him, east and west, north and south, their positions dictating the orientation of the great towers that had been built way above in their honor.

He had never been this close. He had come no closer than the pool surrounding the tombs, but now his place felt up here among them. Standing like a god, while they lay down like the dead things they were. He craved to absorb everything they had left to give. He turned slowly, looking from tomb to tomb, willing them to give up whatever of them remained. He muttered words and phrases he'd heard Phela and her High Order say, but nothing happened. He opened himself up to them, ripping at his clothing until he was naked, standing with arms held wide and soul open and willing. But still nothing happened. He felt the powers he already had surging within him, caressing now instead of hurting, but he wanted so much more. He wanted it all.

"Blane, please," Per Santoger said. The old priest was hobbling toward him through the deepening water, and Gemmy was holding his arm, helping him on his way.

Blane blinked, and a heavy thud sounded through the cavern, sending a series of high waves out from the tombs. Gemmy and Per Santoger went down beneath the first wave, coughing and spluttering as they stood again, wiping their eyes, spitting water from their mouths. The river ran close by, outside this cavern, but Phela's ambition had cracked the world and now the river was coming in.

From around him Blane heard a low shuffling sound. Like something moving against rock.

He glanced at the mass of fallen rock that had tumbled down from way above, and several large boulders lifted from their resting place and clashed together, smashing into fragments.

That shifting sound came again, and this time Blane was ready for it, kneeling with his head cocked so that he could make out where it came from.

It came from all around.

He moved closer to one of the tombs. It was coffin shaped, but larger, carved roughly and displaying no signs of seams or cracks. Whatever it contained was meant to be sealed inside forever. He hesitated for a moment, then laid his hands on the stone.

It was cold, rough, lifeless.

He shouted, sending a shock wave around the cavern that splashed aside the water curtain that always fell, and he felt movement beneath his hands, transmitted from inside the stone coffin.

His heart hammered, his skin tingled, his senses burned, alive and alert and ready for more.

I will be the eternal god, Blane thought. He took a step back and looked around, jumped down into the lake, plunged his hand beneath the surface, grabbed a broken block the size of his head, and climbed back up.

"Blane, please, you don't know what you're doing," Gemmy said from behind him.

Blane ignored her. She was nothing, none of them were anything, and they would soon see that he was *everything*. He was the Kij'tal whose birth had been prophesied. His people would rise with him as their leader and take what should always have been theirs. Quandis would burn, and from the flames would rise a greater place. A Bajuman place.

He lifted the block in both hands and smashed it down onto the tomb.

It only took one strike. Stone cracked and fell away, the block smashed into fragments, and he closed his eyes for an instant against the shards.

Maybe I should never open them again, he thought.

He opened them anyway.

And screamed.

⁓

Daria went down. As an admiral, as a Bajuman, as a sister, she had no choice but to follow her brother into the depths revealed beneath Temple Hill.

She left Lieutenant Skin in overall command until Myrinne could appoint a new commander of the force that would become the new City Guard. While Skin and the surviving rebels retreated through the remains of the temple to secure the area, Daria found a rope and started lowering herself into the pit. She knew that whatever lay below was nothing natural. Or, perhaps, *it* was the most natural thing in the world—the *first* thing. But it was strange and new to her. She could feel it on the air, and smell it, and the sense of some vast thing waiting below with bated breath was almost enough to drive her back up, running from the temple and back through the ruined city to her ship.

It was the sister in her that drove her on. She had spent so long without Blane, and every part of her now needed to know what had happened to him.

Nothing good, she thought. *Nothing good can come of this.*

Deep down was the hope that she would find him dead, but she tried to bury that thought, afraid that if he was still alive he might hear it.

The long rope ended before the bottom of the hole, and she had to climb the wall the rest of the way down. Rocks tumbled away beneath her. Creatures watched from holes in the pit wall, breathing, wafting noxious breath in her direction, and she was always prepared to draw her sword and defend herself against whatever strange things might come at her. But nothing came. It was as if these subterranean beasts knew that greater things were happening.

At the bottom she scrambled over piles of loose rubble, ran through tunnels, always deeper, always somehow confident that she was going the right way. Something drew her on. Something terrible.

"Blane," she heard at last. A woman's voice. And then soon after, an old man called his name as well.

Daria climbed down another steep slope. Some light emerged from somewhere, and she could just make out the lake at the slope's bottom.

The survivors gave her hope, but hearing them call Blane's name frightened her, too. She'd seen what he could do, and what Phela had already done. The city and its people had already sustained too much damage, and perhaps it was mortally wounded, both as a place and a concept. Perhaps there was no going back from the terrible events that had already happened.

But that didn't mean it couldn't get worse. That *Blane* couldn't make it worse.

Daria climbed the rest of the way down, and when she no longer needed her hands to descend, she drew her sword and leaped from rock to rock down the slope of debris. At the bottom, standing in the lake, were the old priest Per Santoger and a novice.

Beyond them, farther into a wide cavern with water falling from the ceiling, Blane stood on a raised area, surrounded by four stone tombs. The water level seemed to be rising.

Daria's blood flowed cold.

Her brother had a stone raised above his head.

Blane, she tried to shout, but her throat was caked with dust, her voice silent. She wasn't sure it would have mattered.

He brought the rock down onto one of the sarcophagi. Rock broke and shattered, and several chunks broke away from the stone structure.

For a moment Blane only looked down, and what he saw was hidden from Daria and the others by the angle. Then he screamed. It was unlike any scream Daria had heard before, pounding inside her head as well as from without, as if it were a voice that had run inside her head to hide, and now sat there, crying out in utter terror. A rush of memories assaulted her—she and Blane as children, fighting, laughing, sad and happy, hungry but content—and such a rush of sadness came over her that she dropped to her knees in the lake, the water coming up to her chest.

When he screamed again, the whole world began to shake.

She felt shock waves through the water, vibrations in the ground, and dust and grit fell from the ceiling. Behind her the mound of rubble shifted and spread, exposing the crushed bodies of those who had fallen with it, the dead finding light again. Great cracking sounds reverberated around the cavern as faults opened in walls, letting in fresh torrents of water.

"Blane, what are you doing?" the novice shouted. "You told me you wanted to help people, not kill them! You wanted to be a savior!"

Blane backed away from the broken tomb and stood between the four of them, looking up at the ceiling as water washed down over his face. His mouth remained hanging open, ready to scream again.

What did he see? Daria wondered. *Do I even want to know? Would I—?*

The world seemed to explode in fire and wind, chaos and destruction, and she realized that everything now was coming from Blane.

And as she was drawn to this place unerringly, she knew with certainty what she needed to do.

Daria closed her hand around her knife and started forward.

∽

It's me, Blane thought, and he looked down at the body of a god.

If anything remained inside these sealed tombs, he'd assumed it would be little more than a shred of dried flesh, a shard of bone. So ancient now, who or whatever the gods had actually been would have rotted away to nothing, and then crumbled to dust.

It's just like me.

The face looking up at him was not his own, but it was so like him that Blane could not tell the difference. Bajuman skin, pale and cool in death. Bajuman eyes, open and staring at nothing for all eternity, their deep blue as endless as the day this being had died. Uncorrupted in death, frozen in a moment.

The terror that clashed teeth together over Blane's heart was from the sudden understanding of just how much magic he *didn't* have. His own power was a mere morsel of what these gods possessed. The potential in them was dreadful.

The dead god did not move its head. But its eyes turned in its skull, fixing on Blane with an icy regard. Awake, somehow. *Aware* of him.

Stumbling back, another scream locked forever in his chest, he looked to the ceiling and felt water flowing across his face, and deeper down he felt the power rushing into him. Power and a joy unimagined.

Were these the secrets from the missing panels of the Covenant of the Four? That the gods were Bajuman? Blane laughed so hard tears streamed from his eyes. The Blood of the Four flowed in the veins of the royals, which meant they'd been part Bajuman all along, somewhere back along the bloodline. This was why the priesthood had always kept magic away from the monarchs of Quandis—out of fear. But what they ought to have feared all along was something more than a queen or a king. They ought to have feared a pure Bajuman.

They ought to have feared the Kij'tal.

I am the true heir of the Four. The only suitable vessel for the re-emergence. Not Lysandra or Phela, foolish pretenders. Not the High Order, dabblers in power they had not even begun to understand.

Me!

The magic flooded into him, and he felt himself open to receive it. Felt it crack him wide and overflow the vessel of his poor flesh. It spilled out and spent itself in the world, and Blane knew, saw, and felt everything that was happening.

From Anselom, great quakes shook the whole of Temple Hill and beyond, shaking buildings to the ground and opening rents in the land, into which people and history fell, and out of which shadows crawled. From Bettika came the storms, sweeping waves down the river to flood boats and drown people, unleashing winds that flattened neighborhoods and swept away centuries of construction. Charin brought fire, flaming, molten rock bursting from the top of Kallistrate Hill in a massive explosion that dropped blazing magma across Lartha and beyond. Firestorms raged as wind streaked along alleys and streets. Superheated air turned rain to scalding steam that stripped flesh from bone. And finally Dephine surged along the river and to the sea beyond, raising tidal waves that washed away fishing ports and coastal dwellings, powering back inland and wiping out a hundred square miles of farming land and farms.

Quandis cracked and burned, death traveled on the wind, and water drowned the screams of the dying.

Blane swallowed the magic because it was everything he had always wanted, and when he at last opened his eyes again and looked down, Daria was climbing up between the tombs. She stared right at him, never blinking, and never once looking aside at the thing he had seen. The terror in her was plain.

"Sister," he said, holding out his hands. She must know what this meant. She would see the magic in him, making him whole and beautiful now instead of making him bleed, and she would revel in it as much as him. He would save their people, and she would be by his side as he did so. "Daria," he said, "it was me, all along. The Kij'tal."

Her left hand held his right hand, and she pulled him close. For a hug, he thought. For an embrace. She felt safe, because she knew that she would be the first Bajuman he saved—

At first he thought she had punched him. He frowned, looked down, saw her hand pressing against his chest, over his heart.

Then he felt the pain, and saw the blood, and every aspect of his new, wonderful magic shrieked at what she had done.

∼⟋⟍∽

Daria was blown back and away from Blane by a spurt of water and fire, a blast of wind, and a ragged detonation, all issuing from the wound she had made in his chest, all carried in his rich arterial blood.

Her knife had pierced her brother's heart, and his blood was thick on her hand. She still grasped the blade. As she flew back through the air she could see him, slumping down between the tombs and trying to hold the fluid that spurted out between his fingers.

She was already crying when she struck the surface of the water and went under. When she surfaced again, the whole world was falling apart.

Stone walls cracked and fell, and river water poured in. Hands grabbed her arms and pulled her back toward the mound of rubble and the tunnels beyond, a priest and a novice dragging her away from her dying brother, and she let them. She struggled to stand and look back at Blane, and the last time she saw him, he was kneeling between the tombs of the Four, blood pulsing from the wound with ever-weakening beats of his heart.

She felt the pain in her own heart, and it was an agony she knew would follow her into death.

∼⟋⟍∽

Blane saw his sister across the cavern, Gemmy trying to pull her away, and he tried to ask her what she had done. To ask why. But he had no voice. His heart was stuttering. His blood was cooling.

He looked across at the god that had turned its eyes upon him, and its body was now old and decayed, its eyes shriveled back into the pits in its skull.

As his heart beat its last, a wall of water surged across the cavern and plucked Blane away, smashing him from the tombs and sweeping him into a deep, eternal darkness.

24

Dawn broke over Lartha with its usual languid beauty, a brightening of the indigo horizon that spread golden light and morning shadows across the city as if nothing at all had occurred the day before. As if somehow the world cared not at all what had transpired there.

Daria watched the glimmer of morning grow and the sky brighten to blue. The rains had stopped, the clouds cleared, and it looked like a fine Growing Season day. It would have been perfectly cloudless were it not for the plumes of smoke still rising from the fires that had burned through most of the night. She'd managed only a few hours of sleep in the small hours and returned to the deck of the *Nayadine* while the night watch still walked the deck. All through the darkness, little boats had passed the fleet, headed downriver toward Suskmouth and perhaps out to the Ring beyond. People who'd lost their homes or who were too frightened to stay, terrified that the ground might begin to shake anew, or that the battle for the Crown would continue. Perhaps their homes still stood but had sustained enough damage that they were now unsafe, uninhabitable. Perhaps they were haunted by Phela's horrors, or by the friends and family who died there.

Either way, Lartha was emptying.

The fleet allowed these boats to pass, but her sailors and fighters had watched each of them closely, wary of some final attack by those loyal to Queen Phela. It did not surprise Daria to learn, in the predawn hour, that her ships had not encountered anyone who still wished to fight for Phela. The knowledge might have given her hope, except that she could now stand at the railing of her flagship and watch as morning arrived, and finally see the true toll that Phela's brief reign had taken on the city.

There would come a time when she might weep, a time when the tears might fall no matter how hard she tried to fight them. But this morning she felt hollowed out and numb, even further away from tears than she was from laughter. The city that lay just upriver, beyond the tumble of stone that had once been the outer wall, was unrecognizable to her. How could this be Lartha? Where there had been Seven Hills, there were now six. Hartshorn Hill had shaken itself apart. The ground had opened and swallowed it, doubtless ending thousands of lives. Of the others, only Clan Daklan seemed relatively unscathed. The other hills bore terrible scars. Whole neighborhoods had burned or been destroyed by the quaking of the earth. Atop Temple Hill, only the Tower of Bettika still stood, and she sensed the irony. If any of the Four had won the day before, it was Bettika, the god of Wind and War.

Then, of course, there was Palace Hill.

The Blood Spire had cracked in half. The upper portion had toppled, but a jagged remainder was a brutal slash against the horizon, a murder weapon. The Bone Spire was gone completely. One whole wing of the palace had collapsed, taking the Archives of the Crown with it. Yet, miraculously, much of the structure remained intact. With great care, patience, and time, the palace could be rebuilt.

Whether or not that ought to be considered a good thing, Daria couldn't be sure.

A footfall on the deck alerted her that she was no longer alone at the railing. Daria glanced to her right and saw Princess Myrinne. Tired as she looked, the woman radiated a strange sense of calm. Tall and strong, bruised and unkempt, she looked far more like a warrior than a royal. For so long, Daria had wondered at the bond between Demos and a princess, but this morning she wondered no more.

"Majesty," Daria said.

Myrinne inclined her head. "Admiral."

They stood together at the railing, surveying the still-smoking city. From somewhere very far off came the sound of a hammer. Though only minutes after sunrise, someone had already begun to rebuild.

"It's so . . ." Princess Myrinne began, before losing her way.

"Horrifying."

"Yes. Though I was going to say it's so quiet. I've never known the city so quiet."

The hammer rang out again, the sound traveling quite a distance to reach them.

"Yes. Quiet," Daria agreed. "But not silent. The night seemed far too long, Majesty, but Quandis wakes now, and we're still here to greet it."

Princess Myrinne gave her a thoughtful glance. "You know, Admiral, I think we're going to get along very well."

"Oh, I doubt it."

Myrinne frowned. "Pardon me?"

Daria met her gaze. "I've just helped you usurp your mad sister. You seem honorable enough, Princess, and I've a deep respect for your husband-to-be, but I was born the lowest of slaves, and you, as the pinnacle of royalty, were the owner of us all. Yesterday I fought for Quandis—*all* of Quandis, not just the Crown. I intend to spend my life doing the same."

"As did I," Myrinne said. "As *will* I."

"I shall hold you to that promise," Daria warned.

"See that you do."

Daria nodded slowly. They understood each other.

And maybe Myrinne's wish that they could get along might eventually happen.

But it wouldn't be today . . . and probably not tomorrow.

Together, the two women gazed out over the city, and the new day began.

$\backsim$

They had no throne on board the *Nayadine,* so a chair from the admiral's quarters had been brought up on deck and deemed satisfactory. Demos had smiled at Myrinne's use of the word. Anything would have been satisfactory at this point—any intact chair, a folding stool, or an upturned barrel. That was one of the things he loved about the woman he'd promised to marry. The entire kingdom had been thrown into turmoil. Thousands of people had been killed, the capital city practically decimated. She had no time for the niceties of monarchy.

Myrinne was going to make an exceptional queen. And it broke his heart.

A lieutenant from the *Breath of Tikra* played the violin as the fleet's officers gathered on the deck of the *Nayadine.* Demos stood at attention with them, watching as Myrinne emerged from belowdecks. With no access to her own clothes, she had cobbled together a selection of clothing from various sources among the fleet. Clean shirt and trousers crisply pressed and close enough to fitting her that nobody would notice. Nothing ornamental save for the ceremonial scabbard that hung at her hip. The sword within it had been the one she'd used in battle yesterday, and she'd vowed to Demos that it would be the one she carried for the rest of her days. He'd wondered if she might be the first monarch of Quandis to wear a sword to her coronation. Myrinne had gone quiet a moment before confessing the certainty that she would not be the last.

She wore the wine-red cloak of a healer. That and the sword would be what people remembered about this moment. Both had weight and symbolism that would resonate for eons. On this day, in this place, the future queen had made an unspoken promise to defend and to heal Quandis and its people. It had beauty and simplicity, much like Myrinne's wardrobe choices, and like the thick braid into which she'd tied her hair. This, anyone watching her would think, this was a leader.

With every step she took across the deck, Demos felt her moving further away from him. The slave brand burned into his right hand was visible to everyone. He wondered how a queen could marry a man with such a brand, but every time he glanced at Daria, this Bajuman woman who'd become the true hero of the Battle for Lartha, he realized that perhaps the old scars and brands had lost their meaning.

It was a sliver of hope he held on to with all his strength.

The violin played. Officers stiffened their spines, trying to give the proceedings as much dignity as possible. Even the injured seemed to forget their wounds in that moment, watching Myrinne stride toward the blackwood-and-red-velvet chair. All whispers stopped. Even the creaking of the ship's timbers and the rushing burble of the river went quiet. Only the violin broke the silence as Myrinne turned and took her seat.

A priest named Per Joli—not High Order, but a woman who'd traveled with the fleet and had conducted weekly services on board the *Royal Dawn*—approached and knelt before the princess. Myrinne gestured for her to stand and the priest rose, then moved around behind the makeshift throne. Per Joli extended her hands, palms toward the sky, and began to pray over Myrinne. Demos found himself wincing as the priest intoned the names of the Four. A restless shuffling occurred among those gathered there, and many glanced uneasily toward the devastated city, where even now uncounted thousands needed their help *and* the help of the gods. But it had been the power of those selfsame gods that had laid waste to Lartha. It was no wonder so many seemed unsettled by the idea of seeking their blessings now.

The prayer ended. Demos had barely heard the words. The wind gusted across the bow and the rigging clanked against the masts overhead. The *Nayadine* bobbed in the river and the entire assemblage seemed to hold its breath. Demos scanned those gathered faces, many familiar and others not. He saw Fissel. The man tipped him a wink and Demos couldn't help smiling. A good man, Fissel. He saw Dafna Greiss, who'd served faithfully as the Voice of the Queen, despite her fear of Phela, and who had stumbled through the ruins last night with a handful of other royal servants to pledge their fealty to Myrinne.

So many good people here, a strong foundation for the future. He saw the young novice, Gemmy, who had helped Daria on the long climb out from the tombs and into the ruin of the temple. They had lost old Per Santoger on that climb, a broken and wounded man. It had been another sad loss. The wide ranks of the Faith had been decimated, but they would rebuild. Novices like Gemmy would be the beginning. Daria had brought her on board because Gemmy had been a friend to Blane. Perhaps it eased her grief, Demos thought, to have someone close by who knew him better than his own sister had. He understood, and he thought Myrinne would as well. All three of them were orphans now—himself, Daria, and Myrinne. No parents, no siblings.

At least you've got family left, Demos told himself.

His gaze shifted into the distance, where Kallistrate Hill still stood, ravaged but still strong. All he had to do was to walk to the top of that hill and he would take up his father's mantle. Slave brand or no slave brand, he would be Baron Kallistrate if he wanted it.

If he wanted it.

Per Joli gestured toward the line of officers, and they parted to allow a small figure to come forward. Demos smiled again, and some of the darkness lifted from his heart as he saw Tollivar approach the priest with a pillow whose velvet matched the coronation chair. Upon the pillow rested the true crown that they had rescued from the archives. Again the assemblage seemed to quiet, to stand a bit taller in the presence of what that crown represented. Tradition, history, the Blood of the Four, the strength of the values the kingdom had shared before Lysandra had tasted magic and spiza, before Phela's ambitions had tainted all that Quandis stood for.

Today, Demos thought. *Today, it's tainted. But maybe not tomorrow.*

He stared at Myrinne, watching her eyes as Per Joli took the crown from Tollivar's pillow and raised it above her head. All he had ever wanted was a quiet life with this strong and beautiful woman, a life of children and laughter, away from the duties of the Crown. Those were meant for Aris, or even for Phela, but not Myrinne. It had all seemed so simple, so joyful, when they were children, and later when they were young and falling in love.

As he watched Per Joli lower the crown, saw it touch Myrinne's hair, Demos closed his eyes, unable to watch the moment when the road back to a simpler time was blocked off to them forever.

The violin went quiet, leaving only the wind and the creak of the ship and the hush of the river. Demos opened his eyes.

"Beneath the gaze of the Four who bless us," Per Joli said, "we see this woman with our own eyes. Myrinne of the Blood of the Four, Crowned Queen of Quandis. Myrinne, Commander of the Five Armies. Myrinne, Queen of Strikes, Honorary Beneficent Leader of Larks, Figure of Nine, and Lady of Fields. Queen Myrinne, the Sword of Lartha."

Daria stepped forward, stiff and formal. Chin raised, she marched along the ranks of her officers and stopped before the coronation chair. A smile touched her lips.

"Queen Myrinne, Sword of Lartha," Daria echoed.

"Admiral Hallarte," Myrinne replied with a nod.

Daria drew her sword, knelt, and placed it at the feet of the queen.

Demos's feet were moving before he'd even realized they might. Three steps in, and he wished he had stayed put. All eyes were on him as he broke every tradition, interrupted the ritual, drawing his sword as he approached. Several of the officers took half a step, as if to stop him, perhaps fearful that he meant harm to the newly crowned queen.

He made sure to stay two steps farther back than the admiral. She outranked him, after all.

"Queen Myrinne," Demos said, his heart lightening as the words left his lips. His love stared at him, and when he grinned, it seemed to surprise them both. "Sword of Lartha."

Just as the admiral had done, he laid down his sword and knelt before the queen. Life would never be simple again, would never be the quiet joy that he'd dreamed of, but Myrinne was his queen now, and as he pledged himself anew, all his regrets seemed to fade.

One by one the other officers on deck followed his example, laying down their swords and kneeling to Queen Myrinne.

Dafna did not kneel. From the corner of his eye, Demos saw her make her way through the officers and come up to stand beside Tollivar.

"Your Majesty," Dafna said, "I served both your mother and your sister. If you will have me, it would be my honor to serve you now as Voice of the Queen."

Myrinne stood, the rough-hewn crown glinting in the sun, her sword hanging by her side, healer's cloak rustling in the wind that swept across the deck.

"You have my thanks, old friend," Queen Myrinne said, "but I will speak for myself."

Demos smiled, still kneeling, until she commanded them all to rise. As one, those who had offered their swords stood and faced their queen.

"The city is shattered," Queen Myrinne said, gazing out over the hushed congregation. Behind her, in the distance, black smoke still rose from the dying fires in Lartha. "Hills have fallen. Noble houses lie in ruins. The priesthood is diminished, and though we all now recognize the truth of magic—its power and its poison—its influence will wane with the unraveling of its mysteries. All that has been in the shadow of secrecy shall be exposed to the light.

"It will take generations to recover from this, but over those generations we will not merely build a new city. We will build a new people—a new *society*—in which service to the Crown and to our fellows will one day be honored in equal measure, and in which that service is offered by duty or fealty or out of necessity, but never in chains. Never in slavery. From this day forward, let the brands on the flesh of all former slaves be a reminder that each of us is entitled to fight for our own future, our own freedom."

Demos felt his heart swell. No matter how eloquent she was, Myrinne's words alone could not erase his shame or the urge to cover the slave brand on his hand, but he felt a deep determination now to combat that shame. What had marked him as a slave—no matter how briefly—would now be a sigil, a symbol of freedom and resistance. He made a silent vow to inspire other former slaves, those who knew nothing of freedom, who'd experienced only the worst of society, to feel the same.

"Yes, the city is shattered," Myrinne continued. Her eyes shone brightly, alight with purpose. "Many have died. Institutions have crumbled along with architecture. But we have built hills and bridges before, and we will do so again. The city is scarred and broken . . . but, my friends, the *nation* is strong. *Quandis* is strong. Quandis endures.

"Quandis is triumphant!"

She drew her sword and raised it over her head, its edge gleaming in the sun. Demos cried out, echoing her words. Other voices joined them, rising in chorus.

Quandis endures!

Quandis is triumphant!

Only a day before he had intended to leave her, and now he knew he never would. Never could. It occurred to him that he wasn't sure which *her* his thoughts referred to—Myrinne, or Quandis itself. But it didn't matter, really, for in the end they were one and the same, and both had his love. Both had his vow, and his sword, forever.

"Quandis endures!" he cried.

And Quandis was triumphant.

ACKNOWLEDGMENTS

Massive thanks to our editor, David Pomerico, for his invaluable input into the creation of this novel, as well as to Priyanka Krishnan and the whole team at Harper Voyager. Thanks also to our ever-supportive agent, Howard Morhaim, and his excellent colleagues, especially Kim-Mei Kirtland. Finally, our deepest gratitude is always reserved for our families. Without Tracey and Connie, and our respective offspring, we'd be cast adrift.

ABOUT THE AUTHORS

CHRISTOPHER GOLDEN is the *New York Times* bestselling author of such novels as *Of Saints and Shadows, The Myth Hunters, Snowblind, Ararat,* and *Strangewood.* With Mike Mignola, he co-created the comic book series *Baltimore* and *Joe Golem: Occult Detective.* He lives in Bradford, Massachusetts.

TIM LEBBON has written more than forty horror, dark fantasy, and tie-in novels, including *The Silence, Relics, Kong: Skull Island,* and the Noreela fantasy series. He's also written hundreds of novellas and short stories, winning several prestigious awards, and has had his work optioned and made for the big screen. He lives in Monmouthshire, UK.